Kathleen Rowntree grew up in Grimsby, Lincolnshire, and was educated at Cleethorpes Girls' Grammar School and Hull University where she studied music. She has written five previous novels, *The Quiet War of Rebecca Sheldon*, *Brief Shining*, *The Directrix*, *Between Friends* and *Tell Mrs Poole I'm Sorry*, and she has contributed to a series of monologues for BBC2 TV called *Obsessions*. She and her husband have two sons and they live on the Oxfordshire/Northamptonshire borders.

D1488996

Also by Kathleen Rowntree

BETWEEN FRIENDS
THE QUIET WAR OF REBECCA SHELDON
BRIEF SHINING
TELL MRS POOLE I'M SORRY

and published by Black Swan

Outside, Looking In

Kathleen Rowntree

BLACK SWAN

OUTSIDE, LOOKING IN
A BLACK SWAN BOOK : 0 552 99606 8

Originally published in Great Britain by Doubleday,
a division of Transworld Publishers Ltd

PRINTING HISTORY
Doubleday edition published 1994
Black Swan edition published 1995

Copyright © Kathleen Rowntree 1994

The right of Kathleen Rowntree to be identified as the author of this
work has been asserted in accordance with sections 77 and 78 of the
Copyright Designs and Patents Act 1988.

All the characters in this book are fictitious and any resemblance
to actual persons, living or dead, is purely coincidental.

Conditions of Sale
1. This book is sold subject to the condition that it shall not,
by way of trade or otherwise, be lent, re-sold, hired out or
otherwise circulated in any form of binding or cover other than
that in which it is published and without a similar condition
including this condition being imposed on the subsequent purchaser.
2. This book is sold subject to the Standard Conditions of Sale
of Net Books and may not be re-sold in the UK below the net
price fixed by the publishers for the book.

Set in 11/12pt Linotype Melior by
Phoenix Typesetting, Ilkley, W. Yorkshire.

Black Swan Books are published by Transworld Publishers Ltd,
61– 63 Uxbridge Road, Ealing, London W5 5SA,
in Australia by Transworld Publishers (Australia) Pty Ltd,
15– 25 Helles Avenue, Moorebank, NSW 2170,
and in New Zealand by Transworld Publishers (NZ) Ltd,
3 William Pickering Drive, Albany, Auckland.

Printed and bound in Great Britain by
Cox & Wyman Ltd, Reading, Berkshire.

To Trevor Hopkins

PROLOGUE

Sunday 14th June

A summer's evening. When the dusk deepens, when, across the grass, white plastic chairs and tables, a white sunhat, a newspaper (memorials to a party that has moved indoors) are reduced to a faint gleaming, the watcher shifts forward, parts the leaves of the sheltering apple tree, takes stock.

Lights blaze temptingly at the ground floor windows. A blur of voices – pierced by shouts of laughter, roars of protest, shrill childish cries – is a heady lure. But this is a farmhouse, there are sure to be dogs (dogs are a menace and the first ·thing to take account of) – strange that after twenty minutes' observation, no bark, no growl, not even a whimper. Though perhaps it is not too surprising: humans everywhere about the place, widely dispersed mayhem going on for hours (today being Sunday), by now any sensible cur has its head down. Forward then, cautiously, slowly . . .

A kitchen full of men, young, middle-aged, elderly; beer set out on the table . . . Oh, and children in the dining room, chasing, crawling beneath the table, leaping on and off chairs . . . Here in the sitting room, women are taking their ease, their heads going from speaker to speaker, now and then flopping and lurching as laughter takes them . . . This room on the end of the house, though brightly lit, is apparently deserted. But, no – full-length on a settee lie a girl and a youth – she trying to rise, he hulking up after her . . . Ah, she gives in – head lolling back, eyes closing,

7

her hands like claws against his back . . . His face so deep in her neck – is he devouring her? Back, *back*. Too late – the girl's eyes are on the window, her face is stretching round a gathering scream.

So *run* – as the row breaks out, as queries and denunciations speed back and forth – across the lawn, through the orchard, over the gate; into the lane as voices erupt in the garden behind, and feet clatter and garden furniture crashes – 'Steady on!' 'Sorry.' 'Over there, d'you reckon? Something move?' 'Where's that dratted dog?'

Just . . . keep . . . going . . .

Breathing getting tight – but the voices growing faint, it must be safe to slow down. Somewhere along here, a path through a cottage garden leads to an alley at the back. Yes, here. Work the latch silently; now, swiftly down the path . . .

'Oi – who's that?'

Dear God – an old fellow by the greenhouse! Run. *Run.*

Three minutes later, men from the farmhouse arrive at the gate of the disturbed cottager.

'That you, Dan? Seen anyone about?'

'Aye, since you ask; going through me garden.'

They pause, swap stories. It is news, it is something to wonder about: 'Kids, do you reckon? Ought we to ring the police?' And something to joke about: 'A Peeping Tom, eh?' 'That's right – spying on our Trisha and her young man. Praps it'll teach 'em to draw the curtains.' 'You reckon she gave him his money's worth?' 'Gave who, Dan? – Gary or the Peeping Tom?' Secure, easy-going village folk. By midday tomorrow most people in Aston Favell will have heard the details.

However, there may be some who will receive the news less lightly. And certainly one to whom it will come as a blow.

CHAPTER ONE

Monday 15th June

The shop smells spicy soapy sweet, and in one corner
quite pungently of wilted cauliflower. Nan Hutton is
placidly stacking tins and bearing with voluble Mrs
Prior; Ted Hutton behind the wire partition on the
Post Office side is stamping pension books; behind
the counter young Debbie Lines is slicing quarters of
ham. Safe, mundane, permanent.

If she stops to think about it, Kate will accept that
her beguiled senses are misled, for Aston Favell's is as
vulnerable as any other village shop, and the Huttons
filling in forms of an evening must often question
whether their long hours are adequately compensated.
This knowledge at the back of her mind is one reason
why Kate, instead of calling at the hypermarket on
her way home this evening, where in any case she
will have to stop off for petrol, is here, filling a wire
basket, before setting off for work. Another and more
pressing reason is her *need* to be here. She needs to
stock up on the commodity the shop gives her for
free: a sense of life chugging on and nothing untoward.
Safe, mundane, permanent.

Mrs Prior sees a chance to widen her audience. 'Oh,
Mrs Woolard,' – catching Kate's arm – 'you too, me
dear. Mind you lock your doors at dusk and draw
the curtains. I was just saying to Nan, you can't be
too careful. Did you hear we've got a Peeping Tom?'

Nan Hutton makes a clicking noise. 'Just one of the

lads at a loose end, I expect. Nothing to get excited about.'

'Oo dearie me, no. Mrs Ellwood – she's the one who reported it – says the police told her there's been quite a spate of this sort of bother on and off over the years. Why, in some of the villages . . .'

'It's the first time we've had anything of the sort in Aston Favell. And I daresay it'll be the last.'

The doorbell pings; another customer steps in; Mrs Prior moves on. 'Morning, Dan. Have you heard about the trouble last night at Ellwood's? You don't say. You hear that, Nan? – it weren't just at the farm, someone ran through Dan's garden. Didn't catch him then, Dan?'

To Kate, the shop has become less immediate. She conducts her business at the counter – selects a piece of cheese, hauls up her basket, finds the money – over a widening distance. Fear, like fog, has closed her in – furry, disabling. Her limbs feel encumbered, throat and vision constricted . . . 'Change, Mrs Woolard!' – the cry startles her out of her skin.

'Miles away already,' Debbie jokes, dropping coins into Kate's hand.

A generalized smile – she can't speak – then very carefully home; one foot after the other across The Green, up Vicarage Hill, and at last through the open gateway to Wayside Cottage.

Kate is moving from room to room, taking time to pause in each, to finger a book, smooth a curtain, pick up and put down a Tonbridgeware box, plump a cushion. She is reacquainting herself with her home's cosy friendly atmosphere. (Well of course it's friendly in the sunlight, snaps a perverse voice in her head; it's later on you've got to worry about, coming back to an empty house, or that moment during a solitary evening in when it's definitely time to draw the curtains.) A benevolent cottage, continues the biddable part of her mind, a charming place to live, full of happy memories, still apt, when the children return, to ring with laughter and argument. And very close to other dwellings. She goes to the window to be assured of this. Certainly within shouting distance. 'Shouting' is not helpful, however. She walks away from the word and out of the room (the sitting room) and into the next (formerly the dining room, but never again a room she would consider eating in).

She stands in the doorway and looks across to the place where Chris died. There is still a gap where his bed stood under the window. The quietness in here is the void in your ears when a loud noise stops suddenly – like sound sucked into a vacuum; negative, but an assault.

Her memory still flirts with the sounds which preceded this silence, sounds of despair, anger, hope, tenderness. But she has learned, catching herself in the act, to blank them out. The impulse to set off down memory lane is a vile trick; it gives a feeling of going somewhere, a promise of finally stumbling on answers – then you discover there are no answers; it is a circular route round the same old agony. Lately, she has managed to prevent herself starting out. That at least is something. She cannot be entirely without resource.

Of course she isn't. Catching sight of herself in the hall mirror she can see how well she has pulled herself together during the last ten months. For a year after Chris died she looked appalling. She assumes she looked pretty ropy all the months of Chris's illness, but was too worn out and distracted to notice. In fact, she has no conception of herself during his last year; looking back, she can only see Chris. Now, getting on for two years after his death, there is a marked improvement. A smile, and it is the same happy-go-lucky Kate grinning out of the mirror as in all those photographs taken while the twins were growing – their second birthday tea in the garden, camping in France, walking in Derbyshire, fun at the village fête. Cheered, she goes into the kitchen. On the table lies further evidence of how well she is coping: a pile of marked essays ready to take with her to school. 'Don't for heaven's sake leave us, Kate,' pleaded Irene Cobb, Headmistress of Lavenbrook Comprehensive where Kate teaches French two and a half days a week. 'With these cuts they'll never let me replace you. They'll think it quite all right if Josie Templar' (History teacher) 'and Mick Davis' (games) 'cobble a few French lessons together from what they can remember of their own A levels.' And Kate promised she wouldn't dream of it. It was when Chris became seriously ill that she arranged to teach part time. They were unable to afford for her to give up entirely, what with the twins soon to start university and Chris's income from consultancies taking a dive. Since Chris's death, proceeds from life insurance have made her feel almost well-off. But she has continued with the part-time arrangement. And not just out of loyalty to Irene and the school. She enjoys working; it is part of her getting-back-to-normal programme. In fact, last winter she taught a class of adults at night school.

Kettle on for coffee, smoked salmon from the fridge, bread from the bin. Drink and sandwich on a tray, she goes into the sunny sitting room and settles with a newspaper in her favourite chair. Her eyes read mechanically, her mind elsewhere. As she eats and drinks, she is going over things Dr Horden said, that there had to be some reaction, some wound to her personality after the trauma of watching a young husband die. Another person might be left with crippling anger (for Chris was only forty-five and she a widow at forty-two); another with a crippling lethargy, or a need to seek potentially harmful comfort in booze or men. Her hang-over is merely an irrational fear of being alone in the house, especially after dark. Dr Horden says it is important to remember that it *is* irrational, and to think of it as a wound. Wounds heal.

Even so, she cannot help feeling disappointed, because until this morning in the shop and that stupid gossip about a Peeping Tom, the healing process seemed well advanced. True, there are certain actions – closing the curtains, turning off the downstairs lights before going up to bed – which bring the *thought* of her fear to mind – indeed, there may never come a time when she can perform these mundane acts carelessly. But recent evenings have found her not so much actively afraid as aware of the possibility of being so. It is rather a let-down, then, to discover that learning of a concrete reason for being afraid can set off a depressingly familiar reaction – her heart leaping and then racing in anticipation of the evening ahead.

Her early lunch over, she takes the tray to the kitchen, visits the bathroom, collects the marked essays and her car keys. The further she drives from her cottage (waving to the postwoman, tooting to Will McLeod who is collecting milk from his doorstep) the more fond she becomes of it. (An hour ago, walking through the rooms trying to coax love and admiration for the place, on the surface she felt totally at ease, only at the back of her mind was a measure of reservation – knowledge that in this place terror can strike. For it was at the bottom of *these stairs* one night that her limbs froze. It was to *this chair* she'd clung with her heart knocking. It was on *this bathroom floor* she'd lain with acid searing her throat caused by too much adrenaline charging her body for too long.) At five miles' distance she remembers Wayside Cottage is home to her children who are in their second year at university and eagerly look forward to returning every vacation to their own bedrooms and their old friends. Twelve months ago, she'd considered selling up and moving. The twins were devastated, and Dr Horden warned that her irrational fear might very probably move with her. In any case, it never became clear where she would move to. Her life is here. Her work close by. She has lived in Aston Favell for fifteen years; she has good friends in the village. She is particularly close to Fiona and Zoë; their children grew up together; they three and

13

their husbands ran the village youth club, organized discos, expeditions, camping holidays. Of course, Will was involved in these things, too – dear Will, who was Chris's best chum, and (let her never forget it) now depends on her. Sylvie (Will's wife) has become so difficult, Will has need of close friends. How can she think of deserting him when, of all Chris's friends, Will was the most stalwart, the most dependable, and in the final stages, the most brave?

At nine miles' distance from Wayside Cottage (and within sight of the school entrance) a dozen excellent reasons for continuing to live there are clear to her, and only one – an irrational one – for running away. Damn it, she is *not* going to run away. She will stay here and beat it, this . . . whatever it is. This wound.

When the shop reopens for the afternoon, the Peeping Tom is no longer topic of the day. The commanding entrance of Mrs Bullivant secures attention for the Best Kept Village Competition. She waves a notice setting out the rules under Nan Hutton's nose; Nan promises to put it in the window. While she is at it, adds Mrs Bullivant, Nan might like to put up a second notice advertising the Bullivant coffee morning a week on Thursday. At this Nan looks doubtful. 'In aid of the church,' protests Mrs Bullivant. 'The Rector announced it on Sunday.'

'All right,' Nan concedes, 'as it's for the church. Just leave the notices there, and I'll see to 'em later. Yes please?' – to a man who has entered the shop, a motorist stopping off to buy cigarettes.

Besides Mrs Bullivant, also present in the shop and searching the shelves are Mrs Critch (close friend of Mrs Bullivant), Mrs Prior (making her second visit of the day, this time on her way home from her duties at The Old Vicarage), and two young mothers (not friends, in fact unacquainted): Karen Watts with her eighteen-month-old daughter in a pushchair; Bel

14

Rochford with an infant son strapped to her designer tracksuit front. Pauline Turner, landlady of The Crown, arrives on the heels of the motorist.

The form is to allow the stranger, whose arrival has had a dampening effect, to be served immediately. Mrs Prior stands back. Nan serves him briskly. Those near enough observe the transaction in silence until, pocketing cigarettes and change, the stranger departs. At which there is a perceptible rallying – Mrs Prior steps forward to reclaim her place, Mrs Critch decides to pop a chocolate bar into her basket, Debbie bends down and tickles the toddler, Pauline Turner (landlady of The Crown) temporarily relieves the pressure on her shoulders by hitching up her bra-straps, and Mrs Bullivant draws in breath: 'I do hope this year *everyone* will make an effort. The front of The Crown is looking very gay, I must say . . .'

'Lovely,' Mrs Critch smiles to The Crown's landlady. 'Such a row of hanging baskets.'

'I suppose the brewery helps out there,' murmurs Nan, in case anyone should be setting the pub's lavish display against the shop's lone tub.

'That'll be the day,' scoffs Pauline Turner.

'. . . but *litter* is the thing we have to guard against. Oh, I do understand, the pub needs the trade, but it's a bit off when the rest of us are left to pick up the pieces. And I'm speaking literally. Last Sunday lunch time, the Major' (she refers to her husband, Royal Engineers, retired) 'saw with his own eyes this *fellow* walk out of The Crown with a bag of crisps, get into his car (radio blaring, of course), eat 'em, toss the bag out of the window and roar away. No time to remonstrate. Lucky for you, I said to the Major. Knock you down soon as look at you, some of these young men nowadays.'

'I can assure you,' protests the landlady, 'Jim goes round every night clearing up, regular as clockwork.'

'Oh, my dear, I know you both pull your weight. You, too, Nan – though, perhaps you won't mind my saying, that bin out there does tend to get over-full. And of

15

course the schoolchildren pile off the bus and come in for their sweets and then just chuck their wrappers in the vague direction . . . And litter travels so. You wouldn't *believe* what I found yesterday in my hedge bottom.'

A general disinclination to be enlightened is indicated by a hoisting of wire baskets.

'That everything for you, Mrs Prior? Shan't keep you a moment Mrs Critch. I think we're all litter-conscious, really,' Nan soothes. 'After all, we did manage second place last year.'

'I know I clear up any clutter in our corner,' Mrs Prior preens. 'You can't fault Pond Cottages.'

'Such a lovely corner of the village, I always think . . .'

But Mrs Bullivant cuts in on her friend. 'I think you'll agree there are *parts* which leave room for improvement?' She looks round, spots a resident of one of these parts, and lowers her voice. 'Penfold Close?' she all but mouths.

The aspersion is not missed by Penfold Close's representative. '*Leave* it,' shouts Karen Watts, venting her indignation on her young daughter. The child's screams waken Bel Rochford's baby. As Bel hurries forward to deposit her basket on the counter, soothing her baby with her free hand, censorious eyes leave Karen Watts to dwell on *her* – a mother of a different sort, they discern, taking in her trim tracksuit, her tall lithe figure, her flaxen hair twisted stylishly into a plait from the crown of her head. 'I think that's the lot,' Bel says brightly. And Nan Hutton, busy reckoning Mrs Prior's bill, smiles and calls Debbie to serve her.

'I hope I'm not pushing in.'

Not at all, they agree, and fall over themselves to admire the baby and its neat sling: 'They think up such clever ideas these days.' 'Yes, I could've done with one of those when our John was a baby; Elizabeth was such a terror to hang on to.' 'Doesn't he look snug, bless him? It *is* a little boy? Oh, Jamie – what a nice name.'

They guess correctly that Jamie's mother comes from The Park, a small up-market housing development. Maintaining a shielding hand round her infant's head, Bel Rochford answers their questions pleasantly, but warily. She has caught the gist of their former conversation and hopes she will not be called upon to pick up litter from or in any other way chivvy The Park, where people prefer to mind their own business, by and large. Also, she is unsure whether her garden would pass muster with these formidable matrons: a once-over with the mower every week during the growing period is as far as husband David will take his horticultural responsibilities, and a spot of weeding plus the insertion of regularly and distantly spaced bedding plants the limit of her own.

'Well, I must get on,' observes Mrs Bullivant as though they are wilfully detaining her. 'You won't forget our little *meeting* tomorrow at The Old Vicarage, Edna?' she calls to Mrs Critch, her tone deliberately mysterious; and though Mrs Prior (employee at The Old Vicarage) attempts to look knowing, in fact only Mrs Critch catches her meaning, is aware that her friend, Mrs Bullivant, is burdened with Big News. For as well as the Best Kept Village Competition and the coffee morning in aid of the church, there is another matter on the village agenda. Mrs Bullivant has learned from an impeccable source (and been sworn to secrecy, which detail she has forgotten) that at long last, after a dozen fruitless applications, Aston Favell may be selected to host an edition of the radio programme, *Gardeners' Question Time*. Nothing is settled, but the news is quite enough to send *ladies who count* in Aston Favell into a preliminary scurry.

'Interfering cow,' Karen Watts spits vengefully as Mrs Bullivant departs. Mrs Critch looks shocked; the others, understanding her fury but reluctant to acknowledge it, maintain carefully blank expressions. Feeling aggrieved, and also that she has failed to express herself with sufficient force, Karen dashes a tube of sweets from her daughter's hand. 'I said, *fucking leave it.*' Brightly coloured discs spatter over the floor.

'Dearie me,' says Nan. 'Give the kiddy another tube, Debbie.' But the child's screams and Karen's ill-temper have hurt the atmosphere as well as their ears; business is briskly concluded, the shop clears.

'Poor little mite,' Debbie mourns, when she and Nan are alone.

As village shopkeeper, Nan knows better than to comment; if a villager committed murder on her door-step, she would risk no more than 'Dearie me.' 'You do the shelves, while I see to the post,' she tells Debbie, and raising her voice to the back room where her husband is skulking over a newspaper, 'Ted, for heaven's sake stir yourself. Fetch in a sack of potatoes.'

Kate is driving home from school on autopilot, her mind going in and out and round about the Will McLeod situation. He looked drawn this morning, she remembers, when she drove past the house and he came out to pick up the milk. She tooted, he waved. Unable to stop in case it made her late, she checked him in the driving mirror: the bottle hung from his hand like a dead weight. He ought to get out more often. Thursdays are not enough.

Sometimes it occurs to her that Will's tragedy is worse than her own. The essential Chris remained un-diminished by illness. To the end he was the man she knew and loved. His last moments of conscious-ness were tender, a leave-taking between two people who were whole to one another, complete in the other's eyes like cut and polished gems. Will, on the other hand, has to watch and cope with a slow de-generation. The brain of Sylvie McLeod has been dying for the past three or more years, starved of its life-blood by solidifying arteries. Premature senile dementia.

Guiltily, Kate admits that she never specially liked Sylvie. Attractive in a fussy sort of way, prone to

18

announce her arrival in the pub with loud (and, she no doubt imagined, tinkly) laughter, to drape herself over some man, to cling and pout and call people darling, Kate found her irritating. Depending on your viewpoint, Sylvie was fun or a bore; unlikely, though, to go unnoticed. At village hops, Will would sit and grin admiringly as his wife hauled successive men onto the floor – flattered, reluctant or downright terrified – to tango, swing or smooch with.

To be fair to Sylvie (the Sylvie she was), Kate recalls the many good things said of her. At first, the nature of Sylvie's disintegration was misunderstood; her behaviour seemed merely exaggerated, as if she had deliberately shifted, or forgotten the existence of, the barrier between acceptably high spirits and being a nuisance. Will and she had rows. He would take her home early. Was driven on one occasion to frogmarching her out of the Elliotts' conservatory (where everyone at the party was trying to ignore Sylvie – except Gordon Byrne who was obliged in self-defence to keep his eyes firmly upon her and even so ended up in the yucca plant). But as she became pathetic – forfeiting her driving licence, ceasing to do her face, forgetting how to dress, how to wash, and what purpose brought her to the village shop – help was sought, the diagnosis made, and people began talking as though she were already dead. Vivacious, lovely, a butterfly; a wonderful dancer, the life and soul, a smile for everyone: these are some of the things they say about Sylvie, shaking their heads at life's perverse cruelty. Though Sylvie was never Kate's idea of a friend, she can appreciate how people were enlivened by her; can guess at the sighs of relief from party-givers as Sylvie appeared on the scene, and how participants at boring village do's perked up with her arrival.

Which is all the more heart-breaking for Will. Everything – the travesty herself and people's sad reminiscence – emphasizing the steepness of her decline; from airy heights to muddy post-cognitive shallows. He is determined not to abandon her. As if the true Sylvie died giving birth to the monstrous infant she has become, he asks constantly what would *she* have wished? Not to be put away, is the answer he arrives at, visualizing flooding tears, clinging hands. So he has arranged his life around caring for her at home; turned a bedroom into a design engineer's office with computer, printer and drawing board, and crams all the visits he must make to clients into Thursdays when Kate comes to spend the day. If for any reason Kate cannot manage a particular Thursday, she has a couple of friends who will stand in. This kindness she performs out of loyalty to Will who was her husband's chum. Of a similar age and outlook, with the same ironic sense of humour, the two men shared a passion for fell-walking and spent several weekends together in the Lakes and Dales.

On her journey home, Kate conjures Will's face which she has always considered handsome. Its cragginess is now deeply grooved and the blue eyes which seemed always lit with amusement reflect weariness. On an impulse, when she turns off the Lavenbrook Road into Main Street, she draws up at High House where the McLeods live – then has to wait before opening the car door for an overtaking delivery van. So by the time she has run round the car and stepped onto the pavement, Will is frowning on the doorstep, blurting, 'Is it about Thursday?'

'No, no. Thursday's fine.'

'Phew. When I saw your car I thought . . . Thing is, if I miss going to Birmingham this week I'll lose the contract. And things are tricky back here,' – he jerks his head towards the house interior – 'I'm not sure anyone but you could cope. Although it's not exactly fair of me . . .'

'Rubbish. Thursday's settled. And look, I've nothing on this evening other than a pile of marking, so why don't I come round here for a couple of hours and keep Sylvie company while you go down to the pub or somewhere?' (He looks bemused, apparently needs time to consider.) 'You'd feel so much better for it, Will – a chinwag, game of darts, even . . .' (A smile breaking out on his face brings his eyes alive, but she scents a refusal.) 'And I honestly don't mind if Sylvie's a bit, er, lively. I mean, the marking doesn't *have* to be finished tonight . . .'

'Thanks,' he interrupts. 'Nice of you to offer. Actually, if I get the chance I'll do some work this evening. I'm rather behind, what with one thing and another.'

A howl, low at first then gaining pitch and intensity, breaks out inside High House – 'Where . . . are . . . you? Where *are* you?' – and Will leaps from the step as though it were red-hot. 'Thursday, then,' he reminds her from the other side of the threshold. 'I'll give you a ring.' And calls as she turns away, 'Thanks, Kate.'

'You *left* me,' Kate hears Sylvie screech before the door shuts.

Feeling flat, she gets into her car, drives home – down Main Street to The Green, then left up Vicarage Hill. The lawnmowers are out in force – diligent villagers engaged in the eternal summer campaign to control lawn and grass verge. Which reminds her, her own could do with a clip. Arriving in her drive, she sits staring at the back garden with mild annoyance. No rain for a fortnight and still green comes thrusting: whatever does it run on, for heaven's sake? After a moment or two, it strikes her that there is more to her annoyance than buoyant grass; she is mad because back there at High House she missed an opportunity. Will said if he got the chance he intended to work this evening. Well, then, she could have offered to go over and keep Sylvie quiet while he worked in peace. She could have made supper. Damn.

She climbs out of the car, collects the exercise books, nudges the door shut, locks it. When she arrives in her cool kitchen and allows the silence and the rational steadiness of the hall clock to bear in on her, she has calmed down, straightened things out. The idea, she remembers, was to release Will, not get herself cooped up with both McLeods. She drops the books on the table, goes to fill the kettle. All the same, it might be a nice idea if, instead of dashing home the moment Will returns next Thursday (as she usually does, twelve or so hours of Sylvie McLeod being quite sufficient), she has supper ready and stays to eat with them. Also, she resolves, when he phones her, she'll repeat the offer to Sylvie-sit one evening. If ever he does feel like getting out, he should let her know – not tomorrow because she has parents' evening at school, and not Wednesday evenings when she goes to exercise class in the village hall – but any other evening would be fine.

Chatting to herself silently in this soothing way (as has become her habit), she makes the tea, takes it to the table, reaches for the uppermost exercise book. Might as well make a start. Then she will mow the lawn, have a drink, stick a dinner-for-one in the microwave, ring the kids, watch telly. Pass the evening. Keep her mind off stupid fears.

In High House, Will, sitting his wife down to table, is recalling Kate on his doorstep – slight and dark, the sun glinting her hair, her large eyes turned up earnestly: he thinks that if by some miraculous arrangement he might have gone to the pub *with* Kate, he would have accepted like a shot. As it is, the thought of desultory conversation with whoever happens to be in the bar this evening does not appeal. Nor does any other solitary expedition. Also, since a recent incident – when Sylvie stole out of the house in her nightdress and made it to The Crown from where he was summoned to come at once and remove her – Will has steered clear of the place. He ties a napkin round Sylvie's neck, absent-mindedly encourages her to eat, and lets his imagination carry him to a better class pub than The Crown – The Woolsack in Carlton, say – where Kate soon joins him by the bar under the old oak beams and together they study a list of succulent-sounding

dishes chalked on a blackboard . . . 'Bluah,' says
Sylvie, pushing out a mouthful of food like a faddy
two-year-old. 'For heaven's *sake*,' he shouts, before
getting a grip on himself. And without another word,
with taut gentleness, starts cleaning her up.

CHAPTER TWO

Tuesday 16th June

Kate has spent a difficult night. The vigilance required the previous evening to pounce on and stifle the merest thought of the Peeping Tom (to the point where, as she switched off the downstairs lights and mounted the stairs, it was her familiar unspecified fear which took hold and caused her to feel for one mad moment that a footfall outside might serve as welcome diversion) proved her downfall once she fell asleep. For liberated from restraint, her subconscious fed on the subject. 'Be sure and lock your doors and draw your curtains, me dear,' quoth a leering and grotesquely enlarged Mrs Prior, tugging on Kate's arm and looming so close as to be smothering; 'we've got a Peeping Tom.' *Peeping Tom, Peeping Tom,* she droned endlessly as Kate fought to wake up (and having done so, discovered the duvet covering her lower face). Further sleep proved impossible until the birds were chirping and the curtains brightening.

Having decided on a recuperative breakfast in the garden, she is preparing toast and tea when the telephone rings. It will be Will, she decides (for no particular reason other than sudden pleasure at the thought of speaking to him), and goes gladly to answer it.

'Hello, Kate,' says her mother.

'Oh . . . Mum,' she says flatly. 'A bit early isn't it?' (She tends to react like this to her mother, striving to discover some justification for pushing her off.)

'Well, love, your dad and I were just saying, we haven't set eyes on you for over two months. It's a lovely day; why don't you drive over?'

A picture of her parents' home looms, the tall gaunt Manse at the side of the grimy road. 'I can't. I can't possibly . . .'

'It's Tuesday, so you're not teaching,' her mother swiftly points out.

Keeping tabs on me, thinks Kate. But even as she condemns her mother, is aware of what drives her to it: that self-serving cry at the crematorium: *But we want to comfort you, dear.* They were returning to the undertaker's cars at the time, turning their backs on the flowers and the smoke plume. Her mother took her arm: 'The twins say they're going straight back to university . . .'

'Yes, I think that's best.'

'So why not come home with your mum and dad?'

'No thanks — if you don't mind. I need to be alone, I need . . .' (It is hard to recall her exact words, only her desperate desire to fend people off.)

But we want to comfort you, dear, bawled her mother, as if her daughter were thwarting her natural right, some huge legitimate maternal appetite.

The cry banged round Kate's skull. It seemed an outrage, on this of all days, to have a demand made of her, an obligation put upon her. 'I don't want to be comforted,' she bellowed back, stating the clear truth; for her raw pain was her last living link to Chris; throbbing, hurting, it maintained him as a physical feature of the present, held off his relegation to the past.

'Well!' her mother exclaimed, gathering herself, as if Kate were ten years old and refusing a role in the Christmas Nativity, thus shaming The Manse and setting a poor example to the congregation.

Insidiously over succeeding months the bitter half-stifled thought has occurred (like a nasty bug poking the tip of its head through good brown earth): how come *they* keep going, on and on, year after year, never changing, never ageing, smug and comfortable and virtuously poor, surrounded by admiring friends, still doing the round of coffee mornings, prayer meetings and Sunday services; how come *they* keep going strong in their seventies, heading inexorably for their eighties, when Chris, oh God, when *Chris . . .*?

Jesus Christ! she once swore at her reflection, catching herself thinking along these lines — You're not seriously suggesting you'd swop them, you're not asking Fate to do a rewrite? *Ye-e-e-es*, she screamed in her head, pushing away from the mirror and her sour face.

How much of this is the desire of a hurt child to punish its mother (who after all is responsible for its presence in a hard and pitiless world), she cannot fathom. With an effort, she now makes her voice conciliatory. 'I'm *sorry*, Mum, but I've got parents' evening later on. And you know how it gets towards the end of term — exam papers to mark, reports to fill in . . .' At her mother's sigh, she breaks off. She is being unfair, she ought to stop being so hard on her. If one of the twins were desperately hurt, wouldn't *she* yearn to provide comfort? Of course she would. 'Tell you what, I'll try and come over next Tuesday.'

'Oh Kate, will you? We do worry about you, dear. We only want to help.'

'Mum, I can help myself . . . Look, I must go now — things to prepare for tonight. But I daresay I'll make it next week. 'Bye, now.'

'Goodbye, dear — let us know,' her mother's sharp voice gets in before, very gently, Kate cradles the receiver.

The Old Vicarage on Vicarage Hill, whose garden wall runs opposite Wayside Cottage and Kate's immediate neighbours, is the grandest house in Aston Favell. The former manor burned to the ground during the last century; the executive housing estate known as The Park has been built on what was once manor parkland, with a few large remaining trees – oak, lime, horse chestnut – indicating what had been the vista. 'Old' as applied to The Vicarage denotes former use rather than age, for it is not nearly so ancient a house as those nearby, but Georgian, built in the days when the Church offered fat livings to parsons born in the right station. The present incumbent (who would not have qualified – and, should this be brought to his attention, would lose not a minute's sleep) has five parishes in his care and resides in a modern house in the neighbouring village of Symington. The Old Vicarage was sold forty years ago to Jock Cunningham, successful property developer and businessman and a very big wheel at county level in the Conservative Party. As *Sir* Jock, he married the actress Fenella Ford who was famous in the fifties for the beauty, wit and elegance she brought to West End drawing room comedies. Their home became the scene of glamorous parties and political weekends. But now Sir Jock is dead. For the past five years, only his widow Fenella and sister Molly have inhabited The Old Vicarage.

The drive to the portico steps is long and curved and sheltered by shrubs; a monkey puzzle tree and a spruce form ceremonial guard. There are wide, trim lawns before the windows, backed by herbaceous borders full of neatly staked blooms and broken by rectangular rose beds. Most clement days find Molly Cunningham at work somewhere in the garden.

The visitors spot her here this Tuesday afternoon, her old straw hat bobbing among the rose bushes, her secateurs reaching to snip off dead-heads. 'Good afternoon, Miss Cunningham,' calls Mrs Bullivant; she waves, too, with her whole body, as if guiding an enormous tanker into a tight parking space. But today Molly is blind as well as deaf. The ladies find this disappointing, for Molly and not Lady Cunningham is the expert gardener. They hesitate on the drive, wondering whether to call more loudly – Mrs Bullivant, Mrs Critch, Mrs Haycroft, Mrs Potton, and the two

Miss Jameses. Their group is entirely *ad hoc*. They do not officially represent Aston Favell Horticultural Society. But news that the BBC is at last seriously considering the Society's long-standing request to host *Gardeners' Question Time* has prompted them to take the initiative, to draw up one or two plans and decide which members should be encouraged – and which not – to address a question to the panel. For the very best must be made of this opportunity. Within the five parish group, Carlton can boast of The Manor, Carlton-le-Walls of The Hall; Symington – the largest and in most people's eyes the least attractive of the villages – has the school and the hideous modern rectory, and Tetchborough is merely a farming hamlet. What Aston Favell has going for it is the Aston Favell Horticultural Society (to which gardeners living in the other parishes also subscribe) and a spanking new village hall in which to house the Society's meetings and slide shows (as well as numerous other functions). The ladies envisage only too well what might happen without such pre-thought: some people unused to the limelight getting carried away with their own importance. As Mrs Bullivant said to Mrs Haycroft only yesterday afternoon: 'You know how the media go for *types*. If we're not careful they'll encourage some dreadful old codger like Barney Coles to hold forth on his allotment. Or Granny Dobbs with her "me dear" and "me duck". It'd be a tragedy if people got the wrong impression of Aston Favell . . .' So *ladies who count* in the village have arranged this afternoon's gathering. No-one has sent them. They know who they are.

'My dears,' – the cry throaty, the arms gathering. Fenella Cunningham tripping down the portico steps so successfully conveys strappy sandals, floaty chiffon, cartoon advertisements for *les parfums Worth,* that she forgets, and they fail to register, her brogue lace-ups, tweed skirt, baggy cashmere jumper. 'Come *in*. Molly, darling,' she trills faintly, 'our visitors are here.' At which a dingy white terrier emerges from the vicinity of the rose bushes onto the lawn, sees who it is and growls.

'Molly will be in directly,' Fenella says firmly and leads urgently, searchingly, through the portico into the hall, and starts peering into rooms. 'Ah, here we are,' she cries at last, spying tea things laid out, evidently by nameless servants who are a law unto themselves and not she and the daily woman an hour earlier. 'Do sit down. Anywhere,' she adds recklessly, herself perching on the window seat, hands thrust into the cushions, stiff arms making wings of pushed up shoulders round her lovely tilted-back head. Her softly waved hair these days is allowed to be as grey as it likes, her powdered skin sags in criss-crossed lines from the famous bones; yet *lovely* is what she projects, and *lovely* is what – to varying degrees – they imagine they see. Like a matinée audience they sit on the chairs and settee ranged before her.

Lovely is not at all what Molly Cunningham sees when, followed by her surly Sealyham, she enters the room and sits at the edge of the group. Maybe this is because, not having been a theatre-goer, she never learned to suspend disbelief. Or perhaps because in the good old days of television when her sister-in-law appeared in genteel plays and parlour games, Molly's preference for American cop shows saved her from being stuck, as are the others, with a mental image of Fenella's head framed glamorously by a TV screen. More likely, she has seen aspects of Lady Cunningham denied to the general public, and these remain uppermost.

Mention of *Gardeners' Question Time* reminds Fenella of her former triumphs. 'Oh, the BBC,' she cuts in, clutching her throat. ''Fraid I can't help you there. Of course, there was a time . . .' Her eyes go sad, the ladies sigh: she shudders – 'Dretful people running it nowadays.'

Patiently, Mrs Haycroft brings the matter into more lowly, local focus; for instance, the problem of who

29

should put which questions, bearing in mind the need for variety of topic and suitability of questioner. Mrs Bullivant repeats everything very loudly for Molly Cunningham's benefit, who, fearful of being called upon to perform publicly in any capacity whatever, pronounces her garden entirely problem free. 'Diction,' postulates Fenella Cunningham, on a different tack altogether. 'So important to find people who know how to speak. Everyone mumbles so nowadays.'

Mrs Potton has a brainwave. 'Perhaps we should all think up some interesting questions and then sort out who should actually put them.'

But the elder Miss James (Davinia), a keen follower of the radio programme, has doubts. The questions, she declares ringingly, always relate quite definitely to the questioner.

'Oh it may *sound* like that,' says Mrs Potton, a cynic, 'but I daresay it's all carefully stage-managed. I mean, who hasn't got problems left by the drought? Who, living round here, isn't plagued by black spot?'

This is too technical for Fenella. Loudly, she suggests it is time to make tea, whereupon Molly goes out to do the making and Esmé, the younger Miss James, follows to lend a hand. Fenella girds herself to entertain the rest – to give of herself is how she thinks of it, regarding this as her artistic duty. Unstintingly, in bewildering succession, she demonstrates herself in several varieties: submissively humble as she offers to share whatever she has learned of her craft with anyone desirous of addressing the panel; graciously magnanimous as she volunteers The Old Vicarage and its hospitality to the BBC; skittish as she confides how she was once guilty of an unfortunate malapropism when a panellist on *Spot The Couple*. Even, when Mrs Bullivant invites her to join their anti-litter vigilante group, convincing them of her fragile unsuitability, despite the evidence of their eyes – that here is a strong-limbed woman, athletic in her movements, of a physical vigour belying her seventy-odd years.

Afterwards will come a savage let-down. For this she will blame not sparing herself. 'Drained, spent, poured away to the very last drop,' she will wail, lying on her bed in despair, carefully not facing up to the true cause of her depression. Which is that the moments when she is on show, the moments she was born for and are the only occasions when she feels truly alive, come far too rarely these days. Once they were all her days – rehearsals, performances, business meetings, the social whirl; and after her marriage (although her career floundered with the new low taste for kitchen sink theatre and people on television taking their clothes off) still continually in the spotlight as the idolized wife, the radiant hostess, the essential guest. Jock dying meant not only losing her most loyal, devoted, generous fan, but also seemed to bring down life's curtain. Sometimes she manages to scrabble beneath it and come up on the other side almost begging for applause and notice, but the plain fact is, she is no longer necessary to the big occasion. At first she thought everyone must assume she was in prolonged mourning, even wondered whether she had overdone The Grieving Widow; but her hints and then direct offers were never taken up. The Old Vicarage, in the absence of the great wheeler-dealer, was no longer a desirable venue for weekend politicking – evidently, her role had counted for less than she appreciated – and parties without Jock were total flops. She had not before grasped how very much he *presented* her – brought her forth to be admired, made of her a rare and delightful centrepiece. Not only a love-match, theirs had been a social partnership, she understood belatedly. Some friends, of course, remained loyal. But overnight her life was reduced and has since run on a very small scale; sunbursts of happiness are eked out in widely spaced lunch dates, afternoon teas, and when she is extremely fortunate, evenings with not-too-late bedtimes. Life during the last two years, during which three old friends have died and several become infirm, has become more minimal still. Their son, Miles, comes to visit when he can (as current wife, girl friends, business deals permit). Often, she reflects glumly, she is dependent for a little brightness on such as these village women – though even in the midst of her depression, she knows better than to lump the James sisters in this category; she has always 'known' Davinia and Esmé, whose social standing led to invitations as a matter of course to The Old Vicarage in its heyday, with dear Jock unfailingly gallant to 'the James girls'. The others here today are a different matter, but she laughingly tells herself that she has become kinder in her old age, more tolerant, less fastidious. Sometimes, when there has been little or no social contact for days and no relief from an aching loss engendered by wilfully flooding memories (other than the chance to annoy Molly or tease her dog), the bleakness of it all throws her off balance. She has to run to her room, fling herself down, cry, punch the pillows, until she has spent her frustration and can wander through the next few days in a dream state of not properly feeling anything.

This afternoon, on top of her form, selflessly bestowing (or greedily enjoying), she is always aware of the cost to come. Afterwards, when they have gone, then it will hit her. But the knowledge only spurs her to greater selflessness (or more desperate indulgence) – to give, give, give (or have, have, have) while she can.

'It's been so nice, Lady Cunningham.'

'Yes, lovely. A treat.'

'Don't forget my coffee morning a week on Thursday in aid of the church. You, too, Miss Cunningham. I SAID YOU TOO, MISS CUNNINGHAM – COFFEE MORNING AT SUNNY BANK A WEEK ON THURSDAY.'

Satisfied with their afternoon, feeling much has been aired if not decided (but these are early days), they depart. At the end of the drive, where the James sisters must turn left up Vicarage Hill to Rose Cottage and the others right towards The Green, they linger for a few more minutes.

                              *   *   *

In the large hall of Lavenbrook Comprehensive, parental interviews are under way. Tables have been placed about the hall at discreet distances; interviews are conducted at these, while waiting parents examine wall displays and information pamphlets or chat to the Head or one of her deputies. By nine fifteen, Kate's last interview is concluded. She is tired, but would not consider leaving until she has helped with the clearing up. Because some members of staff are still busy with parents, she merely gathers up her pupils' work files and sets off to distribute them in the appropriate classrooms.

Her shoes tap with hollow resonance along lighted corridors. On her left, her reflection in dusk-backed windows is the only movement. On her right, though an occasional room has been lit by a colleague engaged on a similar mission, in the main the classrooms are dark and deserted. It feels almost indecent to be here at this time – like spying on an acquaintance who imagines there are no observers and has dropped the guard of public demeanour. Because noise and activity are the norm, this private calm is as startling as the springing emptiness of her dining room with Chris's bed gone from it.

She goes into a fourth-form room and deposits some files, then moves on to the fifth-form area. Entering the lower-sixth, she bumps into Josie Templar, who hangs back for her. They return together through the empty corridors.

'How'd it go?' asks Josie.

'Fine. OK for you?'

'Yes – apart from the Mastersons.'

'Oh, God, I know, I had them too. So over-anxious.'

'You can say that again. Must be terrible for Ben. Fancy having those two for parents, constantly breathing down your neck.'

They chat till they arrive at the staffroom, where Josie elects to make the traditional cups of tea and

                                    33

coffee and Kate returns to the hall to discover who wants which.

By now people are clearing up, folding tables and chairs, humping them across the floor to where George O'Mally the caretaker is storing them in the cavity under the stage.

'Thank you, everyone,' calls the Head, Irene Cobb. 'Refreshments are laid out in the staffroom.'

Cakes and sandwiches — Irene's treat — are fallen on eagerly. They grab their drinks, gossip, joke, sympathize with those who have endured a difficult session. Joining in avidly, Kate's fatigue slips away. She refers a student's problem to Robin Squires, her Head of Department, and exchanges news with Irene Cobb about their daughters who are close friends. At five minutes to ten, recalling that she has further to travel than most, she rinses her cup at the sink, collects her bag, calls 'Goodnight', and without thinking, goes straight to the side door which gives on to the staff car park — then recollects that of course it is locked; all outside doors other than the main entrance are locked at 6 p.m. She retraces her steps, passes the Head's office and the secretary's, goes through the reception area and out through the main swing doors.

It is still not completely dark, though near to the lighted part of the building it appears quite black. Cars are rushing by on a side road. Not until she has turned the corner do her ears detect any further sound — and then she is brought to a halt: a low chortling, stage-whispered exhortation — the croaky tones of male adolescents. Between parked cars jutting shadows dart, pale skin flashes, some object gleams. There is a thud, an impact, then a juddering tearing hissing noise. Tyre slashers! Her first reaction is selfish dismay as the unbearable prospect hits her of hanging around school for hours into the night, sorting out repairs, arranging transport . . .

'Hey, this one's old Dicey's. I seen him in it.'

'Yeah. Let him have it, the plonker.'

34

Lads from here, from this school – otherwise how would they know Gareth Dicey's car? *Gareth Dicey* – the troubles currently afflicting this particular colleague zoom in her head: he doesn't *need* this. 'Stop!' she yells, beginning a dash to the far side of the car park. 'Stop that at once.' The youths, who froze at her first yelp, rapidly recover; two chase off over the darkened playing field, a third ducks down by Gareth Dicey's car. As she runs, she screeches with maximum force (aiming not only to dissuade the tyre-slasher but also to alert her colleagues), 'LEAVE . . . THAT . . . CAR . . . ALONE!' He leaves the car, but steps into her path. He has hitched a looped scarf over the lower half of his face. He is pointing a knife. Even as she falters, she is suffused with rage. Ahead on the playing field, one of the fleers also pauses. 'C'*mon*,' he cries urgently, 'don't be a dick-head.' And then, behind, voices break out, feet come running, someone shouts her name. Her eyes are on the knife, but she calls back defiantly – 'Over here!' At which, suddenly thinking better of the enterprise, her challenger turns and swoops after his cohorts. 'Over here,' she screams again, pounding straight after him. On the lumpy field, the heel of her shoe gets snagged; she flies forward, lands with her face in the grass, the breath banged out of her, frustration pounding her veins, and an image taunting her of the vandals making good their escape into the maze of walkways on the housing estate beyond.

When her colleagues retrieve her, it is some moments before Kate fully comprehends why they are making a fuss. Is she hurt? Is she OK – the yobs haven't cut her? What the hell was she doing going after them? All these tyres slashed – they had *knives*, for goodness' sake – surely she realized? 'You were absolutely mad,' pronounces Irene Cobb.

It slowly dawns on her that – yes – unarmed, slight of stature, single-handed, she hurled herself towards, attempted to prevent, three knife-wielding louts. 'But they were *ours*,' she protests weakly. 'I didn't get much of a look, but they were definitely ours. Third or fourth years, I'd say.'

'With *knives*, Kate . . .'

'Yes,' she agrees. 'But I didn't think, I was so furious. They'd started on your car, Gareth, when I yelled and put them off. At least it stopped them slitting the near-side tyres.'

Understandably, Gareth is too stunned by the existing damage to offer gratitude for its limitation. Satisfied that Kate has come to no harm, they inspect their cars more closely: loud groans go up, curses, commiserations, some muted cries of relief; and for one rare moment Irene Cobb loses her temper. 'Sodding little bastards,' she explodes, kicking her coupé's splayed off-side-rear. 'To think I've been slaving away on their behalf since half-past bloody seven this morning. Now what? Police, I suppose, the AA . . . Christ, is it worth it?' The thankfulness flooding Kate at the discovery of her own car's unscathed condition turns quickly to guilty concern. 'Leave it till morning, Irene. Get some kip – I'll run you home.'

Having had her blow-out, Irene has recovered. 'Thanks, but I think we'd better get organized.'

Robin Squires agrees. 'If we just leave everything, what's the betting their older brothers come back to hack out the engines? We'll have shells of cars by morning,'

'And we can't expect George to mount guard all night. However, there's no point everyone hanging about. You get off, Kate. And you, Josie.'

They demur politely, but are easily persuaded. As they turn towards their cars, Josie squeezes Kate's arm. 'I know I shouldn't, but I can't help feeling grateful you arrived on the scene. I'm absolutely knackered. I'd die if I had all that to contend with.'

'Me too,' confesses Kate, climbing into her car. Her limbs are so shaky, she can hardly fit the key in the ignition or control the clutch. She drives hesitantly to the road, turns left, and a few metres further on pauses at traffic lights. By the time the lights go green, her body has relaxed; she pulls away more confidently.

As she runs out of town and street lighting, her headlights cutting into settled darkness, her thoughts return to her stranded colleagues. How weary, how down-cast they looked. And no wonder: some of them had worked a thirteen or fourteen hour day. She is glad that at least she prevented further devastation, glad she gave the culprits a fright – yes, specially glad about that. In retrospect, it seems crazy, shocking, appalling that she challenged louts armed with knives, but at the same time she gloats at the memory, plays it over and over. It is such a novel view of herself after these fear-ridden months – exhilarating to discover she can still face up to a threat, still refuse to be intimidated. Next time she trembles at imagined terror, let her just remember tonight! Her speed increases, as though she can't wait to get home and exhibit her fearless self. She turns smartly into Aston Favell, zooms along Main Street, swoops up Vicarage Hill, arrives with neat aplomb in her yard, springs out, locks up, and strides, key at the ready, to her kitchen door. As she opens it and before she steps over the threshold, it seems wearily predictable that her mind should conjure a Peeping Tom; but she deals with this sternly – a one-off, she declares, locking and bolting her door; Nan Hutton was probably right, the prowler at Ellwood's farm was just one of the village lads fooling around. She draws the curtains over the sink, puts on the kitchen light, then runs over the house closing curtains, pressing light switches, looking into cupboards, peering under beds. (She does not expect to discover an intruder in the airing cupboard, much less in the few vacant inches beneath the pine-framed beds in the twins' rooms. Simply, this is her evening routine, undertaken to remove the least excuse.) The routine accomplished, she goes bounding downstairs with a sense of expectation, full of the evening's adventure, bursting to report . . .

What an idiot. Stupid, pathetic fool. Who the hell did she imagine she was going to report *to*?

She stands at a loss on the sitting-room threshold, staring at the chair where Chris would sit, feeling the house watching her confusion – a myriad hidden, knowing, eyes. Quickly, wrathfully, she extinguishes all the downstairs lights and returns upstairs.

In the bathroom, she cleans her teeth and scrubs her face and studies her reflection in the mirror over the basin. At last lets herself off. Allows absolution. What it is, she now sees, is that living with someone for years and years, you develop a habit of sharing any significant happening, of enlarging upon it, making extra sense of it, and of discussing, arguing and joking about what other people say and do, and items of news on the telly that particularly strike you, or things you have read in the papers or books; after a while, things haven't fully happened or been properly experienced until this sharing has taken place. The telling is the climax, the peak. The best bit of all.

Now she has given herself heartache, damn it. She goes into her bedroom, shuts and locks the door. Sets the alarm (school tomorrow); climbs into bed, turns off the lamp.

CHAPTER THREE

Wednesday 17th June

In his drop-side cot in the nursery of 5 The Park,
Jamie Rochford is breathing and bubbling through his
afternoon nap. The warmth of the day accounts for
his wearing only nappy pants. He lies on his back (in
the approved fashion) with fat knees lolling outwards,
his chest and thighs smothered in tiny red pimples
which were this morning reassuringly diagnosed as
heat rash. For this reason his mother has propped the
window wide. Net curtains billow, hanging chimes
clank gently, and all the gaily-coloured birds, fish,
and geometric shapes suspended from several mobiles,
circulate like participants in a stately mating ritual.
A tumble of soft toys ranges over an easy chair. A
teddybear has been stationed at the foot of Jamie's
cot. In a box and over the floor at one end of the
room, a large collection of wooden and plastic toys
— to push along, bash, build with, construct with,
and, in the case of the rocking horse, ride upon —
await the day when Jamie is old enough to do these
things. On a table lies a baby changer and a pretty
woven basket full of baby cleansing equipment. Out
of sight in the chest of drawers are sufficient clothes
to accommodate half a dozen babyhoods. For Jamie
Rochford is a planned baby.

Planned, in fact, to arrive three or four years ago.
After a life of nearly thirty years, during which all
essential features occurred promptly on time — success at school and the poly, swift progress through

management college and quickly up the career ladder, handsome and talented husband acquired – a baby failing to turn up was a profound jolt to Bel's confidence. Jamie's eventual and natural arrival (after tests and the hideous prospect of a fertility programme) seemed like Fate letting her off. She has promised Fate (or God or Nature or whichever jealous power is in charge of doling out life chances) never again to take good fortune for granted.

Half an hour has elapsed since Jamie went down. Bel, who has been watching the clock, steals upstairs to check that he is still breathing and whether the heat rash is fading. Breathing is normal, but as she might have known, the pimples look much as before. She stares at this disfigurement and berates herself for having allowed her infant to get over hot. All that strapping him to her – though the doctor said the sling is not the cause of the rash, he probably does not realize how often Bel uses it. The truth is, she cannot stand Jamie's body separated from hers, lives in perpetual fear of some terrible outcome if she is not actively succouring him. After all, you do read of babies suddenly ceasing to breathe for no reason. Night-times are worst. The nursery is equipped with a monitor and an intercom, but Bel knows she would rest more easily if she remained in Jamie's room rather than lying beside husband David in the kingsize bed, straining her ears and chewing her knuckles. The trouble is, David is getting pretty fed up. He resents the way she is often on edge, swears she no longer attends to a word he says. Trying to appear less anxious, to show an interest in her husband's doings, to smile and laugh occasionally, only intensifies the strain. 'Every first time mother gets these silly little worries,' says Bel's mother blithely. 'Do try and relax more, dear, for David's sake. Shall I come and stay again? Your father won't mind, he's ever so good these days, a better cook than I ever was.'

'*No*. I mean, ever so nice of you, Mum, but honestly I can manage.' (Her mother came to help when she brought Jamie home from hospital. A nightmare – her mother completely out of touch, pooh-poohing procedures strongly recommended at baby class. 'Let him cry, he won't hurt,' she soothed; and, comfortably, 'For goodness sake, Belinda, we all have to eat a peck of dirt before we go.' Most alarming of all was, 'But *you* always slept on your tummy.' '*Cot death*,' screamed an accusing Bel, as if her mother putting Jamie down to rest were deliberately engineering his demise.)

A faint rhythmic thumping penetrates Bel's hearing. She goes to the window. Her next-door neighbour, Tina Fairbrother, is sunbathing below in a garden which resembles a beach – sunbed, windbreak sheltering the far side of Tina's prone bare body, towelling robe to hand for emergency cover-up, bottles of sun lotion, transistor radio (which is playing too softly, Bel decides, to adversely affect her sleeping child. She is thankful for this but at the same time alarmed; for if Tina were to turn up the volume for any reason, that insidious thump-thump might affect Jamie's heartbeat. Her mother, of course, would scoff at this idea, but Bel has definitely read somewhere . . .)

A telephone shrills in number seven. Tina's hand shoots out, slams down on a radio button, reaches for the gown. As she rolls off the sun lounger and before she quite covers herself, Bel gets a swift but impactful glimpse of bouncing brown breasts – and immediately recalls the gossip in the shop last Monday morning about a Peeping Tom. She paid scant heed at the time, but now feels there may well be substance to the story. What is more, the scene she has just witnessed removes the prowler from some misty and remote venue, and brings him right here close to home. She almost hates Tina, who is inviting trouble, the thoughtless bitch. Any decent sensible person would be extra careful with a pervert on the loose and a helpless baby next door.

This, thinks Bel, going softly downstairs to check whether the doors are locked, is the sort of thing you just don't foresee when you go house-hunting for a peaceful and private location. The Park is a close of nine substantial detached houses, each set in a generous plot. Compared to many the Rochfords viewed in this price range, it is a spacious development. In any case, paying out that sort of money, you expect quiet and considerate neighbours. Generally, this has proved to be the case. For much of the day The Park is deserted. In the morning, the men leave early, the older children run for the school bus, mothers are usually gone by nine after dropping off any younger offspring at school. Mid-afternoon sees the start of the return – first of younger children and a few mums, then of dawdling older children, around half-past five or six of the women who work full time, and finally of the Volvo, Audi and Citroën driving men. Only Les Fairbrother (who drives a Jag and keeps irregular hours) and his wife Tina in number seven, and Bel in number five, fail to fit this pattern. Tina has two children at primary school and a cleaning woman twice a week, and devotes her days to shopping and body-grooming and researching for these activities in glossy magazines. Of course, Bel must stay at home to look after Jamie: at thirty-two, by no means the youngest mother, she is the only one in The Park with an infant.

The fact that they are the only people at home for most of the day has made contact between Bel and Tina inevitable. Bel, whose career before Jamie interrupted it was in personnel management for a famous and prestigious retail company, knows it will be better for all concerned if they can be friendly. And there are times when she is glad of the contact. Tina is good-natured; she will always bring items back from town for Bel, or send one of her children to the village shop. She has even offered to baby sit while Bel goes to get her hair done, but Bel refused this offer (imagine leaving Jamie with Tina; imagine her handling him with those long painted finger-nails . . .); she prefers

42

to leave him with his father and brave the Saturday crush. Tina is a friend selected by circumstance. This must often be the case, Bel supposes, for women stuck at home with young children.

Although David wrote off Les Fairbrother on first sight of the beer belly, he encourages his wife to be friendly with Tina. He thinks it is healthy for her to have adult day-time company and was glad when Tina recommended the women's exercise class on Wednesday nights in the village hall. ('Fiona's ever so good,' Tina enthused. 'She can teach everything – aerobics, step, yoga . . . And forty if she's a day, but still looks fantastic; her body's a terrific advertisement . . .') Bel always hates leaving Jamie, but once she gets to the class enjoys herself and feels so much better afterwards for the exercise. Also, it has proved a useful plank in her self-defence. When David accuses her of becoming one-track minded and obsessed by motherhood, she can point to Wednesday nights as evidence to the contrary.

Today being Wednesday, Bel wonders whether, because of the heat rash, she ought to stay at home this evening. In the end, decides it would be better to go to the class as usual: David gets so touchy if she implies (without meaning to of course) that he is the less competent parent. Having checked the doors (locked), she goes to the foot of the stairs to listen. No sound issues from above other than the chimes tinkling, so she decides to prepare the evening meal in advance in order to be free to devote her full attention to Jamie's tea and playtime.

Tina Fairbrother, wearing brief white shorts and skimpy top to show her tanned limbs to advantage, jumps into her Golf GTI, drives slowly to the mouth of The Park, turns left, snaps on the car radio and goes bopping down Main Street – bopping, that is, with head and such other parts of her anatomy as driving permits. She passes The Green and the turn into Vicarage Hill, passes

43

the corner with Lovatt's Lane, takes the curve round the pond (backed by Pond Cottages); at which point Main Street narrows and becomes Symington Road and leads, three miles on, to the village of that name where Tina's children are at this moment in school enjoying story and clearing-up time.

Symington is a larger, more sprawling village than Aston Favell. Its large housing development secured the retention of Symington school when other village schools were closing. Children are bussed here from several surrounding villages. Tina wouldn't dream of abandoning Blaize and Sean to the school bus service. Every morning, in jump suit and dark glasses to disguise the fact that she hasn't yet done her make-up, she drives them here, and every afternoon, never wearing the same outfit two days running, collects them. Sometimes she arrives here in the afternoon from a shopping trip, sometimes takes the children on to town or to play at Melanie's house. But because today is Wednesday and she has spent most of it boosting her tan, she must now hurry home to prepare the children's tea, put something in the oven for Les, and be ready for exercise class by seven fifteen.

She draws up. The car ahead of her in the line is a little Peugeot sprayed brilliant yellow – not a standard colour, a customized job. When Tina first saw this she was jealous, but on reflection thinks she is better off sticking to white (so long as the white is deep and dazzling): yellow would clash with lots of the colours she likes to wear. If Les agrees to a respray next spring, perhaps she will have some discreet and pretty transfers added. Freshen it until it's time to trade it in . . . She jumps out of the car and runs ahead to the Peugeot. 'Hi, Melanie.'

'Tina – Hi. God, you're so brown. How d'you do it? I've spent a fortune at Shapers and look at me against you.'

Pleased, Tina allows Melanie to place an arm against hers; swears falsely that she can detect no difference.

When children begin to appear in the playground, Melanie hops out of her car and they dawdle onto the pavement. Here they wait, like two birds of paradise bizarrely caught up in a flock of sparrows, starlings and other common or garden birds – mums on foot with prams and toddlers, mums leaning against battered estates, sitting in decent little saloons, leaning out of Land Rovers, mostly dressed in unremarkable workaday clothes, waiting singly or chatting in couples or groups.

Melanie lives in yet another village, Carlton, in a lavishly converted farmhouse. No amount of reflection has managed to assuage Tina's jealousy over the farmhouse. Maybe we should buy an older property, she said to her husband. You can do them up fantastic. Make them really individual. I mean, these in The Park are nice, but whatever you do, they're basically the same. But Les says there's no way he's going to tie money up in property – not in this sort of market – no way. So Tina sighs and moans to Melanie about how boring it is living in 7 The Park, with no outlet for her creativity; and Melanie, gratified, confides the drawbacks of her own situation – how you can't so much as have a builder call to give an estimate without Mrs Nose next door winging round to ask what you're planning and have you got permission from the Listed Building people. Honestly, Tina, the trouble we had pulling down that old dairy. I mean, it was an eyesore, never mind a danger to the children, and stuck just where we wanted to build the swimming pool . . .

Tina and Melanie met on such a day as this two years ago, waiting to collect their children. From the first they recognized in each other the right stuff for intimacy. Once or twice a week they visit a health club in town together, and on some other day in the week take turns to collect all four children and gossip and drink tea while their children play.

Today, their children emerge singly, Tina's daughter, Blaize, is followed by Melanie's daughter, Tamara. Then

45

follow their sons, Melanie's Ross, Tina's Sean. They pile into their cars. Shout, call, wave. Tina backs and turns, and for the second time that day, begins the return trip to Aston Favell.

Kate is sitting with a detective constable in the Deputy Head's room, staring at photographs of three fourth-year boys — cheap head shots taken in a booth and attached, as the school requires, to the pupil's record. She has already explained — first thing this morning, again this afternoon and now after school — that her view of the tyre-slashers was poor; it was virtually dark, only one of the miscreants actually faced her and he had the lower part of his face covered. Nevertheless, these three lads (promising candidates according to the detective) have failed to come to school today and cannot be contacted at home. Covering the lower portion of their faces, Kate stares into each pair of eyes in turn — the first pair cheeky, the second wide and innocent, the third curiously blank. No memory stirs. She shakes her head, repeats her story for what she hopes is the final time, departs.

Within minutes she is speeding home to Aston Favell. What a day — nothing but interruptions and requests to cover for colleagues still inconvenienced by last night's attack. Constantly recounting the incident has made her tense; her limbs feel cramped and nervy. Thank heaven for exercise class tonight — a good work-out, friendly company, a relaxed and carefree evening. She is glad, too, that tomorrow will bring a change of scene. After today, keeping an eye on Sylvie McLeod will seem almost restful.

By seven o'clock, the children fed and bathed and settled in front of the TV screen, a meal in the oven for Les (cottage cheese salad having taken care of her own needs), a sixth-former from over the road (Jenny) sitting with Sean and Blaize until Les's or Tina's return (whichever is the sooner), Tina is pulling a leotard

46

over her filmy footless tights. She straightens and looks at herself in the long wide mirror. The leotard, in pearlized tangerine to match the tights, is a new one, cut more daringly than some of her previous numbers – perhaps a bit too scantily for the village hall; ought she to save it for Shapers? She turns, looks over her head at her pearlized buttocks, executes a few steps, a few stretches, a few thrusts forward from the hips. The sight of her image precipitates a stomach-fluttering excitement. Thing is, she looks great. She'll knock 'em out, they won't be able to keep their eyes off her, even those who pretend not to notice. Yeah – 'course she'll wear it.

Tina's greatest thrill comes from knowing she is drawing eyes. Whether they are male or female eyes is immaterial, just so long as they're hooked. Eyes are her desire, what she lives to seduce; not fingers, hands, arms, lips: *eyes* – lustful, curious, envious, even unwilling – but *captured*: a conquest with no resulting inconvenience, annoyance or embarrassment; no bespoiling of the image she takes such pains with. This is the reason why Tina loves Wednesday nights. All that speechless attention. Melanie can't think why she bothers when the subscription to Shapers allows up to three sessions a week. What's the point, she asks, in jumping and rolling about on a filthy floor with *that* lot, when you could be having a proper work-out in spotless comfort? Tina smiles virtuously and says you have to support a village when you live in one; and in any case she feels a duty to Bel next door who needs to get out and probably wouldn't bother if Tina didn't. At this Melanie looks impressed. Tina knows what she is thinking – that her friend Tina is a good sort. Which is very satisfactory: a good sort (with amazing looks) is how Tina wishes her friends to think of her.

Time to go. She pulls a loose tracksuit over the leotard, ties on her trainers, grabs her bag, runs downstairs. It is Bel's turn to drive this week, so having called out last-minute instructions to Jenny and her children, she slams the door behind her and runs across her drive and over the lawn which links numbers seven and five. (All the front gardens in The Park are open plan, while those to the rear are separately fenced.)

Looking flustered, Bel hurries from her house and leads to the Rochford car. 'Hi – just made it – Jamie's got a heat rash – I was going to leave it, then thought I'd try a bit of calamine – hope it won't hurt – phew.' She pauses in the driver's seat, catching her breath. Then yanks the seat belt over her shoulder and turns to check whether her passenger has done likewise. 'You look nice, Tina,' she comments, sensing, somehow, that this will get the evening off to a good start.

Bel smells faintly of cooking and baby powder, Tina notices. 'I was pretty rushed myself, what with settling the kids, fixing something for Les, getting ready and so forth.'

'Uhuh,' says Bel vaguely, wondering whether David would have the sense to send for her in the event of Jamie not settling.

They do not have far to go, the hall is less than half a mile from the village centre. They could walk, really, but hardly anyone does. In the winter, of course, it would be too unpleasant, for the streets are poorly lit. You go up Main Street as far as the pub, turn left into North Street, keep going, passing the turn into Penfold Close (which consists of council housing), passing the allotments, and there you have it – a long, low, modern brick building containing large hall, small meeting room, kitchen, lavatories.

The hall was finally built a couple of years ago, funded by ten years' worth of fêtes, bazaars, coffee mornings, jumble sales and donations. As many people bewail, especially elderly folk from long-established village families, it lacks the cosy atmosphere of the old church hall – which the licensing authorities condemned as unsafe and unsanitary and has since been demolished. In theory, the new hall should enhance village life; in practice, several activities (beetle drives, over-sixties' teas, mums' and toddlers' mornings) have trailed off and the only real benefit has been to parish income derived from hiring out the hall for functions and wedding receptions.

Bel pulls into the car park where several cars are already stationed. More arrive. People wave, call greetings. 'Hello,' cries Kate Woolard, springing out of Fiona Nealson's car. 'Oh, hello,' replies Bel, who has mentally marked Kate out as someone she would like to get acquainted with. 'Looks like a good turn-out tonight,' Fiona comments with satisfaction. And Bel feels her spirits rise.

It is the end of the first half. Thoroughly warmed and enlivened, they will have a ten-minute breather before getting down to the serious stuff – muscle toughening, spine stretching, groan-inducing work.

Her friend Zoë flops down in a chair next to Kate's. 'Phew. Tried to get you on the phone earlier. Are you all right for tomorrow? Have you heard how Sylvie is?' Zoë, a medical secretary whose shifts at the surgery vary from week to week, is one of the friends who can sometimes deputize for Kate at the MacLeods'.

'Yes thanks,' Kate replies to the first question; and to the second, 'Actually, I don't think she's too good. I called round there after school on Monday. Will looked harassed, said things were difficult.'

'Mm, I heard she's worse. I was talking to Eilish Gallagher at the Well Woman Clinic – you know, the nurse? She seemed doubtful whether Will can manage much longer.'

This comes as a shock to Kate, the idea of Will's dedication thwarted. His determination to keep Sylvie from being institutionalized strikes her as total, almost fanatical. It is the thought of his relatively young wife incarcerated with the elderly (who form the bulk of Alzheimer victims) which, Kate suspects, upsets him most. 'She's not going into a home,' he has sworn to her more than once.

'I was going to say,' Zoë continues, 'if she gets a bit tricky, give me a ring. I'm off work tomorrow, so I could come over if you find you need a hand.'

'Thanks,' Kate says, not as reassured as she might be. The thought of Sylvie being difficult does not bother her; the prospect of Will's defeat certainly does. She links it with her husband's vanquished ambition to continue living. It is a chilling thought, but the human will in the teeth of circumstance seems to have about as much staying-power as a leaf in a gale.

They are lying on their mats on the hall floor. Fiona is playing a tape of sea music. 'Bing-bong,' chime the tubular bells, 'Ah-hah,' rush the waves. 'Your legs are *heavy*,' Fiona chants, 'so . . . hea . . . vv . . . y.'

This is the best bit, Kate thinks; a lovely way to finish the session. Utter peace. Safe nothingness.

Until this class started, the idea of organized exercise did not appeal to Kate. Fiona, besides being one of her two close women friends in the village, is also a colleague at Lavenbrook Comprehensive where Fiona teaches PE and Dance. Three years ago, when her husband's firm went bust, Fiona began taking adult evening classes to supplement her school-teacher's income. With two teenage children, Fiona needs to earn as much as possible. She takes two classes a week in town, and this one in the village on Wednesday nights. (Once, Kate, Fiona and Zoë were heavily engaged in village activities, particularly those organized for children or which raised money for the new village hall. Then Kate's husband became ill and Fiona's was hit by the recession – events which robbed them of free time and energy, and now only Zoë and her husband Martin continue to beaver away at fund-raising and serving on various committees.) Kate's original purpose in joining this class was to support Fiona, but now she would miss it enormously if it were disbanded. This seems unlikely; attendance is good. Fiona needs twelve participants to break even. Mostly, unless the weather is unusually bad, there are more than twenty.

'Your spine is *soft*, ve . . . rr . . . y . . . sssoft.'

Bliss, thinks Kate, sinking endlessly through layers of warm darkness.

A sudden squawking, as if a hen has been startled from her nest, shockingly impinges on their dozy consciousness – *'The window!'* Some lie blinking, stunned. Others jerk into sitting position. 'What?' 'Where?'

'There,' the speaker, now on her knees clutching her mat to her bosom, shakily indicates. 'Must have been the Peeping Tom. Looking right at me.'

The window, set high in the wall, is blank other than for clouds like pillows in a pink-tinged sky. But sure enough, a metallic clatter sounds outside, as if someone has knocked over a dustbin making a hasty get away.

Marie Ellwood, who had quite enough of this Peeping Tom on Sunday night staring in at her windows and sending daughter Trisha hysterical and all her menfolk out into the night, scrambles to her feet and makes for the door. She is joined by a friend, another equally robust farmer's wife. Their example rouses several others, the more prudent of these pausing to pull on shoes.

Fiona turns off the tape.

Kate's eyes move slowly. Window? Which? There is a whole row of them, high and evenly spaced in the wall opposite. They are all blank, but this is scant comfort. Each, as she checks, becomes a spy; the entire row bears down over her prone body. Hard, baleful. As she returns their glare, the floor widens, runs out of her peripheral vision taking the end walls with it. She is stranded on this large expanse beneath lined-up scrutiny.

Then her heart revives and pounds her into action. She thrusts forward on to her knees, rolls up her mat, lopes over the room to a group of chairs placed against

51

the wall on which people have dumped tracksuits, handbags, trainers. She clears one of these, sits down; hugs her rolled-up mat, hangs on to it.

Eventually, those who rushed out begin to return. Those who stayed – mostly waiting in a group near the door – make way for them and cluster round. The farmers' wives are blaming unshod feet for their failure to get a look at the intruder. Lastly, Bel and Tina, who stopped to pull on trainers but are very fleet of foot, come back – gasping, eyes shining – to report a glimpse of a cloth cap bobbing past a fence on the far side of the allotment. They shouted, but there was no-one around to hear, and by the time they ran up the road and in at the allotment entrance, the place was deserted.

'Just one person?' comments Marie Ellwood thoughtfully. 'Not lads, then.'

Hands on hips, breathing heavily, Bel and Tina agree: just one person.

'Wonder how long he'd been stood there. On a bin was he?'

'Yeah. He must have carried it to the window. It's there now, knocked over.'

'Oo, do you think he *knew*?'

'You mean that we had a class on? Oh I say – that'd make him a local.'

'A pervert.'

'Oh, don't Sue.'

'Bet he was disappointed. It's probably put him right off. One sight of my big bum . . .'

'No wonder he fell off the bin.'

'Got more than he bargained for.'

'Ran home to lie down.'

'Have a stiff drink.'

Their excitement, their turning it into a joke, soothes Kate. The tension slides off her, she leaves the chair and goes to join them.

By unspoken agreement the class has concluded. They pull on their clothes, gather belongings. And sober down when someone points out that the matter ought to be reported. Fiona, because she is in charge of the class, promises to phone the police as soon as she gets home.

'Has everyone got a lift?' cries Kate sharply.

They turn and look at her, gather her meaning, agree that no-one should walk home alone.

'Sue's on foot.'

'But I'm only going to the end of the road.'

'Even so, we'll drive you.'

'And there's May and Louise.' (From the Penfold Close council houses.)

'Huh. Like t'see him try one on me,' growls Louise, who works with May at the chicken factory and spends much of her day wringing necks.

Driving with Kate to Vicarage Hill, Fiona grumbles about how she could do without this added bother. She hopes the police won't want her to go back with them to the village hall to point out the window and the overturned dustbin. Quite honestly, what with her husband seriously depressed, her son in a state over A levels, and the prospect of 4C girls in the gym first thing tomorrow (never what you'd call enthusiastic students, but first thing in the morning positively hellish), she'd banked on a long soak in the bath and an early night. Kate listens – or rather, hears – and makes sympathetic sounds. What she hears is that she cannot confide in Fiona about her own trouble – the fear stirred up in her by this Peeping Tom. As Fiona says, she doesn't need it. Chokiness mounts in Kate's chest, a childish hurt feeling. Seems like, with friends aplenty, it is never OK for *her* to divulge a worry. When Chris was ill, they were all wonderful – her village chums and colleagues at school. In the months following his death they were continually phoning and dropping by, sending her little gifts, urging her that if there was anything they could do, to say so immediately. But gradually she became established as a woman on her own, and there was a perceptible change. They began to have many more and much worse troubles than formerly — or perhaps, now that she has become a single woman, they feel free to let her know their full extent and depth; as if widowhood makes her a natural repository. Another thing: there seems to be a consensus that the time it takes to recover from tragedies such as Kate's has now passed. No wonder they were so keen to urge the old bromide: 'It takes *time*, Kate; it may not seem likely now, but believe me, time does heal.'

'Well, good luck with it,' she finally tells Fiona. 'My turn to drive us next week. See you in school.'

She runs to her door, key at the ready. And the bare-metal roar of Fiona's mini elevates into silence.

Bel and Tina arrived back in The Park some minutes ago but continued to sit in the stationary car in Bel's driveway. Repeatedly discovering some new and entertaining aspect of the evening's incident has made them reluctant to call a halt and go indoors. Tina, who has a wider knowledge of men's strange compulsions (and a potent vocabulary: 'nerds,' she says, 'sickos,') gradually assumes the dominant speaking role, while Bel, fascinated, watches Tina's animated face working, listens and reflects. Tina, she decides, is a blast — fires off exactly what she thinks the moment she thinks it, goes steaming off to confront any presenting threat or insult. She has also managed to dispel some of Bel's maternal anxiety, anxiety which, Bel now sees, has become her habit of mind. A prowler in the vicinity had meant one thing to her — a real and imminent threat to her baby. And the sight of Tina naked in the garden had immediately prompted a view of her neighbour as stupid thoughtless bait. How ludicrous this now seems. Tina passive? — way off beam. She went after the prowler with enthusiasm, and it was sheer exhilaration, Bel discovered, to be winging after the object of her fears — if only a temporary object — directed by a whooping Tina. Which just goes to show: you can learn a lot from an improbable source. Maybe

54

there is a plus side to this business of being stuck at home and landed with unchosen company . . .

'This time of year must be perfect for it,' Tina is saying. 'I mean, look around – hardly anyone's bothered to draw their curtains.'

Turning her head, Bel sees naked windows aglow in most houses in The Park. These nights, because it will soon be the longest day of the year, it is never properly dark before many adults retire for the night, although by nine o'clock or ten the light is too dim for comfort in an unlit room. 'I suppose, in the winter, when it's pitch dark early on, you automatically draw the curtains. In the summer you tend not to bother,' she says.

'Look at my lot,' Tina complains. 'Every light on in the house. The kids ought to be asleep. I'd better go and sort them out.' She opens the passenger door.

Bel gets out too. 'Come and have coffee one morning next week,' she suggests. 'Monday?'

'Great. And if there's anything you want from town tomorrow, ring me first thing.'

'Thanks. 'Night, Tina. And don't forget . . .'

'. . . draw your curtains,' Tina finishes for her. 'G'night, Bel.'

Giggling, they part: Bel to her front door, Tina padding across the lawn.

Yes, every bloody room, Tina marvels. No-one turns off anything in this place – funny how she has never noticed it before; Mr Peeping Tom would have a field day. She starts looking in at her windows to discover exactly what he *would* see. First, the living room: deserted, just the telly playing to itself and sounding desperate (*Hold it – we're coming out.* Bang. Flash. Scream). Next the dining room: deserted and fully exposed. The kitchen: likewise. Finally she peeks into the little room which she seldom enters and Les calls his den. This is more dimly lit, in fact, only by the bluish light of a jumpy TV screen. Les is slumped in a chair in front of the set, remote control loosely clasped in podgy hand. On the floor by his feet lies a tray littered with used dishes and cutlery and a lager can. Tina observes these facts about her husband then studies for a few seconds what he is watching on the screen. Curls her lip. The video's subject matter (she knows it must be a video, no broadcasting authority transmits that sort of stuff) comes as no real surprise; it is merely one more thing to despise about Les. What a lump of lard. He really pisses her off. She goes thoughtfully round to the front of the house, her mind unfavourably, and not for the first time, comparing her husband with her lovely self. Those sleek lines and curves, confirmed at regular intervals throughout the day by her trusty full-length mirror, take the form, in her mind's eye, of a valuable trophy. Truth is, she is letting herself down sticking with a slob like Les. She deserves someone with more class. There are the kids, though, to consider. Mind you, they're growing up fast . . .

In the house, she goes from room to room switching things off. In the kitchen she stops to put on the kettle. Then she goes down the hall passage to Les's den, and puts her head round the door.

'I'm back.'

The screen blanks as his stumbling finger finds the off button.

'Wanker,' she adds loftily – before withdrawing her head and closing the door – lest he fail to appreciate she is nobody's fool.

Quite a different scene in number five. Bel, of course, ran straight upstairs to check Jamie. David caught her arm. 'What's going on? You were ages out there with Tina.'

'We had some excitement.'

Evidently, David thought, in view of her pink complexion, her sparkling eyes.

'Tell you about it in a minute. How's . . . ?'

'Fine. We had a great time together. Then he went droopy so I put him down to sleep. Out like a light

56

ever since,' he whispered, joining her by the side of Jamie's cot.

And here they remain, their hearts swelling and melting at his infant perfection. He sleeps with every sign of peaceful contentment, breathing softly and evenly, his skin warm (but not too warm), his colour rosy (but not florid), eyelashes curling on chubby cheeks, arms raised upwards with little lax fists on either side of his head. David has slipped an arm round Bel's waist. She leans lightly against him. At last, sighing, smiling to one another, they tear themselves away, leaving the door open a few inches.

Finding she is hot, Bel goes into their bedroom to strip off her tracksuit. Finding she is thirsty, she runs downstairs for a drink. All the time David follows and Bel gabbles.

'We had a prowler. The sort that stares in at windows.'

'A voyeur.'

'Yeah, but round here they call 'em Peeping Whatsits.'

'Toms.'

'Mm. Well, there we all were lying spread out on our backs doing our deep relaxation number, when this woman starts yelping . . .' Bel recounts the tale between gulps of milk, every now and then wiping away a recurring white moustache with the back of her hand. David thinks that if this is what it takes to loosen her up, to turn her back into the Bel he used to have fun with, then hooray for a Peeping Tom.

'You know,' Bel goes on, 'I actually heard about this prowler in the shop the other morning. And you know me – started feeling threatened over Jamie, in case it was some sort of pervert. I even got furious with Tina for lying about in the garden, topless and bottomless. I thought, carrying on like that, no wonder we get trouble. Pretty stupid of me when you come to think of it. I mean, spying on women must be light years away from baby snatching, in funny hobby terms – wouldn't you say? Tonight's been a breath of fresh air

– bit of excitement, having a hoot with Tina . . . I know she's flash, but she's really quite interesting . . .'

'Hang on a minute; let's get this straight. Tina lies in the garden . . .'

'Sunbathing.'

'Nude?'

'Starkers.'

'When is this? Perhaps I could arrange to come home . . .'

She swipes him with a tea cloth. He catches it and tugs. 'Cor, mm, you don't half feel nice in this slippery gear. You mean to say, you and Tina gave chase, and this chap *ran away*? Must be a nutter. You wouldn't like to chase me, would you? Say, far as the settee?'

'Er – how about the rug?'

No further encouragement is necessary. He smacks her backside, nips away. Strategically over the Scandinavian long pile, she makes her lunge. Brings him down.

As usual, after locking and bolting her back door, Kate ran round the house drawing curtains, switching on lights, looking in cupboards and under beds. Then she made toast and coffee, and is now sitting in front of a live TV screen with the sound turned down, munching and sipping and waiting for the start of the ten o'clock news. That self-conscious feeling has crept over her again, she notices, pausing mid-munch – as if the house has resumed its scrutiny. She finishes her snack – but discreetly, quickly; then abandons the empty mug and plate on a low table and sinks back in her chair affecting obliviousness. Why does this never happen to her in the daytime? She is not by nature self-conscious; even when she knows she is on show – in front of thirty critical fifth formers, say – she behaves naturally, freely, without any overweening sense of herself. But as the evening settles in, underscoring her isolation, she begins to feel preyed on, observed – so keenly that doing mundane tasks can be like performing on a film set. And she gains nothing by pretending nonchalance; it never fools the watchers. Tonight, although the sensation is not as potent as in the worst of times – six months to a year after Chris's death, when it was often paralysing – it is more troubling than lately. This is due to her earlier panic. For a moment in the village hall she felt personally threatened, as if this roaming spy had sought *her* out, tracked *her* down. Seeing the others deal with the incident in their different ways jolted her into a more sensible perspective, generalized the threat, put the prowler at a distance. Why couldn't she have responded as they did, shown the sort of initiative she found last night in the school car park, instead of lying there like a ninny, terrorized by blank windows? Was blankness in fact the cause of her terror – no-one there to be seen, no threat to confront, no visible challenge, just blankness providing a vacuum which her perverse imagination avidly filled? Well, for God's sake get a grip, she raves at herself. Don't dare start getting jittery about some vague nuisance *outside*. I've enough on my plate battling with some abstract menace *inside*.

She grips the chair arms, as a sense grows of forcing herself up some narrow and precipitous incline where the footholds are precarious; while behind her lies the broad and almost seductive expanse of her eventide fears. She is determined not to set foot in this easier terrain. However, she does need to take a look at it, to stay where she is (even though her legs are wobbling) and, as it were, peep over the fence. Because if she does not examine her fears, how is she ever to get the better of them?

She never was good at being alone at night. Even with the children in their respective rooms, whenever Chris had to be away from home, she would lie awake for hours, her imagination turning every creak and stir of the joists into a sinister footfall, a murderer's tread. She would sleep fitfully; then wake with a jolt in the early hours and strain after sound till her ears burned, reasoning that *something* must have disturbed her. It seems doubly hard to have been left fearful as well as bereaved.

If you knew, if you just *knew,* she mutters to the rocking chair on the far side of the hearth. (Chris's chair. She can see his fair hair jutting above the head-rest, his slippered feet, ankles crossed, propped on their heels on the hearth-rug.) Anger surging takes her by surprise. It's all right for you, she thinks, pain and despair all past. It's not you who's been deserted. *You left me,* she silently screams – like Sylvie the other day unreasonably denouncing Will. Sylvie, being mad, had an excuse. Kate has none. It is wicked of her to accuse Chris who fought to the end to go on living. Even so, she cannot prevent herself. Having had no idea that she *was* angry, the discovery has a force of its own. How dare he go without understanding the cruelty to her? Foreseeing her present agony ought to have racked him on his death bed. Because she was never meant, would never choose in a million years, to live alone; companionship is as necessary to her as food and drink – sorry, but that is how she is; still young, still needful, *still alive, damn it.* With the children gone, they ought to be enjoying their best times together. Shaking, she almost curses him.

And then goes cold with self-disgust. *Darling, forgive me . . .*

She snatches the remote control, jabs the volume button. *News At Ten* is over; the weather girl is standing in front of her chart pointing to unblemished sun symbols, simpering to camera as though she has personally arranged an impossible treat: 'Set fair for the rest of the week!' Kate listens dully for a few seconds, then switches off, rises and unplugs the set. She had better go to bed – coping with Sylvie McLeod tomorrow will take all her energy and concentration.

She rinses her supper things, puts them away; throws out the newspaper; turns off lights. As she performs these final tasks of the day, her mind denies absolutely that she is being observed. But her weak flesh betrays her; mounting the stairs, the fine hairs rise on her forearms.

Later, lying under the summer weight duvet, a more hopeful feeling of having discovered or resolved something steals over. She falls asleep trying to work out what this can be.

CHAPTER FOUR

Thursday 18th June

High House, a tall red-brick Georgian building, stands near the top of Main Street. Its front door opens directly onto the pavement. To the side of the house is a five-bar gate covering the entrance to yard and garden. This has been the McLeods' home for the past twelve years, at first shared with Will's father, now deceased, and until lately their son, Paul, who, having graduated, is now back-packing and odd-jobbing in the Antipodes. Will is glad Paul is not around to witness his mother's present pitiable state. Not that she will ever regain a less pitiable state: Will knows the score; Alzheimer's is irreversible, has only one outcome. No point, though, in loading angst on to their son's early twenties, years which ought to be carefree, years which will not come again.

Kate walks down Vicarage Hill and across The Green to the village shop, running her mind over a list of purchases, items for the supper she plans to cook as a pleasant surprise for Will this evening. When she has filled her wire basket and goes to pay, Nan insists on making her a gift of some ripe peaches. 'Poor Mrs McLeod,' she murmurs, 'I hope you find her improved.' (As village shopkeeper it goes without saying that she knows how Kate customarily spends Thursdays.) 'Remember me to her,' she adds, discreetly dropping the peaches into a paper bag.

At High House the door is opened by today's nurse. Will can be heard overhead, opening and closing drawers, packing his briefcase, starting across the landing, running back for something. Kate and the nurse (who comes from Jamaica and whose name is Joan) exchange looks. 'Killing himself,' Joan says. 'For what? There's no point,' she sighs, 'no point at all. Now,' – she goes to address Sylvie in her chair – 'are you going to be a good girl for this nice kind lady today?' Sylvie stares up blankly. 'I hope so, darlin',' Joan tells Kate, her expression permitting scant hope. 'But if she do give trouble, phone the surgery. One of us'll be there. Bye, bye love – be a good girl. See you tomorrow, Will,' she bellows up the stairs.

'Oh thanks, Joan.' Will comes pounding down. 'Er, have you mentioned to Kate, um . . . ?'

'He means about the toilet,' Joan tells Kate. 'She's not incontinent, not yet,' – at which Will winces and Kate tries to stay cheerful-looking despite her heart sinking – 'but she's getting very naughty. First she won't go, then she goes in the wrong place. Deliberate. Mind you're firm with her. Take her into the bathroom, and if she won't do nothing, just pull down her pants and shove her on the seat. And keep your eyes open. The other day, dear Lord, she used the laundry basket.'

Will lays down his briefcase. 'Kate, I can't. I feel too guilty . . .'

'Look, stop thinking about it and go. I said, *go*, Will.'

He hesitates, face creased, eyes darting. Then, visibly sagging, retrieves his case and goes quickly through to the rear of the house to the back door and yard.

A few moments later, his car passes the window. It occurs to Kate that he made no kind of farewell to Sylvie. Once, he would kiss the top of her head, raise and put down her hand; lately, he has thought it sufficient to call to her from the doorway, emphasizing his later return. But this morning, no acknowledgement at all; he hurried through the kitchen as though it were empty, as though no woman sat slumped in the high-backed chair with dribble coursing from the side of her mouth.

'I must be off,' Joan repeats. 'You'll find she's nice and quiet for an hour or so. Then I should take her outside – up the road if you're sure she's docile, round the garden if she's feeling frisky. Just don't let her see no men. You know how she is – man mad. Now that's *mad*,' she nods, 'that's real mad.' With which, chuckling, she finally departs.

Kate goes to stand in front of Sylvie; shows herself. 'Good morning, Sylvie,' she offers belatedly. Sylvie's unfocused eyes pass over her. Kate pulls a tissue from a box, mops the damp mouth and chin, then goes into the scullery and drops it in the waste bin. The washing up is waiting for her. Glad of this, she rinses her hands, pulls on rubber gloves, fills the sink. 'For goodness' sake don't clear up. Leave something for us to do,' she told Will when she first started the Thursday arrangement. In those days, Sylvie seemed only marginally abnormal, and there were times when Kate would wonder whether the diagnosis could be correct. She and Sylvie would do simple housework together, weed the garden, tackle a jigsaw, play Sylvie's favourite dance records. Then Sylvie's sudden bouts of uncertainty – breaking off to ask 'What am I supposed to be doing?' – became more frequent. Often, in the middle of some shared activity, Sylvie would get up purposefully and stalk away. Following her after a discreet interval, Kate would discover her bewildered in the hall or aimlessly sitting on the side of her bed; when questioned, quite at a loss to recall what had made her momentarily decisive. Over time it has become increasingly difficult to hold her attention. She dozes for longer periods. Sometimes, Kate suspects she is drugged, and though she once disapproved of the idea, as Sylvie became more difficult to manage, resisting persuasion, running off, hitting out, she acknowledges that this may be unavoidable. After all, normal life has to continue; people cannot be expected to drop everything, to neglect their own needs in the cause of permitting full rein to Sylvie McLeod's dementia. And this morning, learning of the latest 'naughtiness', Kate does not care if she *is* drugged. She is quiet, thank heaven. And if she remains quiet for a couple of hours, that is a couple of hours' less anxiety.

When the washing up is completed, Kate makes two mugs of coffee and carries them to the kitchen table. 'Coffee time. Sit up to table,' she encourages. But Sylvie is disinclined to move, so Kate leaves Sylvie's coffee to cool for a while, opens a newspaper, and sips her own. Eventually, Sylvie is persuaded to take a few slurps; then pushes the mug away. Kate resumes her seat. What, she wonders, goes on in that vacant-seeming head? What is it *like* inside Sylvie McLeod? A jangle of tussling memories all fighting to rise to the surface? – and if one succeeds, does it hurt when reality (though a past reality) is briefly restored? – does the pain of this shatter the numbness? – or is what appears from the *outside* like numbness, in fact a blank wall hiding turmoil, clamour, frustration, *inside*?

Suddenly, Kate has a hunch that this is what motivates the Peeping Tom. Pressing up close to lighted windows, peering in, he is trying to fathom what goes on inside, and what, if anything, it *means* – the small routines, the solitary worship of TV screens, and (she recalls the exercise class in the village hall) the peculiar rituals. Perhaps this Peeping Tom is simply bewildered – as she was bewildered watching Chris die, when she would stare into his face, screaming to herself: what the hell's going on in there? – how can his huge vigorous personality be snuffed out by something as pathetic as a failed body mechanism? – and what does the fact that it *can* make of our precious personalities? And here she is, at it again: peering into the face of Sylvie McLeod. Baffled. Maybe this Peeping Tom is not some nasty preying sexual inadequate after all, just some excluded outsider trying to make sense . . . For one minute Kate is high on a sensation of understanding and empathy, she accepts the fact of a prowler with equanimity, can grasp why someone might need to pry; for one brief moment she is fearless, powerful, fizzing with the euphoria of clarity . . .

Then, like a can of opened pop, the zest evaporates. She can hardly recall how she became so excited. Things are back as they were. Tonight when she draws her curtains she wearily accepts that she may be full of dread, wondering whether there is a watcher lurking outside, some 'nasty preying sexual inadequate'. And right now, in her chair, Sylvie McLeod remains inscrutable.

Impatiently, she shakes out her newspaper, starts reading.

Perhaps half an hour passes, maybe forty minutes. Then as she turns a page, some faint movement distracts Kate's eyes from the paper. Draws them to the woman in the chair.

Who is looking at her – hard, straight. And *aware*, Kate registers, horror leaping. The lost face, the blank eyes have come shrewdly alight. Sylvie McLeod has reclaimed herself. Wildly, Kate wonders how to explain what she is doing here, calmly reading a newspaper and ignoring the householder as if she were so much wallpaper.

'I don't know you,' Sylvie declares coldly.

'Of course you do,' rapidly pleads a heated Kate.

'You don't know me.'

The sophisticated alteration (which seems less easily brushed aside) is not lost on Kate. Her thrill of embarrassment peaks – then collapses like a pricked balloon as Sylvie McLeod drowns beneath puffy pink flesh.

'Sylvie?'

Sylvie's tongue darts over her lips. Maybe she is thirsty. 'Would you like a drink now? I'll make some fresh. We could drink it in the garden. Would you like that?'

Doubtfully, Sylvie nods.

*   *   *

It is after lunch. In the main bedroom, Kate is standing on the rose-patterned carpet running her eyes over a collection of photographs, all portraits of the same woman – sweet Sylvie as bride (frothy white lace), swinging Sylvie as Highland belle (tartan sash over flowing white satin), fluffy Sylvie as mum (white angora jumper with baby son as accessory), carefree Sylvie on holiday (strapless white sunsuit), pouting Sylvie as Marilyn Monroe (well, almost – white dress with billowing knife-pleated skirt). No image of Will amongst this iconography, nor of Sylvie's parents, grown son, relations or friends, come to that. Were these portraits always here? Or were they placed around the room with the aim of jogging her memory?

Kate turns to take in the bed with its gleaming white eiderdown and frilly white cushions. Where Will no longer sleeps – a fact she has gathered from observations on previous visits. For instance: she saw no men's pyjamas under these bed covers that dark winter's afternoon when Sylvie decided it was bedtime; and again: that time when she and Joan went racing round the house searching for a gone-missing Sylvie, the small room at the head of the stairs bore several signs of male occupation – shirt and slacks on a chair, shaver and tie on top of the chest of drawers, a single tousled bed. She often brings this evidence to mind and holds for a moment in her inner eye, Sylvie's chaste white bed, Will's narrow rumpled one.

From the bathroom comes the noise of a lavatory flushing. Kate hurries to the door, which opens slowly to reveal Sylvie with her skirt caught up in her knickers. From the way she stands there staring, plainly Kate has once again reverted to stranger. There is none of the shrewd haughtiness which threw Kate off balance earlier in the day, just the painful timidity of someone who hasn't a clue who you are or what exactly are the present circumstances. Kate, who has been stolidly smiling from the moment the door opened, steps forward with an even brighter expression. Something seems to click into place. Returning the smile, Sylvie asks, 'Am I supposed to wash my hands?'

'Yes, that would be good,' encourages Kate, gently tugging down the skirt.

Obediently, constantly checking Kate's face for re-assurance, Sylvie goes back into the bathroom. 'Am I allowed?' – she looks doubtfully at the hot tap – 'Might I get burned?'

At this moment she is three years old, Kate suddenly grasps. 'I'll run it for you.'

'Mm, thank you.'

She is three years old and Mummy's good girl. By the time she gets downstairs some other disjointed memory fragment may have taken over; or, as was the case this morning, knowledge of who she is, or indeed *whether* she is, may have sunk beyond recall.

'Shall we go back outside?' Kate suggests when they have returned to the ground floor.

'Shall we?'

'Well, it's warm and sunny. It might be nice.'

'Yes. Be nice.'

Evidently, still an infant. This being so, Kate takes her hand.

Leading Sylvie round the garden ('Oh, the roses – smell this one, Sylvie. Gorgeous, hm? And the apricot rose against the blue campanula – isn't that pretty?') Kate sees they are being watched. Not overtly; Mrs Bullivant is far too delicate. Nevertheless, she has temporarily reprieved the weeds in her rockery to trim the honeysuckle which garlands the fence separating High House's territory from Sunny Bank's. Turning her back on the neighbour, Kate draws Sylvie towards the patch they were weeding earlier. But perhaps Sylvie is tired. 'Do you want to carry on weeding, or shall we sit in the chairs? I could make us some tea if you'd like. What do you think?'

Too many questions. Too many choices. Kate begins again. 'Shall we sit down?'

'Ye-es?' – a rising inflection indicating a desire to please.

'Or do some more weeding?'

'Ye-es?'

Sighing, Kate reaches for weeding forks. 'All right. First we'll weed, then we'll rest.' She kneels down. Sylvie flops beside her. The garden can certainly stand more attention – speedwell everywhere, even bindweed coming through. 'Let's pull up the speedwell. Put it in the bucket beside you. That's right. That's great.'

A pause as this praise sinks in. Then, lips pursed in a pleased way, as though teacher has awarded her a gold star, Sylvie thrusts in her fork with inspired effort and uproots the dianthus.

Good as gold all day, Kate reflects later, glancing at Sylvie slumbering under the awning of a sunlounger. She has replanted the dianthus clump, also an aquilegia, and watered them well. There was nothing much she could do about the crumpled saxifrage beyond pressing it down, but saxifrage is over for the season, has almost a year with nothing to do but lie quiet and heal. The important thing is, for a time Sylvie was happy. Kate is surprised how grateful this makes her feel, how tenderly she recalls the clumsy diligence of a giant three-year-old. She is glad she decided against taking her into the village. It took her long enough today to feel easy with Kate; meeting other people might have completely thrown her. Similar reasoning prompted Kate earlier to lead Sylvie away from Mrs Bullivant; someone leering or calling over the fence could have proved seriously unsettling. Now, after her exertions, she is sleeping like a baby. It occurs to Kate that Sylvie tires very quickly. Stupid to suspect the nurse of drugging her in the mornings. What happens, of course, is that all the bathing, brushing, dressing and breakfasting wears her out.

Kate leaves her chair and looks cautiously over to Sunny Bank – a modern ranch-style bungalow built six or seven years ago as part of the village in-fill programme. (The planning authorities have decreed there can be no further building at the edge of Aston Favell and any future development must be confined to spare patches of ground within its existing boundaries.) Kate has never seen Sunny Bank's interior, but she has heard about it; its sitting room bar is reputed to be larger than The Crown's. Nor is she acquainted with Mrs Bullivant beyond greetings exchanged in the street or the shop, though again, news has filtered through of her reputation. Thankfully, there is now no sign of the lady.

Turning back, it strikes Kate that High House is too tall for its grounds. She wonders whether the abandoned orchard on which Sunny Bank now stands once formed part of this property. The garden is attractively laid out, though, and well-stocked. It is a pity Will does not hire a gardener. Once a month should do it — perhaps once a fortnight in the growing season. Because if he lets it go now, it will be the devil's own job getting it back into shape in time to sell. Already she foresees the McLeod era drawing to a close for High House. Which is natural enough: those who hold the deeds of an ancient property cannot be unaware that their possession is fleeting, that they are merely passers through. Nor is she uncomfortable to catch herself exploring the consequences of Sylvie's demise. Even in their prime people die. She knows this. Everyone knows it superficially, but Kate knows it from experience; it colours her outlook, she takes it into account.

A man is standing by the side of the house. Kate cannot quite believe it, but there certainly is a man standing there. She shades her eyes. Who is he? What does he want? He is wearing a sort of shabby uniform. His thin plastered-down hair glistens damply. He looks like a bus driver left out in the rain.

'I tried the front.'

'Oh? I'm afraid when the traffic's going by you can't always hear.'

70

'So I came round the side.'

'Right.'

'The last three have been estimates. Time you had a reading.'

Realization comes in a rush: he is holding a torch and a notepad – she can see this now; he has come to read the electricity meter.

'I'll go in this way then, shall I?' – a nod to the back door.

'Of course. I suppose you know where it is? I'm not the householder, you see . . .'

'Under the stairs, i'n't it?' He starts confidently up the path.

And Kate suddenly recalls Sylvie. Who is not always safe with men – or rather, with whom men are not always safe. Only last month she escaped from the house in her nightie and made it to The Crown where she claimed the landlord, Jim Turner, for her long-lost lover. It is still the talk of the bar. *Hurry,* she wants to yell. Oh, why doesn't he get on with it?

'Roses look healthy. There's Super Star, one of my favourites. My wife, though, she prefers Fragrant Cloud. For scent, I'll grant you, I tell her; but when it comes to rust . . . Mind you, if you spray regular . . .' He breaks off, startled by Kate darting across the lawn to urge him on. Backing away, he stumbles into the weed bucket. 'Whoops, sorry.' Torch and notepad are plopped down on the lawn as he stoops to right the bucket and pick up spilled weeds.

Under the awning of the sunlounger, Sylvie has gradually come to. She sits up, takes in the visitor, hurries to her feet. 'Oooo, I'm so glad you've come!' – it is the voice of a stunning young woman to whom flirtatious flattery is second nature and whose advances are unfailingly met with enthusiasm. But to the meter man as he straightens up, this second advance is of an unattractively heavy and patently crazed creature, now flying at him, now pinning him to the wall. 'So *glad,*' squawks Sylvie, grasping her prize and hanging on to it. 'She's been really horrible to me, 'cos she's jealous. But you'll take me out, won't you? Somewhere nice,' she wheedles, 'somewhere special.'

'Sylvie, *get off.* Look, I'm terribly sorry, she'll calm down in a minute.' (But Sylvie is not to be deprived and screeches in protest; Kate and the man struggle to loosen her grasp.) 'Shut the door after you,' Kate shouts after him when at last he wrestles free and shoots away. 'And go out the front way.'

'I shall report this . . .' The back door slams. He doesn't need to be told.

'It's all right, Sylvie. All right. Come and sit down.'

But Kate has just ruined her assignation and Sylvie is beside herself with rage and grief: allowing Kate to propel her towards the sunlounger, she is merely gathering herself. For suddenly, with renewed strength, Sylvie springs.

They are rolling over the grass, first Sylvie on top, hammering; then Kate pinning her down. All at once Sylvie goes limp. Kate rolls away, flops on to her back; lies gasping.

'Er, can I be of any assistance?'

Kate blinks at the sky. Then tips up her chin and surveys an upside-down Mrs Bullivant.

'My dear, your face! Are you all right? I heard such an alarming noise, I came to investigate. Would you like me to . . .' Mrs Bullivant, clutching the top of the fence, has been about to offer to come round in person. In the nick of time she changes her mind. After all, she is no spring chicken, and that creature lying there moaning and sobbing into the lawn was but a few moments ago fighting like a tiger with the strength of an ox. 'Would you like me to call someone?' she amends lamely.

'Oh no. No thank you.' Kate struggles into a sitting position.

'You're going to have a shiner.'

'I don't think so.'

'Indeed you are, my dear. Go and put some ice on it. Though perhaps it isn't safe to leave her. You know I really do think it'd be wise to call someone. Perhaps a doctor . . .'

'No, really. We'll be quite all right.'

Kate goes forward on to her knees and reaches out to Sylvie. Strokes her. 'Come on. Let's go inside and get washed. Then you can watch the telly while I make a fish pie for supper.'

Sylvie raises a tear-sodden face; collapses into Kate's arms.

'It's such a shame,' she is explaining to Will while the fish pie browns in the oven. 'She was good all day. No trouble at all. Nothing, you know, like Joan mentioned. Then this man turned up to read the meter.'

'But your face . . .'

He steps forward, stands right over her. She can faintly smell him, catch his warmth. She takes her eyes off his blue shirt and loosened gold and blue floral tie (which are on their level), raises them to his face. 'It's nothing, really . . .' A strikingly handsome face, as she has had occasion to notice before, though never from as close up as this. His eyes are as blue as the shirt.

He lifts a hand, touches with very light fingers her swollen cheekbone. She swallows, sways. He steadies her with two hands on her shoulders, then allows her to sink against him and wraps his arms around. 'I'm so sorry,' he keeps murmuring.

She no longer protests that it doesn't matter. Who cares about a bruise? He must know it no longer signifies. His heart and hers are pounding like drums.

'Kate,' he says into her hair; 'Kate, Kate.' His lips come down to meet hers, have barely touched, when – 'Where are you? Where've you gone? What are you doing?' – a petulant Sylvie trudges in from the sitting room.

They come apart. Not suddenly or guiltily – ruefully, reluctantly.

'Kate's made us a pie. Isn't that nice?' Will tells his wife.

'I thought you'd gone.'

They cannot tell whether she means Will or Kate. Perhaps both.

'Of course we hadn't gone,' he soothes, putting her into a dining chair. 'We wouldn't leave you.'

During the meal, which Sylvie applies herself to with fierce concentration, Will recounts how well his day has gone. The firm liked his designs, they offered a contract. Nice people, he looks forward to working with them. Animation brings his face alive, banishes the recently acquired pallor; laughing, enthusing, this is how Kate remembers him arguing over maps with Chris when they were planning to walk the Pennine Way. She wonders when he last relished the telling of a day's achievement. She is delighted to be the recipient, and resolves to cook their supper on future Thursdays. Eventually, the talk turns to the village. What's the gossip? It's ages since he went to the pub (excepting that time he had to go and, you know, collect Sylvie . . .). Anything happening? So she tells him about the Peeping Tom, describes the scene last night in the village hall. Her spirits are so high, she tells it like a joke; has him rocking with laughter. She even tells him about Mrs Bullivant hanging on to the fence to get a ring-side view of Sylvie fighting her on the grass. Even the pathetic, they discover, has its hugely funny side.

Then Sylvie drops asleep with her head on the table. Will is adamant that he does not want Kate to help him put her to bed. Nor must she start clearing up. He has all day tomorrow to do that.

So Kate goes. But before he opens the front door, he puts an arm round her and draws her close. Then she is outside in Main Street with the door closing behind; walking home on nerveless feet.

Kate has had her bath and watched the news. She is

bone weary. Tomorrow is a full day at school. Yawning her head off, she unplugs the television and the lamp, then goes into the kitchen to check the back door is securely locked. This done, she checks the front door, too (which is ridiculous because she never uses it). Bending to squint at the bolts (all properly in place), the Peeping Tom springs to mind. He may be out there somewhere. It is good to note that though she is not exactly thrilled by the prospect, her heart and breathing are unaffected. No silly leaps or gasps. Good.

She crosses the hall to the stairs. Watched, of course, but tonight she couldn't give a toss. She can imagine laughing to Will about these fears sometime in the future. Even – and here she stands stock still – even confessing last night's shocking anger against Chris. She imagines he will understand. More than likely he is taken with similar rage. In fact, considering how he runs his life around Sylvie, tends and clears up after her and must be bitterly reminded all the time he is with her of the way life ought to be, Kate is perfectly certain of it. What a relief it will be confiding in one another.

Going slowly upstairs it seems as if she is taking Will with her. They are ascending together. And the watchers can sear their eyeballs on the sight, for all she cares. Very soon – so certain is she of this she is almost gleeful – very soon their time will be over.

CHAPTER FIVE

Friday 19th June

In her dream, Kate is being hammered all over again in the McLeods' garden. Only this time she wants it to go on and on. 'Don't stop,' she begs in Will McLeod's ear, wrapping her legs round his thrusting buttocks. 'More, more. Oh, *yes* . . .'

'Er, can I be of any assistance?' Mrs Bullivant enquires, popping up over the fence.

Damn her, *damn*, Kate sobs as Will desists. She tips up her chin and opens her eyes.

Sits bolt upright.

It is light already. Sunbeams flicker on the outer side of her curtains. Birds are cheeping out there in a fresh and innocent world. Her heart is thumping so hard you'd think she'd just run a marathon. Oh God, though, it wasn't running she was doing. With a groan, she flops back into her pit of shame.

This is not the first time since she was widowed that she has had an erotic dream. It has happened several times, but always she was partnered by Chris and found it wretched to wake up: a sickening memory of false pleasure would hang over her for the rest of the day. This time she merely feels guilty, a far less painful aftermath. Guilt is not so hopeless. You can expiate guilt. She reaches to the cold side of the bed where once Chris slept and smooths the already smooth sheet with her palm. 'Sorry, love. So sorry.'

She rolls on to her side and peers at the clock. Only twenty to six; she ought to get more sleep. When she closes her eyes, remnants of the dream drift through her mind; loom and fade . . .

The alarm clock beeps her awake as usual at a quarter past seven. She smacks it silent, studies the ceiling. How utterly embarrassing, she thinks, stunned by the coupling on the lawn which has returned to her mind in vivid and multi-sensory detail. She wonders how she will ever look Will McLeod in the face again.

Mrs Bullivant is having a busy morning.

Last evening, she very nearly blew everything on a phone call. But even as her finger tapped out Edna Critch's number, she saw what a waste it would be merely to recount her tale – no facial reactions to savour, and all over (given the Major's current obsession with the phone bill) much too soon. 'Hello, dear – it's Daphne. I was wondering if you'd care to pop over in the morning?' she trilled instead. 'Something of interest to report.'

'About the Contest?'

'Oo, no, no, no. An altogether different matter. A thing I did spy with my little eye. Over the garden fence, if you take my meaning.'

'Oo-oo. Developments?'

'Not over the phone, dear. Thing is, I was wondering about the others.' She mentioned the rest of the gang tentatively, her dilemma being as follows. Edna Critch, as her closest friend, has prior right to any confidence going. But Daphne is damned if, by first telling Edna, she will also be handing over the privilege of further broadcasting. Edna (not as innocent as she looks) is perfectly capable of departing from Sunny Bank and scuttling as fast her little legs will carry her to Brenda Haycroft in Lovatt's Lane.

In the event, Edna was perfectly happy for Brenda Haycroft and Dorothy Potton to be present at the first hearing. 'The Jameses are tied up, though,' Edna reported. 'I bumped into their cleaning lady when I was walking doggy. She said they're expecting company to lunch.'

'Oh never mind them.' The James sisters, being not quite of the same ilk, might in fact put a dampener on the proceedings. 'I'll just give Brenda and Dorothy a buzz. About ten-thirty? Chin-chin.'

So here are the four of them: Daphne Bullivant holding forth, Edna Critch, Brenda Haycroft, Dorothy Potton, relishing every word; Daphne inviting her friends to consider whether it can be *safe* having someone like that living only next door – that is, at the bottom of the garden. Because the woman is definitely *violent*. The one who was looking after her – what's her name? Oh yes, Woolard – received a black eye for her pains. It is rather shocking, when you come to think of it. There you are, peaceably at work in your own garden, when all of a sudden a terrible row breaks out, and when you quite naturally pop your head over the fence to investigate, you discover two grown women rolling over the ground, evidently in mortal combat. Of course it's all very sad. Dementia. Horrid. But there are surely places for people like that?

Mrs Haycroft, who has been thinking, comes up with a different angle. What, she speculates, if there's a *reason* for Mrs McLeod going mental? After all, she is still a young woman. Who knows? – maybe she's been driven that way. This Mrs Woolard. Always in and out of High House. You don't suppose there's something going on between her and Mr McLeod?

A long pause as Mrs Critch and Mrs Potton wait to see which way their hostess will jump. Will she accept the Haycroft garnishing?

Though sorely tempted, Mrs Bullivant decides in the end to throw cold water. (She can be very pushy can Brenda Haycroft.) 'Oh, noo, noo, no. I very much doubt it. I've had more than one occasion to observe that ménage, and I can assure you, he is devoted to his wife, and Mrs Woolard is kindness itself. I get the impression she has been a close friend of Mrs McLeod's.'

'She's a young widow,' Brenda Haycroft points out darkly.

'Even so,' insists Daphne Bullivant.

'The village is not what it was,' mourns Davinia James.

Her sister Esmé, who has been recounting the exploits of the newly formed Best Kept Village Contest Committee, subsides deflated. And their guest Marjorie Cluff, who lives in the next county and has a Bentley waiting for her discreetly down the lane with a chauffeur inside eating his sandwiches, confesses that she can well believe it.

'They're a nice enough bunch . . .'

'Friendly, good hearted,' Esmé ventures.

'. . . as neighbours, you understand. But with Clara and Edward gone, and the new doctor not quite what one expects in a doctor (how one misses dear Alec and June) frankly, there's no-one in the place one would ask to luncheon.'

'But, Davinia, we often . . .'

'Tea, I grant you . . . But I simply don't recall the last time we dined . . .'

'We drove over to the the Plums only last month.'

'I'm talking about the village, Esmé!' Re-tuning her tone for the benefit of her guest (who, unlike Esmé, can be relied upon to stick to the point), she reflects, 'In Sir Jock's time, of course, one would dine at The Old Vicarage . . .'

'Yes. Tell me, how is Fenella Cunningham these days? Haven't clapped eyes on her in years.'

'Mad as a hatter,' Davinia placidly reports.

But Esmé hurries to correct her. 'You have always misunderstood the artistic temperament, Davinia. Fenella is the same as always, Marjorie – you know, *dramatic* – only now it's rather sad because there is hardly anyone to observe her. Only poor Molly (and they were never what you'd call close), Davinia and I occasionally, and a few others. One always feels with Fenella that she needs an audience.'

'Well, she is an actress,' points out Marjorie, as though this makes it a perfectly natural requirement.

'She does seem to have been dropped by all those theatre and political people one used to encounter there.'

'A loony,' Davinia insists, and goes on to quote Mrs Cross, their cleaning woman (who is the neighbour and confidant of Mrs Prior, daily woman at The Old Vicarage). 'Flies off the handle and goes galloping up to her room. Shuts herself in for hours, apparently. We only hope poor Molly isn't the butt of her tantrums – don't we, Esmé? Fortunately, Molly is stone deaf.'

'Not *stone* deaf, Davinia. Very hard of hearing.'

Davinia looks sternly at her sister. This nit-picking is frankly irritating; Esmé only does it when they have company; it must be her way of trying to assert herself. 'The fact is, Marjorie, Molly has been "hard of hearing" for years. Most sensible people would now term her "deaf". One used to think, how awful; but with Fenella throwing paddies and so forth, one can only presume it's a blessing. That great barn of a house has a lot to answer for in my opinion – all those rooms to rattle around in; bound to encourage histrionics. They should sell up and buy something suitable. Atmosphere is *so* important.' Her complacent glance takes in their old oak furniture (Welsh dresser, Windsor chairs, oval gate-legged table); the prettily curtained leaded light windows; the brasses in the inglenook; all gleaming from the attentions of Mrs Cross's duster.

Rose Cottage, where the sisters have lived for twenty-five years, was purchased for them by their nephew as executor of their father's estate. Several family friends live in country houses round about, though fewer than formerly and those who remain have become less socially active with advancing years. Happily, the sisters have always taken their village duties seriously (members of the WI, stalwarts of the altar flowers and church cleaning rotas) and as a result can rely on the village network for ready company. In her heart of hearts, Esmé is perfectly content with this state of affairs, though she would not admit it to Davinia who, she knows, hankers constantly for the old crowd. The high point of Davinia's year is their salmon fishing fortnight in Scotland — which takes them the best part of another fortnight to get there and back (both sisters are demons at the wheel, it has been necessary for most villagers at some time to hop quickly out of the path of their oncoming Triumph Vitesse; but their determination to avoid motorways at all costs has led to ever more lengthy and tortuous journeys). Esmé understands that, after Scotland, life in Aston Favell is second best for her sister; and plummets to third when their attendance is called for (as will happen next week) at events such as Mrs Bullivant's coffee morning.

'Come and see the garden, Marjorie,' urges Esmé, rising from her chintz-covered armchair. 'The stocks are out of this world; their scent sends me reeling.'

They lead their guest under the beams, over the rugs, out into the garden; where they affect not to notice Mr Prior, the gardener (whose primary employment is as driver to the Cunninghams), at the back of the rose border, staking and restraining a lusty *Boule de Neige*.

Kate will be glad when the morning is over. She cannot rid herself of tiredness. And the dream keeps recurring: not details — sensations; particularly if she lowers her head for any reason. For instance: when one of the sixth-formers was unable to find the passage she needed to look at in *Le Grand Meaulnes* and Kate lent over the girl's shoulder to point it out, the smell of the McLeods' lawn rose to her nostrils — with such swooning effect that she could not discover the passage either, though she has been teaching the novel for years. When she returned to her desk to consult her own marked copy, there was a taste of grass at the back of her throat, and her rump and shoulder blades remembered their jarring against the lawn's knobbly hardness when Will – of course, she means Sylvie – rolled on top. Will – or Sylvie? Both episodes seem dream-like. With ten minutes to go before lunch break, she resolves to keep her head up; otherwise, those waves washing through her mind, sucking, pulling, aiming to draw her down into the surreal world, may actually succeed, and she will simply reel into unconsciousness.

In the staff room, with exercise books on her knee (a signal to others that she is not available for general gossip or to argue the pros and cons of the school opting out of local authority control), a mug of black instant coffee and a sandwich to hand, her face tilted towards an open window, her head begins to clear. She remembers what did happen between her and Will; and the harder she concentrates on this, the sillier and fainter the dream becomes. What occurred between them was tenderness, a reaching out. Her mind homes in on him – not just on his physical attributes, but things he says and does, on Will McLeod the person. She is filled with a warm yearning.

By the time she gets up to go to the cloakroom one last time before afternoon school, things have been sorted out. All right, she admits it: she is attracted to Will McLeod, fond of him – but he is a very attractive man, for heaven's sake, and it does not necessarily follow that she is in love with him. Nor that she lusts after him. She cannot be held responsible for an over-active subconscious playing tricks on her poor neglected body. So it is all perfectly OK, she informs her reflection in the mirror over the basin. She dries her hands, feels cool and collected; so much so, that she considers calling at High House on her way home from school to suggest they all three take a trip into the countryside tomorrow or on Sunday. It would do Sylvie good. After all, she has accompanied them on several such outings in the recent past.

With matters arranged in their true perspective, and mercifully now wide awake, she goes briskly down the corridor to take the first lesson of the afternoon.

In the principal bedroom in The Old Vicarage, Fenella Cunningham is sorting through her clothes. *Unwanted Clothes – Bed Linen – Domestic Utensils*? enquires a typewritten notice on recycled paper which has been pushed through her letter box by a representative of the relief organization currently housing half a dozen Croatian families in Lavenbrook. Any such items in good condition will be most gratefully collected. Fenella read and re-read the message, standing still as a statue with tears in her eyes. Then raced upstairs to throw open the doors of her three wardrobes and pull out the drawers of her many chests. Unwanted clothes (in excellent condition) are piling up on her counterpane. She works urgently in her petticoat, for, when a hard choice has to be made, she pulls on the garment in question and runs to consider the matter in the long looking glass. When doubt attacks she resolves to be ruthless, and bolsters her resolve by summoning up images of weeping refugee women, babes in arms, hands out-stretched for caressing silk, softest wool, finest lawn. Give, give, she cries, ripping off a straw cartwheel hat, tossing it on to the bed – not an item affording a lot of protection from the elements, but indispensable when it comes to raising the spirits. And may well, she imagines, prove a life-saving restorative to some poor worn-down woman whose morale has been shot to shreds. She reflects on the many times when a new hat or a new hairdo has renewed her own zest for living – infinitely more effectively than champagne and with no horrid after-effects.

When scarcely an exposed square inch of counterpane remains, Fenella sets off to find Molly. Discovers her in the kitchen, scooping Beefy Chunks out of a tin into a dog's bowl, the smelly little terrier prancing and dribbling round her feet.

'Come with me,' yells Fenella, sweeping her arm to point the way.

Molly frowns, snitches up her spectacles, turns back to her scooping. 'Good doggy want uns din-dins?' – at which the dog becomes frenzied, leaps at Molly's legs scattering saliva over the floor tiles, cries, shouts, until the bowl is lowered and he can sink his muzzle into a glistening brown heap.

'Why don't you forget that thundering dog for five minutes and think about human beings?' shrieks Fenella. 'Here, take a look at this.' She thrusts the notice under Molly's nose.

Molly squints at it, but declines to touch it. In fact, places her hands under a running tap, then goes to dry them on the roller towel. At length vouchsafes, 'What about it?'

'Come and see what I've managed to find for them. Perhaps it'll inspire you to make an effort. Come on up,' she commands, striding to the stairs. 'Later on I'll give Prior a ring. I'll ask him to fetch some empty boxes from the shop. Then I'll pack everything ready for these people to collect. There.' (She has arrived in her bedroom.) 'What do you think of that?'

Molly comes trailing in after her vigorous sister-in-law. Surveys the bed. 'Where the devil are you going to sleep?'

'It'll all be gone soon. I've just told you, I shall phone for Prior. Now go and look through your things. Be generous, Molly. Give with a glad heart.'

Molly has moved towards the bed and is now fingering a swathe of chiffon. 'Be better to give 'em money than this old rubbish.'

'Rr-rubbish? I'll have you know that dress is a Hartnell.'

'Wouldn't give you tuppence for it.'

Molly's baggy brown trousers covered in dog-hairs, her grubby check shirt and sleeveless pull-over with frayed welt, are given the Lady Cunningham once-over. 'I daresay some of your things might come in handy for lads. Go and see what you can find.'

Molly shakes her head. 'I've better things to do. And if you're harbouring ambitions to eat tonight, you'd better stop pestering me with bally nonsense.'

Food — typical, shudders Fenella, as Molly plods from the room. No imagination. Finer feelings are beyond some people.

Kate is driving too fast. It is a quarter to five. When school finished there was a department meeting. Now she is burning rubber to get to High House. And brake-pads too — hell, that was a close one; stupid of her, overtaking like that, flat out with nothing to spare — criminal — must have given the oncoming car a stressful few seconds. She slows to fifty and takes in the scenery — shiny leaves in the copse, parched pasture, ripe corn. When last did it rain? No wonder the farmers are moaning about immature crops and premature ripening. Another week and the heavens will surely open, flattening a million sun-dried stalks. Sequence all wrong — ought to be rain first, sun after. Life for you.

Tenaciously, she thinks about anything but Will McLeod. The thing to avoid at all costs is an impression of scheming, of plotting manoeuvres. She hopes to knock on the door and present her idea as freshly formed, her face the picture of spontaneity. 'Hello, Will. I was driving back and I suddenly thought: Why don't we take Sylvie . . . ?'

She slows down for Main Street, turns, then stays in second gear to draw up in front of High House.

But a car is parked there already. Joan's. Which is unusual, at this time of day. Better keep going. Not the right moment. Sod.

When five o'clock arrives and still no sign of Prior, Fenella seizes the telephone receiver. Soon, 2 Pond

Cottages is disturbed by ringing for a second time in the past half hour.

'He's not back yet from Rose Cottage, Lady Cunningham. Like I said: phone him there, I'm sure the Miss Jameses will give him your message. Mind you, I hope it's not a long drive you're thinking of, 'cos Prior'll be tired, working all day in the Miss Jameses' garden.'

Fenella flinches from this unnecessary reminder of how the James sisters use the Cunningham chauffeur. Once it would have failed her imagination to picture Prior out of his chauffeur's uniform, so very much the part he was – discreetly gallant to herself, respectfully confident with Sir Jock. The limousine still reposes in the garage of The Old Vicarage, but these days it gets very few airings. Prior is paid a regular wage to keep it up to the mark, to ferry her and Molly on their unexciting shopping trips and to and fro a rare social engagement, but she cannot invent tasks to keep him occupied. Molly is in charge of the garden and employs Dan Coles to assist her. In any case, gardening is *all wrong* for a chauffeur, who may with impunity soil his hands with engine oil, but please not with garden manure. She knows what goes on at Rose Cottage, but prefers to be spared the details. 'Very well,' says she curtly, 'I shall go myself. Goodbye, Mrs Prior. Oh, and don't forget – clean dusters on Monday morning.'

'But I always . . .'

The shop shuts in half an hour. Fenella cuts off Mrs Prior, pelts through the hall – then darts back again to consult the wall mirror. Thinks: *lady of mercy on vital errand.* Sees: *lady of mercy on vital errand.* Jutting her chin at a brave angle, she strides from the house and along the drive.

In the shop, several people alerted by the draught turn at her sudden entrance. 'Oh, Lady Cunningham,' observes Nan Hutton, carefully without surprise.

'I am here to crave a boon. Not on my own behalf, you understand, on behalf of some poor refugees. Four large boxes, Mrs Hutton, if you would be so kind. I have been turning out my drawers and wardrobes. So many clothes – vanity, vanity. And these poor people with barely a stitch.'

'Boxes,' Nan repeats. 'I'm afraid this isn't the best of days. You see, Ted goes to the cash and carry Tuesdays and Fridays, taking any empties we haven't used to drop off at the tip. If you can wait till Monday . . .'

'Mrs Hutton, this is an emergency. Surely, surely . . .'

'Bob's out there now, unloading.'

Fenella pushes up the sleeves of her gingham frock. 'Then I shall assist him.'

'But Lady Cunningham . . .' Bother! – a silent exclamation; Nan reddens with the effort of keeping it in.

In the yard behind the shop, Ted Hutton, heaving a large carton from the back of a Granada estate, is dumbfounded to discover he has acquired an assistant. Delayed protests are brushed aside as Fenella wraps strong arms round a boxful of tinned dog-food, pulls this into her sturdy stomach, stalks with it into the storeroom. As Ted puffs objections, Fenella unloads two cartons to his every one. At length, rips open four of the containers and strides with an armful of tins into the rear of the shop. 'Baked beans in spicy sauce?' she calls ringingly.

'Excuse me,' murmurs Nan to her customer. 'No, Lady Cunningham. They have to have the price written on first . . .'

'Then pass me the where-with-all.'

Nan sighs. 'That won't be necessary. I doubt there's room yet on the shelves. Oh dear. You'd better stack 'em down there by the potatoes. Debbie, leave that order and help Lady Cunningham.'

'Wouldn't hear of it. I have never been afraid of hard work, and for a worthy cause, you'll find me tireless.'

Soon Fenella is very warm. This rejoices her. She revels in the sweat of her brow (sweat of her brow is how she thinks of her exertions), and wipes at it often with the back of her hand. The onlookers –

customers who have found that they are in no hurry at all – have moved from chuckling amazement to frank admiration. They estimate her age in whispers; hope to be able to do as much when they attain it. Only Nan is annoyed – long past closing time, people still hanging about, a large area of floor-space cluttered, an unexpectedly busy evening ahead.

Returning in triumph to The Old Vicarage with four large empty boxes, Fenella flies immediately up to her room. She packs her discarded clothes, carries them box by box to the hall below. Then retrieves the notice on which is written a collector's phone number and proceeds to dial.

To her chagrin, no collection can be made until Monday evening. This is hard to take in. Three whole days must elapse before the poor wretches can benefit from her generosity. It is too bad.

'Grub's up,' Molly calls from the kitchen.

A bewildered and disheartened Fenella abandons the telephone, turns to survey her boxes. They stand in the gloom, powdery sunlight from a landing window slanting a misty shroud, dismal as suitcases long-abandoned in a luggage hall. A lump forms in Fenella's throat – a familiar impediment which slowly expands to inhabit her chest. She looks into the kitchen, says thickly, 'You know perfectly well I can't dine at this early hour.'

'Put yours to keep warm, then. *Through The Keyhole* starts at seven. We don't want to miss it, do we Henry?'

Hearing his name, Henry wags in agreement.

Listlessly, Fenella leaves them. Returns upstairs.

The most obvious reason for Joan's car being outside High House when she drove past earlier was some crisis with Sylvie. Kate, as she potters about Wayside Cottage, dusting, cleaning the bathroom, choosing a dinner-for-one from a collection in the freezer, dwells on this fact and idly wonders what sort of crisis.

Forking Cod Mornay into her mouth she pictures various scenarios, and promises herself that at eight o'clock – or half-past – she will ring up and enquire, ask Will if she can do anything, and maybe try and worm in the idea of an outing. With luck, Sylvie will be sufficiently calm after Joan's ministrations to make this a possibility. Meanwhile, to pass the time she will go outside and do some gardening.

Buttercups have seeded on the dry stone wall. They were so pretty in flower, she has delayed pulling them out. Now is the time. As she yanks, she recalls Sylvie yesterday – the good-girl three-year-old, aiming to please. Kate's heart twists. Perhaps something bad has happened to her. Genuine concern for Sylvie, for Sylvie's own sake, at lasts permits her to hurry indoors and make the phone call.

'Hello, Will, it's Kate. When I passed your place earlier, Joan's car was outside. I hope Sylvie's all right?'

Will sighs. 'She's quiet now. But it's been a hell of a day.'

'Oh dear. Anything I can do?'

'Not really. I'm about to go up and get some kip. I was awake most of the night.'

'Well, um, I *had* been going to suggest taking Sylvie out somewhere over the weekend . . .'

'Out of the question.'

'Ah.'

'But thanks for the thought. Nice of you to call.'

'Right. Goodbye, Will.'

'Goodbye, Kate.'

He is pushing me away. This selfish and unworthy thought is one she cannot quite suppress. He is worn out, she reasons, worried about his wife and the future. She imagines him surrounded by mounds of filthy washing, by broken furniture (because Sylvie in a paddy is *strong*), with a cut over his eye, scratched, bruised, haggard. Hell, she was a fool even to mention the outing. No wonder she received short shrift.

The telephone rings. Her heart leaps. But it is not Will phoning her back.

'Are you doing anything tomorrow, Kate?' asks Fiona.

'Er, well, not exactly . . .'

'Oh good. Because if I don't get away for a bit I shall end up as miserable as he is. Honestly, Kate, I know it's tough for him, but it's hard on me, too. Here I am, teaching full time at school, taking an evening class three times a week – and this aerobic stuff jolly well takes it out of you, you know – and all I get is my head bitten off. I only asked, why, when I've been out grafting all day and he's been at home, why the hell's the washing up still cluttering the sink? I mean, is it fair? So I thought, I'll ring Kate. We'll go into town and have a damn good spend. Have lunch at the Italian. Maybe stop on for a film. Yeah, why not? The kids are happy enough getting their own – let him fend for himself for once. Pick you up at half ten?'

Kate cannot think of any acceptable reason to refuse. She is free in the sense of having nothing arranged; she has no man in her life, no kids at home requiring to be fed and looked after; she is, after all, just a woman alone.

Eventually, she goes back into the garden and stares at the philadelphus, drawing in its scent. Good lord, whatever is the matter with her; why shouldn't she be available for her friend?

But as she turns to go indoors, a timid and despicably self-pitying voice in her head counters: because it's not what I planned, it's not how I hoped this weekend would turn out. Furthermore, there was not the faintest hint of acknowledgement in Will's voice just now that yesterday they shared a tender embrace. Say what you like, come up with any excuse: the tone of his voice was ever so slightly pushing her off.

An hour before closing time, Major Bullivant finds he is not best pleased with Mrs Bullivant. He leaves The

Crown, having enjoyed with other officials of the Aston Favell Horticultural Society a series of revivers following a strenuous meeting, and having also exchanged words with some of the regulars, in particular, and most disturbingly, with Dan Coles, gardening assistant to Miss Molly Cunningham. Arriving home, he seeks her out. 'Bone to pick with you,' he announces, taking up a precarious stand just inside the lounge, where his wife is watching television.

'Hush, Major, it's my programme.'

'Chap in the pub,' cries the Major, lurching for safety's sake to the nearest armchair on which he sits down suddenly with a surprised expression; 'chap in the pub . . .'

'Do spit it out,' cries Daphne, stabbing the 'increased volume' button.

'. . . Dan Coles, by name,' continues the Major, his voice swooping up and down, 'he said to me: certain ladies, *certain ladies* had a meeting t'other day at The Old Vicarage: subject matter . . .' (He pauses suspensefully, but his wife remains silent: her expression becomes less one of impatience more one of unease, though this is hidden by her continuing to stare at the television.) '. . . subject matter: *Gardeners' Question Time broadcast from Aston Favell*,' roars the Major dreadfully.

Still Daphne says nothing, though she is busy thinking. What she is thinking is, Why can't Molly Cunningham keep her trap shut?

'How did the fellow come to hear about that, do you suppose – a confidential matter, known only to the committee? Good God, woman, how d'you think I felt – hearing this in front of m'colleagues, aye? They dealt me the sort of look you'd turn on a blabbermouth.'

'Don't you "woman" me,' cries Daphne, picking the one fault in his diatribe she can attack with confidence.

'It isn't even official yet, hasn't been confirmed. Yet you get on the blower, round up your coven, and go trying to organize the blessed show before the committee's had time to think about it. Your brief is The Best Kept Village Competition, and I'd be obliged if you'd stick to it. Thought, y'know, a chap could trust his wife to keep mum. I tell you, Daphne,' – a pause, as the bitterness of her betrayal strikes him anew and he heaves up his buttocks and stretches into his trouser pocket for a handkerchief – 'it'll be a mighty long time before I trust you again with a confidence.' With which he noisily empties his nose.

At length, for the first time removing her eyes from the screen, Daphne surveys her helpmate. 'I don't like your colour,' she remarks. 'I'd go and see the doctor, if I were you; let him check your blood pressure.'

It is late. It is Friday night. It is party time, thinks Fenella, sitting alone in her room in the fading light. Her hands are pressed together between her knees, her eyes are fixed on the wall opposite. From down the corridor and a flight of stairs comes the noise of Molly's television – a full-volume falling out among American thieves by the sound of it. Fenella stares at the wallpaper, and *through* the wallpaper. There are thousands of people out there at this very moment, merry-making, flirting, dancing, laughing, exchanging confidences, starting a romance . . . And countless millions settling down in the bosom of their family, round a table, in front of a television, or with friends in the dwindling light of a pub garden. The hotels are full, so are the theatres and cinemas. Cars, trains, planes are conveying people to desired destinations. What she finds, oh, so very difficult to grasp is: these busy millions have not the faintest idea about *her*. They are not even aware of her existence any more, never mind that Fenella, Lady Cunningham is sitting alone in her great barn of a shadowy bedroom. It is rather like being dead. No-one knows and no-one cares. A tear trickles from the corner of an eye. Dear Jock would care, she thinks, roused by the thought to indignation. He would care terribly. He would find it utterly unbelievable that she could be so ignored, so disregarded. How he would snap his fingers, beat the table for attention. Ladies and Gentlemen, he would roar, I give you my wife, Lady Fenella Cunningham.

CHAPTER SIX

Saturday 20th June

'Mm – not a good night,' she observes.

'Er, no,' agrees Will, unable to elaborate for panting. He has been up since six washing bedclothes and rushing round the house trying to reorder it before this visit. Today's nurse is not Joan. She is Eilish. Will calls her 'Nurse'.

Using patients' and their relatives' first names, offering your own in return, is evidently the form, at least in this practice. However, they are presumably taught to apply it sensitively, for his inability to say 'Eilish' to Eilish's face is interpreted as a desire to stick to formalities. Consequently, on Eilish's days he is 'Mr McLeod'. Only his wife is treated informally. 'Good morning, and how are we today, Sylvie? You going to come on upstairs with Eilish, now?' he hears the nurse call brightly. And Sylvie in her nightgown goes meek as a lamb. 'Dear Lord, and aren't we in a pickle this morning?' he overhears when they reach the top – evidently Eilish getting her first view of the bathroom.

He continues to stand in the hall, half listening to the activity overhead (which, wouldn't you know? continues calmly, productively, pleasantly, in direct contrast to Sylvie's previous refusal to co-operate). Because he is low and overtired, his longing for it to be Joan's day and not Eilish's is faintly childish; it reminds him of being bullied at prep school and his chokey despairing hope at the prospect of a weekend exeat or of his mother visiting. He is at ease with Joan.

He likes the way she seems to regard his predicament – as bad luck, as the way life goes sometimes. Eilish emanates disapproval. Will is not sure whether this is aimed at his decision to care for Sylvie personally, or at the job he makes of it. Either way, on Eilish's days he feels inadequate, put upon, misunderstood. Now Joan has three days off. A richly deserved break, no doubt, but please God send Tuesday.

He goes into the kitchen feeling like a peeled fruit, stripped of a tough outer layer, his nerves and juices barely contained by the frail remaining membrane. Very carefully, he lowers his rump onto a hard chair, scoops a portion of the table in front of him free of clutter, lays his forearms on this portion then his head on his arms. Life, he reflects, has been one long nightmare since the early hours of Friday morning when he was woken by Sylvie sobbing in his bedroom doorway, soaked, as it turned out, in urine. Since then she has swung from desolation to manic activity to terror to sullen spite, periodically collapsing into deep but all too brief slumber. Yesterday was the worst of his life. But at least he had Joan's support, which will not be the case today, tomorrow or Monday. Joan saw how things were yesterday morning and returned later in the day for a second visit. She even suggested reporting back to the surgery to try and arrange emergency 'respite'. In other words, get Sylvie booked into residential care for a couple of nights. Tempted, he resisted. Because what Joan is not aware of (since he doesn't dare confess it) is his role in Sylvie's relapse. After all, it can be no coincidence that she lurched into this worsened state a few hours after Kate's visit on Thursday. Sylvie must have seen them with their arms round one another when she came bumbling into the room. Must have sensed they were on the brink of kissing. He had assumed from her lack of expression it had failed to register. But you can only guess at, blindly grope towards, what actually goes on inside Sylvie. She may be incapable of considering cause and effect, but it is not impossible that the sight of him and Kate triggered in some roundabout way her deep insecurity. Insecurity has always been Sylvie's bugbear. She is the least secure person he knows.

What it comes down to is, he betrayed her. If he tried explaining this to Joan, he can imagine how she would scoff and soothe. ('You're tired, darlin'. You can't think straight. I seen it before – folks find they can't do nothin' to help their loved ones so they go tryin' to blame themselves. Make out it's their fault for these bad things happening. Invent all sorts of crazy reasons. You know what I'm saying, Will? There'll come a time when you can't carry on no longer. And you just gotta accept it, love – 'cause you ain't God Almighty. Just a man.') He can mentally write the script from things she has already said during their chats together, but he is not sure such an easy letting off is deserved. A weak moment with Kate may or may not be the cause of Sylvie's suddenly rapid decline; there is no way of telling; but just in case, he has to try reassurance, discover if this buys her time. He is obliged, he is resolved. Nevertheless, like a comfort blanket, he draws on Joan's voice ('A *man*', she says, as though you can't get any lower in the usefulness stakes) and her laughter drowns out the world as he falls asleep.

Despite her expectations, her initial reluctance, Kate is thoroughly enjoying the day out with Fiona. She cannot imagine why yesterday she felt so resentful and taken for granted. Nor why she anticipated Fiona moaning about her husband with total gloom. Of course, the subject is thoroughly aired; whenever did two women out on a spree neglect to discuss their nearest and dearest, their neighbours and colleagues, analyse people's comments and behaviour, speculate as to motive, predict outcomes, weigh points in favour and points against? Fiona concedes that it must be utterly demoralizing for her husband seeing his firm go under and then in quick succession losing two pretty crummy jobs, but honestly, something is bound to turn up sooner or later, once the economy picks up (fingers crossed, but it's got to sometime, hasn't it?); in the meantime, why can't he make himself useful at home, carry out a few improvements? (there's been a tile off in the shower for months, for Pete's sake; as for the garage doors . . .); he could at least tidy up, have the odd meal ready, show more interest in the kids' doings, take up a hobby, spread a little cheer . . . Specially with his wife working her butt off . . .

Fiona's tirade is not continuous. Bits of it erupt during the drive to town and later while they are trying on clothes. It widens into a discussion of how other people they know have reacted to disappointment or stress. They stare at each other in changing-room mirrors trying to decide whether the new long skirts make them feel feminine and young or old and frumpy, and constantly interrupt this sartorial enquiry with new thoughts on the stress-at-work topic. In the middle of agreeing that the bitchiness exhibited by Josie Templar (assistant History teacher) during staff meetings towards Dick Plowright (Head of History) is down to her dashed but justified expectation of being appointed (rather than he) as Head of Department (so though her behaviour is embarrassing you can't really blame her), they suddenly see what is wrong with the skirts. They need to be worn with the new long-line straight tops, not these tuck-in jobs. And so it proves. Skirts plus the right tops are incredibly graceful. Sexy, in fact. At last purchased, and carried off in large bags with a sense of achievement to celebrate in an Italian restaurant.

Over a glass each of the house white, the talk becomes more intimate. Deliciously, hazily, they consider the possibility of new lovers in their lives – in the not immediate future, of course. No candidates are put forward, but the fact that each takes the prospect for the other with perfect seriousness, is ego-bolstering. (And why wouldn't they? Fiona's long body is svelte and firm from constant exercising, her fair hair is cut in the trendiest fashion, skin and eyes gleam; as Kate has often observed at work, Fiona turns heads, men cannot help gazing; in any case, she already has a couple of affairs to her credit. Kate has none. Chris was her one and only. But Fiona, weighing up Kate's undeniable attractions – glossy hair, huge dark eyes, freckle-spattered ivory skin, senses a certain air about her . . .) Exchanged looks, grins, sighs, transmute to a consciousness of their own desirability. They smile at the waiter, sail out onto the street like women with a hand or two to play.

It is hot outside, out of the air-conditioning. Dutifully but listlessly they wander through an art exhibition in the Town Hall. Then repair to the five-screen cinema complex with renewed enthusiasm. In the cool darkness they stuff popcorn from tall cartons into their mouths and hope there are no kids from school in the audience.

It has been getting warmer all day. Now the sky has thickened and turned the early evening sullen; a sudden breeze lifts the leaves of the horse chestnut tree. Standing at the sink in The Old Vicarage, Molly observes this through the window and turns to tell Henry there is a storm brewing. She looks to that spot on the floor a few feet behind where Henry usually takes up position – particularly when she is standing this close to the cupboard housing dog supplies. But Henry is absent. Maybe – the back door is propped open – he has gone outside for a wet.

In the hall, Fenella is standing on the stairs, squinting down over the banisters. All safe, the precious boxes. Planted, waiting, like standing stones. Every hour or so she comes to pay homage. She has a sense of affinity with them, as if she, too, is waiting.

But on this occasion a faint snuffling leads her to suspect desecration. She hurtles down the remaining stairs, darts between two large cartons – as Henry shoots out. Unluckily for him, a draught has blown shut the door to the kitchen. She traps him against it and deals him a kick in the flank.

Aware that his protector is aurally deficient, Henry does not spare himself. 'Whatever . . . ?' puffs Molly, opening the door. 'Oh baby . . .' She gathers him up. 'He's terrified, poor doggy. What have you done to him?'

'He was sniffing round my boxes,' Fenella cries grandly, and continues wrathfully – as a vision of what she might have seen hardens into fact: 'He'd lined himself up and was all set to lift his leg. I prevented him just in time.'

'Nonsense. He's intrigued by the grocery niffs, that's all – sugar, washing-powder, doggy bics. Shall Mummy give oo a nice bicky, then?'

'It certainly is not nonsense. He was positioning himself, the dirty little wretch.'

'Then you'll be sorry to learn some other animal got there first. That's the only possible reason – he sniffed wee and thought, "Here's the place".'

'I'll have you know,' shrieks Fenella, 'those boxes are pristine. *Pristine.*'

'Trouble with you, Fenella, you're not a dog person.' With which irrefutable and damning shot, Molly kicks the kitchen door shut between them.

No, not a dog person. I am for people.

Fenella makes this claim silently, but ringingly, as hand on heart she mounts the stairs. I have devoted my life to Mankind. Every fibre of my being strained to nurture, lighten, lift, inspire. It is my habit, my deepest instinct, to spare, to regret nothing. All that I am, dear fellow human beings, is entirely yours . . . Majestically she gains the landing, her great speech unrolling.

On the threshold of her bedroom, an outbreak of cheering startles by its absence. The silence strikes her as alien. She sinks onto the edge of her bed in a temporary sort of way and is a touch mollified by a distant thunder clap, a rumble of righteous wrath – a sound often contrived to signal moments of high drama and pathos when she was a bright young member of the Shakespeare Memorial Theatre Company. If only there were an audience out there beyond the lights (as she feels there should be), thrilled and moved by her isolation, then she could bear it.

In all her life she was never ignored. Something has gone badly awry. Her fists pound the counterpane – angry, angry. *Why doesn't somebody do something?*

Molly sits in the wooden rocking chair nursing her wounded pet (in dog years he is older than she is), her hand stroking away his shivers until, as his body goes lax, old sinews giving under a tired coat, her hand stills over his ribs and steadied pulse. His warmth, the easy slide of skin over bone, the weight in her lap, his musky odour, send her mellow with well-being. 'Dear old boy,' she murmurs, and Henry's tail thumps against her thigh. Affirmingly. Like applause.

On the way home, with the storm finally broken (exciting stuff – lightning flashing, water hitting the car's underside, and pounding the roof in sudden massive downpours like God playing with taps), Fiona hunches forward in silent concentration. Blissfully irresponsible, Kate settles back and stretches her limbs as far as the little car permits. A most satisfactory day – money splurged, the fat chewed, morales boosted. And a landmark, it occurs to her: she and Fiona are back on their old footing, for Fiona has stopped watching her tongue: in all their frank chat, in their joshing about future lovers, there was never a flicker of embarrassment, no sudden ghastly recollection; Fiona did not feel it necessary to hurriedly assert that Chris, of course, is irreplaceable. Her friend must have caught some signal, thinks Kate. Evidently, without noticing it, she has taken a small step forward. Moved on.

The car slows to make the turn into the village. 'Look,' groans Fiona; 'just look at them.' She sounds offended.

Kate slides upright in her seat, looks to her left, to a lay-by just prior to Main Street and fronting some council bungalows, where, beside a street lamp, stands the village bus shelter. The small brick structure is alive with writhing bodies swinging through the windowless apertures, scuttling over the roof. Lightning flashes, and one figure springs upright, hurls something. It is like viewing the aftermath of a bombing from a position of safety – insulated as they are by the car's speed and engine noise: the ravaging creatures swarm in apparent silence, dark and glossy in the brilliant rain.

'No wonder that shelter's an eyesore. The council might as well pull it down.'

'Where else would they go?' Kate wonders.

This irritates Fiona. 'I hate having that element in the village. Doesn't it bother you?'

'I suppose it might be aggravating to people in the bungalows. But, no, not really. I mean, we know who they are. It's only May's son, and Louise's.'

'And there were girls,' adds Fiona, as if this makes it worse.

'They're just enjoying the storm,' Kate says. She thinks, but keeps it to herself (her last remark having driven Fiona into annoyed silence), of cramped houses in Penfold Close, of adolescents made to share their bedrooms with younger kids: they have to be somewhere . . . The thought prevents her turning her head when they pass High House; they have already gone by before she thinks of it: what, anyway, could she glean from a glimpse of his parked car or curtained windows? She stares ahead, at a picture of dark bodies swarming, interrupted by the monotonous sweep of windscreen wipers.

The car turns left at The Green, goes lurching up Vicarage Hill. In the gleam from the headlights, a figure shoots over the road. 'Hey,' cries Fiona, 'was that out of your place?'

'I'm not sure. Slow down.' But as they pass the spot where the figure merged into shadows on the left, there is no sign of anyone. 'Damn.'

Fiona pulls into Kate's driveway. 'You think it was the Peeping Tom?'

'He was wearing a cap.'

'I didn't see. It happened too quickly.'

'I couldn't swear to it . . .'

'In any case, so what? Loads of men round here wear caps.'

'This Peeping Tom certainly does – according to the women who chased him last Wednesday night.'

'You're not worried? I suppose we could call the police.'

'Forget it. It's not a crime to cross the road. Coffee?'

'OK.' Fiona does not actually want coffee, but can tell Kate is rattled. She feels vindicated, decides that although Kate pretended otherwise, those youths on the bus shelter really got to her.

They dash into the house – the rain has eased off, but the trees are dripping, puddles lie in the yard. Kate puts the kettle on. While Fiona uses the cloakroom, she runs round the house checking all the windows and doors, looking in cupboards and under the beds.

'What else have you got?' Fiona asks, raising her coffee cup.

Kate laughs. 'Look in the sideboard. Take your pick.'

Fiona squints into the cupboard. 'Amaretto – lovely. You going to have some?'

'I warn you, it's a bit ancient.'

'Oh, this stuff never goes off; the sugar preserves it.' She pours an inch into each of two tumblers and passes one to Kate.

It was one of Chris's favourite tipples. Come to think of it, she can remember Chris buying this very bottle in the Duty Free at Pisa Airport. She takes a wary sip.

Then relaxes. The drink is painless. It was the thought that hurt.

'If you're uneasy,' says Fiona, incorrectly interpreting a fleeting look on Kate's face, 'I could stay over. Or you could come to my place.'

'No,' Kate says abruptly (and after a moment's reflection, she fears rudely). But she has not screwed up her courage, refused invitations, forced herself to face out this stupid fear all these months to throw in the towel now. 'Kind of you, but honestly, I'd forgotten all about it. I bet that bloke we saw was old misery guts from up the hill, loping off to The Crown – you know, bloke who used to have the egg round.'

'Oh, him. Yeah. Wife's probably had enough of him, told him to clear out and annoy Pauline Turner. Well, if you're sure you're OK, I'll be off. Get home to *my* cup of joy.'

Kate watches her dart across the yard, climb into the car, start the engine. The moment the car moves forward, she closes the door, turns the key, draws the bolt.

It is odd, but she is not really afraid. All that checking up and making sure – it was just going through the motions. She feels full of optimism getting ready for bed. Even considers phoning Will in the morning. But after all decides against it. Judging from the sound of his voice on the phone yesterday, he is under considerable stress; better give him time to get Sylvie calmed down. In any case, she has a pile of marking to do. She'll clear the decks tomorrow and maybe call at High House on her way home from school on Monday. She could take them a cake – that's an idea; something scrummy from the shop in the Butter Market.

Heart in mouth, Will goes along the landing and unlocks Sylvie's door. He shouldn't have done it, shouldn't have locked her in. He will never forgive himself if . . .

But inside all is peaceful. Sylvie is lying under the white satin counterpane breathing steadily; fast, safely, asleep. So maybe it wasn't such a wicked thing to do. After all, he has to take a shower sometimes, he does have to reckon those estimates for Thursday, he is entitled to the odd bit of peace and quiet.

He knows, however, that these were not the most pressing reasons for pushing her down on the bed and holding her there until she fell quiet, for finally turning the key. Sylvie drove him very close to snapping point this evening. Perhaps the storm brewing excited her; whatever the reason, she was thoroughly wound up, prowling, shrieking, evading, finally chasing outside to whoop about in the rain. His hand goes to his cheek where there are deeply scratched grooves. It is lucky that it *was* raining; at least the deluge sent Mrs Busy-Body-over-the-fence indoors. If Sylvie had gone haywire in the garden an hour earlier the whole village would soon know about it, because then the Bullivants were busy taking preventative measures against the coming storm, he hauling down the sun-lounger, she staking and tying delphiniums.

Even so: *locking her in* . . . He shakes his head, wonders how long he can keep this up.

In the bed, Sylvie stirs and shifts. Her hair falls into the path of rays coming in from the street lamp. The sight makes him catch his breath, roots him to the spot. He stares at the hair until it becomes all he *can* see (gleaming, flowing, essence of the real Sylvie, his wife and Paul's mother), until the dull damaged dying creature lately holding him to ransom is totally expunged. His eyes begin to smart as though the gleam on the pillow is too fierce for them, but he keeps on looking; he needs the image to remind him of what he is sacrificing his life *for*. For Sylvie, he remembers, for lovely Sylvie, unfairly, prematurely and tragically afflicted, who, if she were able, would cling and beg his protection. Impossible that he should see her incarcerated with demented elderly folk.

He remembers also what his priorities are: to re-assure the real Sylvie trapped (and possibly aware:

who can know?) in this alien form, to keep going, *to see her through*. Damn the Birmingham contract, he decides, his eyes still on the pillow as he creeps to the door; he'll phone up first thing on Monday and cancel Thursday's meeting.

In which case, he must phone Kate tomorrow. Put her off.

CHAPTER SEVEN

Sunday 21st June

Ten o'clock — and right on time, the bell-ringers of St Peter's begin the half-hour peal. How nice, how right, thinks Davinia James, putting on her hat — an ancient trilby-shaped object in brownish-grey, chosen many years ago for its ability to go with anything (an excellently judged assessment, so it has proved). The riotous sound would have one believe that none of the lamentable changes of the past twenty years have taken place at all; that the Eucharist is celebrated every Sunday at half-past ten and follows hard on Matins at nine, that there is Evensong at six o'clock, and Holy Communion at seven or eight in the morning throughout the week. Heigh-ho, sighs Davinia, sticking in a hat pin.

The back door of Rose Cottage slams shut. Esmé has come into the kitchen with an inscrutable-looking Sarah (the latest in a long line of cairn terriers). The sisters meet in the hall. They avoid looking at one another, instead study their dog. 'She hasn't done a thing,' Esmé reports. 'I think she's upset after last night.'

Davinia ignores this last contentious remark. 'I expect she did it when I put her out earlier. You know she hates being stood over.'

They contemplate the shaggy little creature, whose black-tipped creamy coat is beaded with moisture from brushing against sopping wet greenery (the morning is bright, but there is still much evidence of last night's downpour). Through her spiky fringe, the terrier regards her mistresses. 'We'll shut her in the kitchen,' decides Davinia. 'Just in case.'

Within the vicinity of the church, only the fast asleep or profoundly deaf can remain oblivious of the bells. Fiona hears them in her detached house on the far side of Vicarage Hill (built in the sixties on the site of an old paddock in an abrasive style which would not be permitted in the village nowadays). She hears them despite the blare of her son's tape recorder and a screaming row going on in the kitchen. She lies in bed, ostensibly reading the Sunday paper, in fact blasted out of her mind by all the turmoil. It is her daughter doing the screaming (Lucy is at art college and comes home at weekends). Her husband merely punctuates the screams now and then with rough shouts. But Fiona does not blame her daughter, even though her noise is the worst. She knows who to blame. *Him*, misery guts.

And to cap it all those sodding bells. She had thought Sunday was meant to be a day of rest – she certainly needs a rest after the day out yesterday with Kate (shopping is *so* exhausting); fat chance, though, with a jangle like that belting out. She tosses the paper aside, jumps out of bed to run a bath.

In Wayside Cottage garden, Kate welcomes the pealing. An hour ago she woke in a bitter mood with Will on her mind, and the trouble and grief very probably occurring right now inside High House. For goodness sake, she silently exploded, sitting up in bed to think about it, why doesn't he ask her to come round and help? If Sylvie is getting worse, this is the moment to call on his friends for extra support. It is simply idiotic to be inhibited by an unguarded moment, an expression of affection – hang it all, they didn't *do* anything. She stomped downstairs, put the kettle on, glowered at the phone. Kidded herself that she would ring him and convey her opinion. She did not, of course; simply ate toast, drank tea, half-read the paper, got dressed. Then the bells rang out, and she looked into the garden where blossom-laden rose stems lay on the grass, battered there by last night's downpour. Now she is raising and tying them to stakes; her mood mellowed by the pouring sound, by the sun's warmth on her back.

The Old Vicarage receives the bells' fullest impact. Even Molly's hearing is penetrated, though their message is steadfastly ignored. She, too, is out in the garden repairing storm damage. A glance up at a bedroom window tells her Fenella's curtains remain closed. She wonders whether she ought to take her sister-in-law a cup of tea and check whether she is all right; but she shoves this thought to the back of her mind. 'My goodness,' she exclaims to Henry, 'just look at the poor scabious. Come on, more stakes needed. We're in for a busy morning.'

Fenella does not hear the bells, despite their proximity. After a tortured night, she fell blessedly asleep at dawn. And sleeps on soundly.

In her house next to the shop on The Green, Nan Hutton hears the bells and endorses their message. Her preparation for church is complete. How, she wonders, is Ted coming along? At the foot of the stairs she harkens for the correct signals – the wardrobe door squeaking (Good, he is fastening his tie in the long mirror), the sound of springs collapsing in the bedroom chair (That's right, he is sitting down to lace up his shoes). Evidently coming along nicely.

It is always rather a headache getting Ted ready for church – not that it occurs to Nan to think it should be otherwise, which would be about as much use as complaining of the weather or the post's late arrival. All men are troublesome. It is in the nature of the beast to prefer lying in bed, or reading the paper, or sitting in the pub, or messing about in the allotment, to sprucing up and attending church. Nevertheless, getting them there is one of life's duties. Success in this reveals a wife's true mettle. And oh, the glory of bringing them in, of having them sit there beside you sleek-haired, close-shaven. Nan pities those women, still in possession of husbands, who admit defeat and attend church unaccompanied. She can honestly say, and take pride in the fact, that it has never happened to her without a cast-iron excuse, such as Ted laid up with the flu or a really bad bout of kidney. Not that she and he bother with the eight o'clock Communion or the half-past three Evensong. This rota business, sharing the rector with four other parishes, results in services being held at nonsensical times; Nan and Ted attend when it is Aston Favell's turn for a nine o'clock or a half-past ten morning service or a six o'clock Evensong, but they draw the line at the other two. It is a pity, really, because letting them off (husbands that is) two weeks out of five can weaken the habit if you are not very careful.

She looks at the clock, which shows a quarter past ten. 'You ready?' she cries up the stairs.

'Aye,' says Ted, and comes thumping down in his least favourite footwear. For the inspection.

At a signal from John Ellwood, the ringing team holds still. Resonance flies out of the belfry, out of the village, over the hills and away; in its wake leaves a buzzing in scalps and eardrums, but this, too, soon dissipates. They hang up their ropes. 'Good work,' says John – to his daughter Trisha and her boyfriend Gary, to Arthur (a farmer like himself) and Arthur's son David. He is particularly proud of Trisha, and squeezes her shoulder as they run down the tower's steps. Arthur and David slip out of the church to return to their haymaking. John, Trisha and Gary join Marie, Gran and the youngsters in their pew; for the Ellwoods are a proper church family.

109

Across the aisle sit the James sisters, whose attendance can be relied upon without fail at every service whatever the hour (excepting, of course, those occurring during the fortnight of their fishing holiday in Scotland).

Arriving breathless and a little late are Zoë Hunter (the friend who will look after Sylvie when Kate cannot manage a particular Thursday) and her husband, Martin. These days, the Hunters come without their children: daughter Penny is away at university (where at this moment, if her religious leanings are unchanged, she is probably attending an earnest and joyless prayer meeting); son Thomas is seventeen and moody and therefore at home in bed. Zoë and Martin are regular but not fanatical church-goers, attending on average about twice a month. But they are staunch church supporters; Martin is treasurer of the church council, Zoë takes her turn on the altar-flowers rota. Now, on her knees, making a hurried and apologetic silent prayer, a vision of earlier Sundays dawns in Zoë's mind, when the children were young and the entire Hunter family charmingly occupied this very pew. She remembers looking down on Penny's and Tommo's glossy round heads. It seemed then that they were a permanently established unit – she and Martin and their two beautiful children. In retrospect, the unit thus arranged was of short duration, a mere few seasons, a brief gleam in God's eye.

The bells are now silent. In High House, Will, who was not roused by their ringing, continues to sleep; even a crash of china in the kitchen fails to penetrate his consciousness. It is the shrill of the doorbell which finally prompts him to sit upright, to stare pop-eyed at the alarm clock – which he forgot to set last night and is now trying to inform him that it is ten forty-five. It can't be, he thinks; then, Hell's teeth, the doorbell! He bounds out of bed, pulls on a towelling bathrobe, pelts downstairs.

Eilish is on the doorstep. She comes straight in. 'Sorry I'm so late, but one of the patients had a stroke in the night. Where is she?'

Will gapes. He hasn't a clue. But then a clatter sounds in the kitchen, and Eilish sets off towards it. 'Holy Mother . . .' she whispers, halting in the doorway.

Will, following, peers over her shoulder.

The fridge door is open, its contents spilled over the floor; there are shards of china everywhere, jam, puddles of milk, scattered rice crispies . . . Sylvie sits amongst this mess with her legs splayed and her face smeared; rank-smelling, Will detects even from the doorway; bloated, he thinks, a monster . . . What the hell is he doing devoting his life, *his precious life* . . .? With an effort he strangles the thought and wrestles to supplant it with an image of her gleaming hair on the pillow, the image which last night successfully stiffened his resolve.

Sylvie is looking up at them uncertainly. 'Hun-gwee,' she says.

'A lovely service,' murmurs Davinia to the rector, as she always does. Stepping from the porch, she blinks in the sunlight, and is betrayed by temporary blindness into turning upon Mrs Bullivant a too-encouraging smile.

Daphne Bullivant is on top form. Hearing Rector for the second Sunday in succession mention the forthcoming coffee morning at Sunny Bank was like hearing her banns read – a heady little triumph. She spots the Major making his escape (already he is passing under the lych gate) but considers this is all for the best. She must now remind her supporters of their blitz-on-litter campaign this afternoon. Penfold Close is top of the agenda. With certain words of the Major's still vivid in her memory ('coven' she considers particularly distasteful) she is glad not to have his critical eye upon her as she buttonholes her friends.

Edna Critch and Brenda Haycroft readily agree to this afternoon's project; Dorothy Potton pleads visitors.

Davinia, who would not dream of an excursion into Penfold Close for any purpose whatever, simply states that she and her sister are unavailable. Where *is* Esmé?

Esmé is unburdening herself to Mrs Cross, their cleaning woman. She feels guilty doing this, but after Davinia's cold obstinacy, found Mrs Cross's insightful and intriguing sympathy impossible to resist. ('You don't look at all yourself this morning, Miss Esmé. I hope you weren't disturbed last night like they were at The Willows. Seems they had a prowler . . .') Esmé led her a little way off and is now eagerly recounting what occurred at Rose Cottage.

'. . . Watching a television programme – well actually, Davinia had nodded off, but I was watching it; it was that nice gardening programme. Suddenly Sarah growled. I looked up. And there, at the window, was this head with a cap on it. I gave a little scream. It woke Davinia. But when I told her what the matter was, the blessed man had disappeared. We got the torches and went outside. Sarah scuttled to the bottom of the garden. Soon came back. Nothing, not a sign of him. Davinia swears I dreamt it, though I know I didn't. And I must say, I feel quite unsettled.'

'Oo, I bet it was that Peeping Tom . . .'

'Esmé,' calls Davinia sharply. 'Oh, good morning, Mrs Cross.'

'I'd better go,' says Esmé, and hurries to catch up with her sister further down the path.

Sylvie has had her evening meal and is now fast asleep in a chair with her head lolled to one side and her mouth open. Will observes her for a moment, then goes to the hall telephone, taps out a number. As he does so, blood mounts in his head, a sense of doom assails him; he abandons the call before it can ring and walks urgently to the front door where he leans on hands pressed against it, arms stiff, head bowed. It is not that he is regretting last night's decision; no, he is still resolved to remain at home for the foreseeable future, to cancel next Thursday's business meeting, to put off the Sylvie-sitters; his difficulty is, how to communicate this to Kate. If he sounds at all hesitant, she may try to dissuade him. If he sounds too warm, she may suggest coming round anyway; which would be disastrous if his surmise is correct – that catching them together precipitated Sylvie's worsened state. Therefore, speaking to Kate he must be decisive and non-inviting. But at the same time friendly, for, heaven knows, he has no wish to hurt her.

Since contact with the front door seems to be neither assisting the problem nor calming him physically, he jerks away and turns his gaze to a framed and glazed water colour – a still life – mauve and yellow flowers in a blue vase on a cream and grey chequered cloth – a pretty composition, competently executed. He frowns at the signature – *S. McLeod* – for several seconds. And abruptly decides to stop the heart-searching, the groping for suitable phrases. To just get it over.

That's it, then, thinks Kate as the line goes dead before she can even manage 'Goodbye.' So he doesn't require her to Sylvie-sit on Thursday; or any future Thursday come to that, not until or unless Sylvie calms down. Of course, what he really means is, he is terminally regretting their brief tendresse.

She is still holding the dead telephone line. 'Dead' is a pretty fair description of how she is feeling. She tosses down the receiver and walks through the kitchen to stare out at the garden. She cannot now be bothered to fork in fertilizer round the base of the rose bushes, but leans against the door frame, breathing in the soft sad evening. Then impatiently steps inside and nudges the back door shut, locks and bolts it.

Half an hour later, the phone rings a second time. Her joy as she bounds from her chair is like an infinitely buoyant ball on an upward bounce – it will be Will, of course, calling to relent. Stretching to answer, she is already framing her response – That's all right, Will; of course I'll be glad to . . .

'Hello, Kate. I hear we're going to see you this Tuesday coming? Is that right, now?'

'Dad – hello,' she says weakly, repressing a childish urge to return pain with pain. 'Tuesday, er, yes, that should be OK . . .'

'Oh, champion. Just checking. Your mam's here.' With countless precedents to recall, his daughter does not need to be told this, she knows he has been ordered to make the call and what to say and what to elucidate, knows he is now nervously complying in the presence of his instructress, who, having achieved the right result, without more ado takes over: 'Hello, love. You said you thought you'd manage to come this Tuesday, so we've been listening out for your call. We were anxious to know for certain. I said to Dad, she's bound to ring us on Sunday . . .'

'Sorry, Mum . . .'

'Well, we know you're busy, love. Never mind, Dad gave me the thumbs up, so I take it you're coming. That is good news. We'll expect you nice and early, mind.'

'Yes, all right.'

'Goodbye for now, then, dear,' says her mother, with satisfaction.

'Goodbye, Mum.'

CHAPTER EIGHT

Monday 22nd June

On Monday morning Bel Rochford is clearing up after breakfast, an overdue chore delayed first by an inclination to sit over her newspaper, then by Jamie's urgent demands. Now, bathed and sweet-smelling and chock full of baby cereal, Jamie is burbling in his pram and dealing mighty whacks to a row of rattly toys. Bel folds up the newspaper, stores away cereal packet and milk jug, stacks used china and cutlery on the draining board. An hour and a half ago, finishing her tea and reading the paper, the house very quiet after David's departure, she developed that Monday morning in reverse feeling — not oh-heavens-back-to-work, but a faintly depressed sensation of being left behind by all the energetic people (people with a stake in the world) rushing away to make things happen; even pictured with a jealous pang her replacement sitting at *her* desk in *her* office. Then Jamie began exercising his lungs and immediately the hub of the universe was established right here in 5 The Park.

Now, cheerful as the sun hitting the window pane, Bel pours hot water into a bowl and adds a squirt of washing-up liquid. Outside everything is gleaming after the weekend downpour; overhead, white puff balls are floating in blue. When the kitchen is tidy, she goes into the large open-plan area her mother warned her against ('No privacy, darling; nowhere you can keep nice for visitors; you'll regret that when Jamie's a bit older and when a little brother or sister arrives.') which contains sitting and dining areas and staircase, and begins setting it straight in time for Tina coming round for coffee.

The long-pile rug is looking flat and dishevelled, and no wonder after the things she and David got up to last evening. Amazing, she thinks, how finding the right place has made her keen and relaxed — a state she could not attain upstairs with Jamie in the next-door bedroom and the intercom switched on (which, superstitiously, she cannot bring herself to turn off in case an unconnected few minutes prove the fatal few minutes). She slides open the glazed patio door, gathers up the rug and drags it outside where, though it is heavy and unwieldy, her strong arms harry it until its pile stands on end (the shag pile, as David now rudely and gleefully refers to it). Then, affectionately, she relays it on the parquet floor, reflecting how a few decent sex-sessions have completely banished David's resentment; for since last Wednesday evening not a murmur of criticism has been directed at her for being over-anxious. Not that she *is* all that over-anxious any more, not like she was.

Tina arrives at five past eleven, harassed-looking. She's late, she's sorry, but the bloody cleaning woman let her down, rang to say she wouldn't be coming this morning because her kid's sick or something. To make matters worse, Les is still at home cluttering the place up. At least she won't have to bother about dinner tonight; Les often has to keep club hours in his line of business . . .

Bel is glad Tina did not arrive earlier. Her house is tidy, the washing machine is doing its stuff in the utility room, the coffee things are laid out, Jamie is taking a nap, and she herself is showered and changed into brand new shorts and T shirt (clothes which do not reek of baby despite thorough washing) — all this has been achieved, but only just.

Tina looks perfectly fine but somehow amounts to less than her norm. After a few moments' observation,

Bel registers that her face is bare. (So is Bel's, more or less, but this is as usual.) Tina's naked face conveys an impression of saving the full works for something better later on. (In fact, a weekend without sun has alarmed Tina for her tan. She and Melanie have a booking at the health club this afternoon; the visit hangs in Tina's mind like a saving goal; she is pinning her hopes on it; rang Shapers just before she came out to make quite sure they will have a sun bed available for her.)

They sip their coffee. Tina refuses to be tempted by a plate of shortbread fingers, so Bel munches her way steadily through to the last piece which she leaves lying on the plate for the look of the thing, in case Tina's unexpectedly busy morning catches up with her and makes her hungry after all. The conversation turns naturally to the Peeping Tom. They recall last Wednesday evening and derive further amusement from the episode. Bel wonders whether chasing after him has frightened him off; there have been no further incidents as far as she knows. But Tina, during a visit to the village shop this morning on her way back from taking the children to school, heard one of the customers report a sighting on Saturday night – in all that rain, marvels Tina; he must've been desperate: two old biddies on Vicarage Hill were watching the telly when one of them raised her head and saw a head at the window. By the time they had gathered their wits and run to investigate, there was not a hair of him to be seen. In any case, it was only a blur, so the other old lady, her sister, told her she must have dreamt it. But the first one stuck to her guns and insisted she'd seen a man's cap. So there you are, declares Tina. Proves it. Must have been the Peeping Tom.

Bel feels a little dismayed. 'I hope it hasn't upset the poor old things,' she says, identifying strongly.

'No-oo,' scoffs Tina. 'Probably brightened their little lives. Bound to be more exciting than the telly – all these flipping repeats . . .'

117

'Wonder who they are?'

'Jones? James? Something like that.'

Both women shrug. (Residents of The Park are notorious for not knowing much about anyone or anything in Aston Favell. 'Might as well not live in a village,' is often said of them. 'They never join in. You never see 'em at village do's. Keep themselves to themselves.')

Bel refills their coffee cups and nudges the lone shortbread finger in Tina's direction. 'Go on.' But Tina remains firm. And so, thinking what a nuisance it would be getting out the tin to put this one piece away, Bel saves herself the trouble, eats it.

Overhead, there is a cry — not of discomfort, more of an announcement: Jamie has woken up. Bel promptly loses the thread of the conversation. (Which has moved on to old houses: Tina is saying she is going off modern ones and Bel ought to come with her one day to visit her friend Melanie's fantastic old place in Carlton — 'Honestly, it'd be an eye opener.') When she can break into Tina's flow without seeming rude, Bel says she will just pop upstairs and take a peep.

'Bring him down, the little pet,' Tina says generously, and while Bel bounds upstairs, rouses herself to cross the room and inspect the curiously large number of books in the Rochfords' possession. On a table by the nearest bookcase, evidently recently consulted, is a volume entitled *Aroma Relaxation Technique*. Inside are many photographic illustrations which cause some surprise to Tina. She carries the book back to her chair. 'Hello, cherub, isn't oo a sweetie pie?' — all the right expressions are murmured when Bel returns with Jamie (who sits on his mother's knee and stares at the visitor in rapt fascination), but what Tina is dying to discover is, how come the Rochfords have a book like this? Is the sort of caper illustrated in here what *they* get up to?

'A bit saucy, this,' she says at last, indicating the book.

Bel blushes. 'Not really.'

'I always thought aromatherapy was something you could have in a health club – you know, like mud baths or massage, with someone in a white overall, and towels covering your bits and bobs.'

'It's a nice way for couples to relax, too.'

'Oh yeah? I wouldn't want Les parking himself on me, thanks very much. Specially with no clothes on.' She taps a photograph with a long red fingernail. 'You wouldn't catch me sitting astride old Les, neither, not for any money. Imagine – oiling all that blubber . . .' (But here, Jamie flinging up his arms and knocking her in the mouth, saves Bel from commenting.) 'Mm, well,' continues Tina, looking arch, 'I always say you never know what goes on behind people's front doors. Mind you, I had a bit of a surprise about goings on behind me own front door last Wednesday evening. I'd just left you after class, right? and I thought, wonder what he gets out of it, this Peeping Tom – well, it makes you think . . . So guess what I did? Went round all the windows, looking in. And you know what? There he was (me lump of a husband) slumped in his chair, eyes glued to the telly, watching one of those, you know, *blue movies* – two women writhing about on a bed, a man doing God knows what to 'em; the women showing everything, and I mean *everything* . . .'

Bel's blush deepens to flame. She is as amazed by this revelation as Tina by her glimpse into Rochford activities. But Bel is more than amazed; she is disgusted, somehow affronted. It would be better to keep her views to herself, she knows, but they still come spilling out – 'God, whatever did you do? Chuck him out? I would have. It's so sick, so *insulting.*' Her voice is rising dangerously. *Threatening,* she nearly shrieks in addition, but manages in time to close her mouth.

'Oh, I *know,*' coos Tina, 'it's blummin' pathetic. I don't mind admitting it, Bel, I'm getting really fed up with Les these days. Do you know, he won't even consider an older property? Wouldn't so much as glance at the brochure I got from the estate agent. Talk about a closed mind – though,' she adds quickly, in case Bel is condemning her judgement, 'he had more about him when I married him, you know. Between you and me – and Melanie (well you have to confide in someone don't you? – I mean, it's not healthy bottling things up): I can't honestly swear to me and Les having a future together. Well, I said to Melanie, I said: it'd only cost him a measly twenty-odd grand on top of what we'd get for number seven . . .'

Bel interrupts. *Where* you live, she feels very urgently, is beside the point. 'Personally, I couldn't live anywhere with a man who, who . . .' her voice trails away; she fears she has gone too far (Tina, after all, is a guest). She squeezes Jamie and buries her undisciplined mouth in his fat little shoulder.

'Don't get me wrong, I've always detested anything near the knuckle – you know, *coarse*,' Tina asserts over a struggling Jamie's squawk of protest. 'Ah, bless him, he wants his din-dins. And I'd better fly. I'm due at Shapers at two o'clock. You should give it a try, Bel. Me and Melanie go twice a week. Keeps you trim. Makes you feel fabulous. Though maybe,' – a coy nod to the aromatherapy book – 'you prefer your own methods. See you Wednesday? Fiona's good, isn't she? My turn to drive . . .'

Bel, showing Tina over the threshold, can scarcely see her. Filling her vision is gross Les Fairbrother drooling over naked women on a TV screen, women exhibiting every bit of themselves, casually, totally available, like things to be used up and thrown away. She closes the front door, then goes to the window overlooking The Park, her lips resting gently on Jamie's fragrant scalp.

Les Fairbrother's Jag is squatting in next-door's driveway like a shiny red toad.

I've had enough of this place, she thinks. I'll tell David tonight. I want us to move. Back to town. Back to civilization.

*   *   *

Kate goes into the staff room, picks up and shakes the kettle. Empty. She fills it under the tap, plugs it in, hunts for a clean mug among twenty or so dirty ones. Sighs, and begins to wash up. 'Want a coffee, anyone?' she calls. Suddenly, with clean mugs coming up and freshly boiled water, most people do.

Gareth Dicey comes in, sees Kate at the sink, saunters over. 'Oh good – coffee.' He dries as she washes, at the same time conducts a conversation with one of his seated colleagues, then falls silent, watching as she spoons out coffee powder. 'I, er, was thinking, Kate: I might get tickets for the Royal Phil on Friday. Do you fancy coming?'

'Sorry, Gareth. I'm, er, sort of otherwise engaged at the moment.' She says this rapidly, and she fears archly, and carries four brimming mugs to the table closest to where most people are sitting.

'Ah,' says Gareth, picking up a couple of mugs. 'Right.'

They are all looking at her, she senses, as she takes her own drink to a chair. 'Anyone we know?' calls Mike Davis; and Fiona's face sends a reproachful message: *You never breathed a word about this on Saturday: I thought we were mates.*

Kate turns to stare out of the window and hears again the expression in her voice when she turned Gareth down. What on earth came over her? And if only what it implied were true. Fat chance after Will's phone call last night. Perhaps anguish over this has sent her slightly batty. '*I'm sort of otherwise engaged at the moment,*' she silently, roughly, mimics herself.

When she has finished drinking the coffee, she turns and smiles across at Gareth, hoping to take the sting out of the rebuff. Of course, another thing which may have led to her blurting out an excuse on a false note, is her decision taken a couple of weeks ago to swiftly and firmly decline should he again ask her out. They have had several dates already on a friendly basis. The last two times Gareth brought his daughters along, and has since dropped heavy hints about how they would adore to visit Wayside Cottage. She feels sorry for him – deserted by his wife for another man, his daughters living with their mother in the new ménage, Gareth missing the girls dreadfully and seeing them when he can. But Kate senses he has a use for her: to create for his daughters an illusion of relaxed family comfort which is no doubt hard to achieve in his one-room flat or sitting in a cinema or eating Sunday lunch in the Pizza Parlour. Though sympathetic, she has no wish to become involved in his family problems, and has decided it would be unfair, therefore, to waste his time. 'How's Caroline's arm – any better?' she asks kindly of his elder daughter who is recovering from a riding accident.

'Much, thanks.'

'Good,' she smiles, and turns purposely to Fiona.

A blast of invigorating air whistles through 5 The Park during mid afternoon.

The phone rings. Bel sets down the iron, bends to unplug it, goes to answer. An ex-colleague is on the line – a woman who was once her junior, phoning from regional head office. There has been an accident in one of the stores; a sales assistant fell down the stairs leading from the rest room. She seems to recall Bel having to deal with a similar incident, and that the shoes the woman was wearing at the time were somehow relevant.

Yes indeed. Memories come flooding in clear-cut detail. Bel can recall the stairs, the shoes, the exact location of certain useful documents it might be wise to consult, which paragraph on which form to pay close attention to, the name of a company solicitor who is a bit of nit-picker, the name of another who is an absolute angel . . . Bel holds forth; her colleague gratefully scribbles. 'Oh thanks, Bel,' she says at last. 'You know how it is. This is my first AAW (Accident At Work). Got to get it right.'

'Phone any time,' Bel says emphatically. Putting the phone down, turning to face the room, she is a new person: resourceful, in command. Jamie is lying on a sheet on the rug, kicking his feet in the air, grappling with a toy which he chunters at sternly – a robust little world-taker-on in the making; the last thing he needs is an over-protective and fearful mum. She returns to the ironing board, takes up the iron, steers its nose with smooth precision round the shoulder seam of David's shirt. (This is a concession – while she is stuck at home she will iron his shirts; when she resumes work they will return to their former practice of doing their own laundry. She reminds him of this quite often. 'I hope this isn't a slippery slope,' she will say, handing him a pile of neatly pressed shirts; 'please don't take it for granted.' 'As if!' he protests, wide-eyed. Bel feels, with men you have to watch out.)

She decides not to mention what she learned this morning. It is nothing to do with David; banging on about it, whining that she has to get away, as if the mere presence of a sleazy neighbour is some-how contaminating, will only make him defensive. She knows too well where an occasional outburst over a case in the news involving some rotter of a man can lead: to a row, to David assuming she is somehow getting at him; implying that because he, David, is male, to an extent he is tarred with the same brush.

She certainly does not want a row over Les Fair-brother. Everything is now fine between her and David; why let a creep spoil it? In fact, why waste another moment's thought on the subject? Aston Favell is a perfectly nice village, no better, no worse than any other in England. What she *will* do, however, is raise her sights beyond The Park.

'Esmé,' says Davinia, coming into the room with a pile of library books and looking (Esmé can tell at a glance) most displeased, 'I am *most displeased*.'

123

There – what did I tell you? Esmé silently enquires of her needlework. 'What is exercising you now, Davinia?'

'You have been talking to Mrs Cross. You spoke to her after church on Sunday. I know you did because she broached the subject as soon as she arrived for work this morning, I wouldn't mention it to you while she was here, but now we are alone . . .'

'What subject is this?' Esmé asks innocently, and Davinia flounders, reluctant to name and thereby give credence to an event which, in her opinion, occurred only in her sister's imagination.

Esmé comes to her rescue. 'I presume you refer to the incident on Saturday night. Our prowler. Yes, Davinia, I did mention the subject to Mrs Cross on Sunday; it was a perfectly natural consequence of her telling me about a similar disturbance at The Willows. Which I rather think proves my case. It is unlikely that both I and Mrs Davis were mistaken.'

'Mrs Davis? You mean that vulgar-looking woman with the henna'd hair and the scarlet fingernails? Then I can't say I'm surprised. However, we had no disturbance *here*,' asserts Davinia, coming out in red blotches.

And Esmé grasps what is troubling her sister. Nasty men in flat caps and dirty raincoats (though Esmé cannot swear to the raincoat) are drawn, one assumes, like moths to a flame, to illuminated windows revealing the likes of garish Mrs Davis. Also, she now recalls, Mrs Haycroft regaled their little tea party the other afternoon with a tale about a Peeping Tom at Ellwood's farm – drawn by the sight of young Trisha Ellwood misbehaving with her boyfriend. Yes, Esmé understands perfectly what is upsetting Davinia; even so, she refuses to be bullied. 'I know what I saw,' she says quietly. 'The fact that you did not is neither here nor there. I am not given to wild fancies.'

'But Mrs Cross will tell Mrs Prior – those two are thick as thieves – in which case one might as well put an announcement in the shop window. Rose Cottage will be the subject of speculation, mentioned in the same breath as The Willows – and half the homes in Penfold Close, I shouldn't wonder.'

Esmé sighs. 'If you keep on at me like this, Davinia, I shall be too agitated to finish these pillowslips in time for Thursday's coffee morning.'

This gives Davinia pause. Not out of concern for Mrs Bullivant, at whose coffee morning Esmé's embroidered pillowslips will star as the prize in the raffle, but for the village church which stands to benefit from the occasion. St Peter's is very dear to the hearts of both sisters. They devote much of their time to caring for its fabric, personally launder the altar linen, and when – about every six weeks – their turn arrives on the cleaning rota, polish the pews, burnish the brasses, remove every speck of dust from stone floor and carpet runners. Mrs Cross's elbow grease may suffice for Rose Cottage, but God's house deserves superior attention. One of their favourite pastimes is to debate the nature of their *in memoriam* gift to St Peter's; whether it shall be an altar frontal or carpet for the chancel, vestments or new hymn books, delightfully passes many a cosy evening by the fireside. Each knows the other has remembered the church in her will, but they seek some extra, tangible, useful gift they have chosen together and paid for in advance, to be catalogued in the Fabric Book as *gift of Miss Davinia James and Miss Esmé James: in memoriam*; bearing witness not only to their devotion to St Peter's but to each other, to their long and loyal companionship. Quarrels they have aplenty, but always adhere to their golden rule: never retire to bed, never leave the house without first making up. This rule is what prompted an unbelieving Davinia to fetch her sister a glass of whisky on Saturday night. It is what now gives Esmé confidence in Davinia speaking nicely to her in a very few minutes (for the clock reveals that it is high time Davinia departed to call on bedridden Mrs Thomas, as promised, with those library books).

125

'Good lord,' says Davinia, 'is that the time? I must fly. Do you know, Esmé, I think the work you are doing on those pillowslips must be some of your finest? Whoever wins them will be lucky indeed.'

'Thank you, dear,' says Esmé.

Kate's irritation with herself continues through the afternoon. During an almost animated session (4C – animated!) – supposedly *au supermarché* complete with shoplifter and a row over change at the till – it nags away at the back of her mind. At the close of lessons she lingers in a deserted classroom, which still faintly whiffs of teenagers who never roll out of bed early enough to shower before school, smiling vaguely at cleaners passing through with mops and buckets, thinking: Right, get to it. Obviously, the nub of what bothers her is Will cancelling the Thursday arrangement. And not just because she suspects he is giving her the brush-off (though the very idea is like a punch in the stomach). No, she is hurt, perhaps even offended, at having been summarily dismissed from taking charge of Sylvie. Hang it all, she has been performing this task for months, from very soon after Chris died. And though her motive in the beginning was simple gratitude to Will for all the time and emotion he expended supporting Chris, since then she has developed, if not rapport (which is probably impossible to acquire with someone plunging through rapid change), certainly sympathy with Sylvie. And a degree of skill. Take last Thursday, a particularly testing day: Kate knows she did a good job.

However, it is up to Will; she cannot insist on continuing to see Sylvie. She must stop brooding and think positively. For instance, now her Thursdays have been returned to her, maybe she needs to fill more of her time. Suddenly restless, she gets up from the desk, gathers her belongings, and goes through the corridors towards the Head's office. She will discuss the matter with Irene, who, as well as being her boss, is a wise and trusted friend of several years standing.

But Irene is busy. A quick word around five-thirty might be possible, if Kate wants to chance it and wait. 'Right, I'll come back later,' she tells the secretary. After all, she has nothing to hurry home for.

At five forty-five, when Kate is at last invited to enter her room, Irene Cobb appears strained and jaded. Kate is shocked: Irene is five years her senior; this afternoon the difference seems more like ten. She feels too solicitous almost to launch into her own affairs, but Irene brushes away enquiries as to her welfare and indicates a wish for Kate to get on with it.

'Well, Irene, I've been teaching part time now for nearly three years. It's nearly two years since Chris died . . .' She gets no further. 'Don't ask me, Kate,' Irene cuts in; then flushes, looks down at her desk, pushes some pens around. And Kate's hearing becomes suddenly acute, she picks up not only the pens rattling, but her own blood coursing.

'I know what you're going say – you'd like to start back full time? I'm sorry, believe me, but it's out of the question – at least, as far as Lavenbrook Comp is concerned in the foreseeable future. Frankly, it's more a case of, Who can I lose? And, no, Kate, I *don't* mean *you*. However, if we go self-governing next year . . .'

'Oh, I do hope we don't,' blurts Kate, and a curtain drops over Irene's face; she continues as though Kate hasn't interrupted.

'. . . we'll need to do some hard thinking. Make some adjustments. Certainly, we can't *expand* the pay-roll.'

Kate is doubly uncomfortable. She should not have blurted her own views. She knows perfectly well the staff room is divided, that certain school governors are pushing hard on opposing sides, that Irene is caught in the cross-fire and is probably subject to God knows what sort of pressure from outside school. 'I, er, understand. Look, forget it. I may find something else . . .'

'Oh, well, you know I don't want to lose you – in the normal way of things I'd jump at the chance . . . But of course, if a full-time post crops up elsewhere, I can see you'll have to go for it – and I'll support you, no question.'

Now it is Kate who goes red. 'I didn't mean . . . No, no, I was thinking of teaching night school, or maybe doing a couple of days at a language school. Though it's not the money, it's more, you know, trying to get back to normal. I might even do voluntary work. As a matter of fact, I've been looking after someone with Alzheimer's one day a week for the past eighteen months. I've become quite interested.'

Irene's face clears. She sits back in her chair, appears more relaxed, more like the friend Kate had expected to consult. 'Mm, yes, I should think taking on something like that could be quite . . . refreshing,' she speculates. 'At the very least it would focus your mind on something other than this hothouse.'

Kate nods, suddenly very glad not to be in Irene's shoes. She gets up. 'I won't keep you.'

'Term's nearly over, the kids'll be back from college soon,' observes Irene. 'You and I must have lunch during the hols.'

'Come out to Aston Favell. You look as if you could do with a day being waited on. Give me a ring when you're free.'

'Thanks, Kate. I will.'

In the outer office, Kate sees, but does not acknowledge, Gareth Dicey who is fingering through a filing cabinet. He waits until she has gone into the corridor, then calls her name. As she turns, he comes out quickly closing the door behind him, and steps ahead of her, leans against the wall on an outstretched arm.

She frowns; his arm is barring her way. 'Yes?'

'Um, I, er, understand what you were saying earlier on; it's early days for you, Kate. But I'd like you to know how much I value your friendship. What I feel is, you and I, we've a lot in common, we can help each other, *communicate* . . .'

'Right, thanks,' she says with stiff finality, and steps purposely forward. To her relief he drops his arm. Passing him quickly, she goes to the door and thence to the car park.

What the hell was that about? she wonders, sitting in her car, not going anywhere. Don't say he fancies her! This is an upsetting thought; it surprises her how upsetting. It would be dreadful, she suddenly thinks, if Will, sensing her feelings for *him*, were similarly repelled.

Now Gareth is coming out to his car. He may think she is waiting for him. Hastily, she turns on the engine, lets off the brake and accelerates past; turns out into the road where, a few yards further on, the traffic lights turn red. She manages in time to halt on the line, then watches in the driving mirror as cars draw up behind, shielding her, thank goodness, from Gareth's arrival. Relaxing, she reassures herself that of course Will would not recoil from the idea of her being attracted to him; for last Thursday he was equally keen, no question; in fact, *he* touched *her* first, when he brushed his fingers over her bruised cheek. Whereupon there was a spontaneous coming together. Oh yes – she remembers the sound of his heart thumping, the feel of it knocking against hers. 'Kate,' he kept breathing into her hair, his arms pulling her closer; 'Kate, Kate . . .'

Wuuur, honks the car behind, and the car behind that and a blaring chorus down the line. She jumps, sees the lights are green, lets out the clutch too fast. *Wuur, wuur.* Sorry, sorry, she moans, twisting the ignition, jabbing the accelerator, jerking across the intersection. Several cars from behind overtake, their drivers (male) sending her outraged glares. Oh me, crime of the century! she mocks through her side screen as they screech past. Then turns on the car radio and applies her burning ears to the evening news.

*   *   *

129

Monday evening at six o'clock finds Fenella, Lady Cunningham in her bedroom anticipating the long-awaited moment. (Which has not been defined with any precision. The man who is to collect the precious boxes could promise no more than 'sometime after seven'.) But Fenella is easy. She has no pressing plans. She is completely at his disposal. She stands on the carpet in her satin wrap, concentrating on a very important matter – how to present herself.

Her preparation routine is second nature, she would not dream of embarking on any kind of scene without first employing it – feet a little apart, hands at her side with fingertips lightly touching, eyes closed. Soon, hazy images float in her inner eye; an atmosphere builds; she strains to grasp what the artist in her is indicating . . . At last she has it – the theme, the key: *wartime; a spacious house commandeered; wounded soldiers arriving (or perhaps they are refugees); the chatelaine, dowdily dressed but abidingly gracious, welcoming the weary wretches into her elegant home* . . . It is enough: she moves briskly to her dressing table with a vision of the effect she must create: with deft strokes draws high surprised forties eyebrows; with combs rummaged from the back of a drawer secures her hair in swept-back wings. These hints are sufficient. The artist in her shuns overstatement.

Now to lay hands on the perfect garment. Ignoring her three wardrobes, she goes purposefully to a shallow built-in cupboard. (Not for one second last Friday did she consider donating its contents to the refugees. The clothes in here are worn and frail; dear shabby mementoes – even, there are a few of Jock's old things. Soon after his funeral, agitated by grief, she telephoned the Distressed Gentlefolk's Association and bade them come as soon as possible and remove his entire wardrobe. 'Take everything – all, all . . .' she urged, adding that though she feared she must spare herself the pain of witnessing the proceedings, her sister-in-law would escort them to Sir Jock's dressing room. Then, the

130

night before the scheduled collection, awoken by a distressing dream, she felt impelled to save just one or two of the beloved effects. Impossible to water down the magnanimity of her 'Take everything – all, all . . .', so she rose from her bed that very instant and removed half a dozen evocative items into her secret keeping. For instance, this tweed jacket: briefly, she takes its left sleeve into her two hands, lifts it to her face and deeply inhales – though expressed in beautiful and studied gesture, her emotion is real; simply, she is a professional; it is beyond her to squander feeling inarticulately.) She removes the garment she proposes to wear this evening and carries it to the bed. Drops her wrap; steps into and buttons the frock.

At five minutes to seven when Fenella goes downstairs, she and Molly pass in the hall. They speak simultaneously, neither attending to the other.

Fenella: 'Simply *dretful* pong; the whole house reeks. Why you must boil cabbage to extinction beats me. And it is particularly annoying when I am expecting a visitor.'

Molly: 'Can't stop, it's my hospital programme. Yours is in the oven. It's that poor little boy's leg operation tonight. All right, Henry, Mummy's coming.'

Only Henry takes full cognizance. Seeing Fenella, he nips to the far side of his mistress; once past her, shoots upstairs.

In the kitchen, Fenella props open the back door, removes a covered plate from the oven and marches with it outside to the dustbin. She had an ample lunch, an elegant tea; will require nothing further this day beyond a digestive biscuit with her bedtime cocoa. To dispel any lingering odour, she goes to the front door and pulls it wide; then stands under the portico sniffing appreciatively at the scented evening.

She is still lingering on the steps when a van swoops up the drive. Its arrival on cue as it were, seems to Fenella an auspicious omen. Gladly, she runs down to greet its occupants.

The driver gets out. He is young, good-looking, and informally dressed – with a dog-collar.

A minister of religion! For a few seconds Fenella is completely thrown. Her mind blanks; then braces. 'Bob Hitchins,' he enthuses, extending a hand. She grasps it, and counters democratically, 'Fenella Cunningham.'

'Good to meet you, Fenella. This is Justin.'

Congratulating herself on not batting an eyelid at his immediate use of her Christian name (she did state her title the other evening on the telephone, but perhaps he has forgotten), Fenella turns with perfect aplomb to the bespectacled youth climbing out on the passenger side. 'How do you do, Justin?'

'Oh, fine, thanks,' huffs Justin.

Walking through the hall, Fenella is fine-tuning her persona – less worldly, she decides, more spiritual; too late now to regret the eyebrows, but thankfully she can rely on robust facial muscles to neutralize the effect as far as possible; in fact, by weighing down her brows and parting her lips she senses a look of concerned sincerity upon her features that is quite perfect for the occasion. She indicates the boxes and throatily begs for details of the refugees.

There are four families, thirteen souls in total, and for the moment they are housed in ones and twos by members of St Augustine's congregation. Fenella thinks it must be rather awful for them, visitors in a strange land, split up in this way. But Bob points out that St Augustine's parish is situated in the more modest part of Lavenbrook, where the houses are small and already adequately filled. Bob and Fenella converse while Justin conveys the boxes to the van. As the last one is removed, Fenella beseeches them to take some refreshment. A cup of tea would be welcome, says the Reverend Bob, so Fenella goes into the kitchen to put the kettle on. 'Do sit down,' she cries, indicating the enormous farmhouse table on which Molly has left unclean cooking utensils, a soil-encrusted *Daily Telegraph*, a trug, secateurs and

Gardeners' Monthly. For once Fenella feels grateful to Molly; the props tonight are rather inspired.

She brings three mugs (not cups) to the table and sets them down. As she does so, is struck by a brainwave: clutching her throat, she offers The Old Vicarage for any new refugees; its numerous rooms would prevent the need to split up families, its extensive grounds and clean Aston Favell air would be restorative. How she yearns to be of *use,* she exclaims, and by way of illustrating her longing, briefly and modestly describes her life of service thus far to the Arts and to Politics.

Bob nods sympathetically. Justin gapes earnestly through his horn-rimmed spectacles. Bob promises to convey her generous offer to the Church Council. Meanwhile, he recommends that Fenella pay a visit to St Augustine's Church, where she will receive a hearty welcome and derive spiritual uplift – singing, clapping, praising the Lord. 'Alleluia,' concurs Justin. And Fenella says that though she doesn't drive, she will do her best to arrange something with her chauffeur.

'Wonderful. Bring him along too. He'll be more than welcome,' beams Bob, and continues in the same breath and tone, 'Let us pray.'

So conversationally does he address The Almighty, and so riveting is her picture of Prior prevailed upon to praise the Lord, that were it not for Justin suddenly dipping his head and clasping his hands, she might have completely missed God's entry into the proceedings. At first she is a little embarrassed. Is it possible, she worries, that failure of perception on her part has landed her in a distasteful backwater? God is told a great deal about her, things which God, one might have supposed, was in a position to be better acquainted with than the intercessor. But as Bob persists on her behalf, she becomes intensely moved; it seems incredibly generous of him to take the trouble. A direct and honest soul, she decides, unable to remove her gaze from his tightly screwed eyes blotting out the world in order to concentrate solely on Fenella Cunningham. 'Thy servant, Fenella,' intones Bob, 'our sister, Fenella . . . , may Fenella find grace . . . , look down upon Fenella . . . with thine eternal love support Fenella all the days of her life, and bring her peace.' This repeated utterance of her name is almost unbearably sweet; tears well in her eyes, gratitude charges her veins. At the prayer's close, she cannot speak. It is left to Justin to make the conventional acknowledgement – 'Amen', while Fenella atones for the omission by extending a trembling hand. Which Bob seizes.

Thus they sit, hand in hand, cast in a dream state; at last slowly rise, and seem to float through the hall, down the steps, over the gravel. And then she is watching them leave, waving, waving. Goodbye, dear friends. Dear, dear friends.

For once there is no let down – perhaps because she is buoyed by the novelty of having received more than she has given. Received in abundance! As she prowls about the garden in the soft evening, the Reverend Bob's face, creased with the intensity of prayer, is more vivid to her than the white Philadelphus stars whose scent she is sniffing. She is conscious, too, of blessings to come. Soon her refugee families may be similarly engaged, strolling along the flower-bordered paths, their children enjoying one last scamper before bath and bedtime. She looks back at the house, where the windows are blank dead veils covering emptiness, and imagines it teeming with life: oh, the cooking (exotic smells of peppery stew), the sewing, ironing, chattering . . . The Priors will be needed here full time again, and another man to renovate the kitchen garden. Molly can restock her hen coop (which will please her). She herself will give English lessons (Shakespeare's English – no gift more precious). Perhaps some alterations to the house will be necessary: for instance, Jock's dressing room might be turned into her private bathroom leaving two large bathrooms for the sole use of the refugees; and a door can be added to close off Molly's quarters. She will consult an architect on these points. Meanwhile, there is no time like the present to hunt for ideas.

She bounds across the gravel and up the portico steps, propelled by the teeming energy which often besets her late in the day and has been known to provoke despair and aimless restlessness. Now she welcomes it. She has a purpose.

Many upstairs rooms are shrouded in dust sheets. (As Mrs Prior said, no point in doing them out every week when nobody uses them.) Curtains and rugs in these rooms are crusty to the touch; sheets covering the furniture have turned grey and fly-speckled; lamp bowls have become urns for the bodies of moths. In one of the larger bedrooms (with potential as a refugee family living room) Fenella sets to: unhooks the curtains, rolls them into bundles, makes off with them to the secluded piece of ground where there are washing lines; flings curtains over the lines, fetches a broom – over the head of which she ties a clean cloth – and proceeds to administer a thorough beating. When the dust clears, she returns indoors to re-drape the windows; then turns her attention to the rugs.

By ten o'clock she is pleasantly exhausted and more than ready for refreshment. How mellow she feels, how well used. And how eager to continue with this vigorous work tomorrow. A desire creeps on her to boast a little of her evening's achievement. Perhaps Molly would enjoy a mug of cocoa.

Most evenings, Molly and Fenella do not set eyes on one another after the evening meal. Most evenings, both women endeavour to ensure this is so: Molly thankfully retires with Henry for an evening's solid viewing; Fenella, who these days despises television (despises, in fact, all the toys of the modern world which, in a telling example of its vapidity, has turned its back on her) prowls about in search of occupation. Tonight, Fenella has an urge to be generous. Poor

135

old Molly's joints get stiffer as the day wears on; she can seldom be bothered to come down to make cocoa, relies instead on an electric kettle and a jar of powdered coffee in her room. Fenella makes two fragrant mugfuls and carries them on a tray with a biscuit barrel up to the landing and then up a further flight to Molly's room.

No response to her knock, of course, the poor deaf creature. Balancing the tray on a knee, she pushes the door open. There is a terrible blare – some man on the television screen shouting into a microphone while behind him people dart for cover; and worse than the noise, a stench. 'Paugh!' she says, turning her head. 'I've brought you some cocoa, Molly . . .'

But her sister-in-law is fast asleep with her mouth open. The stink, of course, is of Henry; the very air shrieks *dog* – old, unwashed, brown-toothed terrier. From a dingy heap curled in a mound of crocheted rugs, ears are aprick, eyes alight, a growl rumbles.

Fenella's throat is full of fur. Rapidly deciding not to bother, she backs out with the tray.

CHAPTER NINE

Tuesday 23rd June

In the morning post, Fenella receives a letter from Mrs Reginald Plum of The Manor, Carlton (a prominent local Conservative and Secretary of the Constituency Association).

> Dear Fenella,
> Just a reminder about the Bring and Buy on Saturday. One of us will pick you up soon after ten. Will Molly be coming? Tell her, the more the merrier! Can't do without you, of course. (Ladies of a certain type simply flock when there's a title doing the opening.)
> Looking forward *so* much to seeing you. (As is Reggie!!)
> Yours,
> Cynthia.

Frightful gusher, thinks Fenella, shoving it away. That horrible barking husband of hers — the cheek of it, presuming to flatter her with the reference. Jock would soon put them straight . . . Ah, but there lies the rub: Jock is no longer here. If he were, she would not be offered these insults in the first place.

Come to think of it, the invitation itself is a kind of insult, for it describes the limit of her usefulness: Lady Cunningham is just the person to send the silly hens into a flutter and bring in the shekels for the Party at a Saturday morning bun fight, but dinner with the MP, or gracing the Association Ball? Oh dear me, no; she can forget about those – never mind that when her husband was alive and memories still bright of her glamorous career, they were simply avid for her. Hypocrites. When she thinks, when she just *thinks* of the kindness of those unpretentious sincere people last evening . . . Well, it's a lesson to her.

Fairly bubbling to the boil, Fenella marches to the telephone. Seizes her personal directory. Looks up 'Plum'.

'Good morning, Cynthia. Fenella Cunningham here. I'm sorry to disturb you so early in the morning, but I thought it better to warn you at once. I shan't be available on Saturday morning.'

'But Fenella, my dear, we are absolutely depending . . .'

'I may as well be perfectly frank: in future you may *not* depend on me. I've finished with the Conservatives. I wash my hands of them. I intend to devote my time to the refugees.'

'The, er . . . Come again?'

'I've put The Old Vicarage entirely at their disposal. I hope to house as many as possible. So you see, I shall be very tied up.'

'Fenella, has someone peculiar been getting at you?'

'No-one "peculiar", Cynthia. A very simple sincere gentleman. It was the most inspiring encounter – I would go so far as to say "spiritual". Do you know, we were sitting talking in the kitchen and suddenly it was the most natural thing in the world to pray together? I suppose one would say The Spirit moved me. At any rate, I was moved to offer my home as a refuge . . .'

'For heaven's sake, you didn't sign anything? Who is this man?'

'The Reverend Bob . . .' – but the surname escapes her.

'The Reverend *Bob*? Sounds very dodgy to me,

Fenella. I think you should talk to the Rector about it, or Reggie, or . . .'

'It may surprise you to learn, Cynthia, how little I care for your opinion. Or the Rector's, or your husband's. Just be advised that from now on the Conservative Party must manage without me. Good morning.'

A minute and a half later the phone rings in Rose Cottage. Miss James, who is a poor sleeper and has been up for hours, answers immediately. 'Davinia James,' is her brusque growl of a reply.

'Oh, Davinia, thank the Lord. Cynthia here. Tell me, have you seen Fenella lately? Davinia, have you *seen* Fenella?'

A pause. Then, 'Cynthia Who?'

'Plum,' shrieks Cynthia. 'Dear-oh-me, have you all gone potty in Aston Favell?'

'You sound hysterical, Cynthia.'

'With *reason*, Davinia. I've just had Fenella on the phone. Said she won't after all open the Bring and Buy on Saturday — as she faithfully promised ages ago. In fact, said she won't do another jolly thing for us. And do you know why?'

'How can I if you don't say?'

'Because she plans to turn The Old Vicarage into some sort of refuge.'

'Refuge?'

'You know — house crammed to the rafters with drop-outs and dossers, battered wives, drug addicts, that sort of thing.'

'Good Lord!'

'She's been talked into it, apparently, by some-one calling himself the *Reverend Bob.* He turned up at the house and wormed his way in. They prayed together.'

'Good heavens. Who is he?'

'You may well ask. I remember the Rector warning us in the magazine about "Jesus People". I sincerely hope he isn't one of those.'

'Never heard of them.'

'Well, they prey on people, turn their minds, get their money off them.'

'Oh I say! Does her son know about this?'

'You can bet he doesn't. We'd better make jolly sure he's forewarned; the moment Reggie shakes a leg I shall put him on to it. Meanwhile, Davinia, you must try and do something your end.'

'What do you propose?'

'Well, how about the Parish Council? I mean, they won't want the premier village property turned into a squalid home for down and outs, will they? – think of the effect on property values; Aston Favell would simply *plummet*. Who do you know on it?'

'I believe Major Bullivant is the Chairman.'

'There you are then. Act now, before this silliness gets out of hand.'

'I will indeed. Actually, the Bullivants are pretty ghastly, but any port in a storm.'

'Absolutely. Let me know how you get on. I'll keep you posted from this end. Goodbye.'

(How busy will be the telephones in Aston Favell this morning, how twisted and knotted their coiling wires, how moistly warm their receivers. Mrs Potton will bang hers hard many times, then ring the operator. 'I think there's a fault. I've been dialling these numbers for over an hour. What? But they can't all be engaged, not for that length of time, surely. Very well, then; I'll keep trying . . .')

When Joan arrives at High House, Sylvie is still heavily asleep after a troubled night. Nurse Eilish, with an eye to her programme, would have roused her regardless, no doubt; but Joan is more considerate, and offers to come back later after paying earlier than scheduled visits to other patients. First though, she says, glancing at Will's white face, she will have a cuppa with him.

They take their tea into the sitting room. By way

140

of reminding him of the outside world, she mentions Thursday. How is business? Has he many visits lined up?

'Um, I'll be staying home this Thursday.'

'Oh, Will, now why?'

'Last Thursday unsettled Sylvie. This bad patch started right afterwards.'

'Love, this ain't no "patch". I warned you, it's the pattern; this is how it goes with this thing. You staying home on Thursday won't make a speck of difference. But Mrs Woolard coming – Kate . . .' She wonders how to put it – that far from hurting Sylvie, a day with Kate might bring her relief; that people with Sylvie's condition, though they seem vacant, are susceptible to atmosphere; that Will, being so worn down and emotionally involved in the situation, can't help showing distress, which gets through to Sylvie and winds her up . . . Deciding on a positive approach, she begins by urging Kate's virtues. 'I reckon it's good for Sylvie to have a change. I've watched that Kate – I remember her with her husband – well, you were there often enough, so you know what I mean: she's a sensible sort, don't get in a flap, got a real sense of humour, gentle and kind . . .'

'She's bloody lovely,' yells Will, punching his knees; 'I even think we might have a chance together – but not if we start something up from this hell hole!'

Silence. Did he really shoot that out of his mouth? The buzzing in his head from constantly disturbed nights has zoomed into crescendo – Take no notice, I'm crazed from lack of sleep, he wants to say – even opens his mouth, but no words come. He cannot believe he said that to Joan; cannot believe he said it at all.

But it is near enough the truth. Staring into the empty fireplace, he silently admits to a couple of genuine reasons for cancelling the Thursday arrangement. First, he really does fear making Sylvie worse by having Kate here again. Second, he has always fancied Kate – no; that's a banal way of putting what he really means, which is that he has always been *aware* of her and (yes, all right) attracted to her, and also liked and admired her enormously. Kate has always struck him as super-alive. He remembers envying Chris (an uncomfortable memory), and trying to imagine what it would be like having a strong woman as a partner, as opposed to a weak one like Sylvie. (Exciting, he guessed.) Oh yes, the thought of Kate has more than once entered his head, and now, if he is honest, a part of him aches to go all out for her. But only if they could then soar free, unshackled by this miserable confusion. His life at present resembles a waste ground snarled over with weeds and refuse, where any delicate plant would be swiftly blighted . . .

Joan leans forward, lays down her empty mug. The movement startles him; his feet shoot out involuntarily as his body rushes with fear and guilt. What the hell has he said? What can she be thinking? Oh God, what sort of effect will this have on Sylvie? – Joan might feel she has to make some report . . .

Joan sighs and stands up, comes over, sits on the arm of his chair and lays an arm round his shoulder. Suddenly he is juvenile again, shoving his face into her blue serge dress. When he can stop gulping and safely raise his head, it all spills out about Sylvie.

Sylvie's mood swings did not start with Alzheimer's. She has always suffered from them; basically, she lacked self-esteem. Presuming her one sure asset was her power to attract men, she would be compelled to make regular checks on its good working order. Her affairs were short-lived and always ended the same way: Sylvie hysterical with fear of forfeiting Will and ready to promise him anything, especially future fidelity. On some occasions he was even called upon to shield her from wrathful and embittered lovers. She was so pathetic; and he was too easily moved. Really, what bound him to her was pity: the thought of Sylvie seriously hurt or adrift was somehow unbearable. Maybe he needed this role as protector – who knows? And she was amazingly lovely. Did Joan ever see . . . ?

Joan, who did not, but is aware of the photographic evidence, squeezes his arm, gets to her feet. She will make a fresh pot of tea, then she must go.

When she brings in the mug, he is sitting exactly as she left him. 'Here, love, drink this. I'll be back later; right now I have to go see to poor Mr Lowe. Then there's that motorbike maniac; got to change his dressings – like to smack his bum for him, the cheeky young so-and-so.'

'Oh God, I'm sorry. All these patients waiting, and here I am holding you up with my stupid troubles.'

'We all got troubles,' Joan says, nodding, patting his arm. 'Other people having 'em don't make ours no easier. Now, if Sylvie wakes up, just do your best with her. I'll be back soon as I can.'

Kate has arrived at The Manse; she has found, after some difficulty, a parking space, she has climbed the five cracked and yellowed steps, and pushed (before remembering that this is the lawless 1990s) on the ever-open front door. As she rings the doorbell, her head is ringing with her father's once proud Welsh Chapel boast: 'A Chrrristian home has no need of locks!' Wrong again, Dad, she thinks – without pleasure, for it took two burglaries and a frightening encounter to convince him of the contrary.

The door opens. He clamps her hands between his own and manipulates them fiercely – 'Kate, Kate.' Though he does not embrace her, tears spring to his eyes. 'Here she is, Mam', he calls, still gazing at his daughter. 'Here's our Kate.' His imprisoned emotion is overpowering; she turns with relief to her English parent – the parent not tortured by inhibition, the parent who, when it comes to bodily contact, is without inhibition at all. 'Oh lovely, hello dear!' cries her mother, running from the kitchen. Kate is hugged, her ears are clapped, she is fulsomely kissed, she is held at arm's length and thoroughly scrutinized. 'Much too thin. You look worn out – doesn't she, Dad?'

'Well, I *have* just driven up the motorway. It was hell around Birmingham.' (Dear oh me, language already. Why is it that the moment she steps into The Manse, no sentence can pass her lips that does not contain some offensive word? Trouble is, in this house there are so many of them.)

When they are seated in the square-shaped front room, under the high ceiling, in the ancient brown-moquette armchairs padded with cushions to prevent injury from broken springs, Kate has time to study her parents. Older looking, she thinks – though she saw them as recently as two months ago; but perhaps on that occasion she wasn't observing too closely, perhaps she hasn't properly noticed them since Chris became ill. Older and bent – particularly her mother whose upper back has a distinct hump. Her father has always had a wasted appearance, but now it is plain how the skin has slipped from his bones. Of course, he ought to have already retired, but when difficulties arose on the local circuit he cheerfully agreed to continue his stint.

'I almost forgot, I've brought something for pudding,' says Kate, reaching into a carrier bag. 'Strawberry cheesecake.'

Her mother takes the box. 'We'll have it for tea,' she says. 'There's stewed apple for pudding.' (Kate had thought there might be, and for this reason had searched her freezer for an alternative.) 'And in any case, it's cheese for firsts – cauliflower cheese.'

This, too, had Kate anticipated (though not that it ruled out her pudding). On Tuesdays at The Manse, cauliflower or macaroni cheese is inevitable; the calculation had comforted her, for she could not have borne to arrive on soup day, when the remains of Saturday's pot roast – after a second appearance (cold) on Sunday – is finally boiled to extinction with carrots and onions for Monday's repast: she could not have borne to have the bowl placed in front of her, full

144

to the brim with dark brown liquor, malodorously steaming and winking with a thousand grease spots; could not have borne to hear her father's traditional cry of approval: 'Be-ootiful soup, Mam!' Wednesdays and Thursdays also have culinary hazards – shepherd's pie on Wednesdays (grey mince, dense potato topping), the cheapest sausages on Thursdays. Fridays are the best days to visit, when fish of some kind is served.

Nothing is allowed to change here, she thinks. The meal rota is as inviolable as weekday Bible class and Sunday services. Nothing has been changed in the room either – same carpet, same wallpaper, same furniture, same pictures on the wall, same modest ornaments. Only photographs of her children bear witness to the passage of time, though these – the shining, grinning, modern faces, the colourful backgrounds – look brashly out of place. When her mother takes the cheesecake into the kitchen, and her father jumps up nervously to search for a book which he thinks will interest her, Kate goes to examine the decorative objects on mantelpiece and sideboard, objects which she once viewed as almost sacred, objects she would handle with awe and wonder – and sometimes clumsily (the line of glue holding together the nodding chinaman is still visible: how she had quaked and gulped when that dropped from her forbidden fingers. 'Oh wick-ed, miser-rable girl!' 'Sorry, Dad. Sorry.') All still here – the miniature brass candlesticks, the Wedgwood bowl, the lustreware vase, the orange and black lacquered boxes, the small china jug with coat of arms and inscription *Pwllheli*; all still here, but somehow diminished and faded, as though years in this room charged with the impossible task of warding off drabness have taken their toll.

'Here we are,' cries her father, thrusting the book at her – and promptly loses his nerve at the prospect of remaining alone with his grown and changed daughter. 'I'll just see if your Mam wants a hand.'

*　　*　　*

Slumped in the leather chair, the tea gone cold beside him, Will stares into the empty grate – Victorian, black-leaded, with original art-nouveau tiles (pounced on by Sylvie in a junk shop) set in two vertical lines on either side. The tiles are cream, painted with brown chrysanthemums. He dislikes chrysanthemums. For one thing they smell bad, for another they decay too slowly; the outer petals die while more central ones continue to flourish, so they are kept too long, allowed to moulder in their vase bit by bit, smelling ranker by the day. Chrysanthemums are for laying on graves by people who are not planning to visit often and know these flowers will last.

The leaves are browning on Sylvie's maidenhair fern – which stands to the right of the fireplace on a shelf in the recess. This is despite conscientious watering. Perhaps he has over-watered, sloshed too much into its pot because he half-resents having to take the trouble. Maybe the plant has detected his attitude. Sylvie always fussed over this maidenhair fern, said they are sensitive plants: maybe this one is so darn sensitive it resents the lack of her personal attention. He has a good mind to chuck it out, blasted thing, going brown and reproachful on him. Why not? Sylvie is way past noticing.

As far as noticing things go: why is he pretending not to know that Sylvie is up and about? Floorboards have been creaking and doors opening and shutting for some time; he has heard these sounds but pushed them away. If she had called out, presumably he would have jumped to respond. Probably, what has kept him inactive is the faint hope that things will be more orderly today, that Sylvie has remembered where the bathroom is and wants to do some things for herself – well, it could be the case; you never know.

Then a new sound, faint but penetrating, has him sitting up in the chair, waiting to hear it again. There it is. Someone laughing, meanly, like *that'll show him.*

146

He leaps to his feet, flies up the stairs and along the landing.

Sylvie has backed into a corner by the wardrobe. He sees she has made a stab at dressing herself; her blouse is on back to front. Her face has a cunning expression; her eyes keep flicking towards the bed. She has attempted to make this, too; at least, she has smoothed over the eiderdown. But something about the bed makes his heart jump. He steps towards it. A small hollow in the eiderdown's centre is like a dark crevice in a gleaming snowfield; curved inside, grinning evilly, is a human turd. A stench gets to him. Stepping back, feeling instinctively for the door, he suddenly remembers that this is *his* mess – no good fleeing, there's no-one else to clear up; she has done this for *him*.

He goes for her – 'Cow! you did it deliberately,' – hands on her forearms, teeth bared, gripping, shaking – 'Filthy, stinking bitch!' – his right hand seizing the scruff of her neck, jerking her to the bed. He shoves her face right down over the turd. *'Look at it!'* (His father did this once to his puppy, and when Will cried for him to stop, explained it was the normal method of schooling a dog.)

The memory hits him like a fist. He lets go of her. She staggers: he catches and steadies her, then drops his hands. She looks utterly bewildered. Also terrified. Her eyes grow unfocused, her hands start chafing her bruised forearms. Very quickly, he walks out of the room, shuts and locks the door behind him.

His heart is banging so loudly it is impossible to think. What, for Pete's sake, is happening? Did he really . . . ? God, he did! – more than wanting to punish her, he had an urge to annihilate her. He grasps the banister rail like a blind man, takes each stair slowly until his feet reach the hall floor, then sits down heavily on a stair.

Sits there with his head in his hands while the hall clock ticks, chimes, ticks.

* * *

While Joan tends Sylvie — bathes, dresses, coaxes her to eat, Will steels himself to deal with the mess upstairs. He finds that while she was locked in the bedroom, Sylvie pushed her nightdress into the crap, evidently attempting to expunge it. He stares at the sight, recalling the time Sylvie pee'd in the laundry basket. It was Joan who discovered that misdeed; she tracked down the pong and laughed her head off (the way she does), then together he and she bundled everything into the washing machine.

Why, then, is he now so outraged? Because he made the discovery and must clear up unaided? No, there is something more serious . . . This white satin bed-cover — chosen by Sylvie, loved by Sylvie, cared for by Sylvie — is the sort of glamorous Hollywood trapping she always delighted in. Testing an idea, he puts her (the real Sylvie, the Sylvie that was) into his shoes, makes her walk unsuspectingly to her gleaming bed, catch sight of a dent in the centre and bend down to peer closely . . . Nothing could be more predictable than her shuddering, horrified, shriek. It is like a revelation; he has to sit down for a moment. Because now he is certain: this person, the person who committed the desecration, *is not Sylvie.*

There is only one thing to be done, he decides when his head clears: chuck the eiderdown out, nightdress and all. Without further deliberation he starts rolling it methodically — fortunately, its thickness has prevented any leakage underneath. It makes a bulky parcel; how the hell to dispose of it? — impossible to stuff it into the dustbin; someone might unroll it and get a nasty surprise. Better seal it in a garden refuse bag and take it to the tip when he gets the chance.

Downstairs, Joan and Sylvie are in the living room. Will bypasses them, carries his burden to the back door and out into the yard.

When the plastic-wrapped bundle is heaved into the back of his Volvo estate, he returns to the house. In the living room doorway he hesitates: 'Can she be left for a moment? I need a word.'

Joan looks at him. 'Sure. Be with you in a tick.' She hands the patient a magazine – 'See if you can pick out a pretty dress, Sylvie,' – and goes to join him in the hall.

'That respite you mentioned last week: any chance of fixing something up right now? It's, um, urgent.'

She looks at her watch. 'If I phone the surgery this minute I might just catch Dr Jeffreys.'

He leaves her to it; goes into the living room.

Sylvie has her back to him. Her head is bent forward. He reaches out, touches her hair. It feels like Sylvie's hair; undeniably it *is* Sylvie's hair; as the hand on the magazine is Sylvie's hand. He steps forward, takes the hand in his, examines it closely: it is utterly familiar, the hand of his wife, of his son's mother. Gently he replaces it on the magazine and backs away. This is what is so hard to grasp: that though this hand is her hand, this hair her hair, the whole is no longer Sylvie. Sylvie has gone. This person is someone he does not know or understand. Someone he has begun to punish for *not* being Sylvie. Therefore, someone he is unfit to care for personally.

He hears Joan hang up. Hurries into the hall with his reasoning fresh in his head to try it out on her. 'I've been thinking: she's changed, I'm not sure I'm right for her any more; maybe other people could do better?'

Joan nods. 'Could be, Will. Could be.'

'Did you fix something?'

'I did. Emergency, I told him – because it is, isn't it? – you've come to the end. This'll give you time to find somewhere permanent.'

His breath comes out hard. He stares unseeingly at the clock. After a moment, asks, 'Will you help me? I mean, if I find somewhere, would you come and check it out?'

'Of course, darlin'. We got brochures in the surgery – some very nice places. Eilish goes to visit Mrs Culham

149

in Brereton House – that's someone she used to nurse. She says it's very nice there, they look after her lovely. Anyway, Dr Jeffreys will suggest somewhere right for Sylvie. Then if you want me to come and look it over with you, that'd be fine. I want to see her happily settled, too, you know.'

Will is still blinking at the clock. He knows what has happened but it feels unreal. Just a couple of tentative questions, he is telling himself, and the agonizing's over. Everything's settled. It's like getting on a plane: you buy the ticket, give over your luggage, go through to departure, and suddenly there's no way back; you're processed for motion, events have moved beyond your control. Thing is though, life tends to force you to travel. When the ground gives way beneath your feet, there's nothing for it but to jump for the next foothold.

Over her meal at the Manse, Kate is questioned for news of the twins – not news of their studies, their health and happiness, but whether they still dress suitably, still have nice friends, are still pleasantly spoken, polite young people.

'You'll see for yourself, soon,' Kate says. 'I'll bring them over during the holiday.'

Because, her mother continues darkly, so many parishioners – good chapel-going folk who have brought up their children in the proper God-fearing manner – are worried out of their minds by the way their children dress and speak, by the hours they keep, by their terrible friends and horrible habits.

So am I keeping control of the twins? – Kate correctly translates. God forbid that Andrew should shave his head and put rings in his ears, or Andrea do likewise wearing Doc Marten boots. 'Oh, I think you'll find them pretty much the same.'

But her father is not comforted. He recounts how two young people of the parish have been seduced into joining a group of squatters in a near-derelict house on the main road. 'A great crowd of them, male and female, all living together . . .'

'Swopping partners, taking drugs,' puts in her mother.

'. . . in *debauchery*,' cries her father with huge relish.

Kate stares at her empty pudding bowl. The thought pops into her mind that she wouldn't be averse to a spot of debauchery herself – in the right circumstance, with the right person. 'Shock-ing, Dad,' she says, mimicking his accent.

Her mother looks at her sharply. 'Been getting out much lately, dear?'

To her fury, Kate feels herself blush.

In Rose Cottage, in the low-beamed flower-and-polish scented sitting room, *ladies who count* in Aston Favell are conducting a council of war. Joint hosts, Davinia and Esmé James, are not altogether happy that this is so. After all, it was Major Bullivant with whom Davinia requested a word this morning. ('Aeoh!' said his spouse, taken aback. 'I must just go and ascertain whether he's available.') As Davinia might have known, Daphne soon made the Major's business her own business, and very soon afterwards that of the entire gang. True to form, she now appears to be running the show. Ah well . . . Something does have to be done. So long as no-one expects Davinia James to do it. Happy though she is to make her sitting room available ('As your house is most convenient for The Old Vicarage,' Mrs Bullivant rather ominously pointed out), and pleased to relate every jot and tittle gathered from Cynthia Plum, she intends to be obdurate in her refusal to tackle Fenella Cunningham face to face. You never know, this Reverend Fred or Bob or Dick or Whoever might already be installed. ('Oh – you don't think so?' gasped Esmé, when Davinia confided this thought. 'How simply frightful for Molly.')

One way and another it was an action-packed morning in the Bullivant household. In order to speed the

Major to the telephone, Daphne had almost to tear him from the lounge window (where he was standing on a pouffe, squinting through field glasses) and swear to continue the observation herself of happenings on the far side of the fence. In the event, Daphne was unable to refocus the glasses to suit her own eyes. This seemed not a tragedy at the time, she was far more interested in Davinia James's business than in whatever was going on at the back of High House. Of course, later she could have kicked herself.

'A body? Oh, nonsense, Major.'

'Bore a damn close resemblance, then. You should've seen him struggling with it, heaving it into the the back of his Volvo. Tell you what, if there's no sign of his lady wife in the next forty-eight hours . . .'

'Oh . . . my . . . goodness.' Daphne's eyes widened as other scenes recently witnessed in the High House garden sprang to mind. About to run to the phone to confide her fears, she suddenly recalled the second matter. 'By the way, what did Miss James want?'

'Mm. Not sure I can divulge. Council business.'

'Rubbish.'

'Well, I suppose strictly speaking it's not *Parish* Council business, but do try this time to keep it under your hat. You know Lady What's-her-name, actressy type, Old Vicarage . . . ?'

'Cunningham.'

'That's the one. Seems she's been impressed by some dodgy religious fella. Proposes to turn over The Old Vicarage to him, let him fill it with the Great Unwashed.'

For one morning this was almost too much. Daphne sank heavily on to the settee, clutching and crumpling a daisy-stitched arm protector. Her knees sagged apart – the Major averted his eyes.

After two minutes' thought, with huge effort, she heaved back on to her feet and made for the phone, ignoring the warning cry, 'Daphers!' The Major would do what he could, no doubt – get in touch with his cronies on the Parish Council, huff and puff over several pints of the best, propose to tip off the District Council which deals with matters requiring planning permission . . . But honestly, as she scoffed to close friend and ally, Edna Critch, what is the use? By the time they've gone through all that rigmarole it will be far too late. An affair like this, threatening the whole of the village, demands immediate action.

'We must nip it in the bud,' she cries now to the assembled ladies, when they have heard from Miss James the details of Mrs Plum's bombshell.

'Indeed.'

'Absolutely.'

'But can't your husband put a stop to it?' Davinia asks. 'He is the Chairman of the Parish Council.'

'Much better dealt with by a man,' agrees Esmé, who has always considered the male sex formed by Nature for the performance of life's awkward, messy, and technological chores.

'But men are so ponderous,' cries the wife to the spinster from the depths of her superior experience. 'Believe me, if they can shelve a decision until next month's meeting, they'll shelve it. I thought, Miss James, you said *Mrs Plum* feared Lady Cunningham intends to go ahead with this plan immediately?'

Davinia casts her mind back. What Cynthia said has been so thoroughly explored it is difficult to recall it in the original. 'I certainly gathered the matter was urgent.'

'You know, what I can't get over is Lady Cunningham refusing to open the Bring and Buy,' marvels Mrs Haycroft, for whom this is the nub of the matter. 'Letting Mrs Plum down – after all the trouble she goes to.'

'I *know*,' moans Mrs Critch, another to whom the Conservatives' Bring and Buy at Carlton Manor is an eagerly anticipated occasion. 'I always say when Mrs Plum does the catering she knocks our WI efforts into a cocked hat.'

'And such a welcome you get at The Manor – all

the ground floor rooms open, you're perfectly free to wander. In fact, were you so inclined,' (Mrs Haycroft's confiding chuckle indicates that she herself is not) 'you could be a real nosey parker.'

'Yes, the Plums are very good,' Esmé rather loftily pronounces. 'I'm glad people appreciate them. I know we always do wonderfully from any affair they host.'

'Which does cast Fenel . . . Lady Cunningham's attitude in a rather dubious light.' (So put out is Davinia by Fenella's conduct, that she will concede as much even in the present company.) 'After all, Sir Jock devoted his life to the Party.'

'He'll be turning in his grave, I shouldn't wonder,' asserts Mrs Critch – feebly in the others' estimation, if a general shuffling of bottoms and readiness to come to order is a reliable sign.

'*What*,' demands Daphne Bullivant, jabbing her knee, 'are we going to do about the threat to Aston Favell?'

And Mrs Potton lends weight: 'I think Daphne is right – about immediate action. Imagine what we'd be up against once these people were installed in The Old Vicarage. We'd have to get up petitions, serve notices. The press would hear of it . . .'

'The press,' gasps Mrs Haycroft. 'Oh my goodness – the village in the newspapers!'

'Reporters banging on people's doors, demanding comments – from all the wrong sort of people, of course. Then it'd be on the television.'

'Aston Favell on everyone's lips – for a disreputable reason!'

'We could kiss goodbye to *Gardeners' Question Time*.'

'And think of the litter: hoards of reporters and busybodies – we'd be ankle deep in it. And bang goes our chance of winning the Best Kept Village Competition.'

'I propose,' declares Mrs Potton, 'that Daphne should approach Lady Cunningham. If anyone can make her see reason, she can.'

Daphne modestly lowers her eyes. 'Well, perhaps I could just call on her; say that as I was passing, it seemed a perfect opportunity to remind her about my coffee morning.'

Even the James sisters applaud this wheeze. Daphne Bullivant is more than satisfied. Having enjoyed the importance of initiating this gathering and the thrill of peering into the abyss, she now relishes a powerful role in the drama's continuation. 'No time like the present,' she says, heaving herself out of her chair. 'Wish me luck.'

Later that afternoon, Fenella's sense of betrayal is deep and many-faceted. For instance, of her innocent and cheerful response to Mrs Prior's summons. (Bullivant? – the name meant nothing; nevertheless, cheerfully to the hall where recognition sprang: ah yes; the stoutest and least appealing of the collection she entertained one afternoon last week in her drawing room, the one with litter on the brain.) For instance, of her decently extending the hand of friendship to said Bullivant. ('Coffee at *Sunny Bank*? – how simply lovely!') For instance, of her presumption that she possessed some choice in the matter of selecting a cause upon which to lavish her energy – particularly in view of the way in recent years, causes she has faithfully served have cast her aside. For instance, of her faith that Cynthia Plum (who has a certain standing) would not bandy her affairs with such as this Bullivant. (What in heaven's name is the world coming to, when Carlton Manor, unjustifiably aggrieved with The Old Vicarage, forms an alliance with – if her memory serves – *a bungalow*?) For instance (and most hurtfully of all) of her courageous refusal to be knocked back by the world forgetting her. Dog in the manger seems to be the attitude: no further use for Fenella Cunningham, but we'll be darned if we allow anyone else the benefit.

These bitter betrayals pierce her heart and heat her blood. She stalks up and down the garden paths (observed fitfully and warily from under a protective wheelbarrow by Henry). With enormous effort of will, she turns pain into resolve: the Plums and Bullivants of this world have a fight on their hands; they will discover Lady Cunningham is not so easily thwarted.

Shortly after six o'clock, Kate arrived home from seeing her parents, took a short walk round the village to savour her good fortune in living here and not in the grimy town she has just visited, and is now sitting at the kitchen table getting on with some marking, aided by a glass of wine.

Lifting her eyes from an ill-inscribed and inscrutably composed lower-sixthform essay, she wonders how Will is getting on. (The back door is wide open allowing scented air and birdsong to waft in; sun is pouring through the window, the hall clock ticking solidly, and far away a dog is barking – impossible in such bright chirpy airinesss to restrain optimism.) For possibly the hundredth time she recalls their brief embrace – lingeringly; a *pas de deux* in slow motion; constant re-enactment has made it more real to her than Sunday's curt and bruising phone call. She has begun to understand that it was not Will's intention to be curt or bruising, and her imagination has busily supplied many reasons for an incorrect effect. For instance, Sylvie may have been tugging at Will's elbow as he tried to speak, or out of reach and committing some vile misdeed; or she may have been out of sight but creating a horrible din, or even an ominous silence. There are many possible scenarios which together with Will's detectable weariness at the time of speaking afford satisfactory explanation. Poor Will, he did sound so tired; and sort of tight, as if reining in desperation. Her mind drifts to methods of administering comfort – smiles, strokes, tender words . . . But these she cuts off – reminiscing about what did happen is allowable; starting to invent things is not. To do so might spoil the freshness of what happens when

– she means *if* – their embrace is eventually resumed, when he draws her close, whispers, 'Kate, Kate . . .'

Stop it, she yells, thumping the palms of her hands down over the essay, as though what is written has suggested her irresponsible thoughts. She removes her hands and surveys the work; is sorely tempted to scrawl *Atrocious* in large letters in red ink. Instead, in black, merely writes *See me.* Then gets up to tackle a more vigorous chore, such as cleaning the windows or mowing the lawn.

CHAPTER TEN

Wednesday 24th June

From the moment Lady Cunningham took up a position outside her shop this morning (it seems on purpose to torment her), Nan's life has not been worth living. Lady Cunningham took herself off at lunch time when the shop closed for an hour; then, blow if she didn't return to annoy the afternoon customers. Nan has spent a large part of the day soothing, apologizing, disclaiming responsibility for and all knowledge of Lady Cunningham's request for signatures – her 'petition'. Some customers have sought to enlighten her, but Nan cut them short. She would rather not know, if they don't mind; she prefers to avoid controversy. Politics have their place, but definitely not inside her shop, thank you. ('Oh, a notice, Mrs Haycroft? The Conservative's Bring and Buy? Certainly. Just leave it on the counter and I'll pop it in the window when I get five minutes. Oh yes, I hope to be there, too. Saturday mornings aren't easy, of course, but our Laura comes home from college on Friday so I expect she'll stand in for me. What's that, Mrs Ellis? Well, I should just say, politely but firmly, "No thank you Lady Cunningham, I never sign petitions." That's my advice. It's very awkward. I can't ask her to move. Not very well. After all, she *is* Lady Cunningham. Now where was I? Dearie me . . .')

Nan senses she is getting one of her headaches.

Fenella's morning proved rather hard going. Several customers declined to support her. A couple of women (whom Fenella thinks she recalls as members of the litter-obsessed Bullivant brigade) were quite unpleasant. She also recognized these as the type who gush and squirm and try to monopolize her when she is opening things – Church, WI, or Conservative things – or giving a speech or simply gracing the occasion. Nevertheless, recognizing them as natural enemies and pretty awful to boot, has preserved her from being overly cast down. At lunch time, Fenella thought she detected a hint of frostiness about Nan switching her OPEN sign to CLOSED. And wretched Mrs Prior, homeward bound from her morning cleaning stint, had the nerve to scuttle past pretending deafness and blindness. (That woman would be well advised to watch her step; daily helps are not irreplaceable.)

One bright spot was the arrival of a young woman with a baby strapped to her chest. A strong-minded young woman. (Until then, the people Fenella approached were either signers or non-signers, both categories united by a desire to have the business over and done with and the exchange steered safely on to non-contentious ground – 'And how are you keeping, Lady Cunningham? Doesn't the village look pretty at this time of year?') This young woman was unique both in a willingness to hear Fenella out and a desire to contribute her own thoughts. 'What sort of refugee families?' she demanded. And on learning they are Croatian, launched into an account of some television programme. 'Oh I never watch television,' Fenella said grandly, anticipating the customary admiring reaction, something along the lines of: 'How very sensible, I wish I could say the same; they put out such rubbish; I always say, wasting time in front of the box is our national failing.' But this person had her own views: 'What a shame! – you miss an awful lot,' and proceeded to enlarge in a manner which brought home to Fenella the haziness of her own knowledge. A bracing encounter. But encouraging – the young woman seemed shocked to learn that Fenella's plans were meeting stiff opposition. 'God, that's pathetic. I mean, it's not like the refugees are going to stay with you for ever. It's only while this emergency's on.' Fenella blinked and agreed that this was so. 'Too right I'll sign,' the young woman declared, and promised to recommend the petition to her husband and a next-door neighbour. Fenella took careful note of the best times to call on these people. It turned out that they live in those horrid new places collectively known as The Park, a place Fenella has never visited (perhaps this is a short-sighted omission). 'And do call at The Old Vicarage when you're passing,' Fenella urged; whereupon, Mrs – that is, *Bel* Rochford – replied that she was keen to know the history of the older village houses and would certainly do so.

This, though half a dozen others signed her petition, was Fenella's only lengthy encounter of the morning. Enough, though, to raise her spirits and keep her at it. And how fortunate that she persisted, for this afternoon has brought a different type of customer and quite remarkable support. The secret seems to lie in early and unfavourable mention of Mrs Bullivant. It works like magic. Ah, here comes a person now – not terrifically prepossessing, but never mind, all grist to the mill . . .

'Good afternoon. May I introduce myself – Fenella Cunningham of The Old Vicarage.'

'Oh yeah?' suspiciously answers Karen Watts, she of Penfold Close council houses.

'What a dear little girl.'

'Shuddit, Kirsty!'

'Might I ask you to add your name to my list of supporters?'

'I dunno. I don't reckon with signing things.'

'Oh, I'm the same. In fact, I'm quite bemused to find myself in the position of being obliged to bother people. Such a bore. But it is a very simple matter. I merely wish to extend a little hospitality to one or two unfortunate families. Refugee families . . .'

'Shuddit Kirsty, or you won't blummin' *get* a lolly! You mean have 'em to stay?'

'Exactly. Yet to my surprise, certain people in this village wish to prevent me. One lady actually came to my house to tackle me on the subject. Er, Mrs Bullivant . . .'

'Oh, her. She's a right nosy cow. She was down the Close on Sunday afternoon, wanting to know could she come through me gate and clear up the rubbish – chip papers and that. (It's not us who leave it, it's the blummin' bin men.) Anyway, what it's got to do with her? I told her to get stuffed.'

'My feelings precisely. Surely it is no-one's business but my own whom I invite into my home. Unfortunately, Mrs Bullivant and her friends think otherwise.'

'Cheek, innit? Go on, then, give it us. What do I put?'

As Karen writes, a bus comes along Main Street and draws up at The Green. 'Hang about,' says Karen. 'that'll be May and Louise back from the chicken factory. They'll sign; they hates her, too. 'Ere,' she yells piercingly. 'Come over 'ere and stick your name on this.'

They amble over: a grey-looking woman (May), hardly able to heave her legs in front of her after a shift in the loading bays; her more robust companion (Louise) vigorously chewing double strength peppermint gum to disguise the taste and smell of eight hours devoted to eviscerating chickens.

'What's this, then?' asks Louise, chewing, grinning.

'You know that interfering cow who was down the Close Sunday, going on about litter?'

'Yeah?' agrees Louise chirpily, looking aimiably from Karen to Fenella.

'Well she's only gone and tried to stop *her*' – Karen indicates Fenella – 'having folks to stay in her own house.'

'No!'

'Some refugee families,' explains Fenella. 'I should

161

like to provide them with temporary accommodation at The Old Vicarage. However, Mrs Bullivant and her friends . . .'

'See?' splutters Karen. 'I mean, it's not on; if you can't have visitors no more without people making objections . . .'

'I would be most grateful if you would both add your names and addresses to my list of supporters.'

'Right-oh,' chirrups Louise, taking the sheet of paper (which Fenella has attached to a large hard table mat), and accepting the biro. 'There y'are. Go on, May, now you.'

'Tell you what,' says Karen, as May obediently signs. 'I bet there's others in the Close who'd do it. Specially after Sunday.'

Fenella squints over May's shoulder. 'You mean in, ah, Penfold Close?'

'I'll ask around, then you come over tomorrer — better make it evening — and I'll tell you which ones'll sign.'

'That *is* kind. Thank you *so* much. Until tomorrow.'

The next piece of excitement is the arrival of the school bus. Children of various sizes emerge onto The Green. Fenella eyes them speculatively, but decides against soliciting the support of juveniles. A few boys call out rudely which she affects not to notice.

After twenty minutes or so, peace returns. Then a small car roars up at a quite demented speed and halts shudderingly outside the shop. A nice-looking woman jumps out. At least, Fenella's first impression is of a nice-looking woman; then she meets a full-frontal view of a glowering face. Oh dear. Perhaps this is someone forewarned about her petition, someone stoutly against. However, she will stand her ground.

'Good afternoon!' (To Fenella's relief the woman's face clears;) 'I'm Fenella Cunningham of The Old Vicarage.'

'I know; I'm Kate Woolard. Can I help you?'

Fenella racks her brain. This Woolard woman evidently knows her. So perhaps she *is* part of the opposition – though not a Bullivant creature – too young, too smart. One of Cynthia's, perhaps. She peers suspiciously at the newcomer. 'Tell me: are you a Conservative?'

'Well, honestly! Don't tell me they've made it a condition of entry into the village shop?' Kate, already overheated from a sighting of Will (alone, in his car, making for Lavenbrook: she is not sure why this sight has enraged her, just that it has) is beginning to boil. '*Since* you ask, no; I'm jolly well not. Satisfied?'

'Oh my dear, yes,' says a relieved Fenella. 'They're against me, you know, they and the Best Kept Village people – though they may be one and the same. They're against my wish to house one or two refugee families in The Old Vicarage. On a temporary basis, of course.'

'Um, good heavens,' stammers Kate, thoroughly taken aback, abashed by her misplaced sarcasm. 'That sounds very, er, commendable. Surely no-one objects?'

'I can assure you! So appalled are they, in fact, by the idea of a refuge in the village that certain ladies dispatched a spokeswoman to my very door . . .'

'But who? Oh, don't tell me, I can guess – *the ladies who take it upon themselves* – right? Amazing how mean some folk can be. So you're drumming up support? Well, I'll certainly sign.'

'You know,' murmurs Fenella as Kate writes, 'I'm sure we've met somewhere . . .'

'I'm your neighbour. I live opposite your gate in Wayside Cottage, the one with the white shutters.'

Now it is Fenella who is abashed. But not for long. 'I wonder: if I call on you later, would your husband sign?'

A pause. 'Well, no, actually. He's, er . . . That is, I'm a widow. My husband died nearly two years ago.'

Taken by surprise, Fenella steps back and blurts ridiculously: 'But my dear, you're too young.'

'Afraid not,' says Kate, handing back the list – 'as

163

it turned out. Good luck with your project,' she adds, and goes briskly to the shop door.

The phone is ringing as she arrives home. Kate curses and fumbles with her back-door key. It will stop ringing the moment she gets within answering distance, of course. Law of nature.

But for once it does not. Though the caller is not Will (how could it be, idiot, since half an hour ago he was driving out of Aston Favell towards Lavenbrook?) but her son, Andrew, reminding her that the university year ends in under a fortnight. He and twin sister Andrea must then move out of their respective halls of residence with all their belongings and come home. Is it still OK if they hire a van? Kate, endeavouring to switch her mind to maternal mode, agrees that it is. In which case, Andrew continues, as these hire firms want money up front, especially from students . . . She gets the picture; she will send him a cheque. Everything else all right? she asks out of motherly duty; exams, essays, friendships, sporting fixtures, proceeding satisfactorily? Everything is great apart from end of term liquidity problems. Right, of course, she will make it a bit extra. She will also send something to Andrea who is probably in the same boat. ('Aw, thanks, Mum . . .') Not entirely trusting her memory, she makes out the cheques at once. Seals and stamps the envelopes, props these prominently on the dresser; then goes upstairs.

She wanders into the children's rooms – first Andrew's, then Andrea's – which will soon be full of grubby clothes, books, files, tapes, transistors, sports equipment . . . But for once the prospect of her ordeal coming to an end for two or three months, of no more jumping at creaks and shadows, of no more hidden eyes watching her, fails to lift her spirits. She is glad that the children will soon be home, she looks forward to their company and the way it relaxes her to have the house full as it used to be; pleasant anticipation, however, cannot dispel her immediate mood of stale anger, of niggling irritation. She closes Andrea's door, goes into her own room.

In the dressing-table mirror she confronts her face. God, but she looks peeved. At this rate there will be deep grooves on either side of her mouth by the time she is fifty. Fifty! She drops her face on to her forearms for a minute, counting the number of years to go; then sits up and grabs her hair brush. This is another thing: her hair has developed a frenzied look; she must get it cut. Disentangling her locks, she remembers how her visits to the hairdresser upset Chris. 'Why do you always cut it when it's looking its best?' he would grumble, which always irritated her and made her snappy. Sorry pet, she sighs now, imagining him plaintively shaking his head somewhere in the ether. She chucks down the brush, gets up and peels off her clothes, then hurries along the corridor to run a bath.

Funny, she thinks, as steam rises, how sharply infuriating was that glimpse of Will McLeod at the wheel of his Volvo, staring ahead, totally oblivious of Kate rushing towards him on the other side of the road. Whereas *her* stupid heart leapt like a schoolgirl's: *Hey – here comes a Volvo. Brown? Yes, brown. Could be Will's, then. Oh, it is. And he's alone, there's no Sylvie.*

So what, she wonders, squirting in bath essence, had he done with his wife? There was no car parked outside High House or in the yard, so presumably there was no-one inside looking after her. Perhaps Sylvie was elsewhere today, maybe having tests at the hospital, and Will was rushing to collect her. This explanation makes her feel better, but now she is irritated with herself for so badly needing to know. For heaven's sake, she is getting as nosy as the Bullivant woman.

At last, sinking into warm foamy water and letting her head loll back, the reason for her earlier fury slides home in her mind like a perfectly crafted and slickly oiled engine part. The truth is, she has a rather desperate yearning for Will McLeod, a fact discovered around 7 p.m. last Thursday, when for a few seconds she would have staked her last pound on Will feeling precisely as she did. Whether he did or did not, he can have no such feelings now; he has allowed nearly a week to elapse with no word of affection. She had better face it and cease all her fond fantasies: he has thought better of his feelings if he ever possessed them, and lacks the grace to acquaint her of the fact as painlessly as possible. She could weep with disappointment, not so much at his change of heart, but at his gracelessness. How awful to have her estimate of him proved so wrong. Will, she would have sworn, was just about the kindest, most sensitive man she has ever known. Oh, *Will*. Oh, *sod*.

The water's warmth is no longer relaxing; instead, seems to have raised her temperature. She stands up, quickly soaps and rinses, steps out. In the bedroom, she remembers it is exercise class this evening; furthermore, it is her turn to drive Fiona. This is a nuisance because she doesn't really feel like going; in fact, for two pins . . . Well, why not? Why not be a bad type for once, a let-down, an unreliable person? She is rather sick of being good staunch dependable Kate. Hell, if she doesn't feel like it, why make herself? Belligerently, she pulls on a comfortable old tracksuit and marches to the phone to give Fiona the disagreeable news.

Later, making herself a drink, she starts feeling regretful. A bit of a heel.

In the spare room of 7 The Park, Tina Fairbrother stops pounding the pedals of her exercise bike (birthday present from Les), wipes herself down with a towel, then goes hopefully to her bedroom to appraise herself in the long looking glass.

Damn, it's not *fair* – hardly swallowed a morsel all day, spent a crucifying half hour on the bloody machine, and it's still sticking out. She puts a hand under her stomach, stares at its profile. It's disgusting, she could be five months gone. Period late is the trouble; water-retention. One thing's for sure: she won't be going to exercise class this evening. She's not going to parade with a gut like that.

She had better phone Bel — not to tell her the truth: lacking Tina's high personal standards, Bel would think she was being funny. (Though actually it is Bel who is funny. Fancy sending Lady Whatsit round for her signature. God knows what it was all about; but never mind, signing seemed to make her happy.) No, what she'll say to Bel is, she's developed a migraine. Sounds sort of intellectual, 'migraine'. Bel should appreciate that.

In a temper, Bel drives to the village hall alone after the most amazing row with David. (What did she think she was doing, he demanded, promising his signature on some daft old biddy's misguided petition? He is not at all sure whether bringing people over as refugees serves any useful purpose. And who precisely is doing the bringing? Are they a proper organization? What are their qualifications? What is the prospect for these uprooted people long term?) God, but he makes her sick — *misguided, qualifications, long term*. It would kill him to just respond, one human being moved by the plight of another. It was wasted breath arguing with him (though she had a fair crack). They have had similar disagreements before, she crying over one starving child, one pleading mother, he choosing to focus on the lousy political set-up. Anyway, she demanded, what did he mean, *daft old biddy*? Making assumptions, was he, on the basis of Lady Cunningham being an elderly woman with no visible bloke in tow?

He had huffed a bit at this. His point was: it is a shame she failed to consider before volunteering his signature, because now, when she arrives, unfortunately he will have to disoblige the lady.

Pig, she had spluttered; it wouldn't hurt him to sign. He could swallow his precious principles for once, do it for *her*. After all, Tina signed, to whom, more than likely, the words Croatian and Martian are interchangeable. With which, Bel had gone running upstairs.

'Hey,' he called after her. 'You want a divorce?'

This was a signal meaning: *shall we make up*? She was supposed to scream 'Yes!' at which they would both fall about laughing and hence into each other's arms. Tonight, she ignored the olive branch and started preparing for exercise class. Half an hour earlier, when Tina phoned to cry off, Bel had been tempted to give it a miss, too; to stay at home and prolong Jamie's bath and playtime. But now the row rendered this a tactical error; it would be stupid to hand David further ammunition. Twenty minutes later, therefore, demonstrating an independent and carefree spirit, she came running downstairs heading straight for the door.

And glad she is to be out of the house. Her limbs just ache for a thorough stretching. She longs to jig and jump, to give that village hall floor a fair old pounding.

For someone who is supposed to be enjoying an idle evening, Kate is remarkably nervy and glum. Unable to settle to her novel, unwilling to put on the TV with the sun still pouring into the living room, she has finished marking the fifth-form essays and watered every plant in the house. The garden could do with a spot of weeding, but the task does not appeal. What she fancies is a cosy intimate natter with some nice person. With Will, actually.

Liar. What she really fancies with Will is a cuddle.

She grabs the newspaper off the floor and turns the pages, searching for an unread item. Guilt is the problem, she acknowledges at the back of her mind. But when was it not? Guilt is a part of her make-up, it was instilled in her years ago, possibly imbibed from The Manse water supply. ('Kate, oh Kate; I am dis-a-ppointed in you,' wails her Welsh father in her inner ear, and she remembers how her heart would lurch and she would frantically wonder, What have I done? – or rather – What have I done that he knows about? For there were always so many sins to her account – at least, as a child of The Manse, this was how she learned to view herself, her soul black as pitch and displeasing to Jesus, her misdemeanours the actual cause of his having to hang on a cross. Please, she frowns to herself, not that old stuff; you are no longer ten years old. 'But when I became a man, I put away childish things,' throbs her father from his towering pulpit. Too right, Dad, she yawns, so give it a rest – and she shakes out the newspaper, dismissing him.) A very tenacious worm, though, guilt. Here it comes wriggling in earnest: *Will is still married. It is wrong to have designs on him.* Yes, never mind her childish guilt, this is the subject of tonight's up-to-the-minute version.

On the other hand, counters the radical side of her nature, Sylvie McLeod may be sound in the legal sense, but surely no-one would dispute that Will's wife has been dead for as long as Kate's husband. Not that she dreams of taking a thing away from Sylvie that Sylvie needs or requires. On the contrary; the healthy Sylvie McLeod may have left her cold, but the child-like bewildered Sylvie tugs at her heart. She would not deprive her for the world.

But surely you see? counters her scrupulous side; Sylvie's needs are so vast that they must absorb Will totally, drive his mind and consume his energy. How stupid to imagine he can have a smidgen left over for anyone else. How wrong of her to try and inveigle a portion.

More pertinently: what the hell is she doing here worrying her head off? She looks up at the clock. Only a quarter to eight. If she hurries she could be down at the village hall before the end of the first half. She could explain a change of heart to Fiona later. After all, she is a fairly recent widow and on that score can be permitted the odd bout of indecisiveness.

*   *   *

Music – *uh, uh, ahhhh* – bats Kate in the face as she opens the door. As always, Fiona is facing the group, performing (Kate, who has enough trouble distinguishing left from right, cannot imagine how) all her actions in mirror image. Tall, slim, glossy, her eyes follow her hands as if these fingers jabbing towards the ceiling offer the most riveting sight in the world. Down she swoops, then rises slowly – and her eyes meet Kate's, her arched brows shooting even higher in surprised acknowledgement. Having mouthed a shame-faced 'Hi', Kate strips off her outer clothing and slips into a space near the back. Because she is small, Kate usually positions herself towards the front. From the back it is hard to follow Fiona's lead, especially now with a giantess in front of her – Bel somebody-or-other, with her plaited hair flying distractingly across Kate's line of vision. During the pause between numbers when people flop and puff or chat to a neighbour, Bel hops backwards, grins at Kate and urges her forward. 'Go on. You won't see a thing past me,' she urges when Kate demurs.

'I talked myself out of a lumpish mood,' she tells Fiona during the interval. 'Sorry you had to drive yourself.'

'No matter,' says Fiona. 'Glad you came. Numbers are down tonight.'

Kate looks round. Some familiar faces are absent. Zoë's, for instance. Kate is glad about this, for it means she won't have to explain about not going to High House tomorrow. Another absentee is the glamorously tarty creature who usually arrives with Bel. (They make an incongruous pair, Kate has often thought; one looking like a performer in a high-class clip joint, the other like a Nordic queen in an illustrated book of fairy tales.) She wanders over to a group of excitedly chatting women, listens to the chat for a moment, and turns away. 'Oh, not the Peeping Tom again,' she groans.

Bel, who is standing next to her, laughs. 'Not *again*, exactly. They're talking about an old sighting. Mrs

Ellwood has brought her daughter – that's her in the blue outfit. Apparently, Trisha and her boyfriend were early victims . . . What's up? Does it bother you?' – for at the word 'victim' Kate gave an involuntarily shudder. 'As a matter of fact,' Bel confides, 'I was a bit rattled myself by the idea of a prowler.' (Kate's face betrays that she finds this hard to believe of such a confident strapping young woman.) 'For my baby,' Bel explains diffidently, 'I'm one of those awful over-anxious mothers.'

'I certainly remember you and your friend taking off after him with gusto.'

'Oh, Tina? She's my neighbour – not here tonight. Yeah, chasing him, *doing* something, was quite exhilarating. It stopped me being anxious. Taught me that if he ever did come anywhere near Jamie, I'd have him,' – she snaps her fingers – 'just like that. Face your fears and you get the better of them, I suppose.'

Kate smiles, but wonders to herself, as Fiona calls them to order, how she would face the hidden watchers lurking near the staircase in Wayside Cottage.

After the session, Bel helps Kate and Fiona load equipment into Fiona's car. 'Fancy a drink in The Crown?' she asks cheerfully as Fiona locks the car boot. (It would be a sound move to arrive home late, she reasons; give David something to think about.)

'Sorry, bath and bed'll do me,' says Fiona.

'All right, I'll come,' Kate agrees. It seems churlish not to.

Not until she is seated in the lounge at the ring-marked table with the Bass beermats and the beige pottery ashtray, does it hit Kate: this is her first time in The Crown without Chris. She has lain several 'first times' to rest in other old haunts – The Woolsack in Carlton where she and the twins like to go for a meal, The Swan in Lavenbrook . . . Tonight it is the turn of The Crown. She observes Bel at the bar; Pauline Turner serving her and hitching her bra-straps as she waits for the money; the string of fairy lights over the liqueur bottles put up one Christmas and never taken down; old Jack Tasker in his usual corner waiting hopefully for someone to join him in a game of dominoes ('Evening, Jack. Yes, hasn't the weather been grand?') – all predictably familiar as if nothing more significant has occurred than the world revolving on its axis, day relentlessly following night and the seasons changing since she last rested eyes on the scene. 'Ta, love,' says Pauline to Bel, and calls, 'You keeping all right, Mrs Woolard?'

'Fine, thanks,' responds Kate. 'How are things with you?'

'Trade's slack in the week. Shouldn't grumble, though; we're run off our feet at weekends doing garden lunches.' With which Pauline goes wearily into the public to round up the empties.

Having confessed earlier to being an over-anxious mother, and reluctant to have Kate think of her as a general worrier, Bel is keen to explain how she developed this particular neurosis. She tells of her difficulty getting pregnant, of her overwhelming feelings when she finally made it. Kate listens and sips her wine as Bel describes her terror of somehow losing Jamie – a superstitious fear of jealous Fate snatching him away; and then of her consequent horror at hearing of a real threat, a Peeping Tom; finally, when she'd dealt with this fear, of learning that her next-door neighbour is a creep with a taste for porn videos. This is the first time she has confided in anyone about Les Fairbrother, having decided to keep the discovery even from David – specially from David. It is a relief giving vent to her feelings on the subject. If there's one thing she can't stand, she declares, it's being made to feel vulnerable. 'Of course, I immediately jumped to the conclusion that *he* was *it* – that Les Fairbrother was the Peeping Tom. But he can't be. For one thing he's fat, and the bloke we were chasing was slimly built. For another, according to Tina, Les was watching his videos at the time. Oh gosh, I shouldn't have told you, should I? –

172

about Les, I mean. But I know you won't blab.'

'Never a safe assumption to make in a village,' Kate warns. Then laughs – 'Don't look so worried; I promise not to breathe a word.'

'Mm, a village . . .' Bel drinks at length from her half of lager. 'As a matter of fact,' she says, setting down her glass, 'hearing about Les made me want to rush back to town. Until it occurred to me that you could live anywhere, next to the weirdest people, and never know a thing about it.'

'You do tend to *know* these things in a village. But that doesn't mean villages collect more oddities than elsewhere. I should think people are pretty much the same in any neighbourhood; or any work place, come to that. You come across some queer fish in a school staff room, I can tell you.'

'And in the retail business.'

'My husband told me . . .' begins Kate, and without any difficulty proceeds naturally, easily, to relate an anecdote of Chris's. Only at the tale's conclusion does she feel a pang. She takes up her glass.

'So what does he do, your husband?'

'Um, oh, he's dead. I'm a widow. I somehow thought you'd know.'

Bel stares. Then collects herself. 'Sorry. It's just that you don't look . . . I mean, "widow" sounds sort of old.'

'Sometimes,' says Kate, setting down her glass, giving it a shove, 'widow *feels* sort of old.' She laughs, but Bel catches a flitting shadow on her face which is sufficient to make her think guiltily of David. She decides he has suffered long enough, and that, by and large and overlooking one or two irritating tendencies, he is rather a darling. 'I have to go,' she says, getting to her feet.

'Me too. It's been nice. I'll do the honours next time. Or why don't you call round for coffee one morning? – a Tuesday or Thursday when I'm not at work.'

'Right, I will. Where did you say you live?'

'Wayside Cottage. On Vicarage Hill opposite The Old Vicarage.'

'Oh, I've noticed it – the pretty one with the white shutters? Funny, I met Lady Cunningham earlier from The Old Vicarage. She said I could call there and see inside.'

'Well, call on me, too. Bring Jamie.'

As soon as he hears the car in the drive, he opens the front door and flicks on the porch light. Stands waiting for her. As she locks the car door, calls, 'Hi. Good session?'

'Great. Went for a drink afterwards – with Kate Woolard from the class. Has Jamie been OK?'

'Fine.'

She steps over the threshold, he shuts the door.

'I say,' he continues, following after her, 'I liked your Lady Cunningham.'

'Oh?'

'I signed her petition, by the way.'

She swings round. 'Oh David, you shouldn't have. Not when you don't agree with it. You were right, I shouldn't have promised you would.'

'Like you said, it didn't hurt me. Completely painless, in fact.'

She puts her hands on his shoulders. They stare, eye-level to eye-level. He slides his hands under her tracksuit top, clasps her slippery, tightly encased ribs – which is the feel he had in mind when he resolved to sign the jolly thing. 'Truth is,' he murmurs, 'I'd do anything for you, Belinda, beloved.'

'Seducer,' she growls, grasping his buttocks.

'I sincerely hope so.'

She pulls him to the Scandinavian rug. 'So you liked Lady C?'

'I did indeed. Very impressive. Marvellous eyes, an amazing voice, a stride like Gary Cooper's in *High Noon* – bet she's got a great pair of pins.'

'That's enough about her,' Bel says severely. 'How about me?'

*   *   *

174

Having delayed to exchange a word with Jack Tasker and his long-awaited dominoes partner, Kate now arrives in her drive; switches off the ignition, unbelts, steps out; shuts the car door, inserts and turns the key . . . Then knows – *knows* – someone is watching her. Someone is here in her garden. There has been no tell-tale sound, but her sense of a presence is so keen that for a moment she peers round – to the road, then across the yard into the shadowy, near-black garden.

Nothing. And suddenly she cannot move fast enough – hurtles to the back door, frantically unlocks it, steps inside and slams it shut. In the kitchen her legs start to give way, but she drives herself to draw the bolts, to pull the blinds, to run round the house closing curtains. At last, sits down heavily on one of the lower stairs.

They steal forward, of course, the hidden watchers; but tonight she can ignore them; it is the menace outside which preys on her mind. Her hand reaches over her shoulder to where eyes bored into her back. The place feels marked, as though she has brushed against cobwebs.

What did Bel say – face your fears and you get the better of them? Ought she to go outside, then, and shake the hollyhock? Or march on the rosemary bush – 'I know you're there, so come on out!' The absurdity of it steadies her. She breathes in and out, in and out. Then goes upstairs to Andrew's room which has the clearest view of the garden and yard.

Head and upper body under the curtain, she stands motionless for some time. The darkness softens, shadows gain shape and outline. But there is no movement, nothing to indicate a prowler. And no sound other than a faint hum of traffic on the Lavenbrook Road. Tense with watching, she gives up; slides down and away from the window, goes downstairs.

Prowling from room to room, she seems to gather up self-disatisfaction – a lump of disgust, a handful of regret, a stony shoeful of impatience. Accusations mount – that she has spent too much time alone in the house brooding (no wonder she is beset by irrational fears); that at school she has been merely half-hearted (not in her teaching, in her participation: once she would have campaigned against the opt-out proposal, not ignored it); that she has shown little interest in her children's doings recently and been churlish to her uncomprehending parents; that she has greedily sought comfort from a man almost submerged by his own troubles . . . She slumps wearily against a doorframe and wonders whether her worst sin is to have allowed herself to feel old. God, she feels ancient. Yet only a few days ago she was out on the town with Fiona, tingling with new-found zest for life, feeling youthful again and capable of fun . . .

It is a surprise to discover herself slumped in the *dining room* doorway, her eyes resting on *that place*. A memory leaps – and Chris is looking at her intently: 'When this gets too much, you must send me back to hospital,' he declares – because he feels obliged to, because this is what considerate patients ought to say in such circumstances. But returning to hospital is the last thing he wants; it terrifies him even to suggest it. His eyes are dilated by conflict – duty against desire, fear against hope, guilt against despair. She reads this accurately (sometimes, intimate knowledge of another person can feel like tyranny) and her knowledge removes all possibility of an honest reply. What he longs to hear is her promise to continue nursing him at home where a semblance of control allows a morsel of belief in his own survival, to hear her promise not to return him to hospital where it is certain that he *will* die. She, however, is by no means sure she possesses the strength to continue with this regime much longer. So she drops her eyes and takes his hand; kisses it.

Now, slumped in the doorway, staring at the space where he eventually died, her inner perspective changes. The focus is no longer on Chris, but on herself. Fascinated, she observes Kate Woolard in an

176

endless performance of back-breaking and gruesome tasks, knowing how her nerve-ends scream, and her dragging weight of despair. She could almost swoon reliving the effort it cost her. It seems like a miracle, but she did succeed. She kept going to the very end.

Tears are stabbing under her eyelids. Rubbing them away, she absolves herself. All those sins mounted a moment ago in self-accusation: they are piffling, she decides, snuffing each one out as she flicks off the lights in dining room, sitting room, kitchen and hall. Her legs mounting the stairs feel strong. Words form in her mind in large bold script – *brave, gritty, resourceful*; pounding along the landing she repeats them out loud – because having earned such accolades, she needs to hear them conferred and in the absence of her former life-companion there is no-one other than herself to do the conferring. But then, pushing on the bathroom door, she comes face to face in the mirror over the basin with her reddened complexion, her faintly mad-looking eyes; and she sinks on the edge of the bath giving herself up to laughter, deep laughter from the belly, rolling easefully through her chest and throat. It is amazing how effectively this restores normality: rising to her feet, squeezing toothpaste on to her brush, she is relieved to discover she is neither heroine nor neurotic, just an everyday person doing her best. She brushes her teeth with vigour, rattles water round her mouth and spits; then creams her face, scrubs, rinses, pats it dry.

In the mirror, her face has calmed down; her eyes regard her coolly. She nods. It is clear to her now that what she misses most in her widowhood is the healthy pleasure of blurting thoughts as she thinks them, describing feelings as they are felt, relating events as, or soon after, they occur. And receiving an equally spontaneous response, such as 'Rubbish, you are an idiot,' or 'Do you really?' or 'Oh, darling, poor you!' All such responses are valuable; they bring a truer perspective, and best of all create that lovely sense of companionable sharing. She would be glad, for instance, to confide her curiously strong hunch that she was spied on when she returned home this evening; she would be glad to hear comments, to laugh and speculate in cosy safety. Particularly, she thinks as she climbs into bed, she would like to share the experience with Will.

She reaches out to turn off the lamp. Blackness falls, and is broken at once by a car's headlights swooping up Vicarage Hill driving brightness over the ceiling. Afterwards, the room settles into familiar patchy darkness, moonlight outlining the curtains and describing their folds. Turning her head, she can just make out the shape of her white bedside telephone. She could phone Will, of course. Though in fact she will do nothing of the sort: right now, Will is either struggling to manage Sylvie or taking a much-needed rest from her, and not for one moment would she consider disturbing him. No: all she is saying is, she *could*. She is playing with the idea, indulging in harmless fantasy, comforting, lulling herself – the equivalent of thumb-sucking or rocking or stroking.

'Hello, Will,' she might say. 'Sorry to disturb you so late, but a peculiar thing happened earlier – or didn't happen – that's why it's so peculiar, I can't be sure. I just wanted to tell you about it.'

'Of course,' he would no doubt reply.

'I'm not worried or anything. It was probably my imagination – which does tend to become over active, specially now I'm alone so much . . .'

'Kate, Kate . . .'

'But I had this terrifically strong feeling there was someone there. It was as if I could touch them – or that this person's stare was jamming into me . . . You know, Will, I'm not sure I'm cut out for living alone . . .

'Oh, Kate . . .'

'Oh, Will, Will . . .'

178

CHAPTER ELEVEN

Thursday 25th June

Thursday does not begin smoothly for Kate. Harmless fantasy? she wryly asks herself as she struggles out of bed at a needlessly early hour in order to foreclose on a night's hectic dreaming. Do me a favour – next time you try a spot of bedtime musing, try concentrating on wind-in-the-beeches, flowers-in-the-meadow, gurgling-stream sort of thing: just keep off any reference to Will McLeod. 'Deprrraved . . . wan-ton . . .' resounds her father's *hwyl* in her throbbing head. You said it, Dad, she agrees, sighing, reaching into a cupboard for the paracetamol bottle.

She dresses quickly, then goes straight outside to search for evidence. Sure enough, a few yards from the kitchen window beside the rosemary bush, discovers a flattened clump of peonies. Flattened by feet, of course; feet belonging to the Peeping Tom. So he *was* here when she got home from the pub last night, he was here spying on her. She shivers, feeling nauseous rather than vindicated. But later, sipping her tea, becomes philosophical. Lots of people in the village have been visited by this wretched prowler; maybe this was her turn, and now he has seen her he will leave her alone. For the next hour or so, when her mind slips into fearful speculation – as it seems inclined to do as she dusts and vacuum-cleans – she returns to this helpful theory.

By half past nine she is regretting the housework. Her headache is back; it would have been better to have pursued a quieter occupation. She makes a cup of coffee, eats a biscuit, and resorts again to the paracetamol bottle. This time last week she was having coffee with Sylvie, she reflects; this time last week . . . Then curses herself. Why must she keep harking back to the McLeods? Where is her pride, for heaven's sake? She ought to bear in mind that whatever his troubles, however distraught, Will's pretence that nothing has occurred between them is cowardly. But this leaves her with an empty feeling; she takes a second biscuit. Damn and blast Will McLeod, she thinks, chewing savagely.

Major and Mrs Bullivant have been hard at it since seven o'clock this morning. Breakfasted by seven thirty, dressed and spruced by eight, they are now preparing for a prime event in the Aston Favell calendar — coffee morning at Sunny Bank. At this moment, Major Bullivant is briskly applying a nozzle to the lounge carpet, the vacuum cylinder following in jerky runs like a spastic dog; his front is protected by a plastic tie-on apron inscribed *The Work Horse* and suitably illustrated. In the kitchen, Mrs Bullivant in flowery overall is prodding a ready-sliced, home-baked Victoria sponge; prodding and thoughtfully sucking her fingers. Almost thawed, she thinks hopefully, making further prods to convince herself of this. She is annoyed that she did not rise at six this morning in order to remove the cakes from the freezer an hour earlier. Last night, she decided against removing them before she retired, calculating that she would be sound asleep when the thawing process reached the optimum moment for cutting into slices. It is a tricky business. Could the cakes, she wonders, do with half an hour in a heatless fan-oven? No; that might overdo things, and one does, after all, like to see a buoyant Victoria, not a saggy affair with oozing filling; better to place them on the sunny ledge in the dining room — yes, that's the ticket — then it'll be the work of a moment setting them in their final resting place on the dining table. Always supposing that the Major has obeyed orders . . . 'You've done the dining room, I trust?' she enquires, poking her head round the lounge doorway and bellowing to drown the noise of the vacuum cleaner.

'What?'

She asks again, but to no avail. Irritably, he stabs the 'off' button. She repeats her question.

'Of course. I vac'd in there first, as per instructions.'

'Just checking. And I should open the patio windows and draw back the nets when you've finished in here.'

'And put out the garden furniture, and lay out the plant stall – I know, I know; I'm not quite in my dotage, I can still keep a grip on a modicum of info. Interruptions likely to cease, by any chance?'

She withdraws. He hits the cleaner's 'on' switch.

From a large carton in the spare bedroom, she selects twenty choice items of her personal handiwork to display on the *For Sale* table in the lounge. This morning's effort is in aid of the village church. Daphne, who likes to make Sunny Bank's contribution distinct from certain others, has taken care over the years to hit the right note. This is a coffee morning, not a sale of work or a bring and buy. And that being so, it is not quite nice, in her opinion, to charge people directly for their coffee and eats – worse still to charge an entry fee into her home; rather, her style is to personally welcome visitors at the front door, indicate the dining room as the place to go for refreshments, and the lounge and garden (weather permitting) as areas in which to socialize – while pretending obliviousness to the fate which actually awaits: namely that upon entry to the dining room Edna Critch will pounce with the raffle tickets; in the lounge it will be impossible to ignore the large table smothered in price-tagged Bullivant artefacts, and in the garden the Major's plants for sale.

Many ladies in Aston Favell are known for their expertise in a particular handicraft, often one they have developed deliberately as their trade mark. For example, Mrs Haycroft creates ruched velvet cushion covers and Mrs Critch knits stuffed toys. Such works form part of their identity – 'That's another pair for Edna Critch,' say ladies who ladder their tights, for tights, well-chopped, are the ingredients of the Critch toy stuffing; just as, 'You know who I mean, she does the dried-flower pictures,' is a method of pinpointing Mrs Potton. Daphne has two specialisms: St Peter's Marmalade (her own recipe named after the Patron Saint of the church destined to benefit from its sale and consumption), and crochet-work pot holders (white crocheted circles soaked in a heavy sugar solution and shaped round a container – jam jar, plant pot, sweetie bowl – then left to dry and harden until miraculously transformed into rigid three-dimensional shapes). Daphne is famed (also feared) for her crocheted holders; there can scarcely be a better class home in Aston Favell lacking the benefit of one or more examples. Their shapes become more varied and fancy as the years go by; their uses (according to Daphne) are limitless. Her intimates feel obliged to demonstrate how amazingly useful they do indeed find them, and many a table bears the stain of their sticky collapse.

The Major, who is permitted on these occasions to man a plant stall – a collection of small specimens specially cultivated for the occasion – meets his wife as he is putting away the vacuum cleaner and she is coming down the hall bearing a tray of her crocheted holders. 'Want a hand with that?'

'No, thank you Major, I can manage perfectly well. If the lounge is now shipshape, just you attend to the garden.'

'Message understood, sir.'

His spirits rising at the prospect of attending to his own province, he returns whistling to the lounge, where, grasping the curtain pulley, he yanks back the heavy and expensive Swedish net drapery – and instantly undergoes one of those 'out of body' experiences, metamorphoses into a stranded creature gulping in an alien environment. For instead of confronting his own immaculate lawn and well-marshalled flower borders, here is a litter tip, a refuse dump. Hand acting independently of brain, he draws back the sliding patio window; at which a paper bag rises on the draught and brushes his cheek. 'Daphers,' he splutters, 'Daphers, old girl,' as his pulse quickens and *heart attack* leaps to his mind's eye in coroner's script. 'Daphers,' he cries more urgently.

She hears him. She hopes he is not about to throw a wobbly on this of all mornings. She warned him against taking that late-night snack – tiresome man; never learns; courts indigestion then swears it's angina. All set to remonstrate, Daphne marches into the lounge, opens her mouth . . . then says nothing at all. She creeps to his side, and together they survey their garden. Wordlessly, they step down onto the patio and wander like lost souls towards the lawn. Empty crisp bags and chocolate-bar wrappers nudge their ankles, rise and billow on the gentle breeze; bright shiny scraps peep like late blossom from the almond tree, shine at the base of thorny rose bushes like crocuses sprung in June. It is impossible to gauge the duration of their wanderings, which is a chunk out of time, so unreal there is nothing to measure it by.

At last, the Major is moved to utterance. 'Jumping Je-hos-o-phat . . .'

'I can't believe it. Whatever has happened? It's not dustbin day.'

'It'd take a whole tribe of bin men to affect this sort of mess. No, it's deliberate sabotage.'

'You mean someone actually *brought* this here?'

'I should say so. When did *you* last sample' (he gropes to retrieve a luminous green wrapper) 'a Monster Kerrunch Bar, eh? If you ask me, it all bears a suspicious resemblance to the contents of the shop's litter bin.'

'You're not seriously suggesting Nan, or Ted . . . ? Out of the question.'

'Kids, then. Or someone with a grudge, or not quite the ticket.'

'Oh, I say, you don't suppose . . . ?' She nods towards the rear of High House.

'You mean the resident loony? Trouble with that theory: lady not sighted since husband observed heaving large parcel into the rear of his Volvo estate. I told you we should have called the police.'

'You won't be told, you obstinate man – I've counted at least four further car loads in the past few days. Obviously, Mr McLeod is having a turn out.'

'And his excitable lady?'

'Probably kept strictly indoors – precisely *because* he foresaw her creating this sort of nuisance. If you'd seen what I saw over the garden fence, you'd realize what she can be capable of. Even . . .' Words fail her, she waves a limp hand over the garden.

'As you say, my dear. But it's no use standing here debating the point; we'd better set to.'

'Oh my goodness,' shrills Daphne, suddenly aware of the time, 'there's not a moment to lose.' And even as she exclaims, the doorbell chimes.

Thankfully, her palpitations prove unnecessary. It is loyal Edna, come early to lend a hand. 'Thank heaven, dear, come in. Oh, you are kind.' She takes a cake from Edna – who, as a mark of best friendship, has been permitted to contribute to what is essentially a Bullivant occasion. 'Quick, into the kitchen. There's been a DISASTER. No, not in here. Put on these rubber gloves and I'll show you where. Now follow me into the garden . . . There. What do you make of that?'

'But what, whatever happened, Daphne? Has the Major had an accident?'

'Don't be ridiculous. These are sweet packets, Edna, soiled food wrappings. We must retrieve every piece – Major, do make haste with the refuse bags – ah, here he comes – every scrap before people arrive. It's even got into the trees; and – oh my giddy aunt – look at the trellis. You'll need a ladder, Major. You and I will work at ground level, Edna. I tell you, if I ever lay hands on the perpetrator . . .'

Panic stations are not entirely over when the doorbell chimes again; the plant stall is not yet erected, the cakes not yet on the table. 'I leave this to you, Major,' yells Daphne warningly and, ripping off her overall, dives indoors.

As it turns out, people are more than happy to purchase raffle tickets. At a sight of the prize – a pair of pillowslips trimmed with *broderie anglaise* – worked by Miss Esmé James, people can tell at a glance – whole strips of tickets are cheerfully purchased. (Though most ladies pride themselves on their particular hobbies, excellence is always accorded due recognition. No-one would dream of wasting a piece of Miss Esmé James's needlework or one of Mrs Grant's professionally iced cakes on a bring and buy stall or even a handicraft or cake stall; such wonderful items go without question for raffle or some other ingenious means of extracting the sort of money true art can command.) But it is a very different story when guests enter the lounge and spy the *For Sale* table. Many feign partial blindness. Some, facing up to the inevitable, rush to purchase a pot of marmalade in order to evade a dreaded crocheted holder. Some utter cries of joy and swoop on the Major's belatedly arranged plant stall.

Most members of St Peter's congregation who do not have places of work to go to put in an appearance, as well as faithful church-goers from the sister parishes of Carlton, Carlton-le-Walls, Tetchborough and Symington; busy farming wives such as Marie Ellwood arrive, even Nan Hutton has left the shop for half an hour with instructions to her assistant, Debbie, to send word to Sunny Bank in the event of an unexpected surge of custom. Nan causes quite a stir of excitement among Mrs Bullivant's intimates. Behind their cups, *sotto voce,*

185

it is agreed between them: Nan's innocence is proved; for it is plain as daylight she lacks the brass nerve to do the deed and come within half a mile – not that any of them seriously suspected her in the first place . . .

The Miss Jameses arrive and are laughingly exempted from buying raffle tickets, which exemption they blithely assume applies to all else on offer (and being the Miss Jameses no-one is prepared to disabuse them). In fact, never mind the gift of pillowslips, the James sisters think they are very good to be here at all.

Daphne Bullivant's cup of joy overflows when Mrs Plum of Carlton Manor pops in ('only for five minutes, I'm afraid') and blatantly proceeds to drum up support for the Conservative's Bring and Buy on Saturday. Few of the present company object to this; most, with the possible exception of one or two from Symington (a predominantly working-class village), are flattered to be asked and only too delighted to promise their attendance.

'Good morning, Cynthia,' says Miss Davinia James. 'I'm rather surprised to see you here.'

'Good morning, Davinia,' Cynthia sighs. 'We have to do our bit.'

They allow their eyes to take in a portion of the Bullivant dining room (where they are now placed), and exchange grim looks. Cynthia indicates that they should step to one side. 'No luck with You-know-who, I suppose,' she asks, when they have withdrawn to the unpeopled area at the side of the fireplace, which, mercifully without heat, is flickering monotonously, artificially aflame.

'Quite the reverse. Our, um, hostess took it upon herself to call at The Old Vicarage,' says Davinia, recklessly distorting the truth. 'With, I am afraid, disastrous consequences. So enraged was Fenella, in fact, that she took up a position on the village green to mount some sort of protest.'

Mrs Plum stares sorrowfully into the flickering flames. 'I fear for Fenella,' she proclaims. But then brightens: 'Fortunately, the Member's wife has agreed to do the honours on Saturday. What *makes* it do that, do you suppose?' she asks suddenly of the lively fire.

'I have no idea, Cynthia,' Davinia says impatiently. 'Oh good, that sounds like Molly's arrival.'

'I decided to bring Henry,' Molly Cunningham is shouting in the hall, stepping briskly past her hostess with her pet tucked under her arm (almost as many white dog hairs on her well-knee'd tweed skirt as on Henry's back), 'rather than leave him with Fenella – who can't come by the way, she's, um, indisposed. She teases him so, and the poor boy's getting too old to stand it. I know you won't mind.'

In this she is mistaken. Mrs Bullivant's face turns sour as Henry is deposited on the midnight-blue Wilton and Molly is effusively greeted by the James sisters and the great Mrs Plum. Daphne's friends, when they see Henry, are astonished and miffed. They think resentfully of Buttons (Mrs Critch's wire-haired dachs) and Chow-chow (Mrs Haycroft's peke) shut up at home. Daphne has imposed an inflexible embargo on pets at Sunny Bank; she says she has to consider the Major's asthma. While other members of the gang are easy-going – Mrs Potton encouraging Buttons and Chow-chow to visit her cottage despite the offence caused to her tortoise-shell cats, and the Miss Jameses, owners of a well-travelled cairn terrier, always able to discover about their person a suitable morsel to offer in greeting, a doggy choc-drop or meaty chew – the Bullivant household is known for its peculiarity in the matter of animals and their place in the world (which is never within the immaculate vicinity of Sunny Bank).

The Major bustles up. 'Do you know,' he demands of his wife, 'that Cunningham woman has brought a dog? – smelly looking beast – nosing about on the dining-room carpet.'

'She won't stay long I shouldn't think. I'll vac thoroughly afterwards. Go back outside.' She gives him a shove as the doorbell chimes again.

Bel is on the doorstep, looking a little uncertain. (A recent encounter in the village shop led to Mrs Bullivant pointing out the notice advertising her coffee morning and Bel, in keeping with her decision to broaden her horizons, promising to come. Of course, in her innocence, Bel made no connection between the Bullivant camp and Lady Cunningham's petition; lacking the self-protective warning system developed by the seasoned villager, she failed to become wary at the conjunction of the words *opposed to* and *plan*; indeed, has forgotten that they were ever uttered.) As usual, Jamie is strapped to her breast. This fact and the way she is dressed cause a mild sensation. Were the gawping ladies to see a similar outfit (sleeveless geranium tunic over sheer black leggings) bouncing out of Penfold Close, 'common' would be the scathing verdict; as worn by Bel, however, it brings to mind such phrases as 'bright young thing' and 'healthy looking gel', and Major Bullivant's 'dashing young filly'. Bel takes a quick look round and wonders where on earth her quest for adventure has landed her; but smiles brightly, nevertheless, and goes forward.

The ladies hurry to coo at Jamie. One offers to dandle him while Bel drinks her coffee. They sense she is rather at sea and help her to refreshments; recommend the raffle, and manage to disguise their surprise when she cheerfully admits to having come without money. They introduce her to Molly Cunningham, another of life's ingénues.

'*Cunningham,*' repeats Bel. 'Any relation to Lady?' Molly looks blank. Mrs Haycroft at Bel's elbow murmurs, 'Sister-in-law. Miss Cunningham is rather hard of hearing.'

'Oh, she's so sweet your sister-in-law,' cries Bel, raising her voice to accommodate Miss Cunningham's handicap. 'I met her the other day. Signed her petition.

Isn't it terrific that she wants to offer these refugees a home?'

'What?' bawls Molly — whose deafness and disinclination to attend to anything other than her garden and telly have preserved her from knowledge of Fenella's intentions. 'What does the gel say?' she demands of Cynthia Plum.

Cynthia draws Molly aside; Mrs Haycroft does likewise to Bel.

'Come and look at the garden,' Mrs Haycroft insists. But in order to reach the patio windows, the *For Sale* table must be passed. Marmalade is sold out. However, there are still many examples of Mrs Bullivant's handicraft. 'Oh, I say,' cries Bel. 'Aren't these pretty? What are they?'

'Er, Mrs Bullivant's crocheted holders.'

'Crocheted — and rock solid. How extraordinary. This one would look nice on a dressing table — for holding cotton wool balls or something. My mum would love it. Would it be OK, Mrs Bullivant, if I paid you later? Gosh, they're so dainty-looking, I think I'll take two.'

'Whatever will she say next?' wonders Mrs Haycroft under her breath to Mrs Potton. 'Better keep an eye on her. I don't think she's safe.'

Finally, flustered, in place of her husband who has been summoned to an unscheduled Rural Deanery meeting, Mrs Robin Jesmond, the Rector's wife, arrives. Because she is also the Reverend Harriet Jesmond, (Reverend, that is, in her own right as an ordained deacon), her arrival causes great dismay among the traditionalists in the present gathering. Daphne is frankly affronted. There is something rather distasteful about a lady vicar she always feels, and she can never, she confides to her friends, bring herself to look one in the eye. Today her suspicion that lady vicars have working-class connotations (after all, they tend to end up in that sort of parish, no doubt because those spineless types are the only people they can be foistered on) is what particularly exercises her. 'Oh, but where's the Rector?' she blurts, thinking bitterly that, rural dean or no rural dean, he would break a leg to avoid missing a function got up by Mrs Cynthia Plum. Pink with anger, she tries to assess the degree to which her coffee morning has been downgraded in certain eyes (eyes belonging to the snobby James sisters for instance, or the said Mrs Plum).

Harriet Jesmond is as depressed to be here as Daphne Bullivant is to receive her. Robin, she knows, is a tolerant man who would argue that Mrs Bullivant is as deserving in her own way of pastoral consideration as any other parishioner. Besides, all five churches in his care have an urgent need for funds: all contributions should be gratefully acknowledged. Nevertheless, as she attempts the chit-chat, sips her coffee, buys her raffle tickets, casts round in vain for her friend Zoë Hunter (in vain because Zoë is on duty this morning at the surgery), her mind goes to the deserted and despairing mother of five she promised to visit today, and the overdose case whose hospital bedside she has recently left. She stares at the *For Sale* table. Recognizes the crocheted holders. Robin brought one of these efforts back from some do or other; Harriet chucked it in the cupboard where she keeps all curious items purchased out of duty. Where do these women get their daft ideas? From magazines probably. Some desperate editor screams, 'Think of something for Christmas, someone!'; whereupon a lunatic hoping to save her job invents sugar-hardened crochet – never guessing that ladies with nothing better to do will thenceforth devote half their lives to its mass production, to the everlasting torment of friends and acquaintances.

'Hi, I'm Bel Rochford – and this is Jamie,' says Bel, coming in from the garden and spying the newcomer.

'Hello – Harriet Jesmond,' says Harriet, offering her hand, gratified to be claimed so cheerfully (she had given up hope of anything beyond subdued politeness from this gathering of mainly elderly and strictly conventional folk.)

'Are you from Aston Favell, too?' asks Bel, and explains: 'I'm a newcomer, so I hardly know a soul.'

'No, from Symington,' says Harriet, chucking Jamie under the chin.

'Oh yes, the village with the school – where Jamie will go, I expect. Have you got children?'

'Two – one at the village school, one at Lavenbrook Comp. How do you like living in Aston Favell?'

'I'm slowly getting used to it. It's my first experience of village life. Mind you, it's my first experience of living anywhere, day in day out – I mean, until Jamie came along, I was always out all day. I suppose that's the hardest thing to get used to.'

'What did you do before you had Jamie?'

'I was in personnel management.'

'Personnel management – my goodness, I could use your expertise.'

'How's that?'

'In a million ways. I work for the parish clergy team. Actually, I'm a deacon, hoping to become a priest.'

'Wow,' says Bel, who is an infrequent church-goer, but a keen supporter of the proposition that women should to be free to participate in any field they choose; 'now that *is* interesting.'

'It's good to hear you say so . . .'

'Attention, everybody,' booms Mrs Bullivant. 'Time for the raffle.'

'That's my cue,' says Harriet. 'Get in touch with me if you like – Symington Rectory.'

'Thanks, I will,' Bel calls after her, the doubts she had begun to entertain over this morning's expedition pleasantly dispelled.

Mrs Bullivant clasps hands under her bosom, clears her throat. 'In the unavoidable absence of the Rector – who has sent word to say how very sad he is to miss our little coffee morning, urgent business having called him away (and we do understand; the unforeseen occurs) – the, er, Mrs, um that is, his wife has kindly agreed to draw the raffle.'

A buzz of excitement, a searching of pockets and handbags.

'Before we proceed to the raffle, ladies and gentlemen,' Harriet begins, nervously confronting some rather grim-looking faces, 'I must confirm how disappointed Robin was to be called away this morning. Also, I should like to thank Major and Mrs Bullivant, not only for their very warm hospitality, but for the contribution their efforts have made to St Peter's fabric fund. A much needed contribution. Thank you both. Now, without more ado . . .' Desperate to be done, she thrusts her hand into a large glass bowl. Draws out number 107.

The confusion lasts for some time. Harriet bleakly waits for someone, *anyone,* to produce the winning ticket. Eventually, Mrs Critch works out that number 107 was a late-sold ticket. Forty pairs of accusing eyes fall on Harriet – who suddenly tumbles: 'Don't say I drew my own? Oh, how ghastly. Ignore that, everyone; I'll draw again.' And to murmurs of polite protest, she puts in her hand for a second time; draws out number 42. Thankfully, a blameless parishioner from Carlton-le-Walls triumphantly waves the matching ticket. Harriet sighs with relief, shakes hands with the winner, shakes hands with both Bullivants, waves to Bel, departs.

'Well, *she* didn't linger,' sneers Mrs Haycroft.

'Gives me the shudders,' snaps Daphne Bullivant.

'I've reckoned up and we've made eighty-seven pounds,' reports Edna Critch breathlessly. 'That's twenty-odd pounds more than the Robinsons made from their do. Won't it look splendid in the church magazine?'

Daphne agrees that it will. But her feet are throbbing. She would like everyone to go.

Though her friends delay to help her tidy up, the Bullivants know this is only surface tidying; later, Sunny Bank will require a thorough going over. 'Tell you what, old girl,' says the Major when at last they are alone. 'You and I deserve a couple of stiff ones. Put your feet up. I'll go and fix 'em.'

Thus, dusters, vacuum cleaner and garden broom win a temporary respite. Very soon, Sunny Bank is at peace; there is only the soothing hum of the refrigerator, the clock's ticking, and deep companionable snores.

Kate is engaged in some gentle weeding of the strip of earth fronting her cottage, when a car pulls up. 'Hi,' Zoë calls, jumping out and coming round. 'Good class last night?'

Kate straightens up slowly. Her headache has gone but she still feels delicate. 'Yes, it was excellent. What happened to you?'

'Oh, the practice manager's sick – I had to cover for her. I'm here to ask if you're free on Sunday.'

It occurs to Kate – as she replies that she has nothing fixed – to wonder why, since this is Thursday, Zoë has called here rather than at High House.

'Then come to us for the day. A business contact of Martin's is staying for the weekend . . . Hey, don't look like that.'

'Like what?'

'Wary. I'm not trying to fix you up; you know me better than that. It'd just take some of the strain out of the occasion if a few chums came round. I've asked the Browns as well . . .'

'It wasn't that. I was remembering I've still got to mark the fourth-year exam papers,' Kate says, not altogether truthfully. 'Don't worry. I'll make a huge effort and finish them off on Saturday. It'll be nice seeing Phil and Margaret again. Haven't seen Martin for ages, either.'

'Great. Come about eleven. Thought we'd go for a good long tramp, then have a late lunch about four.'

'Fancy a cup of tea?' Kate asks – unnecessarily, she knows; Zoë is always one for a natter.

In the kitchen, waiting for the kettle to boil, Zoë picking up and putting down the tea cosy, Kate senses her friend has more on her mind than Sunday's arrangements, which, come to think about it, she could just as well have discussed over the phone. At last, Zoë turns decisively from the dresser. Here it comes.

'Look, one can't very well send flowers to men. I could write, of course, but it's a bit sort of stiff. So when you see Will, tell him how sorry I am, will you? Well, not sorry exactly; I mean I'm relieved he's done it at last, aren't you? But tell him I'm thinking about him, and if there's anything I can do . . .'

The kettle boils, switches itself off. 'I haven't an idea what you're talking about,' Kate says.

Zoë stares, then looks round, draws up a chair, sits on it. 'Oh hell. I was absolutely certain you'd know, of all people. I even thought you might have helped him make the decision.'

'What decision? What?' demands Kate, parking herself on another chair.

'God, this is beginning to feel like the ultimate sin – you know, gossiping about the patients. Eilish Gallagher – one of the nurses – asked after Sylvie last night. She assumed I was in the know, having seen me at High House looking after her at various times. Rather as I assumed *you* . . .' She shrugs, then blurts, 'Oh, why don't I just spit it out? Sylvie's in the annexe at St Michael's – only temporarily. Apparently, things had become horrendous for Will, so they took her in as an emergency measure while he finds somewhere permanent. Which is what he is doing at the moment. Poor Will,' she mourns. 'Don't you just ache for him? It was so pathetic; you could see he was killing himself trying to avoid the inevitable. Must be harrowing, now she's gone – like bereavement but without the proper rites. Christ,' – she puts her face in her hands – '*now* what am I saying? Sorry. *Sorry.*'

'Don't be, please. I'm not fragile. I can stand to hear it talked about – death and stuff.' Kate gets up and busily makes the tea. Wishes she didn't have to. Wishes Zoë would go and leave her alone to digest this news. Then her hands fall still. 'Poor Sylvie,' she says. 'Poor little Sylvie.'

The 'little' puzzles Zoë. 'It's the best thing for her, Kate, really. I thought last time I was there he couldn't cope with her much longer.'

'I'm sure.' She is appalled for Will, and guilt-stricken at having suspected his motives towards her when all the time he was going through hell; but she is loath to discuss him. She pours the tea, brings two cups to the table. 'I had a prowler here last night,' she says, deliberately changing the subject. 'I went to the pub after class with that tall girl from The Park – Bel Rochford. Got back late. Didn't see anything, but I could feel someone there . . .'

'Kate, how hideous!'

'Then this morning I found the evidence – trampled peonies by the kitchen window.'

'Have you rung the police? Because you should. I bet it was the Peeping Tom. I was in the shop just now, and they were saying that Mrs Bullivant – you knew she was having a coffee morning? – well, she was busy getting ready for it, looked out into the garden and found it covered in litter. Loads of it, brought there deliberately. They reckon it must have been the Peeping Tom.'

'Oh, but she's a litter fanatic. Louise was sounding off about her at class last evening. Apparently, she's been turning her attention to Penfold Close; says the state of their front gardens will ruin our chances in the Best Kept Village Competition. What's the betting it was Louise and her friends getting their own back? They could've dumped the litter before they caught the early shift bus for the chicken factory. They'd be pretty safe at that hour of the morning.'

'Mm, maybe. I just wish they'd catch him.'

'Seems pretty harmless.'

'Even so . . .'

They drink their tea and plan Sunday's walk. 'Is he a walker, this colleague of Martin's?'

'Haven't a clue,' shrugs Zoë. 'He'd better be; I can't think what else to do with him in Aston Favell.' She gets up. 'About Will: he's bound to be in touch with you, so give him my love.'

'Of course.' Kate goes with her to the door – where she is surprised to be fiercely hugged.

' 'Bye,' says Zoë, relinquishing her. 'See you Sunday.'

'See you Sunday,' repeats Kate, bemused. When Zoë disappears, she wanders curiously to the hall mirror, where a wan face looks back at her. Mm, yes, she thinks, rather *poor little waif.* She resolves to cook herself a nourishing meal. She has slung too many dinners-for-one into the microwave recently; it is simply not good enough, only cooking properly for friends and the children. What is needed around here is a large helping of self-respect.

Kate has enjoyed her meal of red bean soup with crusty bread (she cheated a bit, the beans were tinned, but included lots of fresh vegetables and a handful of pasta), followed by lemon soufflé. As usual, she made too much for one. She considers the leftovers on the work top. It is a pity Will can't help her out. He could probably do with it . . .

Don't even think of it, she warns, starting to wash up.

In the middle of scouring a heavy orange-enamelled saucepan, her hand falls still. She has a very clear picture of Will – haggard-looking, overtaken by events, torn by doubts, empty. This is easy for her to imagine, aided as she is by memory.

CHAPTER TWELVE

Friday 26th June

Tina, dropping her children off at school on Friday morning, is waylaid by Melanie hopping out of her own car and beetling over to Tina's. 'Hi, been waiting for you.'

'Hi, Melanie. Right, hop it you kids,' she enjoins the squabbling pair in the back. 'Quick, or you'll be late. Tamara and Ross have already gone in.'

Sean makes a dash for it, but Blaize gives a yelp – 'Ow, he kicked me,' and proceeds to bawl.

'Christ, these kids,' Tina complains, getting out, running round to the nearside rear. 'Let's see. Mummy give it a rub.'

'Tell him *off*,' screams Blaize.

'I will, love, later.'

'Say he can't have a lolly or sweets.'

'All right . . .'

'*Say it.*'

'He can't have any, right? Now, out you get.' She hauls her daughter from the car, thrusts her forward.

'Nor watch *Home And Away*,' shrills Blaize, limping pitifully past the iron safety barrier.

'We'll see. Bye-bye, sweetheart.'

'Say he can't. He always ruins it, flicking the channels. It's not fair; it's my best programme.' She turns and glares at her mother – small, stocky, irate. 'Promise he can't,' she shrieks.

'Mummy'll see,' cries Tina, wringing her hands.

From across the playground, an adult appears. 'Blaize Fairbrother?'

Looking sulky, forgetting to limp, Blaize trudges into school.

Tina flops back against her car. 'God, I'm shattered.'

'I know, bloody kids; mine are the same. But, hey,' cries Melanie in a rallying tone, 'I had an interesting visit last evening from the woman who lives at the Manor. You know,' – as Tina looks blank – 'Carlton Manor. Ever so nice, ever so friendly, quite well dressed. She was really taken with our improvements; raved about the conservatory, said the pool made her jealous – that's one in the eye for Mrs Nose, I thought, with her boring local history club and her interfering Heritage Whatsit. This woman has *class*, know what I mean? Anyway, she's having a do at her place tomorrow: apparently you bring something – jar of honey, bottle of plonk – and you buy something. Sounds daft, but it's in aid of the Conservatives. Said she hoped we'd come. Well, I can't promise for my husband, I said; he's a bit tied up at the moment; but would it be all right if I brought my friend? Delighted to see her, she said. So what d'you think, Tina? You could bring your two over to our place and plonk 'em in front of the telly with mine. Mike'll keep an eye on 'em.'

'Great,' says Tina, 'if Mike doesn't mind.'

'Oh, he won't mind; specially if it lets him off the shopping. He wouldn't fancy a do like this, anyway, not at that time on a Saturday. It'd be good having a gawp inside her house. Looks fantastic from the road – that great big window all leaded lights, those velvety lawns . . .'

'Yeah, it does,' Tina agrees, then puts her finger on the vital spot. 'But what do you think we should wear?'

Melanie, who hasn't yet considered this aspect, frowns.

'Tell you what,' says Tina, 'come home with me and

we'll look at the mags; we can get an idea, then go into town. 'Cos honestly, Melanie, I just know I haven't a *thing*.'

'Mm, me neither. Yeah, t'rrific.'

In the midst of squalor, full length on the sofa, clad in nothing but knickers and an old shirt of her husband's, Bel is sprawled with a gripping novel. She was up commendably early this morning; gave David a loving and nourishing send-off, Jamie a playful bathtime and breakfast. Then, as Jamie slumbered, she came to a decision: to hell with dirty crocks, filthy clothes, baby gunge, newspapers strewn about, and general coating of dust; if you can't be a slob in your own house, where can you? Anyway, there have to be some perks in being stuck at home.

But now, peace in The Park is suddenly ruptured by racey engine noise. Tyres squeal, car doors slam; Bel frowns and looks up. Screams of laughter prompt her to roll on to her feet and pad over to the window. Two cars are outside: a yellow sporty job, and Tina's white one.

Tina and another woman are killing themselves on the pavement, doubled over, staggering sideways like drunks. At last, straightening up, they come tottering and laughing up the shared drive. This must be the glamorous Melanie of the desirable and lavishly converted farmhouse in Carlton of whom Bel has heard so much. She takes a backward step. Don't say Tina is bringing her here! Tina is always saying Bel ought to meet Melanie, to visit her gorgeous farmhouse or accompany them to their gym in town. ('And another thing, Belinda,' warns her mother in her inner ear; 'with these open plan arrangements you've got no nice little sitting room to take an unexpected visitor when the rest of the house is a bit of a tip.') Not that her mother's house ever *is* a bit of a tip, but Bel suddenly gets the point. If the doorbell goes now or in the next half hour, she'll pretend to be out. She simply won't answer. And if Jamie makes a sound she'll smother his mouth with a kiss.

It is rather a puzzle to know whether to start on the house or her person, both areas so cry out for attention. In the end, miserably, stiffly, fearing to drop something and cause betraying resonance, she creeps round the dining area gathering used mugs, bowls, plates, cutlery.

Kate slept soundly, woke early; went downstairs to make tea and took a cup back to bed, revelling in a sensation of having deeply relaxed. When did she last feel this rested? So long ago it was hard to recall. She felt lighter, as if during the night some encumbering garment were shrugged away. And an amazing aspect of the night before struck her: that she went up to bed unobserved; there were no hidden eyes round the stairwell – or if there were, they were discouraged observers, shrivelled, retreating, vanquished by Kate Woolard going calmly to bed engrossed in her thoughts – this miracle achieved by her identifying totally with Will's bereavement, forgetting her own.

Now, Kate is listening to the woes of Eve, a sixth-former who is sure she has failed A level French. Never her favourite pupil – blonde and babyish, with heavy moist lips and eyes, given to coyly putting her head on one side and peeping out sideways, today Kate is feeling sympathy for her. She goes over the examination paper carefully, trying to gauge whether Eve's fears are well-founded; eventually decides that perhaps they may be and gently suggests other options and courses. As Eve's face clears, as she confides her thoughts on her future and her struggles with her parents who, she feels, have always entertained exaggerated ambitions for her, Kate watches the puppyish face with the protruding eyes and is put in mind of Sylvie. When a bell announces the end of break, Eve goes off looking cheerful. Sylvie, she finds, stays with her. She reaches for her bag, and wonders how Will is progressing in his search for a refuge. She hopes he will find somewhere sympathetic and caring. Walking to the staffroom for a belated coffee (for she now has a free period), she thinks of the hours she has spent with Sylvie over the past year watching her fall backwards through time. What stage has she reached now – age three, age two? Whatever happens in the future between her and Will, Kate knows she will retain a concern for Sylvie. Allow a couple of weeks for her to settle, she decides, then she will go and visit – perhaps taking Zoë along to save any awkwardness. For it is important, she suddenly sees, not to let other people's scruples hinder you from doing what you ought to do.

Will is up in Sylvie's room. An hour ago he arrived home from a visit to the second of the three institutions the doctor recommended as suitable for patients with his wife's condition; she can stay in the local NHS home only as an emergency measure, so he must quickly find somewhere permanent. The place he saw yesterday was not too bad, though he was unable to picture Sylvie in it or himself visiting. This morning, at Westbrook Court, he couldn't get out of the place fast enough. Its odour – hard to define and no doubt innocuous – reminded him of prep school, made him feel suddenly semi-naked and exposed. He imagined Sylvie breathing it in and becoming desolate, aching as he had once ached. This olfactory message was so intense that it seemed to stun his other senses, and he failed to observe the place properly, to notice whether the residents appeared happily occupied, to hear what the matron said and to take her measure; just went through the motions as swiftly as possible knowing he could not bear it if Sylvie were installed there.

Ludicrous to write a place off because of its smell, he thinks now, pulling clothes from the rails of Sylvie's wardrobe. But what the hell else is he to go on? In the absence of obvious negative pointers, like inmates strapped into chairs or locked in rooms or snoring heavily in the middle of the day, or filth lying about or surly looking staff, what else but gut instinct? Though he wonders uneasily whether he is not searching for a place in which *he* feels comfortable, rather than necessarily Sylvie. Strangely, people appear to expect him to use this criteria. As the doctor said, 'Choose a place where *you* feel relaxed. After all, you've been married long enough; you're sure to have the same tastes.' But Will is not sure about this. He is not sure that he knows much at all about the new Sylvie. Perhaps the importance people attach to *his* impression of a place arises from a recognition that he will be the one paying the fees, he will be the one making any complaints.

This afternoon he must check out the third institution suggested by the doctor – Beresford House. If only he had been able to find someone to accompany him on these expeditions. Alan (Sylvie's brother) phones every week making sympathetic noises, but is always too tied up with business or family matters to pay a visit (possibly because Libby, his wife, has always been wary of Sylvie). One of Will's difficulties is that Sylvie never made close friends of women; he has searched his memory and failed to recall a single one. Which, of course, left *his* friends: somehow, though, Will shied from the idea of taking along a male chum; two men on the case, he suspects, would simply double the embarrassment. Joan, bless her, has promised to check out his final choice, but he is reluctant to take advantage of her good nature; he should not forget that though he and she have become friends, Sylvie is part of Joan's case load; that as well as her patients, Joan has a family to think of and cannot be expected to spend hours of free time helping him with the donkey work. There is no getting away from it: Kate is the obvious person. But he has decided most emphatically against asking her; in fact, he has been dreading Kate getting to hear of what is happening about Sylvie: given her concerned and generous nature he knows she would offer assistance, and this he would have to refuse. For come what may, he will not involve Kate – it would smack of asking the new love to help dispose of the old: maybe that is overstating it, but a superstitious dread tells him that doing anything of the kind would inhibit any possible future together. For this reason, he has also ruled out Zoë – who is Kate's friend – who only sat in with Sylvie on Thursdays as a favour to Kate. If he involves Zoë, Kate will certainly get to hear of it, and then be puzzled and hurt not to have been preferred. No, there is nothing for it: this is a decision he must make alone.

On the stripped bed rests an open suitcase. Into this Will puts any clothes he comes across which might still fit Sylvie (whose shape has thickened considerably this past year). Most clothes he stuffs into gaping plastic bin-bags propped against the wall. Sylvie will never come back to High House in any shape or form; he has a fierce desire to remove all the tailored skirts and flouncy dresses, the gauzy tops and sequinned jackets, the heaps of underwear and rows of shoes, which seem to bear witness to the contrary. He works without pause. He has been clearing up (apart for a few hours spent sleeping and the visits to institutions) from the moment he arrived back on Tuesday to an empty house, clearing up and throwing out, making countless trips to the refuse tip, filling the garden shed with sacks of items destined for Oxfam. Curtains and loose-covers have gone to the cleaners. He has hired an industrial cleaner and applied it to several of the soiled carpets. Soon it will be time to visit Beresford House. Until then, he will carry on with the job of emptying the wardrobe and chest of drawers; folding and packing Sylvie's clothes. Remnants of Sylvie.

In the staff room, Gareth Dicey is sitting at a table marking examination papers. If Kate had known he would be here, she would not have come in. Having done so, she discovers the tenderness with which she is viewing the world today extends even to Gareth; even to his absent daughters after whom she enquires solicitously. Perhaps too solicitously, for Gareth is not only gratified but visibly encouraged.

'Gareth,' she says, breaking in before he can suggest a cinema trip or a concert, and lightly touching his arm, 'Gareth, as I hinted the other day, I am sort of . . . involved. But I'd like you to know if you ever find a need for some quiet place to take the girls, I'd be happy to loan you my cottage for an afternoon – given due warning, of course. I don't know if this helps . . .'

He colours slightly, but when he speaks, sounds grateful. 'Thanks, Kate, that could be, er . . . Thing is, it can feel a bit rootless tramping around, sitting about in cafés. It's OK mostly, just when something crops up. I wouldn't make a habit of it, but it would be nice to know if a problem arose . . .'

'Sure. There you are then. Coffee?'

She makes two mugfuls, but carries hers to a separate table where she lays out her marking. Sits and blinks at it unseeingly. So what? she thinks, I wasn't lying, I *am* involved. It is quite clear that she is in love with Will McLeod (and this is perfectly all right – no betrayal of Chris, no threat to Sylvie, no nuisance – if that is what knowledge of her love would be – to Will). She is glad to admit this to herself at last, to allow it as part of the person she has become. The point is, love does not require reciprocity to be acknowledged as fact. So long as she keeps it to herself until – or if ever – it becomes appropriate to do otherwise, she will even exult in it when the mood takes her. Good.

That being settled, she takes up her pen.

This house is too big, thinks Will, collecting up all the photographs from the bedroom mantelpiece, shoving them savagely into a drawer. Too darn big. He will sell it; get a nice cosy little place; not gaunt and tall, but squat and homey, cheerful and attractive. Like Kate's place, he thinks.

These blasted photographs are all over the place. This is his fault; he put them out. What the hell was he trying to do? — attempting to jolt her memory of who she was; or inflicting punishment, confronting her with what she *had* been?

He closes the drawer on the photographs, goes out of the room. Downstairs in the kitchen, pours himself a beer; takes it into the sitting room and flops into his old leather chair. Of the three possible homes for Sylvie, Beresford House, where he visited this afternoon, struck him as most promising. He rang Joan and told her this, and she has agreed to check it out with him tomorrow before he makes a final decision. It will be a relief now to get everything settled, though he doubts whether he will ever stop wondering whether he has done the right thing. The trouble is, however noble your motives, whichever course you finally take, in this sort of business there seems no escape from feeling guilty. Not to mention sick of the subject. And tired out. Damn near exhausted.

CHAPTER THIRTEEN

Saturday 27th June

Saturday morning at ten to eleven. A small car turns abruptly right on Vicarage Hill, swoops past the laurels and the sentinel spruce and monkey puzzle trees, swings in an arc hugging the edge of the turning circle, pulls up exactly in line with the columned entrance to The Old Vicarage. For once, Fenella is not in evidence. Only Molly and Henry wait under the portico.

'No change of heart, then,' observes Davinia James, the driver, to her sister and passenger, Esmé (meaning no change of heart on the part of Fenella).

'Too late now, anyway,' murmurs Esmé, leaping out. 'Come along,' she bawls, striding over the gravel towards Molly.

But Molly is worried. 'Can't shake Fenella,' she reports. 'She's going to be late. Where's Reggie Plum?'

'You're coming with us, Molly.'

Molly looks at the boxy little vehicle. 'Fenella won't think much of that.'

'Fenella's not coming.'

'Not coming? Don't they want her?'

'She's refused to do it.' She grabs Molly's arm. 'Now do come along, or Davinia will get cross.'

But it is Sarah, the sisters' rough little cairn terrier, who suddenly gets cross. As Molly goes down the steps, the cairn hurls itself at the passenger window. Molly bends down and protectively hauls Henry to her bosom. 'We can't travel in there. Two terriers? – they'd eat each other.'

'Nonsense. Sarah's just showing off. I'll nurse her in the front, you and Henry climb into the back. And when we get there, Sarah will stay in the car on guard. As you always do, don't you, darling?' she cries to the cairn (now restrained by Davinia). She gives Molly's rump a final shove, slams the rear car door, heaves into the passenger seat and relieves her sister of the furious Sarah.

The car takes off like a rocket, its passengers giving forth simultaneously at full blast − Sarah frenziedly yapping, Henry defensively barking, Molly bawling 'But I thought Fenella was going to open the bally thing, she always does; I don't know what's got into everybody.' Davinia screaming 'Shut up, you dogs, or how can I drive? Give her a clout, Esmé.' Esmé yelling 'Quiet, you little brute. Fenella declined to do it this year, Molly. I'm doing my best, Davinia. Bad dog, be *quiet*.' When they arrive in Carlton and park as directed in a field adjacent to the Manor, they lurch from the car (all except Sarah) like refugees from a battering storm. Molly is still unable to make out why Fenella is not to perform her annual duty. When Cynthia Plum has welcomed them, when they have deposited their gifts − after much delving into pockets and handbags − on the enormous Bring and Buy table, Esmé draws Molly aside to explain matters.

'You mean she's asked these people to come and live with us?' eventually shrieks Molly. 'You can't mean it. Then she can't be right in the head, I've suspected this for some time.' The clap of doom shrills so surely in her voice that it convinces Henry and prompts him to pee on the Turkey carpet. Esmé notices this − though Molly in her perturbation fails to − and discreetly leads her friend and the nervous Sealyham away from the tell-tale evidence. If the carpet is still wet by the time Cynthia alights on it, with luck she will assume someone spilt their coffee.

*　　*　　*

'Did you see that?' says Tina through her teeth to Melanie. 'That dirty little dog wet on the carpet. Look at them: scurrying off pretending not to know about it. Disgusting, I call it.'

'They look like two bag ladies,' says Melanie. 'I'm surprised they were let in.' She turns and grimaces in the direction of the wife of the Member of Parliament. '*She*'s a good dresser. I like her jacket.'

'Mm, yeah. But I don't think it's cut quite as well as yours, Melanie.'

'Oh, don't you think so? You look fantastic in that suit, Tina. I reckon we hit just the right note.'

'Yeah. I thought when Mrs Plum clocked us, she looked, you know, *approving*. She's smart too – a bit heavy-handed with the pan-stick, mind. You are lucky having such nice neighbours. There's no-one like that in Aston Favell. There's a lot of snobby old frumps, but you hardly ever clap eyes on real class.'

'Oh, but there's a fair bit of rubbish in Carlton, too.'

'This house is fabulous, Melanie. This sort of place is really me. Shall we go through there? Oh wow, look at that mirror – and the curtains. It's like a picture in *Homes and Gardens*.'

At twelve o'clock in the surgery car park, Will is sitting in the passenger seat of Joan's car. Earlier this morning Will left his own car here and Joan drove them to Beresford House. Joan insisted on driving. Maybe she didn't trust him, he said; thought he'd get upset and cause an accident. Not at all, she countered; he could drive next time, when they go to see how Sylvie is settling in. He feels immensely grateful to her for saying that; it means she is not planning to absolutely abandon them. They have just arrived back, Joan having approved his choice. But now he is attacked by doubt: on his first visit he was not aware of so many dopey-looking dribbly patients strapped into chairs.

'Look at it this way, Will. How would you feel if they threw Sylvie out when she gets bad like that? Which she will, you know, soon enough. You do know that, love? Dr Jeffreys explained how it's progressive . . . how she's been going downhill fast lately?'

'Of course,' he says, shifting his legs. He is no fool. It has been explained to him often enough, so of course he knows. Hasn't he been packing away her things, chucking them out? Would he do that if he didn't *know*? (On the shelf under the dashboard is a child's flute. A recorder. Paul used to play just such an instrument in his primary school orchestra, he can recall the thin uncertain sound it made . . .) But does he *completely*, *utterly*, know? Is not a small part of his mind still unconvinced? All that clearing up he has so frantically engaged in: maybe he was just desperately trying to convince himself that the life of Sylvie – his wife, Paul's mother – is to all intents and purposes over despite the complicated arrangements being made for the care of her breathing body. Really, he does know. But because it is such an outrageous piece of knowledge, his mind tends to baulk at it. This explains why last night, after a day spent clearing her wardrobe and visiting potential homes, he woke from a deep sleep with the thought pounding his brain that all this was madness; that he must go at once and collect Sylvie; bring her home. Snap out of it, he would command her; enough of this playing the fool. He would rescue her the way he did all those years ago when an affair she'd started with her tennis coach got out of hand. ('Will, it's me,' she sobbed on the phone in the middle of the night. 'Please come quickly. I didn't mean it, I'll never do it again, I'll give you anything if you'll only come and get me out of this *now*.')

'Darn it – Shelley left her recorder,' says Joan, following the direction of his frowning stare. 'That girl'll be the death of me – forgets her homework, forgets her sandwiches. I'd better pop down to music school, quick.'

He blinks – 'Oh – yes,' and straightens in his seat. 'You're right, Joan,' he concedes, '– about Beresford

House. Obviously, I'd be upset if they didn't want to keep Sylvie until, you know . . . the end.'

'That's right, love.'

'You thought it was OK, so we'll go for it.'

'Right. I'll tell the doctor. He'll arrange the transfer. You'd better phone Beresford, too, and let them know you've decided.' She reaches out, puts her hand over his. 'We'll give her a couple of days to settle in then we'll go and see her. How's that?'

'That'd be fine. Thanks, Joan.'

She withdraws her hand, turns on the engine. 'Now get out of my car, man. Got to go save my daughter's bacon.'

He unwinds his long legs onto the tarmac. Then stoops and peers into the car. 'Shall I give you a ring later, let you know how I get on?' – he asks this anxiously, as if she is his lifeline and he daren't quite break hold.

'All right,' she calls, slamming into reverse gear. 'See you, Will.'

He shuts the passenger door, and immediately the car swoops round, backwards. He watches it spring forward and disappear, then walks briskly to his own car.

'I really think, Fenella,' (all Molly's shakeable bits are shaking violently – head, jowls, the dewlaps under her eyes, her slack squat body) 'I really do believe you're no longer quite the ticket.'

Amazing to see Molly, normally so reticent and reluctant to engage in exchange of any kind, throbbing with excitement, determinedly button-holing her. Fenella backs into the dresser. Her eyes search out Henry (a sharp kick and its invariable consequence would soon end this disagreeable encounter).

But Henry has planted his four feet firmly to the rear of his mistress. Head bowed, ears cocked, tail at half mast, he listens carefully for sounds of encouragement. 'Bickies' would do, better still 'din-dins', but optimist though he is, Henry knows he is a little previous with this second idea; what he does hear, and does not at all care for, is the note of angry anxiety in his benefactress's tone, a tone which customarily resonates with the unchanging rightness of the world and their companionship, with comfort and strokes and a regularly filled belly.

Fenella throws up her chin. 'It is you who are not quite the ticket, I fear. I shall invite whomsoever I choose into my home. *My home, Molly*,' she emphasizes dreadfully. 'Your position here is what used to be termed "grace and favour".'

Tears of fury start in Molly's eyes. She quivers more violently than ever. 'How dare you? My dear brother left me amply provided for – no thanks to you, I daresay. When Jock died I thought it would be churlish to leave. However, if you do carry out this mad scheme I shall go forthwith. For all I care, you can stuff The Old Vicarage to the gills. I shall leave you to get on with it.'

Spent, half blind, she turns and wobbles away. Henry sprints to keep up on the side of her which is not exposed to Fenella's feet. In the hall, Molly fishes for a handkerchief in her cardigan pocket and loudly trumpets into it, then stares through the open doorway, wondering whether she has the strength for a spot of weeding. After the Bring and Buy this morning, Davinia and Esmé drove her to Rose Cottage for a brisk lunch. Then the sisters gathered flowers from their garden and announced they must drive to the church, it being their turn to dress the altar. They pressed Molly to accompany them, but she declined. Church interiors give her the willies, reminding her as they do of weddings and funerals: she is surprised the James sisters, as spinsters, don't feel this too – oh, the humiliations of the eternal bridesmaid! – but perhaps, because there are two of them, the shame is halved; oh, and the turgid agony of those chokey farewells – to Mama and Pa, to Eric shot down in the war, more recently to dear old Jock. 'No, I won't, if you don't mind,' she told them. 'Trouble with churches, you can't take your dog. We don't think much of places like that, do we, Henry?' So they dropped her off on their way to St Peter's, and Molly hurried indoors to have it out with Fenella. She found her in the kitchen. Skulking, Molly thought.

And much good it did her, she reflects now, with a sigh. It's no good, she's whacked. 'Come on, old boy, let's go upstairs; Mistress needs a bit of a nap. You never know, there might be a film on the box.'

It is Fenella who marches into the garden. With a snort, sweeps out through the kitchen doorway, across the yard, round by the side of the house to stalk up and down the garden paths. Eventually flops down on a slatted wooden garden seat and discovers she is quite shaken.

Why is this? Not that silly Molly, surely?

No, not silly Molly, but the naughty Reverend Bob who has failed to renew contact with her. She has been so busy with her petition and turning out the rooms that it slipped her notice, but, good heavens, nearly a week has elapsed. Perhaps he will telephone this evening. Or tomorrow. Foolish girl, what is she thinking of? – it is Sunday tomorrow, the busiest day of the week for a clergyman. And this evening he will no doubt devote to composing his sermon.

Monday will be the day. Definitely Monday. Not very long to wait. Just till Monday.

CHAPTER FOURTEEN

Sunday 28th June

Sunday – and (Kate lifts her head from the pillow) if her ears report correctly, it is damn well raining. She jumps out of bed, pulls back the curtains – yes, sheets of water falling straight from the sky, hitting the road; Vicarage Hill is a running river. When the phone rings, she turns away from the window and sits on the edge of the bed to answer it.

'Rain,' Zoë yells vengefully down the line. 'Can you believe it?'

'I know,' mourns Kate. 'I was about to ring you. Is it still on?'

'Of course it's still on; don't you dare let me down. I just feel like Fate's socked me one. What am I going to do, Kate?'

'Have you checked the weather forecast?'

'No, have you?' Zoë replies hopefully. 'Our paper hasn't come.'

'Hang on; mine probably has.' Yawning, she puts down the receiver and runs downstairs. 'Rain at first, brighter later,' she reports into the hall telephone. 'So if I were you, I'd get lunch for one o'clock, then with luck we can stroll out later.'

'Yeah, I suppose so.'

'You sound frazzled. What's up? Guest heavy going?'

'Wait and see,' Zoë says grimly; then hurries to correct any off-putting impression which may – God forbid – induce Kate to ring back in half an hour inventing a headache. 'Oh, he's not bad, really. No, it's just that everywhere's so gloomy – you know how dismal these old houses can be when the light's bad. And this rain means Tommo will hang about all day making his usual din. I'd banked on having all the doors open, and maybe sitting in the garden.'

'Brighter later,' Kate reminds her firmly.

'Well, get here early.'

'I'll do what I can. Cheer up.'

Will is driving. Eilish sits in the back with Sylvie. Sylvie, looking flushed, has fallen asleep. Eilish is professionally calm, professionally cheerful. Will's teeth are clamped together so hard his jaw aches. This rain doesn't help, he thinks: water lashing the windscreen, wipers going like enraged insects; it all contributes to a churning stomach. 'Should she be sleeping like that at this time in the morning?'

Eilish leans forward. 'Och, sure, she's just exhausted by all her wickedness.' (She must be joking, thinks Will, darting a look at her in the driving mirror.) 'She led them a fine old dance,' Eilish continues placidly. 'Matron was glad to be shot of her. It was a good job you didn't dither any longer.'

'Well, I hope they aren't going to take that sort of attitude at Beresford House.'

'No, no; and why should they? The staff at Beresford are specially trained. St Michael's annexe – well, it's a bit of a dumping ground, really. She was only there as a respite case.' (Will frowns. It is rather early in the morning, but surely, wasn't *he* the respite case?) 'It's all credit to you; Matron said she can't think how you stood it so long. "The things she gets up to – he must have the patience of a saint," were her very words.'

'It wasn't so difficult,' he objects, as if they have a trying child under discussion, rather than his wife. And he almost believes it. He can remember the facts – the tantrums, the escapades, the deliberate messes – but his reactions to these – his despair, his torn nerves

214

– have become slightly unreal. Basically, all he feels is tired.

Sylvie wakes as they draw up before Beresford House. At least, she will walk inside, not be carried in like some drugged prisoner which would have made a very bad memory to carry away. She lurches a bit. Eilish hangs on to her. A nurse from Beresford comes running out to help (also professionally cheerful). How do you know 'professionally'? Will rebukes himself, bringing up the rear with two large suitcases; maybe this is how they normally are – two nice, competent, optimistic women. Just because *you're* grumpy, just because you seem to have two left feet; just because you feel guilty . . . Yes, in spite of everything, he still feels guilty.

Sylvie is led away. He is relieved of the suitcases, shown her bedroom. He is asked to read and sign forms and given booklets. Then, 'Coffee, Mr McLeod?' asks Sister, and he is taken into a large room with wall-to-wall glazing at the far end. 'The garden room,' explains Sister. 'Too bad the weather's so poor today. But Sylvie doesn't mind. Sylvie has some nice crayons. She's quite artistic, I understand?'

Will looks towards a table where his wife is sitting with a nurse and a couple of inmates, furiously applying colour to a large sheet of paper and looking mightily pleased with herself. 'Oh yes,' he agrees awkwardly. 'She does, did, produce some pretty competent water-colours.'

'There now, Nurse; we must get the paint pots out later.'

Will gulps his coffee, says 'Yes' and 'Indeed' several times and prods himself to smile. As soon as he decently can, he stands up: 'I think we'd better get back.' He is relieved to see Eilish promptly putting down her cup.

He goes over to Sylvie. 'Goodbye, darling,' he says, bending to kiss her cheek, aware of several pairs of eyes watching.

Sylvie's eyes remain on her crayonning. 'Red,' she says with satisfaction. 'Lots of *red*.'

Molly stands at the window in the large spare bedroom, staring at the slanting rain, the moving smoke-coloured sky. It may brighten up soon, she thinks; those speeding clouds are a hopeful sign. Meanwhile, the garden is saturated; long rose stems trail over the ground unable to bear the weight of their sodden blooms. It is very disheartening; almost as depressing as the state of the room behind her. What a shock she received when she came in here. What on earth has Fenella in mind? It appears she has somehow managed to trundle whole pieces of furniture down from the attic – old armchairs, a discarded folding table – and rearranged this room, formerly the best guest room, into a semblance of a bed-sit. And how is it that she, Molly, heard nothing of this activity? Her deafness must be more profound than she supposed.

In a way, this serves her right. Years ago she began sheltering behind her impoverished hearing as a means of avoiding the fuss and bother, the awkward embarrassments, that inevitably befall those who must live in a relative's house. It allowed her to go pretty much her own way. It meant she could wander off in the middle of one of those ghastly political weekends and do some gardening, and people would merely comment, 'Old Molly's had enough, I see.' It was a useful defence against Fenella's exhibitionism (as Molly has always regarded her sister-in-law's penetrating delivery and extravagant mannerisms); she could pretend not to notice, with practice she learned *not* to notice, since apparent deafness excused her from any reaction. So now, if things have been going on behind her back which she would have been well advised to keep an eye on, she has only herself to blame.

'Lord knows what's going to become of us, old boy,' she murmurs. (At which Henry politely wags his tail – twice only, once to the right and once to the left, for like his mistress he disdains inordinate show.) Perhaps she can buy a little cottage; Davinia and Esmé seem contented enough. Then she spies a splodge of yellow in the swirling grey, like broken egg in the sky, and feels a twinge of optimism, suspects that the most likely outcome is the satisfactory one: Fenella will come to her senses and things will potter on as usual. Reasonably cheered, she goes to the door. 'Watch out, come quietly,' she hisses to her four-legged companion as she cautiously steps into the corridor (for Fenella is probably across the way, holed up in her bedroom). It is an instruction Henry is strongly minded to observe.

The rain is driving Fenella to distraction, beating, falling, making the greenery sinister; inflicting too much green – the sort of insatiably hollow green that sucks in and destroys light; the sort of green that makes you heart-sick to look at it. Standing at her bedroom window overlooking the garden, she is filled with an intuition that the purpose has been snuffed out of her life. It was only a puny purpose, still in its infancy, barely able to raise its head; but someone, she is sure, has stopped its breath. That, or from deliberate neglect it has given up the ghost and died. She shivers. Then a sudden slant of light in the sky and diminution of the rainfall incline her to concede that her suspicion may not necessarily be correct. It is still possible that her present purpose will not turn into another of those disappointments which have blighted her life since Jock's death. There may yet be hope that the Reverend Bob will telephone or send her a note. She did adjure herself to wait in patience until Monday. And this is only Sunday, hateful wet Sunday. A little longer, then. Wait, wait.

'No foraging for you today, my dear,' says the Major, staring out at the rain.

'Nonsense. The man on the radio said it would dry up later.'

'But Daphers, old girl, everything will be sopping wet. You can't go rooting under dripping hedges for sodden rubbish. Leave it for another day.'

'What you don't seem to grasp is that they spring it on you, these Best Kept Village judges. They don't announce their arrival; there's no "get set, on your marks and tidy up". The whole point is to keep people on their toes, make them constantly litter-conscious. And I don't mind telling you that after our nasty little surprise last Thursday morning I'm less than sanguine. There's evil about, deliberate wickedness. Some people are out to sabotage Aston Favell. Vigilance is the name of the game, Major.'

'Well, you're a better man than I, Daphers. Shouldn't fancy it, myself. Though I may take the umbrella and wander down to The Crown in a jiffy.'

'I might have known you wouldn't consider it too inclement for a trip to the boozer,' she snorts, hurrying to the phone to rally the troops.

'Now, now, I pull my weight . . .' he calls, then sinks into a chair and shakes open the Sunday paper.

To her annoyance, Mrs Bullivant's supporters incline towards the Major's opinion. Mrs Haycroft simply refuses, Mrs Potton cites her rheumatism and Mrs Critch her arthritic fingers; all think it prudent to postpone the weekly clear-up until a drier day. Suspecting them of planning this rebellion in advance, Mrs Bullivant declares that she will jolly well manage without them; she will cover the whole village single-handed, even if it takes her till dusk. This has no effect; even best chum, Edna Critch, remains obdurate.

In a temper, Daphne stalks into the kitchen to baste the joint.

Kate, putting on storm coat and wellingtons, stuffing walking shoes (just in case) and pumps into a carrier bag, finds she is somewhat reluctant to set off. Now why is this? It takes her only a few seconds to work out the reason: in her secret heart she is hoping for a call from Will; she would hate to be out if by any chance, having settled things for Sylvie, he wishes to contact her. Well! – she is jolly glad to have caught herself out in this piece of self-indulgence, because now she can jolly well smother it. There she goes again, pushing her own wants forward; she would do better to consider whether, when Chris died, she had any spare thoughts, any spare emotion, for anyone else. Honestly, what a fool. She walks at a punishing rate down Vicarage Hill and across The Green, turns left down Main Street and soon into Lovatt's Lane. Making her face cheery, she enters the driveway of the cottage where Zoë and Martin Hunter live.

As the morning drags towards midday, Zoë's earlier panic is well understood by Kate. This friend (or business associate) of Martin's is the type who is excessively fond of his own voice; endlessly and pedantically knowledgeable, he has seen or done anything you have, only very much better. Should you rise and go to the kitchen for a word with your hostess, or look into the rear sitting room to say hello to the teenager watching a video, he will of course follow in order to carry on talking. Kate, having attempted these stratagems, sinks with resignation into her chair and regards him with dulled eyes. Eventually considers testing her theory: that were she to walk into the downstairs lavatory, he would continue talking at her through the locked door, even through the sound of water flushing.

When Martin returns to the room with some papers, Kate seizes her chance; murmuring 'Excuse me,' she nips past him, closing the door behind her. 'Phew,' she says to Zoë, leaning back against the fridge. 'How long's he staying?'

Zoë pulls a face. 'Martin brought him home on Friday night and takes him back to the office tomorrow morning. They talked business most of yesterday. They're planning another session tonight.'

'That lets you out, then. I should go to bed with a good book. Where the hell are the Browns? We could do with some back-up to spread the load.'

Almost as she speaks, a car draws up. Gladly, they go to welcome Maggie and Phil Brown from Carlton-le-Walls.

During lunch the sun comes out. This, and the prospect of getting out of the house, makes the guest seem less dreadful. It is decided that, because the fields will be squelching and the paths through the wood turned to mud, they had better stick to the lanes. This is Kate's least favourite form of walking – ears constantly straining for cars driven by boy-racers, taking your life into your hands round blind bends, trudging on ankle-busting tarmac. Still, anything is better than an afternoon cooped up in the gloomy parlour with its tiny windows (sweetly old-fashioned when the sun streams in, prison-like on dull days), listening to the Hunters' weekend guest.

'We'll clear up later,' Zoë says. 'Let's get out while the going's good.'

When they are ready, Martin opens the front door – then steps back smartly. 'I say, there's a woman out there scratting about in our hedge.'

Zoë pushes past and peers out; comes in and firmly shuts the door. 'We'll go out the back way,' she declares. 'I couldn't stand it; it's Mrs Bullivant.'

'Battering Bullivant of the litter patrol?' grins Kate. 'Why here? Been dropping your fag-ends, Zoë?'

'It'd be just my luck if she's found something really disgusting.' Zoë leads them through the house to the garden, where the bemused guests, following the lead of the Aston Favellites, steal like house-breakers to the back gate.

They begin by walking almost the length of Main Street. As they approach High House, Kate notices the curtains are drawn over an upstairs window on the gable end. This is Will's small room, she remembers; he must be having a nap. Or else he went dashing out in a rush early this morning on some mission connected with Sylvie and forgot to open them. Passing the yard, his parked car confirms his presence within; perhaps, you never know, he will phone her this evening. 'Seen anything of Will?' asks Zoë, falling into step beside her. Kate confesses she has not, and to prevent any follow-up, turns with an expression of interest to hear what Martin's guest is saying. She decides not to linger at Zoë's beyond six o'clock this evening, when, by any standard of friendship, she will have done her duty.

Will opens his eyes on sunny light showing in the curtain crack. It has finally stopped raining, he concludes. He is lying on his back in socks, trousers and loosened shirt, more or less fully clothed. This fact seems somehow surprising, though it would be positively amazing to discover himself in pyjamas or in any way differently clothed, for he paused merely to kick off his shoes and chuck jacket and tie on a chair before collapsing on the bed when he arrived home after disposing of Sylvie. How many hours ago? Raising his wrist, he squints at his watch – and jerks upright in disbelief. Good lord, it is twenty to five. And he has eaten nothing but an indigestible slice of toast first thing this morning and had nothing to drink since that abominable cup of coffee at Beresford House. He is ravenous.

But downstairs, it is hard to find anything palatable to eat. In the end, he settles for soup, cheese, hunks of bread, and a dollop of Zoë's chutney. Halfway through the soup, he jumps up and opens a bottle of beer. Then continues stolidly eating and drinking. At last, sated, leaving the evidence of his meal where it stands on the table, he opens a second bottle of beer, collects the newspaper from the front door mat, and retires into the sitting room.

After a time, the newsprint starts jigging in front of his eyes. He leans forward and turns on the TV.

221

Finds – oh God – a churchful of people singing madly, mouthing the words with ridiculous emphasis (as if God is deaf and needs to lip read), all wearing the facial expression of the school sneak. Ghastly, he thinks, meaning any second to turn it off or switch channels. But before he can do so, falls asleep.

Sun in the afternoon proves irresistible to both Molly and Fenella. Fortunately, the garden is sufficiently large to accommodate any number of sisters not wishing to encounter one another. Molly makes matters simple by sticking to the area of the fruit bushes, where she lifts the nets and shakes them free of water, then begins picking currants for jam making.

Fenella sails past a lavender bush, inhaling deeply; intoxicating steam fills her nostrils – delicious. Now the greenery fairly dances with light, sparkles, dazzles. Her spirits soar. It is as if her own sap is rising. Life, she exults, life! Pooh to patience (on or off a monument); life is for getting on with.

And so she will. Quickly, before second thoughts can undermine resolution, she darts over the gravel, bounds up the portico steps, runs through the hall to the telephone. Just a moment, though – where did she put the card with the number on? After a five minute hunt with her heart in her mouth, she retrieves it from a drawer of the kitchen sideboard. She puts on her spectacles, then stabs out the number.

Somewhere – in a vestry or vicarage hall, perhaps – a telephone rings and rings. No-one comes to answer it. Of course, the Reverend Bob will be getting ready for Evensong – in the church, whose name she forgets (did he mention it?) but where, he promised, she would receive a very warm welcome. *The name, the name* – if only she could bring it to mind. She repeats the name of every saint she can think of, even tries 'All Saints', but to no avail. One thing she does recall: the Reverend Bob referred to a poor parish. Yes, she is certain of this. A poor parish in Lavenbrook should not be too difficult to track down. Prior can drive her through the streets until they come across one; with luck there may be a notice board mentioning the Reverend Bob Somebody or other. Quickly, she puts through a call to 2 Pond Cottages.

'Hello,' says Mrs Prior, 'to whom am I speaking?' (a phrase she has acquired from the present caller).

'Your employer,' says Fenella. 'Put Prior on the line, if you please.'

'We're busy,' says Mrs Prior, 'with visitors – our Annie and her Jack from Mablethorpe.'

'Well, grieved though I am to interrupt your little party, I am afraid I need to go out. I require the services of my chauffeur *immediately.*'

Even 'immediately' uttered *basso profundo* with an athletic drop of the jaw on the final syllable, fails to shake Mrs Prior. 'I'm sorry, too, Lady Cunningham, 'cos Prior driving anywhere is out of the question. You see,' (and Fenella hears her gathering herself to administer the *coup de grâce*), 'Prior's had a skinful – what with it being a day of rest and a family celebration . . . 'Course, if you'd given notice of your requirements I daresay he'd've fitted you in. But there it is. Sorry he can't oblige.' With which the wretched woman puts the receiver down.

Botheration, cries Fenella, turning to the shining afternoon glowing at the far end of the hall in the open doorway – yes, twinkling and dancing as if deliberately enticing her to venture abroad. Life can play some pretty mean tricks.

CHAPTER FIFTEEN

Monday 29th June

On Monday morning, many lights are on in High House when Joan arrives and rings the doorbell; shaded bulbs show beams at several windows, bashfully, as though embarrassed to reveal their measure to the light of lights, the almighty sun. Will opens the door with the startled expression of the newly awakened. Joan steps in, walks past.

'I came to ask how it went yesterday,' she says, reaching into the sitting room to flick off the light switch; she continues to the kitchen and comes to a halt in front of the debris from last night's meal. 'Apart from this,' she concedes, nodding at the table, 'seems you got everywhere clean and tidy.'

Will runs fingers through his hair. 'I can't keep awake,' he says worriedly. 'I went to bed as soon as I got back yesterday, came down and got something to eat, then fell asleep in front of the television; woke up feeling hellish, crawled back to bed and slept till you woke me. Do you think I've got sleeping sickness?'

'Reaction.' (*Reac-shon*, is the way she says it – up, down; it has the effect of declaring his desire for sleep predictable and reasonable.)

'Oh Joan,' he sighs, giving her a hug, 'thanks a million for coming round. Actually, it wasn't too bad yesterday. That is, Sylvie took to Beresford House without complaint, and they seemed pleased to have her – in spite of the reputation she acquired in St Michael's annexe.

The formalities were concluded with remarkable speed. Eilish wasn't too caustic . . .'

'Get away with you,' cries Joan in defence of her colleague, shoving him off. 'Right, then: how does tomorrow morning suit? I'm not on till half twelve. We could go and visit her.'

'Do you mean it? Oh, that'd be tremendous. Got time for a cuppa?'

'I have not,' declares Joan, making for the door. 'I should put some clothes on, if I were you. Seen anything of Kate?'

'Er, no?'

'I just wondered, Will,' says Joan, stepping outside, walking round her car. 'See you tomorrow. Be at the surgery at half nine.'

'Don't forget I'm driving.'

'Lord have mercy,' she mocks, unlocking the car door.

Brisk footsteps sound. 'Good morning, Nurse. Good morning, Mr McLeod.' Damn — it would have to be her, of course, the Bullivant woman, noting his towelling robe and pyjamas. 'Morning,' he growls, closing the door. Then stands where he is, trying to focus on the day ahead.

One thing is for sure: it is time to get back to the drawing board; it seems months since he was last in his study; it is time to take earning a living seriously again. There is probably enough in the various accounts to keep Sylvie at Beresford House for a year or two, and this house, which is much too big (he will buy somewhere cheaper and smaller) will fetch quite a sum; but he does need to eat. More than that, he needs to rebuild his ruptured life.

'This is Fenella Cunningham of The Old Vicarage, Aston Favell. Please write that down. I should like the Reverend Bob . . .' Here she allows an inviting silence, into which the female person on the other end will surely drop his surname. But no: 'Bob isn't

225

here. Want him to ring you back?' the bored voice asks. 'I do indeed,' says Fenella. 'On an urgent matter to do with my refugees. Kindly take a note of my number. Are you ready?'

A sigh. 'Yeah.'

Fenella enunciates each figure slowly, separately, so that only a moron could make a mistake. However, this person does not come over as specially bright. 'Would you like me to repeat that?'

'I got it. That all?'

'You will ensure that he receives my message?'

'Yeah, 'bye-ee,' says the voice, and the line goes dead.

Fenella stands in the hall for some moments, contemplating the telephone. Not entirely satisfied. Not as satisfied as she had intended to render herself. Of course, it was too much to expect to find him in; he is a very busy man, even now, perhaps, visiting the refugees in their different billets – some of whom may be wearing clothes donated by Lady Cunningham. The thought revives her. Oh, she does so *yearn* to be of use.

Jamie is getting too big for his sling; also, rather heavy for Bel's shoulders. With trepidation, she brings out the pram – which is of the folding variety, will eventually convert to a push-chair, and is one of the many expensive items of baby furniture selected prior to his birth. She examines it critically, and wonders whether it was a good choice, after all. Making the purchase, she had tested for ease of folding, for lightness, picturing herself getting in and out of cars and riding in lifts in multi-storey car parks. But is it strong enough, she wonders now, for extended walking on country lanes, for bumping up and down pavements; does it offer *protection*? This is stupid, it is a perfectly good pram. She goes to fetch Jamie. Lifting him from the cot, holding him against her for a moment, one hand supporting his padded bottom, the other his fragrant

226

head, his rubbery limbs open against her and his body moulds instantly to hers. Her fingers on the back of his neck fondle the touching fold of babyhood . . . Perhaps she will put him in the sling, after all. His plasticity, though adorable, fills her with terror; recent newspaper reports, items of sickening news on the television, thump in her brain until life seems a series of traps underscored by evil. What chance for an innocent babe; against all that, what chance? She presses him more tightly, as if she is clasping her own beating heart, and a sob shakes her. 'Blah,' protests Jamie, flexing, kicking. 'Blaaah' – screwing the skin of her neck in his tiny strong fingers. 'Ouch, you monster!' She raises him over her head, shaking him, growling; they laugh in the other's face. 'Yeah,' she agrees, 'what a stupid mother,' and goes to lie him in the pram.

Wheeling her treasure – the pink podge under the pram's sunshade – to the mouth of The Park, she has almost reached the corner with Main Street when a delivery lorry careers past; its weight and speed are conveyed to her hands via the vibrating pram handle. She walks on, determinedly ignoring this threat, but turning the corner, cannot resist embarking on a mental refit of the pram – a steel chassis, a steel surround, pneumatic bumpers . . . Near The Green, it takes her a ridiculous amount of time to cross the road, ears and eyes straining, manoeuvring to step off the pavement first, pulling the pram after (the method recommended by one of her baby survival books). Having tried out this procedure, though, she wonders whether its good sense does not depend on the direction from which the arrival of a rogue vehicle is anticipated, and whether the resulting delay in getting across does not defeat the desired object; considers, in fact, that she might possibly do better to follow the established practice of generations of mothers. So engrossed is she in all this, that she almost over-shoots the turn into Vicarage Hill; but the chiming of St Peter's church clock acts as a kindly reminder, and she swings left and puts her head down. It is a steepish climb.

The clock reminds Fenella of the Reverend Bob's continued failure to return her call. The suspense has driven her outside to pace the lawns and paths (keeping safely within earshot of the longed for telephone bell). When the church clock chimes and strikes the hour, she pauses to count – one, two, three – then in despair resumes her pacing.

All at once a young Amazon appears on the drive. This is how Bel appears to Fenella, rounding a corner: tall, healthy-looking, her hair plaited from the crown, her bare face, arms, legs, gleaming. She is standing beside (Fenella squints through the sunlight) – Good Lord – a pram.

Shielding her eyes, Bel calls, 'Hi. Remember me? I signed your petition last week. We got talking and you said I could come and see your lovely old house. I don't know whether this is a convenient time . . .' Fenella comes slowly over the lawn. And Bel carries on chattering: 'This really was the Vicarage, wasn't it? I mean, this is where the parson lived. Amazing, isn't it? – the house dwarfs the church. You can hardly see St Peter's from here.'

'One can slip into the churchyard very easily. There's a path at the rear through the kitchen garden . . .' For some reason, the visitor finds this hilarious. Watching her laugh (marvellous teeth), Fenella's memory slots her into place. 'Of course, we met on the village green. Later I called at your house for your husband's signature. He was so charming.'

The young woman looks surprised. 'He was?'

'Indeed. Now come along. Let me show you round.'

During the next hour it is as though the silence Fenella has endured – the telephone's silence, Bob's silence – has been in fact a raucous sound (like the piercing drone with which some deaf people are said to be afflicted, like the buzzer on the oven's timer, which, though dreadfully penetrating to Fenella's ears and certain to bring her running, is useless to poor old Molly unless she is actually present at the time in the kitchen); it is as if someone has mercifully turned the volume down in her head, then at last switched it off.

Bel, her young companion, is in turn, surprised, delighted, interested: surprised by the extent of the grounds whose large dimensions she would never guess at from the road; delighted by the variety and profusion of flowers, by the well-proportioned rooms and the beautiful furniture; interested in the photographs placed about the house, in the Vicarage's history, and to discover where Fenella proposes to house her refugees. It does not cause Fenella the slightest pang to enlighten her. She is able to talk as avidly of her plans as she could last week before her doubts set in. This is due to her visitor's confident enthusiasm. Fenella can even bear with fortitude Bel's reference to the opposition.

'I think I put my foot in it last Thursday, by the way. It was at Mrs Bullivant's coffee morning – you know? – in the big modern bungalow down that funny little lane. That's where I met your sister-in-law.' (Bel has just renewed the acquaintance in the kitchen where Molly was discovered making jam.) 'I airily mentioned your plans, said what a good idea it was and so forth – and there was this eerie silence. I was then frogmarched in another direction and when I tried to buy some of Mrs Bullivant's crocheted holders, people sort of stared. Even Mrs Bullivant looked at me weirdly, as if she wasn't quite sure I'd give them a good home. Afterwards, I twigged; it was this lot who were against you, it was because of them you got up the petition. Honestly, I can be so slow sometimes . . .'

Fenella listens, blinking rapidly. 'Come and sit down, my dear,' she says, showing Bel into the large sitting room with the semi-circular window seat. 'We'll have some tea.'

'Gosh, is it OK if I wheel the pram over this lovely carpet?'

'Of course. Now, sit there.' She indicates an easy chair facing the window seat, then returns to the doorway, raising her head to bellow, '*Mol-lay!*'

'Yes?' enquires Molly, putting her head round the kitchen door. 'I suppose you'd like some tea. I've put the kettle on.'

'Thank you so much,' Fenella concedes graciously, and returns to arrange herself on the window seat in front of her guest. 'Interesting what you say about the Bullivant woman. How did she appear at her coffee morning? Flustered at all?'

'Now you come to mention it, she wasn't her usual self. Not like she is in the shop or the street – you know, bombastic. I don't why, everything appeared to be going smoothly. You've been there, I suppose?'

'Once,' shudders Fenella. 'Dretful place. Quite, quite horrid. What is it called? – *Sunny Bank.*' On Fenella's lips it is almost an expletive.

Bel lapses into rather uncomfortable silence, for last Thursday's visit to the Bullivants' bungalow put her in mind of her parents' home; more plush, more spacious, it would probably encompass the summit of her mother's homemaking ambitions. 'I suppose we've all got different tastes,' she suggests diffidently. 'You'd probably hate my place, too. It's open plan, split level; the furniture's modern. My mum thinks it's ghastly.'

Fenella looks thoughtful. 'How very interesting. Ah, here comes tea. Oh, Molly, Molly, do mind the dog!' – and when Molly looks blank: 'Not near the *baby.*'

'Oh,' says Molly, 'well, he won't eat it, he's had a perfectly adequate dinner – haven't oo, Henry?' She puts down the tray and bends to tweak her darling's ear. 'In any case we can't stop, we're about to reach setting point.' And Bel, who has no knowledge of jam making, and imagines she is referring to the onset of some canine disability, politely murmurs, 'What a shame.'

With some ceremony, Lady Cunningham pours the tea. Soon, a couple of questions have launched her upon a vivid account of her stage career. You would think the tea was spiked, reflects Bel, to judge from her increased animation. It is easy to picture the performances she describes – Ophelia, Cordelia, Desdemona, and even Cecily and Marjorie and Lady This and the Honourable Mrs That in plays Bel has never heard of. By the end of it all (Bel judges the end to be near from a certain sadness creeping in) there are tears in Lady Cunningham's eyes. But no: a rallying gulp of what by now must be stone cold tea, and she is off again, cantering through the dazzling country of marriage to Sir Jock, who was apparently an eminent politician. (Bel racks her brains in vain for a 'Cunningham' among the memorable names of past Cabinet ministers.) Sir Jock was the most generous and darling man that ever breathed, and quite crazy about her, his widow girlishly confides; spoiled her, ruined her, life has never, could never . . . But now the tears well up in earnest, great globules bulging at the perimeters of wide, sad eyes. 'Jock understood me,' she whispers hoarsely, 'my need to give and give; *to be of use*!' – this last phrase ending on a note of shocking intensity.

And shocking indeed it proves to Jamie. As Fenella pauses, Bel hears her infant draw a long and shuddering breath which he then expels in a passionately affronted hiccuping bawl – 'A-wah, a-wah,' – repeated until his mother has his mouth smothered against her. 'There,' she coos, pressing him close, rocking, caressing, 'shush, darling, there, there . . .'

Fenella is aghast. She had known, of course, that she was getting carried away, but regarded it as her harmless little treat, well-deserved after twenty-four hours of tortured suspense; and in any case, to be more than adequately paid for afterwards when her mood crashed in the downswing. 'I was too loud, too sudden, I terrified the little fellow,' she mourns, hand to her throat; 'I am a silly old woman.'

Jamie is quickly soothed. Bel smiles forgivingly over his head. 'You don't seem old or silly to me. I've seen less vigorous twenty-year-olds.'

'Yes, I am vigorous,' says Fenella, nodding her head. 'But people won't have it, you know. They've given me up. My husband's death seems to have made me invisible. Yet I still have it in me to do good, to make use of my talents.'

'Then you should. You just should,' Bel says simply. 'Take no notice of these people. Offer yourself – to the Citizens' Advice Bureau or somewhere. Tell them what you can do.'

But Fenella has never heard of the Citizens' Advice Bureau. It sounds rather advanced; its very title makes her feel all at sea; it would be just another institution, she guesses, bound like all the others to regard her as past it. This bright young woman obviously means well . . .

Bel has returned Jamie to his pram, which has not pleased him. 'Shush, darling, it's all right, we're going home now,' she promises. 'It's been a lovely afternoon, Lady Cunningham. You'll come and see me, won't you? I'm nearly always at home during the week with Jamie. But if you want to make sure, the number's in the book. Rochford,' she reminds her.

'I shall be delighted,' Fenella intones smoothly over her mounting depression. She helps her guest down the portico steps with the pram, waves as she disappears round the curve of the drive; droops and returns indoors.

Kate has arrived home from school. She is bending into her car to retrieve a pile of end-of-term school reports which require her attention, when Bel hails her from the top of The Old Vicarage driveway. 'Oh, hello,' she replies, withdrawing her head, waiting as Bel dithers at the kerb, looking right, left – still right, left, as she marches across. 'I don't think I've seen you before with a pram.'

'No, and I haven't quite got the hang of it.'

'Coming in?'

'I'd better not. I've been ages at the The Old Vicarage, much longer than I intended. Any further delay and there'll be an almighty protest.'

'He looks pretty happy to me,' says Kate, bending over the pram.

'I'm glad to catch you, though. Do you know Lady Cunningham?'

'I can't say *know* her. We nod, say good morning . . .'

'I've been with her all afternoon. I'm . . . worried.'

'Really?'

'Mm. She was telling me about her life; she got quite carried away. You'll think me fanciful, but listening to her, watching her, do you know what she suddenly made me think of? – the sort of scatty depressed elderly lady, often quite well-to-do, we used to catch shop-lifting . . .'

'Oh, Bel . . .'

'You see, it's rather sad: she was obviously the toast of the county till her husband died – terrifically in demand, hostess with the mostess (she's got bags of energy; you can sense it, she positively seethes with it); anyway, I get the impression everyone in her circle has dropped her flat. All those people who were simply avid for her don't want to know, now there's no Sir Jock. Isn't that foul? I got a hunch she's bordering on the desperate.'

Kate is nonplussed. 'I hardly know what to say. I mean, you can't very well tap on her shoulder: "Excuse me, Lady Cunningham, but if you're thinking of a bit of shop-lifting, I advise against it." It *is* only a hunch.'

Bel looks embarrassed. 'Yes, I know. Forget it.'

'How are things with you?'

Guessing this is a reference to their shared confidences in the pub last Wednesday evening, Bel looks down at her son. 'Oh, better; I reckon I'm getting the maternal angst under control.'

'Good. From the look of him there's precious little

to be anxious about. Feeling better about living in the village?'

'Loads. I've made one or two interesting visits. For instance, to Sunny Bank.'

'Now that must have been interesting,' Kate says ironically.

Bel's eyes go wide. 'But it was. I met this really nice person, a woman cleric . . .'

'Oh, Harriet – Harriet Jesmond. Yes, I know her through school. She's a parent, but she's also someone we can contact when one of the kids gets into difficulties – problems at home or with the police and so forth. She's terrific. She's a friend of Zoë Hunter's – you know? – works at the surgery, comes to exercise class.'

'Of course. Well, Harriet said she could use my expertise. I'm not sure how, but I'm going to give her a ring. I wouldn't mind getting involved with something – keep my hand in, meet people.'

'That's great, Bel. Well, if you can't stop now, how about Thursday?'

'Fine. But I'll see you at class first.'

'So you will. Bye, then. Bye-bye, Jamie.' Kate watches them move off, then reaches into the back of her car for the school reports and a bag of shopping.

In The Old Vicarage, at six o'clock, the telephone rings.

Fenella can scarcely believe it. Her heart thuds, she stumbles on the hall carpet. 'Hello; this is Fenella, Lady . . .'

'Fenella, hello! How are you? I got your message. What's to do?'

The Reverend Bob! 'Well. I, I . . .' Overjoyed, flooding with relief – because this time, *this time,* things are going to work out right; these people want her, recognize her worth, have a part for her to play – she pauses to steady her breathing, then tries again. 'I wanted to ask you about the arrangements for my refugees. I have made some alterations to the house already, and I thought it would be good idea if you were to come and take a look and advise me on anything more fundamental. I do want to be ready for them . . .'

He laughs. 'Hey, wait. Hang on there a minute.'

'But, Bob, you see I have a good reason for wanting to get on with things. I have encountered some rather unpleasant opposition – chiefly from a woman whose husband is a parish councillor; but I know others are of the same mind. Never fear, they don't deter me in the slightest. On the contrary, I drew up a petition which several people signed in my support. Also, when my husband was alive, we knew a very nice chap on the local rag. If things get nasty, I might look him up – make sure our side of the story gets across . . .'

'Stop right there, Fenella. This is exactly the sort of thing we don't . . .' He stops, then goes on in a gentler tone. 'Look, Fenella,' he coaxes soupily, 'you've got the wrong end of the stick. It's not even certain that we'll have any more refugees. Things have moved on. Our thinking now is more along the lines of a mercy mission – you know, driving a truck over there with supplies . . .'

Fenella's taut and trembling fist is pressing the receiver against her ear with sufficient force almost to weld it. His words explode and boom. Her head swells with their resonance. 'But I thought you agreed . . . ,' she tries weakly, but knows she has already lost.

'Oh no, Fenella. Look. You sound kinda down in the dumps. We're a pretty friendly crowd here at St Augustine's. Why not come over and say "hello"? On Thursday afternoons we have Bible Class followed by Crush – we call it "Crush" because we all crush up and have coffee and biscuits and a bit of a giggle. You'll meet some lovely people. I'm sure you'd find it a help . . .'

'A help?' cries Fenella, bewildered. 'To me? But I am endeavouring to help other people. I simply want to be of use . . .'

'Think it over, eh, Fenella? And there's a lovely

service every Sunday at eleven o'clock. Lots of lively music, lots of happy faces . . .'

'Thank you, I may consider it,' Fenella manages with dignity, but without a smattering of truth. 'Goodbye.' Very carefully, she lays down the receiver.

After a moment or two, Molly looks out of the kitchen. 'Grub's nearly up.'

Fenella blinks at her.

'All right. I'll put yours to keep warm,' sighs Molly, assuming she missed the customary response.

Holding herself tightly, as if at any moment she might fracture into fragments, Fenella giddily mounts the stairs.

In 5 The Park, David gathers transistor and newspaper. 'Think I'll go up and have a bath.'

Good, thinks Bel. She is watching a comedy show on TV: her two favourite female comedians. David chuckles at them politely, but she knows they make him wince. Anyway, this programme is a repeat, they have seen it before. 'OK, love,' she smiles, her eyes on the screen. He runs upstairs; and Bel more thoroughly relaxes, swivels sideways on the settee with her back to the arm and her feet up. She laughs often and out loud; knowing what comes next only enhances her enjoyment. A particularly rude sketch has her gasping and groaning and grabbing a cushion. 'Haw, haw,' she rasps, eyes watering. Oh, brilliant – now comes that bit where they pretend to be blokes on a building site, a couple of horrible greasers fancying their chances with a pair of smart office birds. She shrieks with recognition. 'Oh, God,' she groans, rolling almost to the floor.

Suddenly, recalling Jamie, she springs to her feet, looks round for the remote control, dives for it, and stabs the mute button. Solemn-faced, she listens for a moment or two, thinking what a stupid idiot she is, shrieking her head off right below where Jamie is sleeping. Fortunately, on this occasion, there are no cries of infant alarm. She allows the sound to resume at a reduced volume – and while she is up on her feet, decides to draw the curtains, for it is now dark outside, or at least, the lighted room brilliantly reflected in the wall-to-wall patio window makes it appear dark. She bounces towards her reflected image, finding it more compelling than the boring singer on the box who has temporarily taken over from the comedians. Her image bounces towards her – then splits in two . . . Before her eyes, like amoebic reproduction, her reflection breaks into two separate components, one peeling abruptly away. It is a moment of sheer schizophrenic horror. She and her constant image stand frozen in wide-eyed mutual regard, until, in a sudden coming together, Bel leaps to draw the curtains.

Having safely obliterated the outside world, she turns urgently for reassurance; runs to the stairs, crying 'David! David!' in her head. Halfway up, her ears catch the muffled boom of his financial programme resonating on the bathroom floor. She hesitates, stares back down into the bright brash room. And slowly descends. It was the prowler out there. She was being watched, scrutinized, spied on. For how long? What was she doing, how did she appear? For instance: did she pick her nose, scratch her crotch? No – just behaved like a lunatic, hooting and rolling on the settee; though it would serve him right whatever she'd done, the creep.

The curtains on the front of the house have yet to be drawn. She goes to close them. Headlights come sweeping into The Park, swing into the shared driveway. The car stops, the headlights go out, and an interior light comes on revealing Les Fairbrother leaning over the passenger seat, gathering belongings. He heaves out of the car clutching papers, jacket and a case, nudges the door shut and disappears from view.

Of course, she has known perfectly well that the voyeur could not be Les Fairbrother. Even so, she is relieved to have this knowledge confirmed. It crosses her mind that she ought to warn Tina. But why bother, since Les is now at home? One thing she couldn't stand would be Les hearing about it. If she called round there, Les might answer the door, and even if Tina answered, Les might come to listen. Imagine – Les Fairbrother with lascivious eyes on her, drinking in her distress . . . No thanks. Tina can take care of herself.

Gosh, though, it would be a relief to tell someone. She could ring Rosie (her best friend since school days) or Diana (who was a close chum at work). But both Rosie and Diana live miles away in cities; what on earth would they make of this episode? She finds she is strangely reluctant to phone either of them with this skewed tale of village life; feels, absurdly perhaps, that to do so would be letting down Aston Favell. (Good God, she must be going native.) If only there was *someone* she could get it off her chest to, explain how angry, humiliated and invaded she feels. Her mother is definitely out – she can imagine her reaction: 'Now Belinda, lovie, you've always been a fanciful girl . . .' Why does she shrink from telling David? (Upstairs, *The World Tonight* has started, his favourite evening radio programme.) Because, she finally grasps, telling David she would have to give a jokey account. Revealing her true feelings would encourage his suspicion that she has not so much conquered her maternal anxiety as found a substitute, some new subject for obsessive dread. And as there is no point in making light of how she feels, there is none whatever in telling him.

Her eyes fall on the telephone directory. She walks over to it, picks it up. Looks up *Woolard*.

Kate is sitting at the kitchen table, struggling with end-of-year school reports. An hour or so ago, when she got up to make coffee, she put on the overhead light. It was not by any means dark, but her eyes were tired from staring at so much shiny white paper, from squinting to see what other colleagues have written, sometimes in a hand she admires and envies (such as

Gareth's beautiful italic script), sometimes in a hand she can hardly decode, sometimes in an undistinguished scrawl which makes her squirm on behalf of the school. She needs every scrap of light available to complete this beastly chore. She longs to get it over with and is ploughing on for as long as she can stand to.

When the phone summons, Kate hopes it will be Will on the line. She stumbles stiffly to the hall. 'Kate Woolard,' she says, keeping her voice steady despite her leaping heart.

'Oh, Kate. Sorry to bother you so late. It's Bel, Bel Rochford. It's just, well, I've had a visit from the Peeping Tom. I was watching the telly, hadn't drawn the curtains – it seemed a shame to lose the last of the light. Anyway, when it got darker I went to close them . . . and, well, this *figure* shot away. It gave me such a turn, for a second I thought it was my own reflection taking off – I suppose it was the way he moved, sort of insubstantial, like a darting shadow . . . Then I came to my senses and quickly closed the curtains. He must have been really close up, he could have been watching for ten or fifteen minutes . . . Oh Kate, I felt *stupid*. Taken advantage of. You don't mind me telling you, do you?'

By now Kate has recovered from her disappointment, but is feeling alarmed. She glances through the kitchen to the window, which is still uncovered. And she has left a light on. Writing reports was such a grind she failed to notice how dark it was getting. 'No, of course I don't,' she says, turning her back on the kitchen and its blank window. 'I know how you feel. In fact, something of the kind happened here when I got home from our drink last Wednesday night. I got out of the car, and sensed someone was watching me. In the morning I could see the marks he'd made where he'd been standing.'

'God, Kate, you're so calm, so brave. I feel ashamed. I mean, I've got David here.'

239

'Look,' – she glances again at the window – 'I didn't tell you that to make you feel bad, but to let you know I sympathize. It's a hideous feeling – like you get from one of those creepy phone calls.'

'That's it exactly! Oh, I'm glad I phoned you; I needed to tell someone, and I don't want to tell David, not after being such a pain over Jamie. He'd be worried in case I was going funny again . . .'

Kate laughs. 'Going to ring the police?'

A pause. 'Did you?'

'Um, no. I didn't, as a matter of fact. I suppose I didn't want to dwell on it.'

'I know. On the other hand, it could really frighten some vulnerable person. It could give them a heart attack.' She hesitates. 'I don't think I will, though, actually; because then I would have to tell David . . .'

'Well, it's not as if the police aren't aware of the problem; several people have reported sightings. Look, come over on Thursday and we'll swap notes.'

'I will. Thanks for listening. I feel tons better.'

'I'm glad. Goodnight, Bel.'

Kate puts the receiver down and hurries through the kitchen to cover the window. In a minute, she will go round the house drawing every curtain. First, she must just tidy up; if she writes any more reports she will develop a raging head; it is fortunate she was interrupted. What a nice person Bel is. It is a kind of comfort, knowing someone else who is fighting an irrational fear. How unfair that a prowler arrives on the scene, complicating matters – hell, life is tough enough without having an inadequate prey on you. Why don't the police catch him, for pity's sake?

Well, for one thing because people like herself and Bel are disinclined to report incidents. How many others feel the same? It is a natural reaction to prefer to blot out these experiences; to ask, why let the bastard take any more of your life? Maybe she will ring the police in the morning, confess her delay and report what happened on Wednesday night. They can only rebuke her, she can stand that. It is about time this bloke was stopped. As Bel said, someone may end up seriously frightened and hurt.

A noise sounds outside. She knows exactly what it is. Damn – she left the mower out. Some animal – a cat or a fox – must have knocked against the cuttings box; it is a very distinctive sound, the rocking of bashed-out-of-true metal.

Wait a minute, though: *would* a cat or a fox bang into it? Surely their eyes are designed to see in the dark . . . Her heart jumps; her hands relinquish the papers she is gathering; she stands rock still with her thighs pressed against the table edge. It is the prowler out there; the Peeping Tom who, sneaking across the yard to take up his position near the window (this window – her head jerks towards it) knocked blindly into the grass cuttings box. The wretch has returned to give her a second dose of misery; just as half an hour ago he indulged himself outside Bel's, setting *her* nerves on edge, reactivating the problems *she* has been warring with. Evidently, he has a nose for females with problems. Well, he needs to be stopped. *Now*.

With her skin aflame (as if she is visible to him through the curtains, audible to him through the closed door), she goes to telephone the police. But even before she reaches the hall, the futility of this action strikes her – the police station is in Lavenbrook; from there a call will go out to some patrol car, possibly many miles distant, its occupants already busy at the scene of some urgent crime or disturbance; she will no doubt be assured that someone will call on her later this evening, by which time, of course, the prowler will be gone. She does not require this sort of assistance; she requires an end put to the nuisance once and for all. It would make more sense to phone a friend, she decides; and from habit, it is Will's number which leaps to her mind (the number she would ring when Chris's pain became intolerable or when she was at her wits end to know how to cope with his depression).

But no, she will not phone Will. She cannot allow this pest to panic her into making a move she has already set her mind against. Will initiated the silence between them, he broke off contact; if she were to call him – for however urgent or justified a reason – she would never be sure whether he would ultimately have resumed their friendship of his own volition. She longs for this resumption more than anything in the world, but only on perfectly secure terms. *He* must call *her*. So ring someone else, she thinks urgently (and instantly dismisses Fiona on the grounds of her disobliging husband), ring Zoë and Martin, who can be relied on to come to her aid at once. She stabs out the Hunters' number, listens impatiently to the ringing tone. Tommo answers. 'Oh, Tommo,' she gasps. 'Can I please speak to your Mum or Dad?' 'They're out,' says Tommo, insufficiently interested to enquire who is speaking or impart any further information. She is too devastated to notice. 'It doesn't matter,' she forces out thickly through the suffocating swelling constricting her throat; and bundles down the receiver.

Tears spurt from her eyes. She steps blindly, shakily, into the kitchen and grabs a chair-back; pulls it hard into her stomach; stands there, choking on an overwhelming sense of her life gone hopelessly wrong, of an unappeasable Fate having it in for her, forever demanding more and more and more from her – more courage, more endurance, more patience. Her husband was taken from her in harrowing circumstances, she drove herself to the physical limit caring for him; she was left not only with a shattered life, but a grief-prompted disability which she has since – summoning the prescribed *courage* – struggled to overcome; not once did she give in those nights when every nerve urged her to flee the house and fling herself on Fiona's mercy, or Zoë's, and beg to be allowed to stay while she searched for some other home; but stuck it out, *endured* (as prescribed), for the sake of the children, and because she was advised (and knew in her heart) that it

242

was important to overcome these irrational fears. And then victory hove into view. Even, she was permitted a glimpse of bliss. But now *patience* was demanded: Kate Woolard must contain herself, decreed Fate, before she could be allowed such a prize as Will McLeod. And obediently she accepted, strengthened by signs that at last her courage and endurance were rewarded, in that she felt alive again and capable of pleasure, and had virtually conquered her dread of living alone.

And now this prowler comes on the scene. How did Bel describe him? Insubstantial? Yes, she can picture the type – a specimen like the weed who lives in the unrestored cottage at the top of Vicarage Hill, who used to have the egg round, whom she and Fiona saw in the car's headlights flitting across the road that rainy Saturday night, surly looking under his greasy cap, often hunched over a fag, a furtive mover, a gruff monosyllabic speaker; in a word, pathetic. Whether he is actually the prowler or it is someone very much like him, this much she knows: he is slippery as an eel, fleet as a shadow, and will therefore continue to evade capture and endlessly return to Wayside Cottage. And she will never know *when* – whether it will be tonight, tomorrow night, or the night after . . . It is a new source of dread, further grief to prey on her mind . . . Her life will continue an endless road of painful trial; never, never smooth easeful pasture. *It . . . is . . . not . . . fair.* She would like to grab this wretch by the scruff of the neck, give him a taste of his own medicine; she'd like to jam her face into his and scream out what he is doing to her, that he is thieving her peace of mind, that she wants him to damn well *suffer for it* . . .

She no longer consciously sees the kitchen's interior. She sees the outside, where her rage is a white-hot spotlight illuminating the despicable creature hunched in the peony patch. (Oh yes, it would shake him to know that she *knows* where he is, that she sees him plain as daylight!) She'd like that, that would be good – to go for him, scare him out of his wits so that he

243

would never willingly set foot here again. She'd like to obliterate him altogether so that he could never prey on anyone. *Obliterate*, she snarls in her head, jerking away from the chair – *Smash and obliterate* – dashing to a drawer, rifling the contents – *Smash the bastard* – her inner voice screams, her hand fastening on a steak mallet; *Bastard, bastard* – turning the door key, shooting back the bolt. She bursts into the yard, and the word spews out of her: 'Baaast . . . aaard . . . !'

The watcher, who at the sound of the door being opened, shrank back into the shadows, is shaken to the core by the demented scream and instantly elects to flee; darts forward in the direction of the yard and the saving road – as Kate, like an uncannily guided arrow, shoots straight for the peony patch.

They collide; fall together in the wedge of light from the kitchen doorway. Kate frees her arm, lifts the steak mallet . . . But is never to know whether she would or would not have delivered the blow, for the cap has fallen off, hair has escaped, and she sees that it is not him at all – but a *her*.

It is Fenella, Lady Cunningham.

CHAPTER SIXTEEN

Tuesday 30th June

It is twenty past midnight. Fenella, Lady Cunningham is fast asleep in Andrea Woolard's pine-frame bed. Under the U2 poster, the photograph celebrating a hockey team triumph, under the round glass eyes of Freddy-Teddy sitting stiffly on a wall-shelf, lies Lady Cunningham, out like a light. An observer – Kate – stands in the half-open doorway in an indirect glow lent from a light further along the corridor.

But thank goodness she *is* here, safe and sound where Kate can keep tabs on her. Of course, Kate needs to snatch some sleep herself; she is already half dead on her feet. (Thank goodness tomorrow is not a school day – though even if it were, she would have to phone and say she was sick or something; she has to make that appointment first thing, then make sure Lady Cunningham sticks to it.) The important thing is, Lady Cunningham is here under Kate's roof, which, as well as affording Kate a better chance of holding her to her promise, also provides her with the opportunity to forestall any funny business. Kate must sleep, but she trusts her subconscious, impressed by the night's startling events, to rouse her from slumber should Lady Cunningham try to effect an escape.

Poor old thing, Kate thinks, watching her. This is a considerable change from her earlier attitude. (She might have known – when will she learn? – that full-blown righteous anger inevitably goes crashing into an obstacle – someone else's hidden motive, for

instance, or some unforseen mitigating circumstance.)
In a way, Kate concedes ruefully, so it proved tonight.
Lord, though, what a tongue-lashing she gave her:
'You're not going anywhere, you wicked old bat,'
(man-handling her indoors); 'you're coming in here,
sitting down there,' (shoving her hard on to the sitting-
room sofa); 'until you've damn well explained – first
to me, then to the police – just what you imagine you
were up to. You do understand you *terrified* people
– ordinary, innocent people – made them dread the
evenings, scared to go to bed, unable to sleep for
their ears straining? You do realize the police are
involved? Oh yes. What will you say for yourself?
What will you tell the magistrate – I'm sorry, your
honour, I'm a wealthy old fool with time on my
hands and nothing better to do?'

Kate thinks she will never forget Fenella's reaction
– jaw and mouth slewing, eyes losing focus and rolling
in her head as though trying to keep track of inner hor-
rors. And not a sound escaping her. Kate grew alarmed,
fearing she had suffered a stroke. 'Lady Cunningham?'
she prompted. 'Lady Cunningham?'

'I couldn't stand it,' came out at last – a small,
strained sound, as if *squeezed* out. Then, more firmly:
'I *wouldn't* stand it,' with a chilling ring of finality.
Kate bundled forward in her chair until she was close
enough to tap the other's knee. 'Lady Cunningham?'

The eyes came gradually into focus. 'Yes?' And Kate
realized her captive had been addressing herself when
she promised she *wouldn't* stand it, and had been
referring to the threat of exposure. At which Kate's
view of the situation lurched, her confidence in how
to deal with it weakened. 'Will you tell me please
whatever possessed you?' she asked in a gentler tone,
one permitting the possibility of being persuaded.

Lady Cunningham was quick to pick this up; her
bleak look betrayed that she knew what must be done
in order to save her skin: it was necessary to explain
her actions as honestly as possible without histrionics.

She began, and at first her voice was merely weary: 'It was, you see, my only way. I had been out of things for so long . . . They began shutting me out soon after my husband died – not all at once – slowly. It gradually dawned on me I was no longer wanted. Of course, no-one put it in those terms. It was done politely – "Oh we couldn't ask you, Fenella, not so soon after losing Jock." – "We thought, Fenella that we wouldn't trouble you this year." Sometimes I'd set a little trap: I would suggest that possibly I might not be up to some function or other. You should have seen how they jumped at it – "Of course we quite understand, Fenella." It was plain as daylight they had no further use for me; it was plain as daylight that Lady Cunningham without Sir Jock was not easily seated at an important dinner table. Do you know, I began to understand the *suttee* custom? It was as if unconsciously they expected me, if not to obliterate myself, to at least be discreet about my continued existence. Would they notice it at all if I disappeared, I wondered. For several months I conducted an experiment – kept a very low profile, never initiated contact. My dear, it was a revelation; I should imagine the collected sigh of relief was audible in the next county. Barely a civil enquiry. No real desire to discover how I fared. And I realized I no longer understood the ordinary everyday world. Yet it evidently continued robustly without me; people were plainly engrossed in their lives. I was like a stranded sea-creature without a clue how to re-enter the water. You see, it was so very long ago that I last needed to make any effort – I had been in the spotlight, I was accustomed to others seeking *me* out – simply, I couldn't recall how it was done. I'd lost the art; one does, when one is out of practice. How to get an inkling – was that how it started? Or was it that I teemed with useless energy, that I was desperate to find some release?'

Her voice had risen, she had begun to shake. She collected herself and continued in a lowered tone: 'One evening, I felt utterly overwhelmed. I was so dreadfully hemmed in – Molly shut up with her blessed dog, Mrs Prior behaving as she never would have dreamed in Jock's day, no-one in the wide world to talk to. I had to escape, to get out, take a look at life. I was afraid to be recognized, so I put on these old things of Jock's.' She paused for a moment, and her face took on a transported expression: 'Do you know, it was . . . magical?' she asked wonderingly – 'free to roam, free to peek at the world, to gain an *inside view*. I felt powerful. I could choose where I went, whom I looked at. Everything was open to me, and not a soul knew I was there. It is *amazing*,' she confided, 'what you can see, what you can do, when you are only a shadow.'

'Mm,' said Kate, taken by her use of the word 'shadow', remembering that Bel had used it; and remembering other things – 'Chuck litter over the Bullivants' lawn?' she suggested (but not censoriously).

Lady Cunningham darted her a sharp look, but conceded with a nod of the head. 'That was the only occasion when I was deliberately malicious – but then, you know, the woman had been impertinent.' (She was sounding perkier, she had evidently revived.) 'Generally speaking I was haphazard in my selection, though one does develop a feel for the most likely places. Occasionally, after meeting someone like you, or that nice young Bel, I'd go along out of sheer interest.'

'Oh, thanks,' Kate said wryly, rubbing her arm which was sore from their fall. 'Are you all right, by the way? Not hurt anywhere?'

'No, I think I am unscathed.'

'You're amazingly strong,' she commented curiously – then felt abashed, as the phrase 'for your age' hung rather obviously in the ensuing pause. Perhaps this upset Lady Cunningham, for there was a sudden crumpling of her demeanour: 'Must you,' she whispered, and her hands clenched and unclenched and her jaw wobbled, 'must you tell . . . *the police*?'

Something had been nagging at the back of Kate's mind, and now she recalled it – what Bel had said about elderly women shop-lifters. This sparked a further memory of a much written about case concerning a former celebrity who had been caught pilfering, was prosecuted, and soon after took her own life. Kate swallowed. 'Not necessarily,' she said. 'However, I'd need to be sure the spying had stopped. I'd have to be perfectly certain that no-one in Aston Favell had any reason to live in dread in their own home. Other people have troubles, you know, and it's quite possible that in some cases you've made matters worse. I'm sure you can imagine what it's like to be spied on.'

Their eyes held contact for some time, neither speaking, until Fenella bowed her head. 'Let me think about it,' said Kate. 'Perhaps we could do with a drink. Brandy? Whisky?'

'A little brandy, please.'

The little brandies soon became second brandies. But in Kate's case the drink relaxed her sufficiently to devise a solution. 'No, I won't tell the police,' she announced at last, 'on one condition.'

'Yes?' – tremulously, hopefully.

'Who is your doctor?'

Lady Cunningham looked blank. 'Oh . . . some young fellow they passed me on to when Alec Brownlow retired.'

'At the surgery in Symington?'

'Well, yes, I suppose so. Molly went there once, I believe. Of course, one always used to send for the doctor. Alec always came to us. I really couldn't say about this new fellow . . .'

'My doctor's a partner in the Symington practice. You can consult any of them, you know; it doesn't have to be the doctor you're registered with.'

'Does it not?' Fenella had begun to look lost.

Kate moved forward to the edge of her chair. 'Here's my condition: I won't go to the police, if you come with me to the doctor. In the morning I'll make an appointment and we'll go in together. I'll tell him the facts of the matter, then leave you to discuss them. You must tell him what you've just told me. Agreed?'

'I imagine,' Lady Cunningham said slowly, 'that I have no choice. A little more brandy?' she pleaded, holding out her glass.

It seemed churlish to refuse. But perhaps she should have done, for soon after this the grey head hit the cushion and the glass toppled. Kate was obliged to shake her – 'Lady Cunningham? Lady Cunningham!'

'Mm; mm?'

'I think you'd be more comfortable upstairs in bed.'

'Oh,' the poor woman gasped, lurching to her feet, sitting down again. 'Oh dear. I'm rather tired.'

Kate urged her to her feet and pressed the idea of Andrea's bed. 'My daughter's,' she explained as she helped her upstairs. 'It's all made up. I'm expecting her home soon.'

'Daughter? That *is* nice. Haven't see, haven't seen . . . Miles – my son, you know – since . . .' (evidently too long ago to recall).

'Bathroom, Lady Cunningham?'

'No, no. Um, oh perhaps I will.'

'In here.' Kate waited outside with her fingers crossed.

The brief visit seemed to rally Lady Cunningham. 'I say, shouldn't I be going home?'

'I should stay here. Look, the bed's all ready.'

'Really, there's no need to impose . . .' But the feel of a bed under her buttocks seemed to settle the matter: 'It's ver', ver' kind . . .' Her last words. Kate did her best – pulled off the trousers, the shoes and socks, drew up the duvet.

Still in the doorway, Kate detects the breathing is less strenuous – quieter, slower. She staggers into her own room to set the alarm for the morning. Decides to leave both bedroom doors open.

The alarm clock wakes Kate at seven. She turns it off and flops back on her pillows, utterly stunned. Discovering a headache, she lies holding her brow and wondering what the point of sleep *is*, if in the process you end up feeling more shattered than you felt the night before. God, but those were some wild dreams — that fight again, over and over, with Lady Cunningham, with Sylvie, then finally, of all people, with Chris, her husband. And a grimly silent Chris at that — she grappling to hang on to him, to keep him with her, not let him go; he fighting like a beast to escape. She can remember how steely his hands felt pushing her off, how his body throbbed with the desire to be free of her. Crazy, she thinks; weird. Why should she dream such a thing of Chris? She will have to think about it. Not now, though. She crawls out of bed, staggers to the bathroom to shower and dress before thoughts of the daunting programme ahead inhibit her; if she considered it in detail, she might just give up, get back into bed and pull the duvet over her head.

By half-past seven, fresh and decent, she is peering cautiously into her daughter's semi-darkened room where Lady Cunningham has this moment opened her eyes — eyes which light upon Kate and promptly close. Kate goes to draw back the curtains. 'I'll bring you a cup of tea.'

In fact, in the kitchen she sets out a proper tea tray, one her grandmother would have approved — embroidered cloth, cream jug, sugar basin (non-matching teapot, but you can't have everything). She carries it up to Andrea's room, where Lady Cunningham is sitting propped against the pillows with the duvet drawn to her chin — aware that she looks a fright, concludes Kate, considerately keeping her eyes averted. 'There we are. Take your time; come round slowly. You remember where the bathroom is?'

Lady Cunningham mumbles agreement into her coverings.

At eight o'clock sharp, which is the time the surgery appointments system opens, Kate picks up the telephone. She needs, she tells the receptionist, an urgent appointment, not for herself, but for Lady Cunningham, whom she has promised to bring this morning to see Dr Horden. Never mind which doctor Lady Cunningham is registered with, Dr Horden it must be.

'That's all right, Mrs Woolard. Dr Horden's booked up, but he always keeps the last slot of the morning free for something unexpected. Ten to twelve, then.'

Kate lets out her breath. She was prepared to do battle. Perhaps the ease with which she has achieved this much is a happy omen for the coming morning. Confident, optimistic, hopeful: that's the way to play it – friendly but firm; for they have to survive the morning together. She returns upstairs.

Lady Cunningham, in Sir Jock's shirt (fully buttoned) and trews (likewise), is sitting on the side of the bed. 'I'm stiff as a board,' she says accusingly. 'I may have broken something.'

'Then why have you dressed? You need a good soak in the bath.'

'But I haven't any clean clothes.'

'Right. I'll walk over with you to The Old Vicarage and we'll collect everything you need.'

'I'm quite capable of accomplishing that by myself, thank you.'

'Oh, no; I'm not letting you out of my sight. I've arranged for us to see Dr Horden at ten to twelve, by the way. Now, we'll go across the road together. If you like, you can bathe and dress there, but I'm coming with you.'

Evidently deciding she has no other course, Lady Cunningham rises, with a grimace, to her feet. 'Thank you for the tea,' she says loftily, hobbling ahead. 'It was delicious.'

Kate is glad she thought to bring a newspaper. It is embarrassing to sit in the bedroom of a mere acquaintance while ablutions are performed in an adjoining bathroom with the door left ajar at one's own insistence.

'Oh, but I forgot – Mrs Prior will be here soon,' Lady Cunningham wailed as they arrived. 'And she *talks*.'

'What time does she come?'

'Half-past nine.'

'Get a move on, then,' Kate said. 'We can be out of here by quarter past. We'll have breakfast at my place.'

In fact, she is too tired to read the newspaper; it is simply a useful shield. Her headache has been dulled but not dissipated by paracetamol tablets; her bruised left arm is throbbing. Fortunately, if the vigorous sound of water swishing and a flannel slapping is anything to go by, her captive is unharmed and has recovered her energy. She contemplates a photograph on the nearby dressing table of a jolly old cove, presumably Sir Jock. Ah – the bath is emptying. Kate pretends to study her newspaper. Soon, Lady Cunningham returns to the room in her robe. 'I suppose it's all right with you if I take these to the dressing room?' she says, gathering clothes from a drawer.

'Look,' says Kate awkwardly, thinking maybe she is taking watchfulness too far (for in the light of day, nobody could look less suicidal than Lady Cunningham); 'you stay in here, I'll go elsewhere.'

'In that case, why don't you pop over the landing? I've recently turned that large front room into a sitting-come-bedroom.'

'Of course,' says Kate, remembering, 'for your refugees.'

'Another disappointment, I'm afraid.'

'So they're not coming? I am sorry.' Kate goes thoughtfully to the door. 'When did you learn it wouldn't come off?'

'Yesterday, as a matter of fact.'

That explains a lot, thinks Kate, leaving the door ajar.

'Will I do?' It is fifteen minutes later, and Lady Cunnningham has presented herself in the doorway. She looks marvellous, Kate thinks ruefully, having recently examined herself in a mirror – a grazed left cheek, dark shadows under her eyes, raggedy hair. 'Terrific,' she says, admiring the smart navy-blue linen shirt-waister clearly signalling on the part of the wearer an intention not to be intimidated.

They pass Mrs Prior in the drive.

'Good morning, Mrs Prior,' calls Lady Cunningham, striding purposely past, her stiffness evidently cured. 'What a beautiful day.'

Mrs Prior gawps.

'Good morning,' murmurs Kate.

'G'morning, I'm sure,' replies Mrs Prior.

'Rather a sourpuss, I'm afraid,' comments her employer without troubling to lower her voice. 'Always has been. Poor Prior. One wonders how he has stood it all these years. Of course, in the old days when he was fully engaged driving Sir Jock to his appointments and keeping the cars up to scratch, I doubt he saw very much of her. He repeatedly complains how sorely he misses those times, and I can well believe it. Poor, poor Prior. He goes as a gardener, you know, to the James sisters. Purely to escape. He has no need — I still retain him. I must try and think of some nice little trips . . .'

No sign here of flagging, thinks Kate, wearily unlocking her door. 'Right, then: sit down and I'll get breakfast. What do you fancy?'

'Oh, I have the appetite of a bird.'

Kate, whose heart has been sinking at the prospect of cooking, is glad to hear it. 'Toast, then? Marmalade? Tea?'

'Toast and marmalade would be excellent. However, coffee, perhaps?'

'Toast and coffee coming up.'

Sunlight slanting through the latticed window, chintzy curtains billowing, dust floating, the hall clock beating time, birds chirruping. And we two sitting placidly as quiet old dames who were here yesterday, will be here tomorrow and so on *ad infinitum*, with no excitement

254

ruffling our lives beyond trips to the village shop and the next-door neighbour popping in. Who would guess, passing by in the lane and peeping through the window, the scene last night, or what has lately been the preferred pastime of the senior occupant – or the dreams of the younger? thinks Kate (who, on the verge of nodding off, became suffused by waves of an old dream in which she and Will were making love, and had to nudge herself awake).

Throughout, Lady Cunningham has remained engrossed in her newspaper. When St Peter's church clock strikes the half hour, with the manner of one who has been thinking deeply, she lifts her head. 'You, of course, have had your sadnesses.'

Kate is startled. 'You mean – I lost my husband?'

'You seem remarkably well adjusted.'

Congratulation or criticism? 'I won't pretend it's been easy. I've felt incredibly bitter; bitter at being left alone, bitter for Chris losing half his life – I'll never be reconciled to that; I'll always feel it's unfair. But life is unfair. At least I'm able not to dwell on it. When certain thoughts jump into my head, I stop them up.'

'I think you're splendid.'

'No, I'm not. I've just learned to survive.'

Lady Cunningham lowers her newspaper and blinks rapidly at the empty fireplace. 'I hope I may learn to do as much,' she says, her voice wobbling.

Kate leans over and takes her hand, squeezes the long bony fingers. 'Come on: time to go.'

They treat Sylvie like a three-year-old, thinks Will, observing the scene.

This visit is not quite the ordeal he anticipated; in fact, his dominant feeling is one of relief, for the change in Sylvie after less than three days is quite remarkable. Her 'foreignness' seems more marked; that is, she is more firmly settled into her new persona, even further removed from any vestige of her former self. But she appears placid and content. And not drugged, thank

255

goodness – when Sister called just now, she hurried over eagerly to show them her drawing. 'Oh, isn't that pretty,' cried Sister, glancing meaningfully at Will. He took it into his hands, swallowed. Until seven or eight years ago, Sylvie regularly exhibited her work in the local artists' exhibitions; her water-colours did not disgrace the walls of Lavenbrook Town Hall. What he now holds is infantile scrawl. He is still staring at it when Joan gives him a poke. 'Good, isn't it, Will?'

'Oh, yes, yes. Very.' He hands it back.

'Roses,' says Sylvie, pointing.

'Roses – of course.'

'Pretty,' coos Joan. 'Clever *girl*, Sylvie.'

Sylvie claps her lips together in a prim pleased smile, and catching sight of a passing nurse, bustles off to show her the drawing.

This, thinks Will, was where he went wrong; he failed to respond appropriately to the child she has become; he would let his pain and irritation show, which must have been very disturbing to her. He blows out his breath, passes a hand over his brow – in relief that in the end he made the right decision. Joan and the Sister are talking together. He watches Sylvie in the doorway until, without a backward glance in his direction, she leaves the nurse and goes off into the garden room. She has forgotten him already; probably never registered him at all.

'Anything she needs? Anything I can bring next time?' he asks the Sister, who smiles and shakes her head. Sylvie, it seems, has everything a child could need or desire.

'Thanks a million for coming with me,' he tells Joan as they drive away. 'I'll soon get used to coming. But it was good having you there today.'

'I was glad to see her myself; glad to see her looking happy and settled.'

'Yes,' he sighs; 'happy and settled.'

They arrive back at the surgery where Joan has asked to be dropped. She opens the door, puts her feet to the ground, then tilts her head round coquettishly. 'You know, Will, it's time you attended to other things. Life out here has to go on.'

A pause, as he gathers her meaning. 'Mm, does it, indeed? You're not angling for a date, I suppose?' he asks, wilfully misunderstanding her.

She splutters – 'You cheeky monkey!' – and staggers raucously to the surgery door.

Grinning, he turns the car. Then stops – isn't that Kate's parked car? Maybe she's sick. He leans over the steering wheel. It is definitely Kate's car: should he wait for her? But perhaps she wouldn't welcome this if she's feeling rotten; it might be more tactful to phone her later. Yes, that's what he'll do. He drives off slowly, wondering what ails her. Poor Kate, he thinks, poor love.

Her arm hurts, her throat aches, there is something loose banging about in her skull. What can be going on in that room? Lady Cunningham and Dr Horden have been closeted for more than forty minutes. He has made at least one outside call. 'Your line's free now, Dr Horden,' she heard the woman on the switchboard say. What can he be doing with her? Her mind reels, conjures the doctor pinning down a crazed Lady Cunningham while he barks into the telephone a request for a straitjacket.

She shifts on the seat; picks up her book, puts it down again. She is glad that she managed to get all her points across. She had anticipated awkwardness achieving this in front of Lady Cunningham, or worse still, interruptions; but her captive sat in silence while Kate gave a brief account of what occurred last evening and on other evenings, touching upon the unpleasant experiences of several villagers and the interest of the police. The hard bit was conveying her dread of what Lady Cunningham might do if faced with public exposure. Phrases such as *under a strain* and *danger of being driven too far* were the clues she offered. They seemed to do the trick. 'Quite,' said Dr Horden, as he rose to escort her to the door; 'Stop worrying,' as she stepped into the corridor. He took her arm (at which she managed not to wince): 'You've delivered her into safe hands. Now make an appointment for yourself, will you?'

She stretches her legs; lets them flop. She will make the appointment another day. Right now all she hopes is not to draw attention to herself, for Zoë's room is down the corridor and Zoë would want to talk. There has been too much talking.

'Kate?'

Oh my God!

'Goodness, you're jumpy,' says Joan. 'Are you all right? Hey,' – taking a closer look – 'what's the matter? You waiting to see the doctor?'

'I've, er, seen him. I'm waiting to run a neighbour home.'

'Come and sit in my office, then.'

'I can't. I don't want to miss her.'

'Is she in with Dr Horden?' (Kate nods.) 'Sally,' Joan calls to the woman behind the desk, 'give me a shout when Dr Horden's patient comes out, will you?' then firmly propels Kate along the corridor, past Zoë's room, to her own, where she indicates a chair. 'Sit down. Now, what's been happening to you?'

'Well, er,' sighs Kate, knowing she has to somehow account for her grazed cheek and a washed-out appearance. 'Last night, I, er, apprehended a prowler.'

'You did *what*?'

She laughs feebly. 'It wasn't as bad as it sounds. Um, as a matter of fact you can do me a favour, Joan. Will you look at my arm? It's a bit sore.'

'Dr Horden seen it?' asks Joan, carefully looking, prodding, manipulating. 'Nothing broken; a bad bruise, I'd say. What did he think?'

'Oh, the same.'

'Rest it. Listen – tell me what happened. You were attacked last night?'

'No, *I* did the attacking. There'd been a prowler in the garden before; I was sick of it, so I went to sort him out.' (Joan widens her eyes, shakes her head.) 'How's things with Will?' Kate asks, carefully casual.

'You know about Sylvie?'

'I know she's gone somewhere.'

'Beresford House. I've just got back from seeing her, as a matter of fact.'

'How is she?'

'Fine. It's the right place for her. Will made the right decision. It was tough for him, though. Real tough.'

'I can imagine. Um, and he's all right?'

She snorts. 'I'll tell you something, that man's lippy. Sign he's getting over it, huh?'

There's a tap on the door, and the receptionist looks in. 'Patient's come out of Dr Horden's, Joan.'

Kate springs to her feet. 'I'll have to dash. 'Bye for now.' She clasps Joan briefly, and runs.

Lady Cunningham is looking testy by the reception desk. 'Oh, there you are,' she says, as if Kate is a servant she has caught backsliding. 'I am ready to go home.'

Me too, thinks Kate, pushing on the swing door.

Lady Cunningham sweeps past. 'You'll be relieved to learn I haven't broken anything,' she announces ringingly to the car park. 'Although Dr Horden did think it quite amazingly fortunate for a woman of my age.' Waiting for Kate to unlock it, she glares over the car's roof.

Kate gets in and leans across to open the passenger door. Then sits up straight and for a moment stares motionless through the windscreen. Is tiredness warping her receptivity, or was there reproof in the woman's tone? Did that glaring expression really intend to convey: *so you see it would be better in future if you ceased this practice of knocking down old ladies*? She turns to her companion.

Lady Cunningham has fastened her seat belt and settled back comfortably. In a rather beautiful gesture she raises a hand in a brushing movement along her neck to her cheek. 'Though of course,' she continues, 'as I remarked to him, I have been blessed with quite wonderful bones.'

At half her normal speed, her last scrap of energy focused on the task of observing the road, Kate is driving back to Aston Favell.

'Dr Naidoo,' Fenella is reporting excitedly. 'A delightful man. When he had finished speaking with Dr Horden, he asked to be put on to me. Wasn't that kind? He wanted to reassure me, you see. Old-world courtesy. Charming. The Indians are, you know; nowadays, one has to look abroad for a proper gentleman. His English is immaculate; a beautifully modulated tone.' (Fenella modulates her own to convey some idea.) 'According to Dr Horden, Dr Naidoo is very highly thought of, a most eminent man in his field.' She falls silent for a moment, contemplating what this field might be; she supposes, for she has never been one to shirk matters, that it is batty old ladies. Never mind; she can feel in her bones, in her tingling fingers, a rewarding and enriching experience awaits. This cribbed little world will be opened wide for her. The East! And, of course, the learning is not to be sniffed at – how impressive was that long list of letters following his name. 'By the pricking of my thumbs,' she chants gleefully in her best witch's voice – which, oh dear, causes poor Mrs Woolard to take her eyes off the road and cast her a doubtful look. 'Don't worry,' she soothes, 'I'm not off my head. And if I am, I daresay Dr Naidoo will soon put me together again. Oh, how I relish the thought of our Thursday afternoons. There will be several of them, apparently, at his private clinic.'

'And you'll be able to get there easily, will you?'

'But of course. My chauffeur, Prior, will convey me. Oh, *won't* he be pleased! I told you I should devise some nice little trips.'

*   *   *

260

Was she ever as glad to get home! Kate unlocks her door, stumbles into her kitchen; pulls out a chair, flops down – lies her head on a crooked arm on the table; allows the feel and sound of the place to lap her like lulling water.

Even now, Lady Cunningham comes wheeling into her brain (blast her), going into raptures about her psychiatrist's charm (for presumably psychiatrist is what this consultant is), keenly anticipating her therapy visits: Kate hopes the poor woman isn't building for another disappointment, that this won't turn out to be a case of transferring her passion from one inappropriate project to the next. Listen, she berates herself, this man is a *professional*, he'll be aware of the pitfalls; for heaven's sake stop worrying, and concentrate for a change on number one.

Like, for instance, on her churning hunger pangs. She heaves out of the chair, humps over to the fridge, but finds she is too tired to fancy anything; all she desires is to crawl into bed. In the end, she heats some tinned rice pudding and spoons it into her mouth from the saucepan in order to quieten her stomach while she gets some sleep. Leaving spoon, bowl, saucepan in the sink, she takes a gulp of water, unplugs the hall telephone, and at last, not quite on her hands and knees, climbs the stairs.

In the bathroom, cleans her teeth and scrubs off her make-up; in the bedroom, pulls off her clothes. Climbs into bed – then gets out again to unplug the bedside telephone and pull the curtains across. Back in bed, she turns on to her side and falls asleep.

Will has finished his lunch. He intends to wash up and then phone Kate. There are a great many used mugs, glasses, plates and saucepans on the table and draining board, last night's supper things and this morning's breakfast things. Before he can complete the chore the telephone rings. Kate is so much to the fore in his mind, that he stupidly assumes it must be her calling, and rushes with wet hands to pick up the nearest receiver.

In fact it is a business contact: Gordon Byrne, who is also a friend. Will listens intently. This could be important, it could possibly save his skin. Although it has been hard to develop a proper sense of disaster, the Birmingham firm decided not to implement his contract; his cancellation at short notice of last Thursday's meeting shook their faith in him. So he really does need more work. 'Sounds interesting, Gordon,' he encourages. 'Hang on a minute; let me take this in my office.' He bounds upstairs, grabs pen and notepad and scoops a chair under him. 'Yes; I'm all ears . . .' He scribbles like fury, interjects the right phrases – 'Of course; absolutely; no problem. *Sure* I can have something by tomorrow,' he declares. 'Look forward to seeing you. And thanks, Gordon.'

He drops the phone and at once turns on the computer. Three hours later, he has a respectable proposal ready. The old keenness is making a comeback – and about time, too; he had better not let this opportunity escape. Of course, Gordon, he supposes, will have heard about Sylvie. Oh hell, though, he remembers now: Gordon was the fellow Sylvie took a fancy to some years back at the Elliotts' party, pursuing him with embarrassing singlemindedness, backing the poor sod into a yucca plant. That settles it, then: Gordon has not approached him out of sympathy for Sylvie's plight, but in spite of Sylvie, because Will is the best man for the job. Whistling, he goes optimistically downstairs to make some tea.

And to finish the washing up.

A job he seems fated not to complete. Another interruption – this time from the doorbell.

Joan sweeps in, ignores his quip – 'Hey, you *are* chasing me,' and makes straight for the kitchen, where with her usual style she rounds on him with some force. 'Shuddit, you; and listen. You ever rung Kate?'

He gapes. 'Um, no, as it happens . . .'

'Well, I *seen* her. And she weren't looking good. She was down the surgery this morning – you want to know why? Last night she had to beat off a prowler. Her face is hurt, her arm's bad; she looked shocked out of her mind . . .'

'Good God, Joan. I wish I'd . . .'

'I felt real sorry for her. You know, that girl's always worrying about someone else. And there she was this morning, worrying about giving some neighbour a lift.'

'Look, sit down for a minute; I've made some tea. Thing is, before I could get round to it, this guy called up.' Joan sits, Will reaches for another mug. 'It was about a job, which I truly need. For the last three hours I've been flogging the computer. Soon as we've drunk this, though, I'll give her a ring.'

Joan shakes her head. 'You men, you're all useless.'

'I know,' Will says humbly. 'One sugar, isn't it?'

One minute he is chatting about this new job, half his mind on Kate, looking ahead, feeling normal and one of life's participants; the next, Joan is banging down her cup, screaming about the time and how she'll be late picking up her daughter, and – *wham* – he is reduced to a sunken mess. 'Keep in touch,' he almost begs; but swallows the words. He leaps up, cracking his knee on the table leg; the shout of pain in the joint as he hobbles after her to the door seems fair judgement.

''Bye, Will,' she calls, not looking back, jiggling her keys, waiting impatiently for an overtaking van to clear her car and allow her to jump into it. She moves off, waving. He shuts the door.

The thing to do, he decides, standing in the hall, is pick a day for visiting Beresford House, then forget about it; he has to cast off from the Sylvie situation, put it out of his mind. How about Sunday, for instance? Yes, he'll visit on Sundays. Now that's settled, he must get back on track, concentrate on the job – and concentrate on Kate who has been in the wars – whom he has shut out for nearly a fortnight, deliberately, like forbidden fruit, because the timing was wrong, because he longed to dwell on her and couldn't risk a distraction. Well, right now a distraction would be welcome. Eagerly, he seizes the phone.

It is a shock to hear the unavailable tone. He tries again, with the same result. Shaken, stands with his hands in his pockets, wanders into the kitchen, sits down.

She is cut off from him. The knowledge brings his mind to focus solely, intensely on Kate. Experimentally, cautiously, he crawls inside her brain; looks around; finds he is not enchanted by the perspective. He recalls their embrace when they were last together, and measures his silence against it. The result feels shabby. The excuses are easy to recite – that he had to concentrate his mind ferociously, had to put away his wife, damn it, and deal with the painful aftermath. Even so – *silence*?

Hell, he can't stand the suspense. He'll go straight round to Wayside Cottage; he has to know she's all right; he has to know whether she's still speaking to him. But as he looks round for his keys, his confidence in the exercise wanes. He had no right ever to assume confidence. You can't (he now knows) just barge in and out of people's lives. You can't hold someone in your arms and caress them, then put them on hold for a fortnight. At the very least he should have tried to explain, should have kept her informed. Of course she'll be cool to him; he couldn't blame her. God what an idiot, what a pathetic loser.

He pockets the keys and hurries out. All the way down Main Street he is trying to think of an excuse for calling, to parry her displeasure and play for time in which to make amends. Reaching The Green, he hits on the wheeze of asking to borrow one of Chris's walking books, and this elaborates, as he turns up Vicarage Hill, into a need to consult the literature in order to prepare for a break he is planning, a short walking holiday. It sounds reasonably plausible, he considers, crossing her drive.

There is no reply to his first rap. He raps the door again. After a second or two, raps even louder, then stands back and surveys the windows. Her car is here, so she must be at home. Hell's teeth – she had a fight with a prowler, remember? Maybe she's collapsed, or something's happened to her. 'Kate?' he yells, hammering hard on the door; 'Kate, can you hear me?' and hammers and hammers again. 'Kate, are you all right? Kate, Kate.'

Kate wakes, and swings out of bed, disorientated. *The children,* she thinks, then remembers there are no children at home. But the banging? She turns to look at the clock, which indicates that it is ten past six. But ten past six when? How long has she slept? That banging on the door – someone is very impatient. She pulls her old silk kimono from the door-peg, wraps and ties it round her naked body, then goes shakily downstairs in her bare feet. From the hallway, she peers cautiously through the kitchen to the window. Fiona? she wonders, Zoë? If it is Lady Cunningham, she won't answer; she's had quite enough of Lady Cunningham to be going on with.

She jerks out of sight as a head zooms up against the glass. But then cranes forward . . . Oh, it is! – he is calling her name . . . 'Will!' she cries, stumbling across the kitchen, 'Will!' turning the key.

There is no need, he discovers, to say anything at all. The delight on her face, her arms reaching, are signals. All you do is respond.

EPILOGUE

Thursday 10th September

Fenella lifts her head and sniffs the air. Autumn: she can smell it already in only the second week of September. She is waiting under the portico for Prior to bring the car round. Molly, she sees, is hacking branches off the buddleia, with that dirty little dog maintaining a low profile beside her. Fenella had to scoot the little beast a few minutes ago; he'd been through the wet grass and was shaking himself by the steps as she emerged dressed to go out. This afternoon's outfit – a jade green frock, and a jacket, with shoes and bag to match, in orangey-brown – has been chosen with her usual care. The ladies will approve, she feels. She does so like to please them. Already she can hear their cries of pleasure, their hands clapping together, their silken bustle – 'Oh please to come this way, Lady Cunningham, we ladies are very glad to see you.' Her dear, dear friends . . .

Here is Prior; here he is. Tap, tap, tap, go her feet down the steps. He has climbed out of the car and is walking round to open the rear door. His turnout today is excellent, smart, one might almost say burnished. 'Well done, Prior,' she says, complimenting him as she settles on the long seat in a voice resonant with satisfaction. 'Thank you, my lady,' he murmurs, and closes the door with a soft clunk. (It is always 'my lady' with Prior, never 'Lady Cunningham'.) Her satisfaction with his appearance is not primarily for herself, but for her ladies, who are very curious about him. As Mrs Ginwala so hilariously enquired: 'Who is he, your man?' 'He is Prior,' she replied, 'my chauffeur,' – and developed from this a useful exercise in vocabulary. 'Who is *that* man?' she kindly reproved Mrs Ginwala. 'Not *your* man, or *her* man. Repeat after me: *Who is that man?*' 'Who is that man?' they chorused obediently. 'He is Prior,' she beamed.

'He is Prior,' they echoed, greatly animated.

Afterwards, she dropped him a little hint. 'I think Prior, my ladies find you rather intriguing. The full works, I think, on Thursday – cap, gloves, etc, you know the form.' (Since the demise of Sir Jock, Prior has inclined – or his wretched wife has forced him to incline – towards a lesser standard of formality.) 'So nice,' she encouraged, 'to give people pleasure.'

They have set off and now reach the top of the drive. The car's nose emerges slowly, slowly on to Vicarage Hill. All is clear. As Prior swings to the right, his eyes and Fenella's glance quickly to the left. Oh yes, that Volvo estate is parked in the drive of Wayside Cottage, as usual.

('It's a permanent fixture, that car,' Mrs Prior proclaims repeatedly to her husband. 'It's there morning, noon and night, unless he's gone off to work for a change. And there's a *For Sale* sign up outside High House. Blatant, I call it. Disgusting. No sooner has he packed off his wife than he's got his feet under the table at Wayside Cottage, living over the brush with *her,* even when her children are home – what sort of example is that to set youngsters, eh?') It is these and similar observations which now cause Prior to turn his head.

Fenella observes the presence of Mr McLeod's car with more tolerance, even with affection, for she likes Mr McLeod. She often waves to him. She first made his acquaintance the afternoon she called on Mrs Woolard, soon after their little *contretemps,* with a rather beautiful raw silk scarf (a gift to show she harboured no ill-feelings; for she has never been one to bear a grudge). Mrs Woolard bade her come inside and be introduced to Mr McLeod – without, Fenella recalls, batting an eyelid – but isn't that the way of the world these days? Mr McLeod seemed very much at home in Wayside Cottage. However, she found she approved of him; his eyes were steady, dark and kind under straight strong brows. Yes, she quite took to him; he is perfect for poor Mrs Woolard, who certainly deserves this solace – widowed as she was at such a tragically young age.

Ah, but it is a blow at any age to lose one's beloved companion. Thank heaven for clever Dr Naidoo who found this wonderful work for her to do. Such valuable work. As Dr Naidoo explained, elderly Indian ladies are sometimes very isolated in this country, for they are shy and lack the opportunities afforded their menfolk and their younger sisters to make contact with the native people. Some of them are very intelligent. How greatly they would benefit from the regular company of a kindly, cultured, patient English lady. Sadly, such a lady is not easily come by . . . Fenella cut him short. Dr Naidoo, she declared, need look no further, for she longs, yearns, *to be of use.* How he had twinkled at her. 'Dear Lady Cunningham, you have put the matter in a nutshell!'

'Here we are, my lady,' murmurs Prior, turning into a side street in a run-down part of Lavenbrook. Terraced houses line the road; Prior draws up smoothly outside number 43. Fenella gathers her large bag containing items she has selected as talking points – a photograph album, old theatre programmes, a piece of antique embroidery for the ladies to compare with specimens of their own. 'Now, Prior, don't vanish too abruptly,' she commands as he opens her car door. 'Give people ample time to be admiring. Be back at four-thirty – and please don't lose too much at the bookie's or I shall have your wife complaining again.'

Her welcome is everything she anticipated. But even

their lovely warmth cannot quite match the thrill which leaps into her throat when she enters the small front room — silks in pinks and reds and peacock blues and greens, a tiny goddess in a gilded sepulchre, golden chimes tinkling. 'Oh, it is lovely to be here again,' she cries, setting her bag down.

The ladies, carefully not stinting their welcome, are nevertheless edging towards the window overlooking the street.

'Is Prior still there?' she asks casually, indulging them. And when they agree eagerly that, yes, Prior is still there, asks, 'How does he look today?'

'He is looking very nice.' 'He is looking most splendid.'

'Prior looks very nice, he looks splendid,' she corrects them. She joins them at the window. They let her in and crowd at her side, obediently chorusing, 'Prior looks very nice, he looks splendid.'

And so he does, thinks Fenella, watching Prior and the long black car go gliding off. How glad she is to be here where she is valued, amongst her ladies, her dear friends; in this darling gem of a room — inside, looking out.

THE END

TELL MRS POOLE I'M SORRY
Kathleen Rowntree

'ROWNTREE PINS DOWN THE INTIMACIES THAT WEB
BETWEEN TEENAGERS: THE THINGS THEY FIND FUNNY,
EMBARRASSING AND NATURAL'
Sunday Times

*'It was as if at the age of eleven, caring little for the families
they'd been landed with at birth, they took on one another
instead. Not always with happy consequences. But that was
the way with families; it was pot luck whether or not you
thrived in them'*

The friendship between three grammar-school girls, intense
and inter-dependent as a blood-tie, has repercussions
throughout the rest of their lives. And always they remember
the first heady romantic and sexual love affair with Mr Poole,
the music master, experienced by only one, but shared
vicariously by all three. As adults, their paths diverge – a
glittering career for one, a demanding profession and secure
marriage for another, a heavily domestic and social role for a
third. Miles separate them. But one thing never changes:
when one of them hits trouble, the others come to her aid
and the bonds of youth hold firm.

0 552 99561 4

BLACK SWAN

BETWEEN FRIENDS
Kathleen Rowntree

'THE FUNNIEST PORTRAIT OF VILLAGE TRIVIA SINCE
E. M. DELAFIELD'S *DIARY OF A PROVINCIAL LADY*'
Cosmopolitan

Wychwood was a charming and enthusiastically organized
village. The women, with their pine-fitted kitchens and
glowing Agas, ran everything with tireless efficiency, from
the W.I. meetings (Dress a Wooden Spoon, and How to
Decorate an Egg) to Brasso-ing the church lectern and making
mock-crab sandwiches for the Christmas Bazaar. One hardly
expected a *liaison* to flourish in such exemplary
surroundings.

But when Tessa Brierley discovered that her husband was
having an affair with Maddy Storr, she was doubly perturbed
– for Maddy was not only the life and soul of the village and
President of the W.I., but was also her very best friend, a
friend whom Tessa did not want to lose.

Stoically, resourcefully, observed by a community
celebrating crises, tragedies, and local festivities in its own
eccentric Wychwood way, Tessa began to plan how she
would keep both her husband and her friend.

'A HUMDINGER – SHARP AND DELIGHTFULLY
ENTERTAINING. A VILLAGE STORY IN THE SPLENDID
TRADITION OF JOANNA TROLLOPE'
Publishing News

'SPARKLING . . . A DELIGHTFUL SOCIAL COMEDY WITH
UNDERTONES OF REAL PAIN'
Cosmopolitan

0 552 99506 1

BLACK SWAN

A SELECTED LIST OF FINE WRITING
AVAILABLE FROM BLACK SWAN

THE PRICES SHOWN BELOW WERE CORRECT AT THE TIME OF GOING TO PRESS.
HOWEVER TRANSWORLD PUBLISHERS RESERVE THE RIGHT TO SHOW NEW
RETAIL PRICES ON COVERS WHICH MAY DIFFER FROM THOSE PREVIOUSLY
ADVERTISED IN THE TEXT OR ELSEWHERE.

☐	99564 9	JUST FOR THE SUMMER	*Judy Astley*	£5.99
☐	99565 7	PLEASANT VICES	*Judy Astley*	£5.99
☐	13649 2	HUNGRY	*Jane Barry*	£6.99
☐	99537 1	GUPPIES FOR TEA	*Marika Cobbold*	£5.99
☐	99593 2	A RIVAL CREATION	*Marika Cobbold*	£5.99
☐	99602 5	THE LAST GIRL	*Penelope Evans*	£5.99
☐	99622 X	THE GOLDEN YEAR	*Elizabeth Falconer*	£5.99
☐	99589 4	RIVER OF HIDDEN DREAMS	*Connie May Fowler*	£5.99
☐	99610 6	THE SINGING HOUSE	*Janette Griffiths*	£5.99
☐	99590 9	OLD NIGHT	*Clare Harkness*	£5.99
☐	99506 1	BETWEEN FRIENDS	*Kathleen Rowntree*	£5.99
☐	99325 5	THE QUIET WAR OF REBECCA SHELDON	*Kathleen Rowntree*	£5.99
☐	99584 3	BRIEF SHINING	*Kathleen Rowntree*	£5.99
☐	99561 4	TELL MRS POOLE I'M SORRY	*Kathleen Rowntree*	£5.99
☐	99598 3	AN ANCIENT HOPE	*Caroline Stickland*	£5.99
☐	99529 0	OUT OF THE SHADOWS	*Titia Sutherland*	£5.99
☐	99574 6	ACCOMPLICE OF LOVE	*Titia Sutherland*	£5.99
☐	99620 3	RUNNING AWAY	*Titia Sutherland*	£5.99
☐	99442 1	A PASSIONATE MAN	*Joanna Trollope*	£5.99
☐	99492 8	THE MEN AND THE GIRLS	*Joanna Trollope*	£5.99
☐	99549 5	A SPANISH LOVER	*Joanna Trollope*	£5.99
☐	99126 0	THE CAMOMILE LAWN	*Mary Wesley*	£6.99
☐	99495 2	A DUBIOUS LEGACY	*Mary Wesley*	£6.99
☐	99592 4	AN IMAGINATIVE EXPERIENCE	*Mary Wesley*	£5.99
☐	99639 4	THE TENNIS PARTY	*Madeleine Wickham*	£5.99
☐	99591 6	A MISLAID MAGIC	*Joyce Windsor*	£4.99